Dragon's Guide to Slaying Virgins

Otherworld Realms Book Three

I0638480

By Isabelle Saint-Michael

Otherworld Romance, LLC

Copyright © 2015 by Isabelle Saint-Michael.
All rights reserved.

Published by Otherworld Romance, llc
www.otherworldromance.com
www.elvenlife.com

ISBN 978-0-9908665-9-6
Trade Paperback
Fonts Licensed through FontSquirrel for commercial use

For all my fans that cheer me on, for the patient husbands that forgive our late nights, for the cover designer that always makes it happen, and for Lisa and Kenzi who ride this roller coaster with me every day - Thank you.

Chapter One

I studied the wall as it swung by me again. There were exactly twenty-one cracks and one missing stone. It took approximately three swings to make a full rotation to see the wall. I looked down at the bubbling cauldron below me. It was an interesting vantage point considering I was hanging upside down from my ankles. The golden broth steamed and bubbled, causing the vegetables within to dance in its waves.

The air smelled conspicuously of singed hair and unwashed Trolls - a very distinctive scent. From my left I heard the blood-curdling scream of Agshi's latest victim. The Troll was preparing appetizers for his game night and the main course was Virgin Soup. Lucky me, I was the virgin.

"Agshi dearest, I think the soup needs more pepper," I called to him.

The Troll whirled on his heel to face me. "*Dinner should not talk. Dinner should contemplate meaning of life and watch as it flashes before eyes.*"

"Sure, sure, I'll contemplate it. Could you add some pepper though? I want to be well seasoned. I would hate for your guests to feel like you served bland virgin." I nodded approval as the large Troll sighed and dumped black pepper into the pot below me.

"Thank you, Agshi," I chirped lovingly at him. The large Troll turned, giving me a warning glare.

The bubbling broth below me started to take on a smell much more befitting of a savory soup. I inhaled, happily soaking in the array of flavors that would mingle once I, the main ingredient, was added.

"Pssss." I heard the familiar sound of air being released surreptitiously nearby.

"You there, girl!"

The swinging had mostly stopped so I was forced to turn my head to locate the source of the air leak. To my left, about five feet away, sat a young man who looked to be in his late teens. Once again he began to hiss like an angry snake.

"Pssss, girl?" The harsh whisper of a desperate youth escaped him.

I looked at him pointedly. "Yes?" I said in a soft, disinterested tone.

"Has the Troll knocked you in the head or are you under a spell?" he asked, confusion written across his young face.

"Neither. Why do you ask?"

He eyed me warily. "You do realize that Troll plans to make you into a stew, right?"

"Soup," I corrected.

"What?" he said, taken aback.

"Soup, I'm being made into Virgin Soup. It's light and delicate." He furrowed a concerned brow at my words. I chose to close my eyes and ignore him. I should be contemplating my life.

I could hear the young man struggling nearby. With a heavy sigh I opened my eyes and turned my head to look at him again.

"What are you doing?" I asked.

"What does it look like? I'm trying to escape. *You* may be perfectly fine with throwing your life away, but I'm not." He struggled against the ropes again, his face turning red from the effort. When he finally stopped he was breathing heavily.

"You'll never get out struggling like that," I told him.

"Says the girl claiming to be a virgin, dangling upside down above a pot," he bit off angrily.

My temper flared. "First off, I *am* a virgin. Second, getting out of ropes is easy if you go about it the *correct* way… which you're not."

He shot me an angry glare and went back to trying to struggle out of his bonds. He eventually gave up and looked back at me. "Well, I guess I'm dessert," he said defeatedly.

I tried not to laugh at his dejected tone. "Yes, well, Agshi is very good at tying knots," I reassured him.

He laughed in a way that sounded like he was more than a little angry. "You're on a first-name basis with the Troll that's going to eat you?"

"Of course. We have a long history," I explained.

"Did a Troll court you?"

"Oh, heavens no. I slew his entire family." I would have shrugged, but the ropes that bound me prevented it.

"Oh, so he captured you to take revenge." He nodded in understanding.

"No."

His head tilted to the side in confusion again. "No what?"

"No, he didn't capture me."

The youth shifted his gaze from side to side. "My Lady, I hate to dispute the soundness of your mind, but I really am beginning to question your mental stability. You are, in fact, captured. Perhaps the horror of it has sent you into shock and denial?"

"Did you hear the part where I said I slew his entire family?"

"Yes, My Lady, it must have been difficult for you to order such an action, but I'm sure you had good cause." He was placating me. He thought I had lost my mind.

"Agshi!" I snapped. The Troll angrily whirled around to face me again.

"What are you doing, Lady Loon?" called the young man on the floor.

With heavy, thudding footsteps the Troll crossed the room coming towards me. "What does annoying virgin warrior want?"

"Tell that lad about how I killed your family."

The Troll sighed heavily and looked at the other prisoner. "Virgin speaks truth. Slew both brothers and mom. She cut heads from bodies."

I smiled at the memory. The heat of battle, the glory of the kill. The youth looked horrified. "And why did I slay your brothers and mother?"

The Troll rolled his eyes. "They ate four farmers, two horses, mayor, and tax collector."

I snickered. "I almost could have forgiven you for the tax collector," I added.

Agshi reached out and gave me a firm shake. "You be quiet now. Broth almost ready." He wandered away from me to return to chopping vegetables or whatever a Troll does in the kitchen.

"So if you are some great warrior woman, why did you let him capture you?"

I looked back over at the lad who was once again struggling against his bonds. "I handed myself over. I'm ready to die."

He froze and looked up at me in disbelief. "What?"

I sighed mournfully. "I was in love. We were going to be bound and he died. It's as simple as that. Now I have no reason to go on."

"I'm sorry for your loss, My Lady, but I believe that anyone who truly loved you would want you to go on with your life. Live on for both of you." His eyes were apologetic.

"He told me to join him soon. I miss him so much."

He shook his head. "So you were in love with a sentimental asshat. Got it. Why didn't the two of you ever… you know."

I blinked at him.

"De-virgin-ize you," he offered.

I thought about what he was saying. "I didn't have time. So many people across the realms needed my help."

"It just seems like a waste to me."

"What does?" I asked him.

"Dying a virgin." He shook his head. "I just think you should give life a chance. Besides, it sounds like people count on you. Isn't it sort of selfish to just off yourself? Won't your mother miss you?"

"No, she doesn't really talk to me since the pickle incident when she died." I shuddered at the memory. I had smelled like vinegar for a month.

"Ok, what about friends? They'll miss you for sure." He smiled at me in a patronizing way.

"What part of 'didn't have time' did you not understand?" I snapped at him. How was I supposed to die quietly reflecting on life if he didn't shut up?

"Maybe a horse?" he suggested.

"What's your name?" I asked gruffly.

"Young, at your service." He dipped his head.

"Hey, Young, do me a favor?"

"Sure, My Lady."

"Shut up so I can die peacefully." I closed my eyes again. I could hear Agshi knocking plates around in another room. When his heavy steps headed back in my direction, I was prepared for my fate.

"Leave me alone, you brute! Even now, I swear my brother is looking for me, and he'll slay you quicker than that lass did the rest of your family."

I peeked out through one eye. Agshi had Young in a chokehold and was preparing to snap his neck.

"Stop struggling, little man," Agshi said as he tightened his grip.

I looked at Young, whose eyes were filled with terror, and sighed. "Agshi, leave the lad alone and cook me."

The Troll and the young man stared at me like I had snakes growing out of my ears. "I serving two virgins for dinner tonight. You are soup, he is casserole." Agshi pointed at Young, who was growing increasingly paler.

"Well that sounds decadent, but I refuse to share the table with him. I must insist you cook him another night." I would have stomped my foot if I wasn't upside down.

Young cleared his throat. "For the record, I'm not a virgin."

Agshi and I exchanged looks and broke out into fits of laughter.

"I'm not! I forfeited it to a Fairy maiden two summers ago." I let the laughter drain from me, but was still smiling.

"So you were fourteen? That seems far too early an age." I eyed him carefully. The light that occasionally bounced off his skin reflected a strange shimmering pattern. His eyes were large and set at the slightest angle, almost like that of a cat. He was without a doubt handsome, and I had little doubt he had his choice of female Fairies and Nymphs.

A small waft of smoke dissipated into the air as he huffed at me. "I'm twenty-four, and I am not a virgin," he snapped this one last time at Agshi, who seemed mildly annoyed by the banter his food was exchanging.

Agshi turned Young in his grasp. "Agshi won't tell if you won't. He still call you Virgin Casserole." As he tossed the lad over his shoulder, I watched the play of emotions on the boy's face.

I rolled my eyes. *This will be my* last *heroic deed before I die, I thought to myself.* "Agshi!" I bellowed. The Troll turned around, startled. "I told you I will not share the table with that whelp."

"Soup, shut up," the cumbersome Troll commanded.

I began swinging on the rope I was suspended on. I used the brief moments the rope would go slack on each swing to wiggle free of the knots. I heard Young "ooompf!" on the countertop as Agshi slammed him down. Finally, I had freed my hands and made quick work of getting down. I carefully avoided the large, bubbling pot of broth as I descended.

Agshi was turned away from me. He was trying to stuff an apple into Young's mouth. I quietly snuck up on him from behind, picking up a large skillet as I went. I walked up to stand beside Agshi, nodding my head as he rambled as if agreeing with his own madness.

When Young saw me standing there nodding, his eyes flared in surprise. The large Troll whirled around to face me. His blue and grey skin looked oily even in the dim light of the lanterns. A look of surprise crossed his dull face.

"If you put an apple in his mouth you're roasting him, not making a casserole," I said, correcting him on his error.

"What is soup doing?" he asked.

"I told you, I won't share the table. I am a bit of a drama queen and I DEMAND that the table be all mine."

Young struggled to sit up but was held in place by a single large blue hand.

"What is soup going to do about it if she's dead?" the Troll bellowed as he struck out at me with a large kitchen cleaver.

Using both hands I swung the skillet up to meet the cleaver. The weight of the cast iron was hard to compensate for. He was able to recover much faster than I was. I had to jump back to avoid the next swing he threw at me. I was ready for the following attack, sidestepping it easily, and with both hands and all my weight I swung the skillet. It connected with his skull, rewarding me with tingling pain up my arms, a loud clang as if it had hit stone, and my foe dropping to the ground unconscious.

"That was amazing," Young cheered.

I picked up a nearby knife and cut Young free. He sat up on the counter and looked at me with admiration. "My Lady, thank you for saving me."

"It was nothing. I suggest you get out of here before big and ugly wakes up," I told him.

"I think that's an excellent idea. One I must insist on, actually," a deep, masculine voice said behind me.

Young's face lit up as he looked over my shoulder. "Vallen!"

I turned around to see the face the voice had come from. There before me was a man who could have easily been an ancient god. His hair was black as night with streaks of blue and green dancing through it. His eyes were large, the color of sapphires, and had the same cat-like quality that Young's had. His jaw was strong and seemed suited to the rest of him. He was a tower of a man, every bit the height of an Elf or a Werewolf. His skin shimmered as he moved, reflecting bits of black and blue.

I felt myself blush and berated my heart for increasing its volume and speed. *He's just a man!* I told myself and wanted to scream for him to stop looking like that in my presence. My knees almost gave out from under me the closer he came. *How dare he stand there in a cloud of hazy white smoke and look like sex incarnate?* I resisted the urge to growl at him.

Young slid forward and hugged him warmly while avoiding the sword he had drawn in one hand. "Brother, you came for me."

"We should get going," Vallen said, sliding his gaze from his brother to me. "My Lady, you are free to go. We will see you safely to the next village."

He held out his hand to me. I just stared at it. With a shrug I turned away and walked over to the counter where I hopped up to perch on the edge. He narrowed his eyes at me and pursed his lips. "My Lady, are you injured?" he asked as he glided towards me.

I shook my head and picked up the apple beside me. "No, I'm fine. You two should run along before the Troll wakes up. He is not going to be happy about the knock to the head."

Vallen looked shocked, as if I had slapped him. "Do you mean to stay here?"

"Yes, I only escaped to save Junior over there." I looked down at Agshi and tsk'd. "His friends should be here soon and then they'll eat me. It was nice meeting you though."

Vallen turned to look at his brother. "She's daft," Young told him with a shrug.

Nodding as if that explained everything, Vallen turned to walk away. I took a bite of the apple, happily munching.

"We can't leave her here! I took an oath to protect the young, old, infirm, and physically and mentally disabled! And so did you!" Young exclaimed.

"Yes, you can," I said indifferently.

"Even if she is a nut job, she saved me," Young argued. Vallen stopped and turned back to look at me.

Young closed the distance between them quickly. He leaned close and whispered something in Vallen's ear. The older man's eyes flared and his gaze locked on me. He nodded and approached me again.

Standing close enough I could feel his breath, he reached down and captured my wrist. I struggled to pull it free, but with no luck. His grip was stronger than anyone I had ever encountered. He held it to his nose and took a deep breath, smelling me. His eyes met mine and he turned my hand over in his grasp. Pressing a courtly kiss to the back of my hand, he released it.

"My Lady, to whom do I owe the debt of my brother's life?" His words were as graceful as his body, which was way too close to ignore.

It was hard to swallow the bite of apple in my mouth. I blinked rapidly, unable to remember my name.

Finally choking on the apple, I coughed it out.
"Morgan, my name is Morgan," I managed to
squeak.

He chuckled. "Well, Morgan, it would seem Young
told me the truth and you are, in fact, a virgin." I
blinked. "You see, we're Dragons, and virgins that
are full-grown adults are a bit of a commodity
among us. I would normally carry you away to our
nest where I would lock you in a vault until I
decided what to do with you, but…"

I cut him off. "Dragons?" I perked up. I slid off the
counter, accidentally pressing myself against him.
"Good, then you can eat me and we can be done
with all this nonsense."

Vallen took a large step back. "What I was going to
say was that I would allow you to return home
because you saved Young."

"If you want the debt to be paid, *you* will eat me.
You can even set me on fire to crisp me first." I
lunged for him.

Grasping me by the shoulders, Vallen backed up to
hold me at arm's length. "What's wrong with her?"
he asked over his shoulder.

"Some asshat she was in love with died and he told
her to meet him on the other side." Young seemed
disinterested, already making his way to the door.

Vallen looked back at me. "Lady Morgan, I know better than most the pain of heartache, but I'm afraid this is a foolishly made plan. I cannot allow you to sacrifice yourself, nor will I eat you to repay the debt."

I stopped struggling against his grip. "Then leave," I said, pulling free of him and turning away. "I'll wait for Agshi to wake up and he'll eat me."

I heard an annoyed sigh from behind me. Vallen stepped closer, and when I felt his hot breath on the back of my neck, I thought for a moment he may have changed his mind. Every hair, even the green and purple ones atop my head, stood up on end. I gasped when he grabbed my arms and turned me around to face him.

"You're behaving like a child," he said flatly. Before I could react, he threw me over his shoulder and turned towards the door.

I kicked and struggled against him, but just as before his ironclad grip didn't budge. He didn't even seem to notice my weight as he walked. And with only six inches separating my face from his backside, I was in the perfect position to appreciate *how* he walked.

Once outside he set me down carefully on the ground. Looking at me cautiously, he reached out and grabbed my upper arm. I winced a little at the sudden bite and he immediately loosened his grip.

"Will you stop speaking madness and come along to the nearest village where we can get you some help, or will you fight us every step of the way?"

My eyes lit up and I started to say something, but he cut me off with an exasperated sigh. "I should have known better."

He pulled me close to his body, pressing me against him. He lowered his head as if he was going to kiss me and my traitorous body leaned up to meet his lips. Instead he took a deep breath and all the air seemed to leave my lungs. In my moment of sudden panic he reached up and quickly tilted my chin back with a flick of his fingers. The world went black as I lost consciousness.

Chapter Two

When I awoke it was to a pounding headache. A marching band that was badly out of step had taken up residence in my skull. It hurt so bad I contemplated not waking up at all. *I could stay unconscious forever,* I thought to myself.

Once I realized that there was no help for it and I would eventually have to wake up anyway, I began contemplating how best to do it. Surely if I just opened my eyes the sudden light would be enough to cripple me with even more pain. I began to take stock of my surroundings with my other senses.

I was somewhere soft. My fingers curled around linen when I flexed them. A bed? Curious, I hadn't expected Agshi to be so kind. Next I smelled the air. It smelled clean and fresh and not at all like that of a Troll's home. I was no longer at Agshi's. The Dragon had taken me with him!

I squinted and opened one eye. The room was totally dark and my eyes flew open. I flung myself up in the bed, ignoring the world as it danced and swooped around me. After a few deep breaths the outlines of the room settled back in place and my dizziness subsided. Ignoring the throbbing in my head I stumbled off the bed, and felt for anything that resembled a door or window.

After tripping over a chair and stubbing my toes on various furniture I located a door. Just as my hand closed around the handle it was thrown open and light flooded into the small room. In the doorway was a large woman who was as round as she was tall. Her figure blocked a fair portion of the passageway.

"I thought I heard you up in here, I did." The words were spoken with an accent like nothing I had ever heard. She bustled in and busied herself, flitting about the room lighting lanterns with a grace that didn't match her large stature.

"Excuse me, madam, where is *here*?" I asked, squinting against the light.

With more light in the room I could better see the woman before me. She was as tall as any man I had met, with perfect chocolate-colored sausage curls. Her cheeks were rosy and her dark eyes sparkled brightly.

"You're at Everwood Inn, love." She considered me for a moment. "The Lords who brought you here said you sustained some shock in your earlier adventures. That you might be a bit daft still."

Ever-wood-Inn? I rolled the words around in my head for a moment while I looked around the room. *How many realms have Everwoods? Vesaria, Everbloom, Braedeen...* I began counting. Then I snapped back to her earlier words. "The Lords who brought me, are they here? May I speak with them?"

She clicked her tongue. "I just knew they had a mischievous look about them. They didn't seem dishonorable. Did they take advantage of your heart, Miss? They were a handsome pair, I daresay."

I shook my head to put her at ease. "Nothing like that. May I speak with them?"

"I was just trying to tell you, Miss. They left not long after seeing to a room for you."

"WHAT?!" I shrieked.

"They said they had to be on their way." She reached into the front of her bodice and pulled out an envelope, handing it to me.

With haste I broke the seal that depicted a dragon with its tail wrapped around a sword. My hand shook in fury as I read the letter.

Dear Lady Morgan,

I regret to inform you that by the time you read this letter we will be long gone. I have brought you to this new realm so that you may have a fresh start at life. Beneath your pillow you will find a purse with more than enough gold to allow you to start over, or to locate a wizard who can transport you back to your own realm.

My hope is that you will see that your life is worth more than the soup course of a Troll's dinner party, or at least have enough time to contemplate a better way to die while you look for a wizard to transport you home. Either way, I have repaid our debt to you. Your life for the life of my brother, Young.

Please take care, Lady Morgan. If we should meet again I hope it will be under more pleasant circumstances. If not, then have a nice life.

Sincerely,

Lord Vallen

Dragon

P.S. At Young's insistence we have paid for your room and board for the next few days. Please eat heartily as they are gouging us on the price of food and I would rather not think that we overpaid for your welfare.

I crumpled the letter in my hands, seething with anger. The sausage-curl woman eyed me carefully. "Would you be hungry, Miss? Dinner is nearly ready."

"Do you know where they were going, Mistress?"

She thought deeply for a moment before shrugging. "They didn't say, but perhaps one of the other customers or the bartender Douglas heard them mention something?"

I nodded in understanding. "I'll be down shortly"

The woman started to leave. "Ah, Mistress?" I called after her.

She turned, giving me another smile. "Yes, My Lady?"

"May I have your name please?"

"Of course, dear. My name is Neta Dreki. Mistress Dreki is fine." She turned and disappeared out of sight.

I closed the door to the room behind her and latched it. Walking over to the bed, I moved the pillow. Sure enough there was a blue leather purse. Just picking it up, I could feel its hefty weight. He didn't just leave me enough to start over; he left me enough to live on for years. Curious, I opened the purse and peered in. True to his word, the entire purse was filled with gold.

I knew I'd make myself a tasty target by carrying all that gold around, so I removed a few pieces and tucked them in my belt pouch. I left the rest in the purse and hid it underneath the mattress, then straightened up to survey the room. Aside from the bed there was a water basin for washing up, a small round table with two chairs, and a wooden stool next to the bed. The room itself was clean and decorated in reds and oranges. It reminded me of the colors trees change to in the fall.

Beside the door sat my boots, along with a dagger, sword, and bow. The weapons were well cared for and bore the dragon seal I had seen earlier on the note from Sir Vallen. I grabbed my boots and flopped down on a nearby chair to tug them on then slid the dagger into my belt and strolled to the door.

Downstairs was a tavern that housed four long tables that could each comfortably seat ten, and a bar that could seat another half dozen. A crowd of what I guessed were standard clientele filled many of the seats. Three maids ran mugs of draft to the waiting patrons while the bartender did his best to keep up with the demand.

I located an empty seat at the bar and requested a drink and dinner. A deep wooden bowl was brought out to me, containing what appeared to be lamb stew. Along with it I was served a fresh loaf of bread, still warm, and a small pot of honey butter. The beer was a dark stout that sat heavily in my stomach. I ate quietly, trying to take in the people around me.

For the most part everyone looked Human, but time and experience had taught me that frequently what you see isn't what you get. In my own realm I was one of very few Humans. My father had been tempted by the Fairies to cross over into their realm, lured by promises of steady work and lack of war. He had owned and run a successful wood-cutting business for years until he retired. My mother was one of the Fairies that had tempted him. They had both passed away in a fire seven years ago thanks to a pickle-making experiment gone horribly wrong.

Okay, so technically I was only half Human, but after growing up constantly teased about how I didn't have wings, couldn't fly, and had no magic, it was just easier to call myself Human. Fairy parents have a much more hands-off approach to raising a child than most Humans, so my father did his best to raise me in the most Human ways possible.

I took another sip of beer, listening to the conversations around me. Many people were discussing a band of highwaymen that had caused a lot of trouble for the town and surrounding areas recently. I almost went over to introduce myself and offer to help, but then remembered that being a hero only leads to heartbreak.

I waved the bartender over for another pint. When he came over I figured I had best start asking questions.

"Did you by chance speak with my traveling companions earlier, when they brought me here?"

The bartender eyed me closely. "I did. Good looking lads they were. So brave to bring you through the lawless forest to get you safely here to the town."

"I didn't get the chance to properly thank them for their help," I lied. In honesty I wanted to punch them both in the nose.

"That's unfortunate," he mumbled, turning to fill another order.

I waited patiently for him to finish and motioned him back over. "You don't happen to remember where they said they were going?" I asked.

He scratched his chin for a moment. "I'm not sure I remember."

I rolled my eyes and pulled out a single gold coin and laid it on the bar. He raised his eyebrows and reached for it. I quickly clapped a hand down over it.

"Perhaps you can try and remember?" I asked again with a smile.

He glanced over each shoulder before leaning close over the bar. "I heard them mention they were headed for some place close to Maht."

I had never heard of Maht, but that didn't surprise me, considering they had skipped realms with me. "How far away is this town called Maht?"

The bartender smirked. "You're not from around here are you?"

"No, not really," I admitted.

"Maht is a city in a different realm, Drakemoore. The closest portal to that realm is a three-day ride on horseback, then another two once you cross through."

My heart sank. *Maybe I should just head home,* I thought. "Where can I find a wizard or the closest Fairy Circle?"

"Fairy Circle?" The bartender eyed me again. "Do you know how to use those things? I'm not sure Maht is a Fae realm, so I'm not sure there are Fairy Circles there. As for a wizard... we haven't seen one in these parts in at least a hundred years."

"Ugh." I was tempted to pound my forehead against the bar in front of me. "How do I get to the portal?" I finally asked after I fought back the urge.

The bartender grabbed a quill and paper and began explaining while he drew a map. An hour later I had consumed another pint of beer and had directions to work from to get to the portal. Considering the bartender's extreme glee over a single gold coin, I had a sneaky feeling I had over-tipped him.

Feeling the effects of the alcohol warping my perception of the world, I stumbled back toward the stairs. I was just sober enough to notice a hooded figure following me across the room and up the stairs. They took extra care to make sure not to get too close. When I struggled with the door to my room, the figure rushed me.

I was prepared for the speed but not the power behind it. The figure hit me like a loaded wagon, knocking me off my feet. When it pounced again I rolled out of the way and drew my dagger, lashing out at my attacker.

There was a yelp, followed by a low growl. The attacker crouched, preparing to attack again. "What do you want?" I asked, readying myself.

The form stiffened for a moment. There was a slur of growls and grunts that I couldn't make out.

"I'm sorry, I have no clue what you just said."

My attacker sighed and pushed the hood back. I watched as the head of a wolf shifted into that of a Human.

Her vivid green eyes were enough to unnerve me, but knowing that seconds earlier she had been half wolf had me raising my dagger again. "Try saying that again. Use words, not teeth," I directed.

"My name is Heather, Heather Grant. You reek of Dragon, so you must know where I can find them," she said with a sly tone.

"If you had been paying more attention, you would know I am looking for Dragons as well. If I knew where to find them, I would have already left."

She rolled her eyes. "You shouldn't protect them. A Dragon killed several members of my pack. They need to be brought to justice."

"Dragons don't normally attack unless provoked. Were your clansmen threatening one or trying to steal his treasure? Those are the only two reasons I can think of that they would attack your men."

"What would you know, Human?" She spat violently.

"I've had a few run-ins with Dragons. I also used to be the Knight villages would call to get rid of them. So believe me, I know about Dragons."

"All I found were their charred remains." Her voice was little more than a whimper now.

"I'm really sorry about your loss, but it's really no concern of mine." I cracked the door to my room and pushed it open.

"You've slain a Dragon before?" Her eyes considered me carefully. "In their Human form or their lizard form?"

"In their big, scaly, fire-breathing forms. Until recently, I had never seen Dragons in Human form. I knew they had them, just hadn't seen it." I stepped inside my room and started to close the door behind me.

"WAIT!" Heather pleaded. "Look, if you're a Dragon slayer, then you must take money. Help me find the Dragon that killed my family and my clan will pay you well." I stopped and opened the door again.

"I'm not a Dragon slayer. I don't use or want the title. I'm just a hired Knight, and I help those who need me. I have trouble believing that a big, bad Werewolf clan needs my help. Go home and talk to your chieftain. I'm sure he or she will be able to handle it." This time I closed the door with a click. I wasted no time in securing the latch either.

I heard whining and scratching on the other side of the door. I ignored it and sat down long enough to tug off my boots. When the whining continued, I sighed and returned to the door. Flinging it open, I stared down at the girl who was crouched beside it giving me large puppy eyes. "What!?"

"Can I come in?"

"No!" I grated abrasively.

"Five minutes, then I'll leave, I swear," she promised me.

"Fine, but I am counting." I glared at her as she came in and pushed the door closed behind her.

With a deep breath she started telling her tale. "I can't tell my chieftain because he doesn't know where we are. A few months ago fifteen of us broke away from our clans and skipped realms. The idea was to form a new pack."

I rolled my eyes. "How old are you?" I asked.

"Seventeen," she replied, puffing her chest.

"Great, runaway Werewolf teenagers. How could anything possibly go wrong?" I didn't mean for my words to sound as bitter as they were.

She glared at me before continuing. "When we arrived we were met with more hardships than we anticipated."

"Of *course* you were." I sighed. "Go on."

"Before long we were starving in the forest. We are all proud Were, but... sometimes you do things you're not proud of to keep from starving." She hesitated. "We began robbing travelers on the road - but only the ones that looked like they had plenty of money to spare!"

I waved her on to continue. "Then about a month ago, a set of really hardcore thieves arrived and began working most of the roads. They even killed people who didn't cooperate. When a local merchant wound up dead, the sheriffs were called, prices were put on all the thieves' heads, and we were forced into hiding."

"Then let me guess? A few of your boys went looking for the other highwaymen, thinking to capture them and collect the reward." She nodded. "Only they found a Dragon instead?"

She winced. "Not exactly. They found the highwaymen." I quirked a brow in question before I could catch myself from showing interest. "The highwaymen are led by a female Dragon named Avery."

I froze. I could feel my blood run cold within my veins. "Avery? Avery, are you sure?"

"Yes, My Lady. She has dark golden skin and a large, golden tattoo up one side of her. She is also missing an eye."

"The tattoo is new, but that sounds like Avery. But she should be dead."

Heather shook her head. "I very much promise she is alive, and she killed my clansmen and my brother."

"I killed her when I pierced my sword through her eye six months ago."

"You must help us. We don't have much, but we'll pay you well," she pleaded.

I considered her for a moment. "Keep your stolen money. Before I agree to anything, I want to see if it is truly Avery." I walked over to the door. "Your five minutes are up."

Her face fell. "So you won't help us?"

"Meet me downstairs just after dawn. I'll need to secure a few things before we leave town."

"If you tell me what you need, I can get them," she offered.

I let a feral smile split my lips. "That won't be necessary - I come by my belongings honestly. We will buy them or I won't help you. Do you understand?"

With a defeated sigh she nodded. "I'll see you in the morning." She started to leave, then turned back to face me. "I'm sorry, My Lady, what is your name?"

"I'm Lady Morgan, Knight of Queen Mab's Court."

Her jaw dropped but she didn't say anything, she just closed the door and left silently.

Chapter Three

I did my best to sleep, but I was haunted by memories of my last encounter with Avery and the love I had lost. I awoke with his name on my lips and tears streaking my face. If Avery was here in this realm, still alive, I was going to find her and end her.

Using my sleeve, I wiped away the tears that burned on my face and forced myself out of bed. I quickly dressed and gathered all my belongings. After a few short minutes I was stumbling sleepily down the stairs back into the pub below. Sure enough, Heather was waiting at the bottom of the stairs for me.

I dropped onto a seat at one of the large tables and signaled to a barmaid. She approached with a bounce. "Morning, My Lady, what can we get for ye?"

I smiled at her. "How about a meal to break my fast?" She nodded and started to walk away. I caught the look on Heather's face as she glanced around the room hungrily and I let my hand dart out and catch the barmaid by the elbow. "Make that two meals and a pot of tea as well." *Tea makes everything better.*

Heather blinked at me with her large green eyes. "I'm going to wait outside," she announced.

"No, you're not," I told her. I kicked the chair across from me out from under the table. "You're going to sit down and eat a real meal. It will slow us down if you're coping with hunger pains all day."

She shook her head. "I can't afford it and I can hunt once we hit the woods."

"I'm paying, have a seat," I told her.

Hesitantly she sank onto the chair across from me. The barmaid returned shortly with a large selection of meats, eggs, bread, butter, fruit, and cheese. She also brought over a large teapot and two mugs. Heather watched hawk-eyed, all but salivating at the food before us. "Uhh, thanks," she said, eagerly waiting for me to take the first bites for myself.

"Please, go ahead and eat. You're no use to me if you are hungry, cranky, or off your game." I motioned to the food in front of us.

"Don't you want to eat first?" she asked, belying her words by taking a large hunk of bread.

"I'm perfectly capable of eating at the same time you are." I began slicing an apple and collecting bits of cheese to eat with it.

Through a mouth full of food Heather mumbled at me. "So what is your plan?

"Get supplies, buy a horse, find and kill Avery, then head for the portal, where I'm going to go track down the two Dragons that dumped me here against my wishes." I poured a mug of hot tea, taking a moment to sit back and study her while I sipped.

"So you plan to slay three Dragons?" I watched her face pale as she considered it. "Do you have a death wish?"

"I *had* a death wish. Now, I have a pissed off and seeking revenge wish." I smiled sarcastically at her, taking a certain amount of pride at how hard it was for her fathom just how serious I was.

"What did the other two Dragons do to make your list?" Her trepidation reflected her age and gave away that she lacked the experience of the cold-hearted warrior she tried so hard to portray.

"They rescued me from a Troll that was going to eat me and then dumped me here." I threw my arms wide to indicate the inn.

"That doesn't really seem like a punishable by death offense. I daresay many people would feel thankful towards their heroes."

"You're right, many would be thankful. I, however, was *trying* to be eaten." I found myself starting to grumble about the arrogant, lizard-faced jerk who had insisted on rescuing me.

"Excuse me, but you wanted to be eaten? What's wrong with you?" Heather had started to push away from the table and was surreptitiously looking for the nearest exit.

I sighed heavily and started to recount what had led me to Agshi. "Where I'm from I'm a hero and an adventurer…"

"You mean you're a heroine," she corrected. I stared blankly at her in annoyance. "What? I just happen to think if you're going to tell a story you should do it correctly." I felt my eye twitch once but shook it off.

I began again. "Where I'm from I am known as an adventurer and a heroine," I paused deliberately, waiting for her to nod approval. "When people need things handled, they come to me. I led a small band of men that shared similar interests to my own in adventure and peace-keeping. About six months ago my fiancé Simon was alerted to a string of attacks involving a Dragon. After some research, we took on the assignment. We spent over a month tracking the beast and were fortunate enough to locate its lair."

I paused. Heather was leaning over the table, resting her cheeks on her hands. Her eyes were wide with interest as she nodded along with the story. "We can finish this while we are running errands," I told her. When I stood up to pay the innkeeper for Heather's meal she almost tumbled off her chair in haste to follow me.

We made our way around town. I found a grey wool cloak, a change of clothes, a small pot, a set of bowls and mugs, bed rolls, and various other camping gear we would need. I also picked up several bundles of arrows and a sharpening stone. After a few hours we had managed to get everything we would need. I had to admit, I was enjoying having my very own Werewolf to carry my purchases.

By the time we made it to the stables, Heather was breathing heavily under the weight of the purchases but refused to complain. I located the stable master. He was a short man with darkly tanned skin and a bald head. All of his hair had clearly migrated down to his face, where he sported a long beard and mustache.

He looked me over carefully, his lips drawing up in devilish grin that he attempted to make friendly and charming. With a loud clap he rubbed his hands together. "What can I do ye for, My Lady?"

I smiled warmly. "I need to buy some horses. Do you have any you might be willing to sell?"

Without speaking he turned and walked into the stable, motioning over his shoulder for me to follow. He showed me a pair of mares that were young and had been raised as work animals. "These are a good pair for a Lady such as yourself. They are gentle and don't spook easily. One of them is spoken for already, but I would let you have your choice of the two of them." His offer was kind.

After a few serious minutes spent inspecting the animals, I chose the one I believed would serve our purposes best. Her name was Dabble. "This one will do fine. Do you have any others for sale?"

The man chuckled. "I have Slayer, but he isn't for a lady. We broke him for a knight who wasn't fortunate enough to return for him." The man grimaced as he remembered the knight and the bad deal.

"May I see him?" I asked.

"My Lady, he's a killer. Even broken he is large and wild. It would take a skilled knight or warrior – even they may not be able to handle him." His eyes narrowed as he looked towards the back of the stable. Without waiting for an invitation I brushed past him and made my way to the dim back corner.

There stood a black horse that must have been nearly nineteen hands high. He towered over me, breathing heavily, annoyed that I had entered his territory. I reached for his nose but the stable master caught my hand.

"Are you daft? That horse could kill you, My Lady!" I pulled my hand free and glared at the little man. To prove his point the man reached out and the horse reared high, voicing his displeasure.

"Saddle him, please. I want to ride him before I take him." I turned, starting to walk away.

"No, I won't let you hurt yourself."

"Your chivalry is wasted on me." I strolled calmly back towards the beast that was still rearing and dancing in his stall. Without fear I reached up and caught hold of the reins. With a good tug I pulled the horse's head towards mine. I stared the beast in the eyes and allowed my Fae to show through them. "You will behave yourself for me. Do you understand?" I hissed at him. The horse instantly stilled and quieted. "Good boy," I told him as I stroked his nose.

"How did you do that?" I could hear the stark amazement in the older man's voice. I hoped he hadn't noticed any change in me. I've heard it said I glow when I let my Fae out, but most animals easily fall under our spell with little more than a gaze.

I smiled widely. "This is a very special horse and I am very special type of knight," was all I gave as an explanation. After a short test ride I paid the man for Dabble and Slayer, along with the needed food and saddles.

When I finished, Heather met me at the stable entrance, wide-eyed. "Why did you buy two horses?"

"We'll cover more ground if we are each on our own mount," I explained as I finished packing the last of our supplies.

"I don't ride," she said curtly.

"Do you want my help?" I asked, letting a sardonic smile cross my face again.

"Of course, but…"

"But? But nothing. If you don't know how, I will teach you on the way out of town. If you don't like it, then you can suck it up and deal. Dragons fly, so they can cover a lot more land than we can on foot or with only one mount." I pulled myself up into the saddle and watched as she clumsily did the same.

Dabble, full of energy but still a work horse, happily trotted along beside me, following Slayer's lead more than the directions of her rider. The town was about two hours behind us when Heather finally spoke again. "Will you finish telling your story now?" There was a pleading tone to her voice that sounded almost like a child whining.

I smiled slyly, knowing I had her hooked. "Where did I leave off?" I asked, knowing full well where I had ended, but grinning as she all but bounced with glee on Dabble's back.

"You had just found the Dragon's Lair," she supplied.

"Ah, yes, now I remember." I stroked my chin for added effect as my father had always done. I realized that without stubble this was a pointless action. "We had tracked the Dragon to its lair. When we arrived, I led a small team of men inside. We were surprised to see the mounds of treasure the beast had collected, and left unguarded while it was away." It was the first time I had retold the whole story from the beginning since I had first explained it to a bartender all those months ago.

"We agreed to watch the lair and wait for the Dragon's return. After two days had passed I became restless. I decided to take two of the men and see if we could track down the Dragon. While we were gone, Simon was going to keep the rest of the men there and wait for the beast's return." I suddenly found it harder and harder to speak. "Simon and the others decided to go in after the treasure, and that was when the Dragon returned."

Tears stung my eyes and Heather leaned precariously over to squeeze my knee reassuringly. "Most of the men were killed. One managed to escape and came to find us. When we returned, I found Simon dying. The beast hadn't been kind enough to finish him off as it had the rest of my men. I gathered Simon into my arms and promised I would join him on the other side, once I had avenged him." I sobbed.

"Oh, Morgan, that's horrible," she cried.

"I spent another two months tracking down Avery, and when we finally met I drove my sword deep into her eye and used it again to pierce her heart. She fell to her death from a cliff. After that, I spent time trying to figure out what to do with my life, but everything felt so hollow. I decided I would join my Simon so we could be together. I took every suicidal job I could find, and when none of them helped me meet my end, I surrendered myself to a Troll so he could eat me." I smiled at the memory of Agshi running to hide when I showed up, begging him to eat me.

"That's when the other Dragons showed up and saved you? That's odd - it doesn't seem like Dragons are the heroic type without a reason."

I laughed. "The younger of the two was a squire and had been captured. We were both virgins to be served on the menu. I saved him when he had a meltdown about dying. When his older brother showed up to save the day, they 'rescued' me as thanks."

"A Dragon passed on a chance to have a virgin? And how old are you? How can you still be a virgin, especially with having had a fiancé?" Her questions were a bit biting and starting to irk me.

"I was always busy. Simon and I would often take different assignments, so we would sometimes spend weeks or even months apart." I shrugged. "We talked about it several times, but just never did anything. I think he was waiting for our wedding night. He was an honorable man." I used the back of my sleeve to wipe away the tears.

Heather watched me closely. I could see she wanted to say something, but she refrained, most likely trying to avoid sending me into another fit of waterworks.

I looked out at the sky. The story had taken longer to tell than I had realized, because the sun was already sinking toward the horizon and would no doubt be setting within the next hour or so. I urged us off the trail and into the woods, riding carefully while looking for a good place to set up camp. As the last rays of light disappeared we finished setting up at a good spot. It was tucked away out of sight behind a hill, near a small stream and a handful of large boulders.

Stripping down to nothing more than my bare skin I used the icy stream water to wash away the day's travel dust. I sucked in big gulps of air as the water numbed my skin. Heather sat on the bank watching me skeptically.

"Do you bathe every day?" she asked.

"When I can. I learned years ago you should bathe when you have the chance, especially if you're living on the road, because you don't always know when you'll have your next opportunity." I ran the rose-scented soap over my skin, then held the bar out for her.

She sniffed at it. "Wolves don't bathe unless we have to."

I shrugged. "That's fine when you are with other wolves. If you get too rank I will drag you out into the water, wash you, and then beat you dry." I smiled wickedly at her.

She grabbed the soap from my hand where I still held it out in deceptively peaceful offering and began tugging off her clothes. "Stupid… knight… woman… thinks… she… knows EVERYTHING!" The last word was snapped loudly.

I chuckled as I stepped out of the steam and began to dry off. "You'll get used to it, I promise." She growled at me.

Once we were both clean I made us hot tea and pulled some jerky and bread from a saddle bag. We munched in silence before extinguishing the fire. I pulled a few pine branches over the tops of our bedrolls and then snuggled into mine.

"What are these for?" she asked with interest.

"They serve two purposes. One, they help mask our scent, and two, in case people are stumbling through the woods, it helps camouflage us some."

Heather absorbed this new information for a moment, then tugged her bedroll close to mine. She wiggled under the covers, then shifted into her wolf form and snuggled close. I looked into her eyes and was reminded of the tales of how wolves sleep with their packs. While I had met a few Werewolves, I had never traveled with one.

I fell asleep stroking the fur on the back of her neck, the sounds of the woods serving as a soft lullaby. The night passed uneventfully. When you are looking for Dragons, you want your nights to be uneventful.

The next morning came all too early and started with me dreaming of being suffocated. I awoke to a face full of fur. Sometime during the night Heather had draped herself across my chest while we both slept. Now the combination of her weight and her fluffy grey fur in my face left me struggling to breathe. At least she smelled clean, I thought to myself as I shoved her off.

She yelped as she rolled off of me, and ducked into the woods to relieve herself. When she returned she was in her Human form… and naked. Her hair frizzed out in every direction and she stared at me through slit eyes. "Why are we up this early?" She was pouting as she tugged on clothes.

"Because we need to keep moving if we want to find Avery. How is that nose of yours doing this morning?" I asked her as I headed to the horses to check on them and get them fed before we started to travel again.

She sniffed the air. "Pretty good, I think."

"Good enough you think you can pick up the Dragon's scent?"

"Probably," she answered with a shrug.

"Excellent, that's what I like to hear. When I finish with the horses, we'll eat some food, pack up, then head out. Sound good?"

She nodded.

"Are we supposed to be meeting up with any of your clansmen?" I asked, already knowing the answer.

She shifted back and forth uncomfortably. "No, maybe later."

I didn't meet her eyes, wanting to let her hold on to her last few shreds of pride. "Alright, that's fine by me."

An hour later we were on the move again, heading north. If we happened to find Avery close to the Fairy Circle, I wasn't going to complain. I rode atop Slayer, quietly watching Heather's bushy tail bounce ahead of us. Dabble's reins were held securely in my hand as I led her along. She seemed content to follow at the quick, steady pace I set.

As we were starting to consider stopping for lunch, I noticed smoke in the distance. Several small clouds created by chimneys filled the air. "Hey, Fuzzy. You should shift back and get dressed. We'll stop in the next town for some food and to rest the horses."

On cue Heather stopped abruptly and shifted by the side of the road. I swore under my breath, looking around to make sure none of the locals had seen her careless change.

When she was fully clothed and mounted we rode into the village. The locals seemed to ignore our arrival, which I preferred over being the talk of the town. I found the local inn, which had a tavern attached to it. We stabled the horses so they could eat and rest, then wandered into the establishment. I took a table that allowed me to put my back to a corner and assessed the crowd.

Most people ignored us, but a handful of men noticed the two unaccompanied women sitting alone. It wasn't long until we had a half a dozen offers to buy us a round of drinks. Heather seemed to thrive on the attention and swung fully into flirtation mode, but I was content to sit in silence and enjoy my soup.

After a free lunch and a few more free pints than we should have consumed, Heather and I headed back out into the village in hopes of gathering information that might allow us to track down our target. I sent her to talk to local youth while I tried my hand with the shopkeepers.

I had given up hope and was heading back to the inn to meet up with Were-girl, when I overheard a farmer and the blacksmith talking about a recent attack. I stopped abruptly and stared at the men, finally piecing together the all-important fact that I had been moved to the realm of Everbloom. Realms really need to stop using the name Everwood for their forests.

The farmer was an older gentleman whose darkly tanned skin seemed to glow in the sun. The blacksmith was younger, maybe in his late thirties. He was as broad shouldered as any knight and covered in a heavy layer of soot. When he finally noticed me staring, he wiped his face with a cloth and offered me a friendly but obviously flirtatious smile.

"Well met, Lady. Please come join us. We so rarely have the privilege to meet a traveler of your beauty." His deep voice sounded saintly to my ears and I had little doubt that this was one of the village's heartbreakers.

Not needing a second invitation, I crossed the short distance and offered both men my own smile. "I'm sorry to eavesdrop, but I couldn't help but overhear you mentioning an attack. My travel companion and I are moving on shortly and any knowledge we can arm ourselves with would be helpful."

The old farmer blushed when I made eye contact with him. "My Lady, you're only traveling with one other companion? I hope he is a mighty warrior, because one of the thieves controls a Dragon."

"How many thieves are in the party?" I asked politely, avoiding the explanation of two women traveling alone.

The blacksmith and the farmer conferred a moment before finally deciding on a number. "At least six plus the Dragon, but groups like that always have more waiting in case they need them."

I nodded my head. "Has word been sent to the king that your roads aren't safe?"

The blacksmith scoffed. "Yes, but the royals have so much on their plates these days it will take weeks before they send anyone to clean up the mess, and by the time that happens the thieves will have moved on."

In my own realm the plight of the villages was always heard. The Elven Prince, Tallyn, spent years working with each kingdom in our lands building up a guard that was quick and effective. When there weren't guards to handle things, there were bands of warriors like the one I had led that also were hired to resolve issues. "Was there any word on which way the thieves were headed?"

"Yes, My Lady, rumor has it they are headed north towards the Fairy Circles. Chances are they will do their worst along the way, then hop realms to terrorize another realm of people." The farmer shook his head sadly.

"I think they are headed towards the realm that has Maht in it. I've heard there is a huge Dragon's nest in that realm. Maybe one of the largest ever. The Dragon is probably headed home." The blacksmith leaned closely to me. "I would avoid that realm if I were you. Dragons love beautiful ladies."

"Not enough to eat a virgin when you ask nicely…" I mumbled under my breath. Both men looked at me in confusion. Squaring my shoulders back, I thanked them both for the warning and let them know that my traveling companion and I would plan so we could avoid a mishap with the thieves.

When I finally arrived back at the inn, Heather had already had the stable hand saddle our horses. She munched an apple where she leaned against the grey stone wall of the stable. "Any luck?" she asked between bites.

I shrugged. "Just a little, how about you?"

She smiled slyly. "Three local boys have run away, and my guess is it is to a life of thievery and adventure."

"Why, is that what you would do?" I teased her.

Heather's face turned red clear back to her ears. "I left with the hope of finding peace and a better tomorrow. The realm of Caymod is full of displaced Weres always plotting against one another. We only did what we did to survive."

I held up my hands in defeat. "I was just picking on you."

"Well, don't. People I love are dead, and I've done things I'm not proud of." She sniffed, wiping her nose on the back of her sleeve. I wanted to tell her that was a gross habit, but ended up letting it go.

"Are we ready to leave then?"

She nodded at me and I tipped the stable hand before mounting up. Heading out the northern end of town,

I pulled her to a halt once we were out of sight of the town. "It sounds like this group could be pretty large. Is there any way we can try and stay downwind and away from the main roads where they are probably hiding?"

Heather slid off Dabble with the grace of a dancer, landing in a low crouch. She peeled her clothes off and stuffed them into the saddle bags, then shifted into her wolf form. Tying the reins of her horse to Slayer's saddle, I followed behind her as we left the road and made our way into the forest.

We hadn't traveled more than a few hours when Heather flattened her ears and darted away quickly. I pulled the horses to a stop and waited for her return. Moments later she popped back into sight and shifted. She held up her hand, telling me to wait.

With a nod I slid from Slayer's back and made quick work of securing the horses. I pulled my bow and quiver free and secured my sword to my belt. As quietly as possible I slunk across the distance, crawling on the ground beside Heather, who had returned to her wolf form. Carefully, I peered over the top of the hill to investigate her discovery.

Chapter Four

Vallen stretched out to his full length beside the fire. He did his best to ignore Young, who was currently torturing a lute. The squire's voice cracked as he sang, attempting notes too high for his now deeper voice. Why his little brother continued to dream of taverns filled with screaming women chanting his name after a musical performance never ceased to amaze him. He had no interest in destroying his brother's dreams, but most people preferred the sounds of a poorly tuned violin in the hands of a child over his brother's singing.

When Young hit a particularly sour note, one that made him fear his ears would bleed, Vallen wished desperately for his friend Dani's ability to turn off sound. Taking the cue that it was time to be anywhere but here, Vallen pushed himself up out of his chair and headed towards the many personal chambers off the North and East sides of the great hall.

With some distance, walls, and several heavy doors between him and the strained caterwauling of diseased nightingales, he finally found peace in his own chamber. It was a large, round room with two smaller chambers off of it. One led to a bathroom, which had a pool fed by a hot spring. The other served as a closet and housed a spiral staircase that led deeper into the black stone of the mountain. Below lay his personal vaults.

Giving into the calling, Vallen followed the stairs down into the heart of his vaults. One housed riches, and the other... well, the other housed something even more important than treasure. It was a promise his bloodline had made over a thousand years ago. It gave them purpose, and separated his family from the other Dragon clans that shared this nest.

Drawing the small dagger he kept tucked in the top of his boot, he made a cut at the tip on his thumb. He watched closely as a red bubble of blood came to the surface. He pressed his hand, blood and all, to a large stone slab in the wall. Around him the air was filed with whispers and the sound of stone grinding on stone. The large door slid away to reveal the chamber behind it.

To the untrained eye it looked like an almost empty room. A large circle was carved into the floor, and within it sat a large wooden chair and a white boulder as large as he was tall. He stepped inside, walking around the full circle. "I remember my oath," he whispered. Then he crossed to the boulder and rested his hand against it. "I remember my promise."

He turned to face the door and it closed behind him, sealing him in the vault. Sinking into the hard chair, he stretched his body out as best he could, crossed his arms over his chest, and focused on the boulder.

"Well, old friend, it would seem I am here to keep you company in the silence… and avoid Young's singing."

There was no voice to answer him, but his face split into a smile, as if he had heard the punchline of an old and comfortable joke. He knew that nobody else could bear his burden or understand the oath he had taken. His entire life would be spent in service to a king that may never return.

Try as he might, eventually Vallen's eyelids grew heavy and his head bobbed forward. Soon his chin rested against his chest as he quietly snored. Visions of glorious battles and brothers made in blood and honor both called to him and haunted his dreams.

The fog cleared and there he was, kneeling. *He* stood before Vallen, sword held in hand before him. Leaning forward, Vallen pressed his lips to the blade, swearing an oath that he would carry with him for the rest of his days. "I swear my life to uphold the laws of chivalry. To serve my realm and my king as long as I draw breath. I will defend my brothers with my sword and very life in the name of honor. This Oath I swear to you and Avalon."

Keeping his head bowed, eyes focused on *his* boots, he breathed easily as his life was given over to another. The sword touched his left shoulder. "The Kingdom, Avalon, and all Realms honor you and your commitment." The blade touched his other shoulder. "From this day forward know that we are brothers, all of us." There was a pause. "Rise, Sir Vallen of Avalon, and greet those you serve."

Tears burned like fire down his cheeks as his chest puffed with pride. Turning, he saw her. She, who he would forsake all others for. She, who drove away the beast within him. Her golden hair tumbled down her back. Her eyes were warm and welcoming. His Pixie, his love from this magical Kingdom. She inspired him when he thought there was no possible way he could carry on his legacy of serving the Order.

Capturing her in his arms, he held her close. "Melody," he whispered. She was named for the sweetest part of a song, the part that would haunt you long after the music ended. The sky darkened around him, and as quickly as she had appeared she was gone. Lifeless in his arms, he laid her to rest.

Vallen knew he was in a nightmare but was unable to awaken. All he had to do was open his eyes, but that seemed like an impossible task. Melody reappeared before him, only for him to realize it wasn't her. Dani... to see her was to see Melody all over again... but it wasn't her, and never would be.

Vallen awoke sobbing, begging for forgiveness from a ghost that held no mercy for him. With a glance at the boulder in front of him, he stood and used his sleeve to wipe the tears from his eyes. "I have kept my promise as did my family before me, but I will not subject my friend to the fate of my love. That would be too great a price to pay." As he touched the boulder his handprints glowed a soft blue color.

"Time is growing short. My allegiance belongs to Lord Hudraer now. When the time comes and he steps into the destiny before him, I will be at his side and yours no longer. Awaken, if you plan to." With those words he turned and willed the vault door open. He was ready to return to the world of the living, where Young sang horribly as if to court Banshees, and the ghosts of his past could not reach him.

Chapter Five

Lounging just at the bottom of the hill were three armed men. Deep into their cups and singing raunchy drinking songs, they sat unaware that we were spying on them. I almost signaled for Heather to turn and leave when the last song ended and a discussion broke out about cuts of loot. My eyes gleamed as I settled in to listen closer.

"I don't think it's right," said the first man.

"Shhh, you don't want Avery hearing you talk like that," warned another.

"Why shouldn't I say it?" the first argued. "Who stands the biggest chance of winding up captured or dead? We do. Who gets the biggest cut?"

They all answered: "The Dragon."

The second man opened his mouth again. "But you try to explain that, and what happens?"

"Crispy criminal," answered the third.

I looked at Heather, pointing away from the hill to indicate for her to back away from the camp. It was then that one of the idiots opened his mouth and continued with, "At least the women are good." I froze, turning to listen again.

"The last one I got screamed and fought, but once I showed her my knife and held it right up against her throat real close, she opened her legs for me. Didn't have to beat her snot-nosed brats or nuthin." The creep stood proudly with his hands on his hips.

My hand was already on my bow and I saw Heather baring her teeth from the corner of my eye. Rising up on one knee, I drew my bow and took aim. I loosed the arrow and aimed for the man telling his story. I was rewarded with the gurgling sound the arrow made as it embedded into his chest. Ducking low again, I could already hear their pounding feet racing up the hill. I prepared myself, standing up again and firing off multiple shots. Where I thought I had only seen three, at least another half dozen were giving chase.

I glanced over at Heather who was now running away. "Great," I mumbled, reminding myself to chastise her for being a coward later. When I ran out of arrows, I drew my sword and slid down the hill to meet my assailants.

I slid past the first two, swinging up between them. As I plunged my sword deep into the chest of the first one, I let go long enough to draw my dagger, step under the blade of the second, and then drag my dagger across his throat before retrieving my sword in my main hand. I felt a smile spread across my face. Making my way through the remaining three was a dance of kiting their bodies into places that allowed me to dispatch them at my will.

When I finished with a grin still on my face, I decided to take a quick walk through the encampment. I saw now that it was larger than I first thought. I picked up a few bags of food and coins I thought would be helpful along the way then headed back up the hill, taking care to retrieve arrows that were still usable from bodies of the fallen.

Heather sat at the top of the hill, with a mixed look of both shock and awe. "You killed all those men?"

I looked back down the hill and gave a shrug. "Just six by arrow and five by blade. Nothing all that impressive."

"You obliterated them. Do you even have a scratch to remember them by?" she asked, still in shock.

I tossed her the bags of loot then patted myself down. Looking up, I shook my head. "Nope, not this time. I may have a bruise on my arm from the guy I put in a headlock, but I won't be sure of that until tomorrow."

She started to poke through the bags, her eyes gleaming brightly. "What's this?"

"Their loot," I said quickly as I cleaned off my blades, tucking them back into my belt and boot.

"You sure have a weird sense of ethics. You'll kill them and take their stuff, but you'll judge me for being a thief." She tossed the bags over her shoulder and followed me back to the horses.

"We should ride on," I told her.

"What about Avery?" She tucked the bags into the saddlebags on Dabble.

"What about her?" I asked, pulling myself up into the saddle.

Awkwardly Heather followed suit, riding up beside me. "I thought the point was to find and slay Avery."

"It is," I said, nudging Slayer along faster.

"Then why are you so intent on leaving the area?" She was persistent.

"Avery is a coward that will hide behind her men first and only fight when backed into a corner. I know she wasn't there because she wouldn't have missed the chance to engage in a fight that would be unfair in her favor. Meaning she isn't there, meaning she has even more men with her, wherever she is. Do you understand?" I sighed heavily.

"Not really, couldn't we have stayed and waited?" Heather argued.

I pulled hard on Slayer's reins, dragging him to a quick halt. "Why didn't you stay and fight back there?"

"Because we were way outnumbered and they were rapists and murderers. In case you haven't noticed, I'm young and pretty."

"And a coward," I bit out. "Avery probably has twice as many men with her. Let's estimate twenty for a good round number. Then there is Avery herself: big, mean, and fire breathing. Can you tell me with certainty that you would charge into a battle with those odds?" She blinked at me and started to shake her head. "I didn't think so. Here we had the luxury of surprise. Dragons can smell blood almost as well as you can. We don't know when she was coming back, but I can promise she will know we were there."

"Oh," was all she was able to say.

I kicked at Slayer to increase our pace and we pushed on. Night had fallen and riding through unfamiliar woods in the dark could prove treacherous. More than once I had to pull Slayer up short because a path seemed to end in a twenty foot drop or so. In time the darkest part of night came and went, and with dawn just touching the horizon, I could see the markings of a town just beyond fields of farmland.

At some point during the night Heather had nodded off, leaving me to guide Dabble. As the sky started to light up I tugged on the reins, causing Dabble to whinny and wake up the sleeping wolf. She jerked back to consciousness, almost falling off her mount. Sighing heavily I pointed at the town just barely in sight. "How do you feel about a nice warm breakfast, a hot bath, and a nice comfy bed for a bit?"

She shrugged. "I can do without the bath and bed, but food and a place with a lock while we sleep would be a nice comfort." I eyed her closely. "What? I don't have fleas… at the moment."

"Ugh." I pushed Slayer on, urging him to move faster. Soon the horses were at a gallop. When I peeked back over my shoulder it was to find Heather holding on for dear life with her arms flung around Dabble's neck and her face buried in her mane. "Seriously, how does a Werewolf that has grown up in a realm full of horses not know how to ride?" I muttered to myself.

We arrived in town just as the sky had started to lighten to a vivid blue and people were already starting their day. It took only moments to locate the inn within the town. Unloading our bags, we stabled the horses. I tipped the boy to assure they were fed well and watered with fresh water. I also requested that they be hooded and put in the shade. He looked at the coin in his hand and back up at me with a toothy grin. "May I feed them apples with their oats, My Lady?"

"Of course," I answered.

"May I buy an apple for myself as well?" His hair was an unwashed mess and his face was covered in dirt, but still his cheer shone through.

"Absolutely. Go crazy and buy yourself two apples."
I watched as he cautiously lead Slayer and Dabble
away.

Heather followed at my heels expectantly as I
entered the inn. The innkeeper greeted us with a
wide smile. "Are you ladies just looking for food, or
lodging as well?"

"Both, and baths if that's possible," I said.

"Ten copper for the water that's already up there, a
full silver if you want fresh water drawn." He
reached behind the desk to pull out a towel.

"Fresh and hot please," I said, paying for the bath,
food and room.

"As you wish, My Lady. I will have the boys boil
some water and bring it up immediately. In the
meantime please enjoy your meal." He left to go
oversee the preparations of our baths.

Sinking onto two stools at a large table we waited
patiently as a selection of fresh bread, cheese, meats
and stew from the prior night were brought out for
us. I breathed a little easier when the tea kettle
appeared. Sipping on a hot cup of tea, I watched as
Heather gobbled down her food like it was the only
meal she would see in a year.

She looked up at me with meat hanging from her
mouth. "What?" she mumbled at me.

I set the cup down carefully. "Would it hurt you to be more ladylike?"

She shrugged, and using the back of her sleeve, she wiped her mouth. "Where I'm from manners don't mean that much."

"There is always time for good manners and they are always appreciated. Do you see the MacGregors behaving this way?" She paused mid-bite and looked at me.

"They are a ruling pack. They have to be more... polite. They mix more with the Humans and other races." She reached for another chunk of bread but I snagged out it from under her. She growled at me.

"Ask me nicely and I will share." She rolled her eyes at me and leaned back, crossing her arms over her chest. To prove a point I pulled off a small piece and popped it in my mouth. "Mmmm, this is *sooo* good." I could see her mouth watering from two feet away.

With a heavy sigh she sat up straight, rested her hands in her lap, and looked at me with feigned politeness. "May I please have some of that bread?" I looked at her with amusement.

"That was downright civil," I said, passing her the bread.

"My mother went to great pains to try and teach me, but I have seven brothers and often times being polite meant going hungry at our table," she explained.

"Well, you haven't that fear with me," I assured her.

When next the innkeeper reappeared, we had devoured most of the food brought to us and were ready for our baths. "Your water is hot and ready for you ladies. Is there anything else I can assist you with for now?"

"No, breakfast was grand, thank you." We left the table and climbed up to the third floor of the establishment.

Our room was larger than I had expected, and came with a lock on the door and two beds. It was modestly decorated and the linens smelled like lye soap but at least they were clean. I quickly disrobed and sank into the small tub. I pointed to the door. "Make sure it is locked and move the table and chairs in front of it. I want warning should we have unexpected company."

"You worry too much." Said the Wolf girl who was afraid of everything.

"I plan to get a good rest. You may do as you please if you would rather not sleep." I ran my rose-scented soap over my skin, watching as the bubbles melted away, leaving pale golden skin where there had been fine layer of dust and grime. Before I could argue, Heather had stripped and climbed down into the tub with me. "The tub is too small for us both," I argued, pushing her.

"Look, if you want me to bathe I want to enjoy hot water too." Rolling my eyes, I handed her the soap and stood up. I used half the water to rinse off then dripped my way over to my bags. After a moment's digging I was rewarded with a clean tunic and leggings. I tossed another set on the bed across the room. Heather watched the flying clothes with interest. "What are those for?"

"It doesn't make sense to put a clean body back into dirty clothes." She shook her head but said nothing. I put some of the remaining clean water in a basin and rinsed my other tunic and leggings. Before she could argue I did the same to hers, noticing the water turned a murky grey when I did. "Yuck!"

"I told you we don't bathe. When our clothes get gross, we get new, less-gross ones." She took her cleaner clothes from me and copied me, arranging them at the foot of her bed so they could dry. Then we slid without further words under the covers, and I, for one, fell asleep.

Chapter Six

The world was a peaceful and warm place. Vallen lay in bed at the hazy border between dreamland and sentient consciousness. Tugging the covers further up, he decided that someone else could play hero for a few days and that he would play Sleeping Beauty. The thought of all the ways he could possibly be awakened danced through his mind and curled his lips into a smile.

As he buried his face into his pillow again, he heard pounding. At first he thought it was in his head, courtesy of his brother's bardic "skills" the night before. The next round of banging was even louder, and this time it echoed off the walls of his chamber. Sighing heavily, Vallen sat up and slid to the edge of the bed. "I'm coming, I'm coming," he called grumpily to the door.

Vallen flung open the door just as Geren raised his hand to knock again. The Dragon stood half a head shorter and had long golden waves falling down his back. His constant scruff, combined with his actual high level of personal hygiene, made him look like the cleanest Viking ever.

"Lord Vallen, there is an issue of great importance I need to discuss with you." Vallen tried not to roll his eyes at the sight of his friend who currently had a flower tucked behind his ear.

Stepping aside Vallen motioned for him to enter. "Come in I guess." Geren rushed into the room, pushing the door closed behind him. Vallen strolled to the table in the corner and poured two glasses of a dark blue liquid.

"Avery has been sighted again," Geren quickly mumbled. Vallen was so taken aback he almost dropped the glasses before handing one to Geren.

"What? When was she last seen?" His blood began to run colder and colder in his veins.

"She's been seen in Everbloom, but all my reliable sources say that she is headed towards the portals and Fairy Circles to the north. We suspect she's hoping to make the jump to Drakemoore and start by pillaging Maht." Geren looked at the contents of his glass for only a moment before tipping his head back and downing the entire thing.

"Damn it!" Vallen swore, before copying Geren.

"What is it?" the other Dragon asked.

"Young and I were just in Everbloom on our way back from Vesaria. If I had known..." Vallen's head dropped to his chest.

Geren reached out to squeeze his shoulder. "You didn't know and that's not your fault. We all thought that Fae Knight did her in last year. Avery is a tricky one."

"How many have suffered? How many have died because of her?" Vallen's heart ached at the thought.

"You're beating yourself up over something that you have no control over. She is not the same knight you once knew." Geren spoke truly, but it didn't change the fact that they had squired together and been knighted together. They had been nearly as close as blood siblings.

"I can no longer appeal to her or continue to hope that she will see the light. She must be destroyed. She took an oath of honor and has broken that oath over and over again in the worst ways possible. She is of my Order, and so the task should fall to me." Vallen let out a slow, painful breath.

Geren set down his glass and turned toward the door. "When do we leave?" he called back over his shoulder.

Vallen's head popped up. "We?"

The shorter man flashed a deadly smile over his shoulder. "Yes, we! I'm not letting you face her alone. Hudraer would never approve of such a thing."

"Are you going to strike fear into the hearts of her cutthroats with that pretty daisy in your hair?" Vallen knew it was a pointless jibe, but he wanted to lash out any way he could.

"My baby sister picked it for me. Don't be jealous just because it adds to my good looks." Geren's grin was pure wickedness as he closed the door behind him. Vallen rolled his eyes in spite of himself and sank down onto a nearby chair.

"Avery, what are you doing? Why do you wish so much for death?" Vallen was lost somewhere between tears and disbelief. "What was the point of it all? Our King will never rise again in any realm but the Forgotten. The traditions and the Oath is *our* way of life. It is the code by which we exist." He buried his face in his hands, refusing to weep for the job that must be done.

There was a gentle knock on the door. Vallen looked up from his misery at the creature that entered. A vision of loveliness, Dani quietly opened the door and stepped in. "Vallen?" She came to stand before him. "Are you okay?"

Reaching forward, he wrapped his arms around her waist and pulled her close, resting his head against her. She started to pull away. "Just give me a moment. I need to believe that there is still goodness in others." She relaxed in his grip, reaching down to stroke his hair.

"What's going on?" Her voice was tender as she asked the question, but it only pushed him closer to tears.

"It is a personal matter for me and the other Dragons. I don't wish to burden you with it." He knew he should let her go, but he couldn't just yet.

"Well if you decide you want to talk about it, let me know. I am always your friend, you know that." The words meant in the kindest regard cut deep into him, acting as the needed motivation that allowed him to drop his hands from around her and lean back.

Capturing her hand in his own, he kissed her fingertips before letting it drop. "Surely, you didn't come into my Dragon's Lair just to comfort me. What can I do for you?"

Tucking her hands back into the sleeves of her sweater Dani glanced around the room. "I was hoping I could borrow your books on Draconic Arthurian Lore."

Vallen looked up to meet her eyes. "Is this personal research for the Princess or are you doing the council's dirty work again?"

Her smile was so warm it melted straight through the ice in his veins. "I'll have you know I love my job researching for the OAC. This project, however, is of a personal nature, and yes it is at Princess Alizeyah's request."

Vallen pushed off the chair and crossed the room to his shelves, which lined all available walls. Books on every subject imaginable surrounded them. To some Dragons the greatest treasure was gold, but to

Vallen the greatest treasure was knowledge. With careful consideration he pulled down four books. All of them were bound in leather, trimmed in gold leaf, and though they were ancient, each shone brightly from excellent care and love.

He handed them to Dani carefully, watching as her eyes widened with delight. "I will take excellent care of them," she promised.

"I know you will," he said, handing her the last of them. "Is there anything else I can help you with?"

"Oliver and I are taking a trip to Italy this summer. I was curious if I could leave Sheldon with you? We could take him along, but I can't see a Fae cat enjoying the company of Vampires that much. He likes Oliver well enough, but an entire den…" Her face showed her concern.

Vallen waved away the thought of her surrounded by so many dangerous Vampires. "Yes, he seems to always do well for himself here. That shouldn't be a problem." He hesitated for a moment. "How will you do in a Vampire den?" Dani's chosen partner was a powerful blueblood from a powerful family.

"Oh, me? I'll be fine. We aren't staying with his family. There are a few functions he must attend, but I'm going along because, well… I've never been to Italy." She gave him one last smile and headed towards the door. "Thank you again." Vallen walked her to the door and closed it behind her.

"Well that was certainly awkward," he muttered to himself.

Turning from the door, he went to his closet to start preparing for yet another trip. "One of these days I'm going to be one of those grumpy old Dragons that refuses to take a Human form anymore. I will sit in my cave, eat fattening things, guard my treasure, and read books. If anyone comes to bother me, I'll set them on fire then send them on their way."

"Good news, brother - you're already halfway there!" Young's words stiffened Vallen's spine.

"I didn't hear you enter my chambers. What do you want?" Vallen demanded.

"You know why you didn't hear me? Because bards are light on their feet." Young danced quietly beside him.

"They have to be to dodge all the things thrown at them on stage and all the fathers running them out of town," Vallen mumbled under his breath.

"What?" asked Young, a bit surprised his brother wasn't speaking clearly.

"Seriously, why are you here?" He didn't overtly care as he tugged bags free from piles.

"Because you are going out to slay your old knight sister and I thought you may need a squire for this adventure."

"Dani refused to let you help with the research project, didn't she?" Vallen didn't even have to look up from his packing to know he had hit the nail on the head.

"Princess Alizeyah said I should find a way to be helpful or she would find one for me. Last time she did that I was forced to take all the Whelplings on a camping trip." He leaned back against the closet door, crossing his arms over his chest. "Stupid fire ants, how was I supposed to know they would bite baby Dragons?"

Vallen sighed heavily. "Do you really want to help?"

"Yes," Young answered eagerly.

"No complaining?"

"No," Young answered, less enthusiastically.

Vallen tossed two heavy packs to him. "Load one of those with food from the kitchens, load the other with things you will need for the journey. When that's done, go prepare our horses."

"I have to ride?" squawked Young.

Vallen looked up at him. "Is that going to be a problem? I did secure your training as a squire with one of the finest knights across the realms. He trained me, Prince Tallyn, and our father, you know."

Young swayed uncomfortably back and forth. "Oh, no, I'll be fine. I mean, I'm very good at weaponry, and dancing with the ladies is fun, but I'm still not the best rider."

"Then I guess this will be a great chance for you to practice," Vallen told him as he turned his attention back to packing. Young gulped but didn't say anything else. Instead he left to loot the kitchens and do his own packing.

A few hours later Young and Vallen sat astride their horses waving goodbye to Geren, who looked less than happy to be left at home again. Vallen felt bad his friend had to miss the adventure to take care of the Nest, but this was Vallen's fight, not Geren's. Turning south, they headed towards Maht and from there on to the Fairy Circles that would return them to Everbloom.

"Do you think that crazy virgin is still running around in Everbloom?" Young asked as they rode.

"Perhaps, or maybe she went back to her own realm where she is currently plotting her next suicidal adventure. Either way, she is of no concern to us." Vallen pictured her finding Avery and begging to be eaten, and grimaced. Avery would gladly put the girl out of her misery if for no other reason than to shut her up. Putting a face on a victim was cause enough for him to spur his horse into a gallop towards Maht.

"Where are you going? Slow down!" Young called after his brother. Grumbling, he pushed his horse to catch up, holding on tightly to the reins. "If he was in such a hurry we should have flown like we did when we came home. Hmpf."

Several miles down the road, Vallen pulled his horse to a stop and waited for Young to catch up. The fork in the road ahead of them split, taking them either southwest or due south. "If we go due south we can cut two days out of our journey, but it would mean skipping the city," Vallen explained to his brother.

"If we ditch the horses all together we can be at the portals by sundown," Young offered.

"We'll need them on the other side. With a Dragon already running around, I can't see King Aiden liking the addition of two more. Besides, do you think angry villagers know the difference? May I remind you of the pitchfork incident involving you and your Troll friend?"

"He's a half Troll, and no. I can live without recalling that memory." He shivered. "You accidentally set *one* barn on fire and suddenly you're public enemy number one."

Angrily Vallen snapped, "I had to pay to replace an entire year's worth of supplies. It wasn't a barn, it was the town's storehouse!" A puff of smoke floated by as Vallen huffed out his nose.

Holding up his hands in defeat, Young tried to placate his brother. "Fine, fine, we'll take the horses." he pointed to the south. "We have enough food for a week provided you don't take up binge eating to cope with your emotions. Let's head directly to the portal and hope to cut off Avery."

Chapter Seven

I awoke to the sounds of yelling on the floor below. Heather, who had retained her Human form this time, snored like a wild hog, loud enough to shake the room. I couldn't help but wonder if the screaming below was about how to slay the wild animal making such noises on the floor above.

Quickly I rose from bed and quietly moved across the room to wake up Heather. When a gentle shake didn't rouse her, I put my foot against her hip and gave her a push that sent her rolling off the bed. She landed with a thud. She peeked over the bed at me with sleep-filled but irritated eyes. "Was that really necessary?"

I held a finger to my mouth to silence her before tapping my ear. She quickly caught on, lowering her head to the floor to listen closer. Her eyes enlarged and she grinned widely. "Someone's wife just found him here drinking and flirting. She wants to know where he's getting the money for it since he obviously isn't working," she whispered. She shook her head like a dog who had just sniffed out a bone and pressed her ear back to the floor to listen more.

I rolled my eyes and moved away from the bed to start packing up our gear. "C'mon, we should go eat and be on our way."

"Wait!" she hissed at me from her spot on the floor. The yelling had softened quite a bit and now all we could hear was a muffled conversation from the room below. Her head shot up. "Lady Morgan," she motioned for me to come closer. "Here," she pointed at the floor. "There's a gap in the boards and you can hear," she whispered. Shaking my head, I crouched on the floor and pressed my ear down against the wood.

"I told you, lovely, I got meself a job. I'm one of Avery's men now. I do what she tells me and when and the money is good," said a heavy male voice.

"I told you no more get-rich schemes, Henry. What's wrong with working an honest job for once?" His wife was clearly not impressed with his new line of employment.

"Honesty don't pay the bills," he argued.

Lifting my head, I looked at Heather and motioned to the door. "We should gather up and leave," I mouthed to her. She seemed to understand because she nodded and began packing very quietly. Soon our few bags were carefully filled and we had quietly returned the table and chairs to their rightful places. I was beginning to think we would make it out without any trouble when I opened the door and saw the innkeeper standing there with a wide smile.

"I was just coming up to check on you ladies. Did you rest well?" he asked, in a manner that struck me as overly cheerful.

"Yes we did, thank you. We were just packing up," I said quickly.

He blinked in confusion. "The sun will be going down in a few hours. Surely you can't be thinking of leaving already. The roads are dangerous for just the two of you." He took my hand and patted it. "You'll stay here tonight. Molly is making her famous tarts and we are serving wild boar for dinner. Stay the night and leave early in the morning."

Smiling graciously, I carefully extracted my hand from his grip. "We are meeting with our traveling companions this evening." I smiled at him. "We arrived earlier than expected. They went to scout ahead, having heard about bandits on the road and in the surrounding area."

The innkeeper leaned closer and lowered his voice. "It would be unwise for you or your companions to travel the roads today or tomorrow." He gave me a wink.

"Why are you telling us this?" Heather asked in a whisper.

"Because dead customers are bad for return business," he replied. He leaned back with a smile. "Come downstairs, enjoy some warm tarts. Have a nice *safe* evening here with us, yeah?" Heather was already nodding her head in agreement.

Stealthily I moved down the stairs and about the pub, looking for a good vantage point that would offer me a view and the protection of a wall at my back while also keeping us tucked back out of sight. Taking up a table in the corner of the pub downstairs, I watched the stairs closely, trying to identify Henry when he came down from his little private meeting. All I saw were a couple barmaids running pints up and down the stairs to unseen patrons behind closed doors. The innkeeper reappeared with a young woman bearing a large tray. Two loaded plates of boar and vegetables, a couple loaves of bread, a homemade soft cheese, and a small mountain of tarts were piled on a tray. I held up a hand to ask, but the innkeeper was a step ahead with a kettle of tea. "Are you trying to fatten me up?" I asked him with a grin as the maid unloaded the food.

"Nah, I just noticed this morning that your companion still eats heartily, being so young." Heather, who had already shoveled in a mouthful of food, scowled up at him. He smiled at her. "You have nothing to be angry about, girl. My own daughter used to eat like you when she was still around."

I took a sip of tea and considered him. "Is she married, or dead?" I asked bluntly. Heather winced at my words, quickly taking stock of the food on the table as if to see how much she could inhale before the innkeeper took it all away.

"In truth, I do not know. She left here when she wasn't much more than seventeen. Many of the friends she had grown up with were already married, and some even had babes of their own. She didn't want that for her future. So I told her she could stay here and learn the business so I could retire, but she didn't want that either. We quarreled over it a few times. I really only wanted her to be happy, but she just didn't want anything to do with any of it: the town, settling down, or responsibility. I woke up one morning and she was gone." I moved over on the bench so he could take a seat beside me. Heather had stopped eating.

"I lost my own parents, and there are times, even now that years have passed, I wish I could talk to them about things going on in my life. My mother and I were never close, but my father... he was the greatest man in the world." I felt tears prick at the back of my eyes and when I looked across the table I discovered Heather's eyes were also watery.

"But parents just don't get it," she finally let out. "They want you to be them, not yourself. They expect perfection at every turn." Tears glistened as they ran down her face even though she obviously tried to fight them back.

The innkeeper pulled a handkerchief from his pocket and leaned across the table, dabbing away her tears.

"There now, it's nothing to get worked up over. Parents are children too, just with a few more laugh lines. All they really want is to see their children happy and healthy. Sometimes in anger things are said that aren't really meant." Heather accepted the handkerchief and gave the older man a little smile.

"Thank you," she said. It was the most subdued I had seen her since we met.

Halfway through the meal I looked up to see a man dressed in dark browns doing his best to come down the stairs unseen. Luckily Marvin, the innkeeper, also noticed him. "Henry! Henry Hobbard, is that you trying to sneak out without paying your tab?"

Marvin did his best to jump up from behind the table. It did little good as Henry took off like a rabbit out the front door. Marvin slumped down on the seat, defeated. "Excuse me Marvin, I'll be right back," I told him before climbing over the bench and table then bolting out the door.

As I came out the front entrance of the inn I saw Henry duck around behind the next house. Sighing to myself, I gave chase, pushing my legs and full stomach to move quickly. As I rounded the corner of the house, I saw just enough of him duck into an alley that I was able to follow him. When I reached the alley however, it was empty. "Come out. I know you're hiding, Henry, but really it will be much easier on you if you just cooperate." Silence was my only answer. "Fine," I muttered, taking my first few steps into the alley.

I listened carefully for the sounds that would give away his position. With a few more steps I heard his movements to my left rear. He stepped out of a building's shadow behind me, grabbed a handful of my hair, and held a knife near my throat. I didn't move. "Now, my pretty little thing, you're going to tell me why you are following me."

"You're new at this, aren't you?" I asked flatly.

"I'm a regular criminal," he said, pulling the blade closer to my throat.

"No you're not," I said and I used my right shoulder to knock away the arm with the blade, threw my left elbow back into his gut, and stomped on his foot. I stepped out of his hold easily. When he lunged at me I grabbed his wrist and brought my knee up between his legs, dropping him to the ground. I picked up his knife and slid it into my belt before rolling him onto his stomach and sitting on him.

"Who are you? What do you want?" He struggled under me, but I yanked his arm back and bent it at an angle that caused him to scream out in pain.

"It's not important who I am, Henry. What is important is that I am saving your life. I am doing you a favor. If you can't handle me, then a life of crime is not for you. Why don't you make this easy? Answer a few questions for me, go back and pay your bar tab, and then explain to your wife why she was right. Sound like a good plan?"

"Like hell I will, lady," he spat at me. I grabbed a handful of his hair and bounced his face hard on the stone street. I heard the telling crunch of a nose being broken.

Shall we try that again?" I asked. He struggled under me but I tightened my grip on his arm and waited for the yelp of pain. "Where and when are you supposed to meet Avery?"

"She'll kill me for telling you," he garbled out.

"You should know I have killed men before. Really, you have no less to fear from me." To prove my point I grabbed the back of his head again.

"Wait! I am supposed to report tomorrow to the old mill, just after lunch." He breathed heavily as I held his face off the ground.

"Interesting. And what's the plan from there?" I asked, already nursing a growing suspicion.

"We're traveling north to the portals. She wants to completely sack the town of Maht."

"To what end?"

He sobbed in pain. "I don't know, I'm a new recruit."

"Fair enough. It would be foolish for them to reveal their master plan to a newcomer," I said to him. I stood up, still holding his arm to help him to his feet.

"Now you'll lemme go, right? I mean you aren't a sheriff or anything, right?" I pushed him back towards the inn.

"Nope, you will pay your tab, and then after that you will have a nice chat with the sheriff," I partially led, partially dragged him back to the inn.

When we entered the door the entire pub went quiet. I walked him up to Marvin, bloody face and all. Marvin's eyes were full of surprise. "Oh, son, what have you done? Did you trip running away?"

"No, the monster behind me drug me back. I'm here to pay my tab." I kicked Henry in the calf and he whimpered in pain. "And apologize. My actions were not gentlemanly and I see that now."

Marvin leaned up on his toes and peered over Henry's shoulder at me. I offered my most innocent smile, which caused him to look at me with suspicion.

After depositing Henry with the local sheriff and explaining the importance of holding him for forty-eight hours, I went back to the inn. When I returned, Marvin met me at the door and ushered me into his office where Heather was already waiting. He closed the door behind us and bolted it twice before motioning for me to take a seat across from him.

"I'm not entirely sure who you are, miss, but for as thankful as I am, I also need you to understand Henry has fallen in with a bad crowd. You may have made some enemies tonight." His eyes were filled with concern.

"I'm Lady Morgan of Queen Mab's Court in Vesaria." Marvin's eyes widened at the information. "Henry has been hanging out with a very dangerous woman named Avery, am I correct?"

Marvin leaned closer. "It's said she controls a Dragon," he whispered.

I smiled and leaned in equally close. "Avery *is* the Dragon."

The man's body began to shake. "I had a Dragon in my inn."

"Wait, when?" I hadn't realized she was so close.

"Yesterday, she came in with a man she claimed was her husband. They wanted me to pay them money to make sure my patrons would be safe for the next few days until they left." He looked down at his hands. "It was all the money I had on the books, but luckily I had deposited most of it a few weeks ago in the storehouse."

"YOU PAID HER?" I asked, outraged.

"Of course. The safety of my guests is paramount. That's why I wouldn't let the two of you go riding off tonight. Henry is no thug, but my understanding is she is not in short supply of them." He reached across the table and took my hand. "My Lady, I am thankful for what you did, but please think of your own safety."

"Marvin, I'm truly touched by your concern. That's why we are staying the night." The older man sat back in his seat and breathed easier.

"Wise choice, my dear." He started to stand up, but I stopped him.

"I just need you to promise me one little thing, though." He nodded at me. "When they ask you about me, and they will, make sure you let Avery know that her first eye wasn't enough to quench my thirst for vengeance." I stood up, ignoring his shock and fighting hard against the grin that so desperately wanted to sneak onto my face.

When we reached our room on the third floor I immediately bolted the door and began moving furniture in front of it. "Help me move one of the beds over, would you? We need to be quiet and quick about it."

Heather stared at me as if I had magically become a Troll, but did what I asked. I extinguished all the light in the room and moved to the window, opening it just enough to peer out. "Why are we doing this?" she asked.

"If he really cared about his guest's safety he wouldn't be encouraging people to stay - he would encourage us to turn back. He would know his place isn't safe." I turned to look back out the window.

"So he's in on it?"

"Yes," I whispered. "First chance he gets he will tell the right people and we will have an angry mob of thugs here to teach us a little lesson."

It wasn't long before the stable boy went back out to the stable to sleep with the horses for the night. Soon after that, even with all the fun still going on downstairs, I saw Marvin's figure slipping off into the darkness. "C'mon. This is when we need to make a break for it."

I quietly pushed the window open, slung my bags over my shoulder, and grabbed the lattice beside the window to quickly climb down. Heather was hot on my heels, for once not asking a thousand questions. We slid silently into the stables and I caught the young stable boy by the arm. He grinned widely when he saw me. "I will pay you five gold to run away and not be here at the stable tonight. There are some bad men coming and I don't want them to hurt you." I felt the Fae in me rush to the surface and the boy stared at me, transfixed. "Will you do that?" The boy nodded yes and I pressed the coins into his hand before he darted off into the night.

I grabbed the saddles, flopping them over Dabble's butt, and pulled myself onto Slayer bareback. I looped a lead around Dabble and led her out of the stable and onto the main road. "Heather, get to a dark corner and shift. Meet me at the edge of town and stay out of sight." I blinked and she was gone.

With patience I worked my way out of the town mostly unnoticed and skirted its edges. When I arrived at our rendezvous point I dismounted and started preparing the horses for hard travel. If Avery had a small army big enough to take an entire town, I needed to get to Maht and warn the people. A lone warrior wouldn't be enough to defeat a Dragon with an army.

Chapter Eight

"Can we slow down?" called Young.

Vallen slowed his horse's pace to match his brother's. Young's lack of riding skill was showing again. "Every moment that passes innocent lives could be lost," he said, glaring at the younger Dragon.

"That's all well and good, but if your intention is to keep these beasts alive long enough to ride them in Everbloom, then I suggest we slow down. Horses are *not* Dragons. They cannot go for hours at top speed and not pay a price for it." Young reached over and tugged on Vallen's reins.

"We must keep going," Vallen argued, looking down the road ahead.

"We have taken very few breaks today. It's getting dark and there isn't a town that we can to stop at. I say we push into the woods, set up camp, feed and water the horses, and get some rest ourselves." Young's words made complete sense, but that didn't make it any easier to hear. Vallen wanted desperately to put an end to his fear and protect the people of his own realm.

"You're right," he admitted.

Young looked shocked. "Can I get you to sign something saying that?"

Vallen smirked with a huff. He ignored his brother and scanned their surroundings. The closer they got to the coast the more the tree line thinned out. "We don't know what we are walking into tomorrow. Avery could already be at the portal here or just on the other side in Everbloom."

Young processed that information. "So she may be lying in wait for us on the other side and we have no way of knowing?"

"None," answered Vallen as he started to turn his horse off the road.

"Doesn't that worry you in the least?"

Vallen looked over his shoulder at Young. "Are you losing your nerve already?"

"Me? No!... psch.... Besides, ladies *love* Heroes." A smile split his face from ear to ear, revealing the gleaming rows of perfectly white teeth.

"Save it for the ladies, Prince Charming," was Vallen's reply. Though he would never admit it, he too remembered a time when being a hero meant the world to him. He also remembered what it meant to one Lady. Though the memory was bittersweet, it made him smile.

Winding through the trees that made the forest a twisted maze, they were finally able to find a place where they believed they would go unnoticed for the night. The greenery was heavy, but the path through the woods led them to a stream where the water ran clear and clean. Caring for and securing the horses for the night seemed to lighten both their spirits.

Vallen saw to the small fire and dinner while Young unpacked their belongings from the horses. Sinking down by the fire, Young began humming. "So help me, if you start singing, I swear when this mission is over, I will take you back for the Troll to eat."

Young's humming stopped immediately, but the threat wasn't enough to completely silence him. "Why are you letting Dani court that Vampire?"

Vallen considered his brother as if examining his face for signs of the dreaded and dreadful Tactless Disease. He took a drink of ale while pinning him with his gaze. "First off, I am not 'letting' her do anything. Dani is a person and therefore has as much right as anyone else to live her life as she chooses."

"Second...." Young prompted.

"I was getting to it," Vallen snapped. "Dani may or may not be Melody's reincarnation. Either way, this is a different life. I don't expect her to remember me."

"I'm sorry, but that's horrible. You made a deal with a Mage to have her reincarnated. She should remember she loves you."

"I made a deal because her life was cut short because of me. I didn't make the deal for myself, I made it for Melody. I knew that there was a chance she wouldn't come back in my lifetime. I knew ahead of time that if she came back she wouldn't recognize me." Vallen sighed. "Dani may just be from the same bloodline and looks a lot like Melody. It doesn't matter."

"Why didn't you just do what Alizeyah did?"

Vallen glared at Young. "Because what she did goes against the laws of nature. She herself goes against the laws of nature. I don't have such a luxury. I *am* the law, as you will also be one day."

Young rolled his eyes. "So you aren't even going to try for Dani?"

"We have a connection and I do love her. I will always love her, but she is a different person in this life and so am I. If we are destined to only be friends, then I will embrace that relationship and be thankful for it every day." He thought about his outburst the day before.

"Why don't you tell her? Let her choose. She may choose you if she knows the truth." Young was getting worked up over all of this.

"No, I can't tell her, and neither can you. If we are meant to be, we will be. I must trust that there is a plan for me and if I am meant to have a mate, I will find her when the time is right." Shifting the blankets around, Vallen laid out his bedroll.

"One last question." Young waited for Vallen to grunt in agreement. "Let's say she isn't the one and never was. Let's say your true love is still out there. If you are still carrying this flame for her, how will your heart be able to burn for another?"

Vallen rolled the words over in his head, unable to really form an answer. Finally he shrugged under the weight of it. "Faith."

Both men sank into their blankets and closed their eyes. Dawn would come sooner than either would like, but there was work to be done and heroics to get underway.

The sound of dawn in the woods is unique. First the sky lightens and slowly reminds us of warmth, even on the coldest of days. Then the woods wake up. Birds sing, animals rustle, and even the water makes more noise, as if to greet its neighbors. Dragons… don't care about any of that.

Left to their own devices Dragons embrace a safe, dark place to sleep and only venture out for the prospect of food, treasure, or a combination of the two. That's why nests are so important - they allow Dragons to socialize while not having to leave home very often. Vallen was one such Dragon. Young was not. Young needed adventure, friends and attention. Young needed LOTS of attention.

Vallen awoke to the sounds of Young singing, off tune, again. "What are you doing?" Vallen grumbled, resisting the urge to pull the blanket back up over his head.

"Singing while I pee, my favorite morning ritual." Young turned around, having just finished watering the local flora.

"Of course it is. Why ever would I have a brother who conducts himself with a measure of grace?" Vallen forced himself to sit up and take note of their surroundings. As he suspected, they had spent the night uninterrupted. Vallen tugged on his boots and fought his way to his feet to stagger to the stream.

"Are you ready to get going?" Young bounced around behind him, pulling a light coat on over his tunic.

"Are you always this chipper in the morning?"

"No." Young thought about it. "Actually, today I think I'm sort of quiet." Vallen mentally sent a heartfelt apology to Sir Leon for having to train Young.

"If your squire brothers smother you in your sleep I will know it was justified and not insist on seeing vengeance served." Vallen rolled his bedroll back up and gave his younger brother a cutting glare. "It makes me thankful I was out defending the realm in your early years and Grandmother was left to deal with you."

"I was an adorable Whelpling. She thought I was a refreshing joy after the years of boredom she had with you." His mocking tone did little to soothe Vallen's morning mood.

"It's going to be very hard to be a bard if you're missing your vocal chords." Immediately Young shut up.

It took about an hour, but the boys fed themselves and the horses, packed up, and headed out. By the time the sun was dancing in the midmorning sky, Young was already whining for a break. Despite his best pouts, that had obviously worked so well on his riding instructor, they pushed on. Vallen told him repeatedly that they could rest when they arrived at the portal, but Young knew better.

"So what if we see the crazy girl again? I mean, if she's still alive."

Vallen shot his brother a warning look. "She isn't our concern. Avery is our target. Our mission is to go in, put down Avery, disband her men, and then go home. It shouldn't take all that long."

"Yeah, but let's say the crazy girl... what was her name?" Young asked, snapping his fingers.

"Lady Morgan."

"Yes, that's it. Her. What if she's there and is all, 'Oh, Dragon, eat me,' or something like that. What then?"

"The eloquence of your words astounds me." Vallen resisted rolling his eyes. "We keep her from killing herself if she is there. She is an innocent and thus should be protected."

"I don't know about that. She is evidently some all-powerful warrior or something."

Vallen snorted. "You think everyone is an enchanted warrior. You think I am."

"You are!"

"Fine, I'm a bad example. Why are you so sure she was?"

"Because she was hung upside down, tied up tightly, and she managed to escape without a sound in the blink of an eye. That Troll Agshi knew how to tie some tight knots. I'm a Dragon and I couldn't get out of them, but she could."

"Ok, so your personal inadequacies make her an *all-powerful* warrior?" Vallen knew he shouldn't tease his younger brother like this, but he had missed a major chunk of the young Dragon's life. Besides, there had to be some perk for not eating him when he was still a Whelp.

"She killed Agshi's entire family; removed their heads herself. I'm telling you, if she's not enchanted, then she is just one hell of a warrior." Young huffed and looked like he was considering a pout.

"If she is still alive and that solid a warrior, perhaps we will recruit her to help with Avery. At the very least we can use her as a distraction." Vallen was growing tired of this conversation. The young woman had been stubborn, beyond insane, and absolutely maddening to be around. While he hoped she was alive and well, he truly wished she was nowhere near Avery and her army of thugs.

By lunch time they had reached the path that departed from the road and led to the portal. As soon as they hit the trail, Vallen spurred his horse until they galloped down the dirt path. Within minutes he could see a lush blue circle set among the sand. Trees grew tall in a ring, and at the center stood a large white stone that seemed to glow in the midday sun.

"Remember, when we go through, stay in the circle until I figure out the best path of exit."

Young nodded and followed him into the sacred grove. All noise of the outside world faded away until all they could hear was silence. Dismounting, Vallen approached the boulder. He reached deep into his pockets and pulled out an offering of a Fairy Fire gem and laid it on top of the stone. "Ancient portal between the realms, we seek safe passage to Everbloom."

Vallen rested his hand upon the stone and the entire circle started to shimmer. The air grew thicker and soon they were surrounded by darkness. It felt like their feet had been pulled out from under them and their stomachs did flips inside them. Then the light returned and the shimmering faded.

The Dragons stood at the center of a Fairy Circle looking at the forest around them. Cautiously, they inspected their surroundings, unsure of what to expect. In silence they rode into the woods around them, on the lookout for any signs of a trap or other beings.

"I think the coast is clear," whispered Young.

"It's better to stay quiet to be sure for now." When his brother quietly acquiesced Vallen silently rejoiced. They pushed on until it became too dark to ride safely, by which point they were too tired to try anyway. Finding what they hoped was a safe place, they made camp for the night.

Chapter Nine

"Why would you tell her you were here?" Heather shouted from the back of Dabble.

"I want her to know that she is my prey," I explained.

"I'm a born hunter. Word of advice, it's easier when the prey doesn't know," she retorted.

"Avery is, or was, a member of a VERY old order of knighthood whose roots go clear back to the Original Dragon. I will never be considered a serious opponent if I don't challenge her." I strained my eyes against the darkness. Even with my senses and awareness heightened by my Fae blood, it was difficult to see

"Explain the whole Original Dragon thing to me. I know for a fact that Dragons existed before Arthur."

I smiled and thought to myself. My mother and I had never been overly close, but there was still a time when she had made sure I knew the legends of our peoples. "Tarell is the Human realm that Arthur is from. It is also the realm that is believed to have had the first Dragons. In the beginning, Humans were lawless savages, but not without a measure of passion, creativity, hope - and fear. For many years the Fae of the realm ruled over the Humans, but Dragons believed that they could be trusted to rule themselves."

"So Dragons and Humans were friends?" Her question reflected a common misconception.

"Not really. I'm surprised you don't know this, considering your own ancestry." When I glanced over she just shrugged at me. "Dragons are the only race that is believed to be as old as the Elves. Fairies evolved from the Elves, but they would never willingly admit that. Anyway, back to the story."

"The Dragons knew Humans showed great potential, but they had always followed the path of magic for guidance. They didn't see the difference between Fae and Gods. The Dragons knew this wasn't right, so they searched among their ranks for one that held all the best qualities of leadership and had no evil in his heart. When he was found, he shared his blood with a babe so pure he would only grow into a man of good. That babe was Arthur, who taught the ideas of Dragon chivalry to the world. He became a leader of legend." I smiled. I had always thought it would be exciting to belong to the Order.

"Ok, but that still doesn't explain the whole 'Original Dragon' thing. There is more to the story, isn't there? There has to be," she pushed.

"The bloodline of the Dragon who was pure of heart and gave magic to the Humans, has properties in their blood that leads those with it on to greatness. They are skilled warriors, just rulers, and often more powerful than they know." I looked at Heather, who was finally nodding in understanding. "There is an

Order of Knights, most of whom are Dragons descended from that bloodline. They are gifted with powers beyond that of most Dragons or other creatures."

"And Avery is one of these Knights?" I could hear her growing fear.

"Let me put it this way. I took her eye and ran a sword through her heart and she still lives. I can't think of too many creatures that can survive that, can you?" I bit my lip thoughtfully. If I was going to defeat her I needed a new plan.

"So are you a member of this Order?"

"Me? No, not at all. I'm just a Halfling." I always felt like less of a person, telling others that.

"What kind of Halfling? I've seen my fair share, and most don't shred encampments of bandits like you did two days ago." Her words sprang from curiosity, but for the first time in a long time I had a swell of pride in my chest.

"My father was Human and my mother was a Fairy. She oversaw a portal to Tarell. That's where she met my father and lured him through to Vesaria."

"I could be wrong, but normally that doesn't come with the title Lady." Her sharp wit made me smile.

"No, I wasn't born a Lady. The title was bestowed on me by Queen Mab for the peace I brought to her Kingdom. It was the first time in my life I ever felt like a member of the Fae." My mind shifted from riding to remembering the day I had been presented in court. I didn't notice the branch right in front of me. It caught me square across the chest, knocking me backwards off Slayer and sending me flailing to the ground.

The air was knocked from my lungs and I struggled to breathe. Before I could utter a word Heather had dismounted and was kneeling beside me. "Are you going to live?" she asked, with only a slight edge of sarcasm.

Accepting her hand, I regained my feet. "Thank you." I caught hold of Slayer's reins and pulled myself back into the saddle.

"How much longer are we going to ride tonight? Neither of us knows this forest well enough to ride blindly and my night vision is hampered by staying in Human form and riding on this beast." Heather's complaints were valid, but I wanted to be sure we were well out of harm's way before we rested.

"Soon. We don't know if she has thugs hidden in the forest or in the town. We are leaving the region she is likely to be keeping men in. Once I am comfortable with our safety, we can make camp," I told her.

We rode on for another few hours. The darkest part of night had come and gone and I was waiting for the first rays of sun to start warming the horizon.

When the woods grew completely silent, at that time just before first dawn when nocturnal animals were settling in but fluffy woodland creatures hadn't yet begun to stir, I pulled Slayer to a halt so I could close my eyes.

The sound of life was all around me but the world felt silent, like I was the only one listening to it. Ahead and to the right there was the softest noise of running water. I opened my eyes slowly, breathing in the smell of nature, tasting my surroundings. "There's a water source ahead. We should set up camp here."

"Finally," Heather grumbled. I heard her kick her leg over and slide off her horse.

The flickering light of two lanterns was all we needed to make beds near the base of a tree. The surrounding underbrush offered protection from the elements and camouflage from passersby. Heather pulled the food and weapons free of the horses before tugging their saddles off. Dabble seemed to sigh in relief at its removal. Quietly I led them in the direction I believed the stream to be until I suddenly stepped knee-deep into water. "Well, I guess I found the stream," I told the horses before securing and feeding them.

When I found my way back to Heather she had already sliced an apple and stripped down to bare skin. I rolled my eyes but decided not to say a word, gladly accepting the half an apple and soft bread she handed me. I ate quickly, more for the promise of a warm, dry bed than from feelings of hunger.

With a full belly, I peeled my wet boots from my feet and buried them in the folds of my blanket. Tugging it up over my shoulders and head, I allowed myself to relax. The long night of travel had worn on my body, causing it to ache in places it hadn't in a while. I took a deep breath, flexing my muscles in a static stretch, and smiled. I felt more like me than I had in months.

I came awake in a panic when a hand clamped down over my mouth and another jerked me into a sitting position. The sun was up and it looked to be mid-morning. Heather tapped her nose and pointed to the south. Without regard to my shoelessness, I rolled to my feet, staying crouched low. I nocked an arrow and waited to see what was coming.

I heard the rustling of bushes ahead of me. I started to draw back, but Heather's gentle touch on my arm stilled me. A rabbit ran across our trail and I breathed a sigh of relief. I drew the bow and in a single shot felled the rabbit. I had started to rise when Heather tugged me back down and pointed. There, no more than thirty feet ahead, two men lumbered through the woods, unaware of their surroundings.

They were just far enough away that we couldn't overhear their conversation, but I quickly understood their plans when they both dropped their pants and squatted near the ground. One passed gas so loudly we could easily hear him and they both burst into laughter. After what felt like an eternity the men finished and went on their way. I glanced at Heather and we exchanged looks that said the exact same thing: "Let's get moving."

The journey was pleasant and uneventful. It was enough to almost make me forget that I was on a mission to slay a Dragon and avenge my fallen love. "What are you going to do after you slay Avery?" Heather interrupted my thoughts.

"I don't really know, to be honest with you. I was going to track down the Dragons that rescued me, and I still may, but I'm not sure how many more Dragons I really want to face in my lifetime." I sat perplexed. For the first time in months I felt like I almost had my life back, and in many ways it was thanks to Sir Vallen and his brother. Though my blood still boiled when I thought about how they had dumped me in another realm.

"Do you think you will keep fighting, or settle down?" She was full of questions this morning.

"I have been waging war for most of my teenage and adult life now. I'm not entirely sure I want to do that anymore, but I'm not really good at anything else." What other work was there to do? I wasn't a farmer. Fae or not, I had a black thumb that made anything that wasn't a weed shrivel and die within days. I couldn't see myself crafting as an artisan did, or even building. I shook my head. "I really don't know," I said again, but this time more for my own benefit than hers.

She sat in quiet contemplation of my words. When she finally spoke again it was with a new perspective of the world. "I don't know what I want to do with my life when this 'adventure' is over. It makes me feel a little better that you don't know either. I thought something was wrong with me for not knowing."

"I don't think not knowing makes you lost. I think not caring does. Whatever I do when this is over, I will still help others. I've never heard anyone regret their life when they lived it showing kindness and helping others" *As long as I am helping people, I know I will find joy in what I do*, I thought to myself.

Just ahead there was a fork in the road. The left led to another small town and to the right the forest became denser. Somewhere within lay the Fairy Circle that would connect Avery with Drakemoore. She must never be allowed to cross over and terrorize another realm. The circle itself was sacred ground, but outside the circle all bets were off. "We should stage our attack before the circle. Not close enough they can make a run for it, but close enough that they think we aren't coming and it lures them into a false sense of security."

Heather nodded agreement. "So, the woods?" she asked with a grin.

"Yes..?"

"Excellent! Here, hold these," she said, handing me her reins and slipping off her horse into the woods. Moments later the dark figure of a large wolf appeared at the forest's edge, her clothes clamped firmly in her mouth.

Smiling, I rode into the woods away from the path. "Ok then, you lead the way. Find me the Fairy Circle, wolf girl, and I will make sure we have fresh meat for dinner tonight." Heather's dark, furry head bobbed in comprehension before she turned and sprinted into the woods. With extreme care, I navigated the horses through the treacherous trees where there was no trail, I did my best to keep pace with an anxious Werewolf.

Chapter Ten

Vallen awoke in the middle of the night to the smell of roasted meat and the sound of his growling stomach. His eyes slid open to scan the surrounding area. Young was sound asleep, and damn if the smell wasn't tantalizing. Concluding they were safe for the moment, he closed his eyes and did his best to squelch the sounds of his roaring tummy.

He rolled over, drawing his knees up closer to his chest and tugging the blanket over his head. He hoped the smell of the wool would cancel out the smell of the roast rabbit. After a few minutes of this futile attempt, he pushed back the blanket and sat up. Perhaps he should investigate the smell, just to make sure they were safe. It could belong to Avery's men, after all.

Belting on his sword, he quietly slipped from camp and allowed his nose to guide him. Around a few trees, over a hill, across a stream, and up another hill he finally located the source of the smell. He could see a fire's glow reflecting on some rocks at the base of a steep cliff. He slipped through the shadows, darting along the edge of the trees, hoping to get a closer look.

The large boulders surrounding the encampment kept its inhabitants hidden from view. After several failed attempts to spot them he gave up and began stripping off his clothes. Folding them neatly, he tucked then into the crook of a tree, then looped his sword belt around his neck and sighed. "I was hoping to avoid this," he mumbled to himself.

With a moment of focus and a swirl of magic, his body shifted into its powerful Dragon form. His claws gleamed like blades. His blue and black scales glittered in the moonlight – and itched like he had wandered through a patch of poisonous plants. Looking around, he leaned back against a nearby tree and rubbed up and down against it until the itching stopped. "Ahhhh," he quietly growled.

Glancing around again to make sure all was clear, he pushed into the air with a few light flaps of his wings and glided along air currents until he had seated himself on a ledge above the camp. The shadows kept him hidden from sight. Curious, he looked down at the camp activities below.

A young woman with dark skin and large eyes sat cleaning a rabbit and adding it to a pot over the fire. Vallen smiled because she took extreme care with the fur and meat. He leaned his head down, taking another deep breath of the roasting meat and vegetables. His stomach growled again and this time the woman's head shot up. She glared in his direction and growled back. He held his breath, afraid he had been found out.

Just then a movement at the edge of camp caught his eye. Fearing it was an intruder, he softened his knees, prepared to rush to the woman's (and dinner's) rescue. Just before he pounced, the woman turned to face the intruder, a look of annoyance crossing her face.

"Yuck, I can smell the soap from here. Really, what is your obsession with bathing so much? It can't be healthy." Her voice was slightly gravelly and it caught Vallen off guard. He examined the young woman more closely. An aura of animalistic power seemed to radiate off of her. *What are you?* he wondered to himself.

"You know what? It's way easier to convince villagers you're the good guy when you smell like one." Something about the voice seemed vaguely familiar. He racked his brain trying to remember where he had encountered it before, then he turned his attention to the newcomer and his coherent thought ceased.

There in the glow of firelight stood a woman of lithe frame that was covered in tightly coiled muscles. Her breasts were high, pert, and more than a handful each. Her legs were long and carried her with the agile grace that could only belong to a Fairy. Her long hair hung in a wild ponytail from the crown of her head, a fantastic mixture of blue, green, and gold. The best were her eyes. They were large, and even in the dark seemed to sparkle when standing next to firelight. The most unsettling thing to him, in that moment of desire and awe, was that he recognized her. There, before him in all her virgin glory, stood Lady Morgan.

His thoughts were interrupted by the sound of splashing water, a yelp, and laughter. "Ugh! I can't believe you!" the other young woman growled.

"Oh, poor Heather. I'm forcing you to take a bath anyway." She danced around, holding a small bucket as the animal girl batted at her. Her spirit seemed far lighter than it had a week ago when he first met her.

"I told you, I'm a Wolf! We are self-cleaning." She charged at Morgan, who sidestepped the attack again.

"Calm down, Wolf girl. Here, take the soap and go clean up. You know the rule if you're traveling with me." She handed the Werewolf the soap as the girl peeled out of her clothes and headed in the direction Morgan had come from.

"Yeah, yeah, just don't let dinner burn, ok?" Her voice came from around the corner.

Morgan dug through a bag, pulling out leather leggings, a tunic, and bandages. He stared with intrigue as she turned, revealing a beautiful backside and two large scars along her shoulder blades. He realized in an instant that those marks were where her wings should have been. She bandaged her chest down and pulled on her clothes before silently padding across the ground to check on the food.

Vallen shifted on the ledge to view her more closely. She appeared to be in full possession of her faculties. She seemed happy and light-hearted. Maybe she had carved out a new life for herself here. It would seem she had made quick work of finding a traveling companion.

Just then Heather reappeared, bared for the world to see. Didn't these women have a sense of modesty? Then he remembered that he was the one peeking and they were definitely not openly inviting it. Shamed by his actions, he looked away, studying a stone on the cliff's face and wondering when he could look back to find them both dressed again.

"You smell so much better!" Morgan teased. The Werewolf responded with a low growl.

Just then the wind shifted. It fluttered through Vallen's wings and across his body, causing a chill to skim his scales. All of a sudden Heather's head shot up and she sniffed the air. Her eyes pinpointed his exact location. "We're not alone," she said in a low voice, motioning to the cliff.

With the skill of someone well-trained for battle, Morgan rolled for her bow, picking it up and drawing it in one motion. Her eyes scanned for Vallen's location. "Come out!" she commanded.

Vallen didn't move. She quickly lunged, positioning herself between the threat and the Werewolf. The wolf sank back into the shadows behind her. "I won't tell you again. Come out!" When he didn't respond she loosed her arrow in a warning shot. He flinched, trying to pull away and stay covered, but was too slow as it cut into his shoulder.

"That's enough!" Vallen growled, more irritated than he should have been. He stepped off the ledge, swooping down into their small encampment. The cowering wolf yelped loudly and could be heard tearing through the woods on all fours.

Morgan stood her ground, letting another arrow fly. This one missed the Dragon by mere inches as he dove around the fire to avoid it. Her next one bit into his wing and Vallen let out a pained screech and dropped to the ground. Morgan took advantage of the moment, discarding her bow and diving for her sword.

She wasted no time in pressing Vallen back. "Who are you and why are you here?" she bellowed.

Vallen continued to retreat backwards. Her last thrust came dangerously close. The pain in his shoulder and wing was slowing him down. She approached quickly, and, desperate not to die from being a peeping tom, Vallen swiped his tail under her feet and knocked her to the ground.

In a swirl of magic he shifted back to his Human form and pulled free his sword, tossing the belt and scabbard to the side. When her next attack landed it met steel in an echoing clang. "Lady Morgan, it's me!"

She looked at him, her eyes searching his for a moment before recognition hit. When it did, she threw another blow at him, but this time with anger behind it. She charged at him full force, with her sword pointed directly at his throat. Vallen ducked under the blow before jumping back at the next.

"Lady Morgan, I mean you no harm," he hissed at her.

She stepped back, placing both hands on her hilt, no doubt planning her killing blow. "You saved me from myself, but dumped me in a completely different realm far from home. I should kill you." She lowered her sword slightly. "But, thanks to you I have another chance for revenge."

"Glad I could be at your service, My Lady." Vallen shot her his best woman-winning smile. She raised her sword again.

Suddenly Vallen heard the sound of a branch snapping in the woods behind them. Dropping his own weapon, he lunged, grabbing Morgan and pressing her against his body as he rolled them behind a rock just in time to see an arrow fly by.

Morgan struggled beneath Vallen, trying to shove him off. He reached down and pressed a finger to her lips, silencing her immediately. She strained to hear what was going on. Carefully Vallen rose, helping her to her feet, then cautiously he peeked around the boulder they had taken cover behind. He didn't see or hear anything.

Morgan stood pressed between Vallen and the stone. She became suddenly aware that the body pressed to hers was not only firm and masculine, but also naked. Her memory flashed back to Agshi's kitchen and the strange feelings she had experienced there. She felt heat rush over her skin and clear up to her ears. She had seen many a naked man in her time camping and leading her men. She had never seen one quite this close.

"Give me your sword please?" Vallen asked, prying the metal from her hands. "If something goes wrong, escape and find my brother."

Vallen started to pull away to investigate their attackers, but Morgan's hand to his shoulder stopped him. "You're injured and bleeding," she said, touching the wound on his shoulder. "Let me go instead. I'm whole and can fend them off while you make your escape."

He looked down at her and studied her for a moment. "My Lady, it is my duty as a Knight. There would be no honor if I escaped while you put yourself in harm's way."

"Screw your honor. Use some logic. I earned my Knighthood through years of training just like you." She reached out, grabbing the sword with lightning-fast reflexes, and dove out from behind the rock. An arrow narrowly missed her, but she pushed into the shadows towards the direction it came from.

Vallen, remembering himself, found his own sword on the ground a few paces away and followed suit, chasing her into the forest. He snagged his pile of clothes from the tree as he ran. It didn't take long for him to find her. He managed to stumble into the enemy camp just in time to watch Morgan take on six men.

She rushed the first one, catching him by the elbow and using him as a thug shield. The second and third goons charged, running through their colleague. Morgan sidestepped and plunged her sword into the second enemy. She turned, taking the first enemy's dagger, and tore it through the third's throat. Pulling her own sword free of the second, she was just in time to raise it to defend against thug number four and thug number five. She kited the two around the fire, doing her best to interfere with the sixth's aim, who now was trying to get a shot off with his bow.

Vallen was about to step in and lend a hand when Morgan gave the archer an opening. As if by pure luck, she ducked low, dropping to a knee as the arrow plunged deep into the chest of assailant number five. The archer was stunned enough that she was able to throw the dagger at him, burying it deep in his hand and sending him screaming in pain to his knees. She defended against the fourth quickly and landed a deep blow. As he pulled back, Morgan reached out with her free hand and caught the archer under his chin, slamming him back against a tree. He slid to the ground unconscious. Morgan was preparing to strike at bandit number four again when he threw his sword to the ground, dropped to his knees, and begged for mercy.

"Who do you work for?" she demanded.

"We're part of a group headed for the portals to the north. We're scouts to make sure the way is clear," he said with a shaking voice.

"That's not what I asked." Morgan kicked his sword away and crossed the ground between them, grabbing the man by the ear and pressing her sword to his throat. "Who do you work for?"

The man began to cry. "Please, ma'am, if she finds out what I've done she'll kill me."

"Do you really believe you have less to fear from me?" she growled.

"Avery!" He cried out as her grip on his ear tightened.

Vallen's ears perked up as he began pulling on his clothes. "Where do we find Avery?"

"Seriously, ma'am, she will kill me," he pleaded.

"If you don't tell me I will save her the trouble. Cooperate and I will give you a head start when you begin running."

The man mumbled a set of directions, placing Avery and her small army of thugs less than a day's ride away. "Please don't kill me ma'am?" He was expecting her to say no.

She grabbed a length of rope nearby and tied the man's hands behind his back. He sobbed, pissing himself where he knelt. Morgan walked over and secured the unconscious man as well. "You can save you friend or run as you are. If I find you again though, rest assured that I will personally take great care in killing you."

The man stumbled to his feet and kicked the other man until he was conscious enough to speak. Within minutes both men were running through the woods with their tied hands behind them, trying to escape the maniac woman with a sword. Morgan sank down on a fallen tree and looked at her handiwork. Shaking her head, she looked up at Vallen. "Let's go back to my camp. I can patch you up there."

When Vallen and Morgan stumbled through the darkness back into camp it was to find both Young and Heather chowing down on the roast rabbit and vegetables. Heather looked up with a grin. "Don't worry, I saved you some, but you may want another bath." Her eyes took in the dirt and blood smears covering Morgan from head to toe.

Morgan's eyes narrowed at the Werewolf but she said nothing. Grabbing one of their bags, she urged Vallen down onto a blanket beside her and helped him tug off his tunic. The arrow that had ripped through his wing had left a nasty gash in his back along his left shoulder blade. While it didn't need stitches, he would certainly need to be careful with it.

The worse of the two injuries, though, was his shoulder. He hissed in pain as she poked at it." You need stitches in this one for sure," she told him.

"Bandage it, I'll be fine." Vallen tried to sound confident and reassuring.

With hands far gentler than he would have expected, she removed the broken arrow tip and pressed a cloth soaked in alcohol to his wound. It burned as much as any Dragon Fire, and yet he didn't notice. He was too transfixed watching her care for him. Her stitches were tiny and neat. They would most likely leave little to no scar. When she finished, she bandaged him tightly with clean bandages. "Thank you," he said as she stood.

Moments later she returned with a bowl full of roast rabbit and root vegetables and handed it to him. She watched for a moment, making sure he was eating, before pulling out another set of clothes and a bar of soap. "I'll be back," she announced, and disappeared into the shadows towards the sound of running water.

Vallen eyed Heather as she pulled the pot off the fire. "You should leave that on so it's warm when she gets back."

"So what's warm?" asked Heather, rotating the pot so Vallen could see it was empty. Guilt stabbed at his stomach when he realized he had just eaten her dinner.

"I just ate her dinner," he said weakly.

Heather shrugged. "I wouldn't worry about it. I get the feeling that's just the way she is."

Young had somehow known to bring the horses and supplies with him. He now lay sleepily on a pallet of blankets near the fire. Heather had shifted into wolf form and was pressed closely to his side.

Vallen waited at the fireside for Morgan to return. He had questions for her, but also an apology and more thanks. He couldn't decide whether he was in awe of her or, for the first time, a little terrified. Lady Morgan was shaping up to be more of a mystery each time he met her.

Chapter Eleven

I waded into the small stream, letting the icy water numb my body. I closed my eyes and tried not to focus on death, but rather the lives that would be saved. There were people in a city just on the other side of that portal that were counting on me, and they didn't even know it. Peaceful lives would come to an end if something wasn't done.

"Snap out of it!" I told myself. "You aren't in it to be a hero. You're in this for revenge. Pure revenge on Avery." Though I told myself that, I already knew that it wasn't the case. Sure, I hated her, but this had stopped being about revenge the moment I realized innocent people were in danger.

I ran the soap over my body and did my best to clean everything away in the darkness. Taking a deep breath, I knelt down and dunked my head under the water. My face felt frozen and my scalp tingled. I continued to hold my breath under the surface until my lungs burned with their need for oxygen. Finally I pushed up through the water, gasping in the cool night air.

"Are you well, Lady Morgan?" A rich male voice startled me. I jumped back, scrambling for my dagger on the bank.

"Who's there?" I demanded.

"I apologize for startling you. You were gone for quite some time and I was concerned, considering tonight's earlier adventures." Vallen stepped into view but averted his gaze, choosing to look at the night sky.

"I'm fine," I assured him.

He continued to stare at the sky. "Very well then. I will head back to camp."

For a moment I looked up at the sky above. It was missing moons. The stars shone brightly, but there were no moons to be seen. "Is Everbloom always lacking in moons?" I wondered out loud.

I heard Vallen's steps slow and stop. Had he heard me? I strained my eyes against the darkness to see him but I heard his steps resume shortly and fade into the distance.

I relaxed a bit and began working soap into my multi-colored tresses. Of all the useless traits to acquire from my mother, I had hair that changed colors sporadically. Most Fairies could control the changes to their appearance to suit their needs and tastes. Not me. Sighing heavily, I leaned back and dunked myself underwater again, rinsing away the suds, grit, and blood.

Then a thought hit me. Had Vallen seen me naked? My blood boiled in my veins. I found myself gasping for air to calm myself. "That- that peeping poop!" I growled angrily. I climbed out of the stream, furiously tugging on my clothes as I headed back to camp. By the time I arrived I was running.

Without hesitation I kicked Vallen's sleeping form. "Hey!" I yelled.

Startled, Vallen did what any good warrior would do. He leaped up, drew his sword, and placed the tip on the hollow of my throat. "Is there a problem, Lady Morgan?" he panted, catching his breath. Obviously I had given him a bit of a scare. I took a certain level of pride in knowing that.

"You dirty Dragon! You were sneaking a peep at me!" He looked at me with mild annoyance. "Admit it!"

"Admit what, exactly?" he asked.

"Admit you came to the stream so you could watch me bathe! You wanted to see me naked. You and your high horse about being a knight of honor." I tapped my foot angrily.

He glanced over at Heather and Young's sleeping forms. Removing the sword point from my neck, he stared down at me through half-open, sleepy eyes. "Lady Morgan, I know that you have no doubt spent much of your time surrounded by men; some of them probably of less savory character than myself. That may be why it is hard for you to believe that when I went to the stream, it really was just to check on your wellbeing."

"I'm perfectly capable of taking care of myself. I would have thought tonight's show would have confirmed that," I snapped.

He held up his hand. "I know you are capable of pummeling an opponent. Call it being old fashioned, call it being honorable, or call it annoying. I just have a habit of making sure those I keep company with are safe. If you had been my brother or Miss Heather over there I would have done the same." Sighing, he slid his sword back into its sheath.

"And if I had been in distress or drowning, then what? Would you have rushed in and saved me? Touched me while I was nude?" My mind started to race with pictures of what he would do to me if I were naked. I blushed, finding some of them less despicable than others.

"May I remind you that earlier this night I had you pressed against *my* naked flesh?" His nostrils flared angrily. "I'm not sure exactly what you are accusing me of, but rest assured that other than to save your life, I would not touch a woman who had not first invited me to do so. Contrary to what some scoundrels may have led you to believe, males *do* have the ability to control their instincts."

"Likely story. How do I know you won't try something while I sleep? Your brother looks really cozy with Heather over there." I jabbed a finger in their direction. I heard rustling movement behind me and turned to look at the two-sleep addled youngsters.

Young held up a hand. "For the record, she cuddled with me. And she's warm." Heather looked at me, snorted and gave a head nod before she rested her head back against Young and closed her eyes.

Vallen rolled his eyes and climbed to his feet. I watched as he gathered up his blankets and belted on his sword. "What are you doing?" I asked.

"What does it look like, Lady Morgan?" He motioned to the bedding in his arms. "You feel threatened with my presence in your camp. I am going to go find another place in the woods where I can rest the last few hours before morning." With that he turned and began walking away.

Guilt pricked at my stomach. I watched him march into the forest where darkness swallowed him up. Cursing myself, I marched after him. "Vallen, wait!" I called. He didn't answer. I leaped into a run. He had just left - how far could he have really gone? What if he fell off a ledge? What if he bumped his head and was knocked unconscious? What if the men in the woods caught him off guard and dispatched him?

I was so lost in thought I didn't see the tree in front of me. I hit it full force, causing me to fall backwards onto my hindquarters. "Ooph!" I said as I went down hard.

"Lady Morgan? Are you sure you are well?" Vallen asked. I looked up at my "tree", only to realize I had run into a tightly-muscled wall of Dragon.

"Yes." I accepted the hand he offered me and was surprised at the way he seemed to effortlessly pull me to my feet despite his injuries. "Why didn't you answer when I called?"

"I must apologize, I didn't hear you call. All I heard was the sound of someone rushing through the forest in my direction. In the event that it was one of our friends from earlier, I didn't wish to give away my position." I hated that his answer made sense. My hand tingled in his grip. I was mesmerized for a moment, before I jerked it away.

"Thank you," I mumbled as I returned it to my side. Taking a deep breath, I looked up at him. "I'm sorry. I have no reason to doubt your honor or your word. You have done nothing other than what you said you would at every turn since we met."

"If you are uncomfortable with my presence I can sleep elsewhere," he offered.

I sighed and rolled my eyes. "No, Sir Vallen, please come back to camp. Besides, there is safety in numbers that way."

He grinned at me. Even in the darkness it was rather dazzling. "I wouldn't want to be a bother to you should you need to rescue me from assailants." He motioned for me to lead the way. "Oh," he paused.

"Technically, I am Lord Vallen. I'm landed *and* titled."

I stifled a laugh and headed back toward the encampment. "So what are you Lord of?"

"The Lake," he answered simply.

"Which lake?"

"The only one that matters," he muttered under his breath.

I decided to let the question go. "How is your shoulder feeling?" I was looking for any distraction to fill the awkward silence.

"As well as can be expected." I grimaced in memory of putting the wounds there. Then something hit me. "Wait!" I stopped walking, grabbing his arm and turning him around. He winced and gave me his undivided attention. "Why were you snooping on us earlier tonight? Why didn't you answer when I called out to you?"

"I woke up very hungry and smelled something delicious, so I followed a scent to discover where it was coming from. When I came across your encampment, I didn't know if it was bandits or well-meaning citizens of the nearby town. Rather than alarm anyone, I shifted into Dragon form and investigated." He shifted uncomfortably on his feet.

"Why didn't you identify yourself when I called out the first time?" I pushed.

He cleared his throat. "I was ashamed by my actions. That, and being in Dragon form tends to frighten people. Just because you know something exists doesn't mean you want to see it up close and personal."

"What did you have to be ashamed of?" I asked. He just stared at me, guilt written across his face in the starlight. "You saw me NAKED!" I jabbed an accusing finger into his chest. He winced again.

"I did," he admitted. "But it wasn't my intention," he quickly added.

"If it was innocent you could have come down and explained yourself," I accused.

"To do that would have meant leaving Dragon form. Leaving Dragon form would have meant facing you naked myself. I didn't think that would be welcome either." He made total sense, but I still hated the fact that he had seen me naked.

He stepped closer and bowed his head. "I will wear the scars of your arrows as reminders of my poor choices."

"Wait! I'm not saying you deserved to be hurt for making a mistake, just that you're an ass for making the choices you did. I don't usually wish harm on others." I thought about that for a moment. "OK, I don't wish harm on most."

He nodded. "We should get back to camp." He stepped past me to walk back.

When we returned, the last of the embers were glowing. Vallen rolled out his bedding again, this time as close to the embers as possible. I went to settle into my own, but couldn't find them. I looked through my bags on the ground where I had left them and over by Heather, thinking she had snagged them for added warmth. "That's strange," I commented.

Vallen watched me search. "What's wrong?" he asked.

"I'm fine," I stated.

I heard some rustling and then a light shone brightly behind me. "What are you looking for? We are more likely to find it with two sets of eyes and a light." He held up a small lantern, the likes of which I had never seen. It was a small cylinder, and its light source didn't seem to come from a fire.

"My bedding is missing. It was right here last I saw it." I pointed at the place on the ground next to which my boots now sat alone.

He shone the light into the woods and around the base of the cliff. As he turned I noticed his shirt was stained with blood. "I don't see it anywhere," he called back to me. "You may use mine," he offered.

"Vallen, may I see your lantern for a moment?" He blinked at me, but handed it over.

I carefully took it, expecting it to be hot from the fire within. I was surprised to find it cool to the touch. I urged him to turn around and pushed his tunic up. "My Lady?" he asked.

"You've bled through your bandages. I think I may need to stitch this wound as well. I would have thought your Dragon blood would have started the healing process by now." He went rigid under my touch. "Does that hurt?" I asked.

"For some reason in here in Everbloom, Dragons don't heal easily. A friend of mine lost a wing in battle here and died quickly of blood loss." I was taken aback at this knowledge. "I hate to be a burden, but I would be grateful if you would close the wound."

I went back and recovered my first aid supplies, then urged him to sit on the ground. As gently as possible I removed the bandages and cleaned the wound again. I stitched the gash shut then applied healing salve before re-bandaging him. "I'm sorry," I told him.

He turned, looking at me in question. "You're injured and it's my doing."

Vallen shook his head. "I assure you, Lady Morgan, I don't hold you responsible for these injuries. I earned them through my own actions." He reached over, lifted his blanket, and wrapped it around my shoulders.

"You are healing, you need to stay warm and rest. I'll be able to handle the cold better than you." Already I was shaking as a cool mist began settling in. "Besides, there is only an hour or two until dawn." I pushed the blanket back into his arms and urged him down. "Please, rest."

He sighed and lay down. He pulled the blanket over himself then held it up. "Come share it. I swear I will be nothing but an honorable gentleman." He looked at me standing there, shivering. "Otherwise, I will insist you take it."

Grumbling, I slid onto the ground, clothed, beside him. He turned onto his non-injured shoulder and encouraged me to come closer, then lowered the blanket over me. I grew warmer immediately, but I wasn't sure if it was the shared heat of our close proximity or my embarrassment. It was strangely unsettling that the two most physically intimate moments of my life had both been shared with this Dragon. My breathing became ragged at the realization. He moved behind me and clicked the lantern, which extinguished the light.

"Is something the matter, Lady Morgan?" His warm breath fanned my forehead.

"No," I shook my head, trying not to sound like I was panicking.

"I have promised not to put an unwelcome hand on you. You have my word." True to his word already the arm with the injured shoulder lay pressed tightly to his chest.

"I know." I bit my lower lip for a moment, struggling with how much to say.

"Then what can I do to put your mind at ease?" he asked, his tone softer then I had ever heard it.

"I've never slept with a man like this before," I explained.

"Ah," was all he said for a long moment. "Were you not engaged, once?" He shook his head slightly. "I know you're a virgin. I think I just assumed that because you had a fiancé you must have had moments... alone." I could tell he was trying to choose his words carefully.

"Not really." I shrugged.

"I'm sorry that you are sharing this moment with me." Something about the kindness in his voice relaxed me.

I snuggled closely and he froze as stiff as he could. "Please put your arm over me. It will be better for the injury and will allow us to share more warmth." He hesitated for a moment before wrapping his arm over me, resting his hand on my back. I took a deep breath and it was like inhaling him. There was something smoky and woodsy about him.

"Vallen," I murmured as I closed my eyes.

"Hmmm?" he answered softly.

"You smell wonderful." He chuckled softly. The sound vibrated in his chest and caused me to smile. His grip tightened ever so slightly on me and I passed into the dreaming world.

Chapter Twelve

I slowly grew aware of the world. I was floating in a warm cocoon of comfort. The pillow smelled like what I always dreamed home would be like if I were willing to ever settle down. The blankets were surprisingly heavy, their weight encouraging me to sink in deeper. The smell of food wafted through the air to tempt my stomach. I slowly opened my eyes to the bright light of late morning or early afternoon.

Heather and Young sat eating around a warm fire. I refocused my gaze closer to where I was sleeping. Vallen was flat on his back, still sound asleep. My head rested on his chest, with the rest of me draped across him. To his credit, the only hand that touched me was that of his injured shoulder, and it still rested on my back. The other was outstretched, partly free of the blankets.

I shifted, feeling my face glow bright with a blush, and tried to carefully free myself from his grip without waking him. He moved under me, raising his head to look at me. "Lady Morgan?" he asked.

"Shhh, you're fine. Rest some more," I encouraged him. As I slid from his grip he winced but closed his eyes again.

Outside the warmth of the blankets and Vallen, the air was still crisp. Heather looked at me with a definite smirk and handed me a warm mug of tea. I looked down at it with surprise. "Morning sunshine," she said in a chipper voice that seemed designed to irritate me.

"Thank you," I mumbled, talking to the tea.

I sank down on the ground next to Young and took my first sip. He grinned at me like I was the punch line of a joke. I shot him an annoyed look but he just shrugged it off with a laugh. Rolling my eyes, I decided that no good could come from asking what they so desperately wanted to talk about. "So how exactly did you two kids find each other?"

Young's brow furrowed and he looked over at Heather. "She ran me over, fleeing for her life."

"It wasn't as bad as it sounds," Heather cut in.

Young shook his head. "She plowed over me and scared ten years off my life. When I collected myself enough to put more than two words together, I realized my brother was missing and she was babbling about a Dragon. So I gathered our stuff up and came to return her from where she came. I also wanted to see what trouble Vallen had caused."

I glanced back at Vallen, who let out a soft snore. I grinned despite myself. When anyone was stretched out like that, it was hard to picture them as a threat. I looked back at Heather. "Why do you keep running away? You've seen me fight; you know I can protect you. What's more, you're a Werewolf! You're a born predator."

She blushed and looked anyplace but my eyes. Finally she gave up. "Someone I came here with said they would protect me too, but that didn't really happen. I just don't want to die, Morgan. I wasn't raised to be a coward."

I waved it away. "I am not like others. I will defend you with my life. Please know that."

Young's chest puffed. "As will I," he informed her.

I resisted the urge to roll my eyes and opted for a smile instead. "So what brought you two adventurers back?" I asked him.

Young's eyes shifted to Vallen, who still slept. "The story isn't really mine, My Lady. My brother has taken on the responsibility of hunting down a rogue knight who has turned her back on the Order."

I paused and considered this information for a moment. Things all of a sudden clicked into place. "Your brother is part of the Order of the Original Dragon?" He seemed shocked by my knowledge. "You're hunting Avery too?"

Young blinked. "You know of her?" he asked.

"Of course."

"Wait, hunting her *too*? As in also... as in, you are also out to find her?" He seemed very confused. "I thought you were over your whole suicidal phase."

"I am. That's why I am going after her. My goal is to stop her before she reaches Maht. I destroyed her little scouting party last night, which should slow her down for another day or so while she waits for them and sends out another." I was already calculating our time and distance.

"You can't face Avery. She's a Dragon. She'll kill you," he said, panic in his voice.

"I came a lot closer to killing her then she did me last time." I reached for the kettle and poured another mug of tea.

"What are you talking about?" he demanded, with a look in his eyes that made me wonder if his head would actually explode. I hoped not, as I was running short on clean garments and I did hate being dirty.

"When last we met, I drove my sword through her eye, then into her chest. Then she tumbled off a cliff. We all thought she was dead. I was rather surprised to find her still living." I took a sip of the black brew.

Young stared at me, slack-jawed. "No, that can't be right. She was defeated by a mighty Fae Knight."

Heather burst out of her quiet stupor. "A few nights ago she took out eleven or twelve bandits in the woods all by herself. When it was done she didn't even have a scratch on her."

Young looked back and forth between Heather and me. "I'm not doubting your skills, Lady Morgan, but are you sure it was Avery you faced?"

I nodded. Vallen had woken and was sitting up now. Young quickly moved to hand his brother some food. I let out a slow breath. "I know it was Avery. She killed half my men and my fiancé. I'm not saying that they made a wise choice in entering her lair without all of us, but it doesn't change that she was raiding and killing throughout the countryside. We went there with the intention to stop her."

Vallen coughed and cleared his throat before he solemnly met my gaze. "I am truly sorry for the losses you have sustained." There was a hurt there that went beyond mere sympathy. It made me strangely uncomfortable.

Clapping my hands together and looking away, I pushed up to my feet. "Well, we have a lot of work ahead of us. Just because we got rid of a scouting party doesn't mean that we can take it easy. She will send more." I stretched and snagged an apple from the bag, taking a large, unladylike bite. "We need to be ready," I said the best I could around a mouthful of apple.

Vallen shook his head. "We? No no no, this isn't your fight. This is my responsibility."

"Well, considering you are recovering from multiple arrow wounds, it's probably better you had some help," I offered.

"That's what Young's for," he said.

"What? Me?!" Young choked through his breakfast.

"Yes, you. You came to act as my squire."

"Yeah, but I thought you would talk some sense into her or kill her on your own." Young stuffed more food into his gullet.

"Young, we have a responsibility," Vallen insisted.

"Then we will do this together. Avery has assembled a small army. She plans to take Maht in the realm of Drakemoore. We need to stop her before she gets through the portal." I began packing things around the camp, trying to stay busy.

"You steer clear of Avery and leave it to-"

"Leave it to whom? You, the injured Dragon that heals like a Human in this realm, or the squire that doesn't want to face a foe?" I cut him off. "Or is it that you doubt my abilities because of my gender? Is that why you foolishly only brought one squire with you to battle her? Do you underestimate *her* because she is a woman?"

"Are you done?" he asked, his voice flat with annoyance.

"Well?" I pressed.

"No, I do not underestimate your abilities or hers. She was my squire sister. We trained together under the same knight. I came with only a single squire because I know that she will face me on an honorable field of battle where I will best her fairly." He stood up and began to stretch, wincing a little when his stitches pulled.

"Have any of her recent actions led you to believe she still holds to any of her teachings of honor and chivalry?" I walked over to him and encouraged him to put his arms down before he re-opened his wounds. "This isn't an honorable battle. This is us against a monster."

"I swore an oath to protect those that need my protection," he protested weakly.

"And that differs from the code I live by?" I urged him to sit so that I could check his bandages. To my surprise he complied rather easily. "I trained under Prince Tallyn in Vesaria. He came into Fairy lands and helped to build defenses against the marauders, bandits, and monsters that threatened our citizens. I traveled with him for ten years, as his charge."

Vallen grunted as I pulled a bandage free. "How's it look, Doc?" he asked in a surprisingly jovial tone.

The wound was red and looked angry. "Are Dragons like Fae in that Iron can burn, poison a wound, or cause it to heal slowly?"

He paused for a moment. "I don't know. It has never proven to be an issue in the past."

I dug through my supplies and pulled out a salve that would help with the inflammation. As I opened it, the smell of clove and pine permeated the air around us. "Where was I?" I asked, gently working the medicine into the stitches.

"You trained under Prince Tallyn," he filled in the gap.

"Yes, and in my travels with him I developed a greater passion to help and protect, not just my own people, but all people who had to fear evil. I was elevated because of the works I did to protect my kingdom. Just because I don't share the blood of the Original Dragon doesn't mean I don't have a responsibility to protect." He became still under my touch.

"You are familiar with the Order, then?" he asked.

"I am. I make it a point to know my enemies. When Avery appeared in Vesaria, causing chaos and harm everywhere she went, I did all I could to learn everything about her." I finished bandaging the wound on his back and moved around him so I could better inspect his shoulder.

"I applaud you for your research, but if you know the Order I belong to, you should understand why it is so important I be the one to take her on and not endanger you." He winced, sucking in a deep breath when I pushed on his wound.

"And that look on your face is exactly why *I* should be facing her and not you. You're injured and for me, this is unfinished business." I examined the injury closer. It didn't look good. "Besides, I think it might be better for you to get back across the portal and to a doctor in your own realm. These injuries are showing signs of infection."

Vallen looked down at them, then back to me. "Treat them and wrap them. The sooner I finish here the sooner I can return home." I growled when he climbed to his feet as soon as I finished. He really was the most impossible man.

"Heather, let's get packed up." I paused until she gave me a nod of understanding. "Out of curiosity, do you know where my bedding went?"

She looked at me blankly and shook her head. "I'm sure it's around. If not, you can use mine tonight. I prefer to sleep in wolf form anyway."

Vallen and Young were also packing up but everything came to a halt when Heather screamed. Grabbing my sword from where it rested, I charged through the forest in her direction, the sound of the Dragons on my heels following me. I burst through the trees near the stream and looked around for the threat. "What's wrong?" I asked.

"The horses have been stolen." She looked crestfallen.

"Are you sure they didn't just wander off?" asked Vallen. "We can give you a ride back into town."

"No we can't," corrected Young.

"Be a little considerate," Vallen snapped.

"Ok, are we going to shift into Dragon form and carry them?" he asked his older brother.

"Of course not. They can ride the horses with us." Vallen looked at Young, who continued to shake his head no. "When you brought our horses, you secured them here with theirs, didn't you."

"Yup," Young said quickly.

Vallen sighed deeply and pinched the bridge of his nose. "Well, then I guess we will *all* be walking back to town together."

"And give away our position so easily to the enemy?" I asked. "Sir Dragon, I think you are getting rusty." I motioned for Heather to follow me and brushed past the boys.

Within moments I was easily a story and a half up in a tree, securing our nonessential items out of sight. It took three trips but I managed to tuck everything away. When I finished, I pulled on my boots, secured my sword, bow, and pack, and then looked at the others. "Heather, you ready to play bloodhound?"

She nodded and stripped unselfconsciously in front of the group. Vallen and Young both found other things to look at but I held out my arms to take her clothes. She smiled at me slyly. "I'm impressed, not even a little peeking," she teased the boys before shifting.

She led the way back to where we had secured our mounts. She sniffed at the ground, then splashed through the stream to the other side, where she carefully inspected the ground again. With a small bark she took off through the woods and I chased after her.

We wound our way through the trees for at least an hour before she stopped. She ran a little ahead then returned quickly. She shifted into her Human form and stayed crouched close to the ground. Her voice, no more than a whisper, had us all leaning in closely. "The horses are ahead with the people that took them. When I was tracking I only smelled two. Now that we are here, though, I smell a dozen or more scents from others."

I nodded at her as I pulled my bow free and started working my way closer. A hand on my wrist stilled me. "Lady Morgan, we should try a bit of diplomacy first. Perhaps they will return them without the need for bloodshed," Vallen offered.

"Either way, I'm staying here," inserted Heather.

I rolled my eyes and pulled my hand free. "Fine, how about you go in and try to be diplomatic, and Young and I will hang back ready to give you cover when you need it?"

Vallen considered the proposal for a moment, looking back and forth between his brother and me. "Fine, but I think you will be surprised at how negotiating can be a peaceful way to settle things."

"Yes, because I always think peaceful when I think about horse thieves." Finally he relented. Young took cover from a low vantage point and I climbed a tree near the entrance of what we could only assume was a hideout.

As expected, Vallen walked up like he owned the place. Two men immediately approached him, the first pulling a dagger. "Good day, gentlemen. I believe you have taken my horses by mistake."

The men exchanged glances with one another. The first's face split into a wicked smile while the other drew his sword. "I think the mistake sir, is that you came looking for them."

Vallen stood his ground. "No, I believe your mistake is that you are under the impression you can take things that are not yours."

There was movement and the muffled sounds of a struggle from where Young had stationed himself.

The men in front of Vallen glanced in the direction of the noise. Vallen took advantage of the distraction to draw his weapon with one hand and with the other slam his fist into the nose of the man with the sword. He yowled in pain as Vallen side-stepped him and shoved him into the path of his friend's dagger. Vallen plunged his sword into the man with the dagger before turning towards his brother. He had taken three steps before his body jerked from the arrow that planted itself into his left thigh.

"That's far enough, hero," called a voice from the trees. Five men stepped into sight, dragging Young with them. Two held Young, his body limp between them, another two held bows at the ready, and the fifth stood with a sword drawn, its tip pressed to the squire's throat. The man holding the sword seemed familiar... "Henry," I whispered to myself, remembering him from the pub a few nights before.

I drew an arrow from the quiver at my hip and aimed it for the closer of the two archers. I knew once I let it fly that the standstill would break and things would get messy. I glanced at the tree base below me to confirm that I was still alone. I let the arrow fly and was rewarded with the gurgle of pain that comes from piercing a heart. I quickly drew again, dispatching the other archer that tried to flee to cover. He managed one shot in a direction nowhere near me.

A shout went up for reinforcements that I ignored, taking aim next for Henry. My shot missed, but caused him to dive for cover, away from Young. I wanted Henry alive so we could chat again. I managed to take out one of the two men holding Young before Vallen got to them, but a common thug is no match for a trained knight.

Vallen reached for Young, trying to pull him out of the way of the battle that was undoubtedly coming. I could hear the pounding of feet coming down the pathway that had to be at least two dozen armed men. One thug may not be a match for a knight, but an entire hive of them can be a challenge for any hero.

Chapter Thirteen

Young began to regain consciousness just as a small army of men appeared at the tree break. Clumsily he drew his sword and took a defensive stance with Vallen at his back. Reaching into my quiver, I realized I only had five arrows left and that I had best make them count. The first wave of men arrived, quickly swarming the Dragons. I scanned the fighters, looking to do maximum damage with my limited ammo.

Two archers, they only had two archers in a crowd that big. I drew the first arrow back and released. It found its mark and the first archer fell. The second on the other side of the group hadn't been scanning the surrounding area like the other had. He was my next mark and easily fell. With both archers down I needed to choose my last few shots. There was already a small group fanning out in my direction hoping to find where the arrows had come from. I quickly fired, taking down two of the men closest to Young and landing a hit to the one facing Vallen.

There was a shout from below me - my position had been discovered. I looped my bow on my back and sprinted down the length of the tree branch I stood on. I held my breath as I neared the tip, hoping the extra air in my lungs would make me lighter when I jumped for the roof of the hideout. I pushed off the tree branch with all my strength and focused on the building ahead of me.

My hands extended in front of me as I stretched beyond my limits. The distance seemed even greater now that I soared over the ground below. As I felt the pull of gravity begin to tug on me, my fingertips connected with the rough wood of the roof. I tightened my grip as my body slammed into the wall of the building and pulled myself atop the structure. Breathing heavily, I watched as the main group divided, part of them storming into the building to come after me.

I quickly looked around the rooftop and found the door that no doubt led to a ladder below and the floors within. I pulled my quiver free, using my dagger to cut away the heavy leather strap on it. I fished the strap through the door handle and the door's outer frame twice before knotting it as tightly as I could. Returning my dagger to my boot, I made my way to the edge of the roof closest to the fight with the Dragons.

Sixteen men lay dead at Vallen's feet as he held off three more, as well as guarded his brother's back. I looked at the ground at least three floors below and sighed. I sent up a silent prayer to whatever deity that might be listening not to let me break every bone in my body. I took a step back and could hear the men beating at the door behind me. I was lucky that it was small enough to limit the number of them able to pound at it at one time. The strap held. With a deep breath, I took a running step and pushed off the roof.

I seemed to hang in the air forever. I was able to look around and see the Dragons below, men in the woods busy with something else, and a man dressed in black with a golden Dragon emblazoned on his tunic hiding on the outskirts of the battle. His face was hidden by a black mask and a hood. His gaze seemed to be glued to me.

Suddenly the ground came rushing at me very quickly and I tucked tightly and rolled as I touched down. I groaned at the abuse on my body but came to my feet quickly, drawing my sword. I was only a few steps from Young. I raced forward, grabbing the closest man by the shoulder and pulling him around. His shock at my appearance was short-lived as I pushed my sword through him before twisting it and yanking it free. He fell to his knees.

I pushed my way into the fray, dispatching villains as I went. By the third felled assailant I found myself at the center of the fight with Vallen and Young. Young had a dozen or so light wounds that stained his clothes. I had no doubt Vallen had ripped his stitches, as his back and shoulder had all but dyed the cloth black. He gritted his teeth as he smashed his fist into the face of another man before bringing his sword up to defend against an incoming attack. Around him lay nearly a dozen and a half men.

Yet another man stepped up to replace the last to fall, I stepped in, bringing my own sword up to protect Vallen's exposed right side. Realizing I was the more immediate threat, the man turned his attention to me. He swung widely, almost catching me across the stomach. I stepped back, bumping into Young but doing no damage. I lifted my sword to deflect the next blow, then quickly pulled my sword back. The man's scream and a spray of blood as his hand, still holding his sword, detached from his arm told me all I needed to know. He dropped to his knees before me, clutching his wrist with his other hand. I used my foot to push him to the side and advance on Vallen's next attacker.

Catching the thug totally by surprise, I buried my sword deep into his side. The man fighting next to him had just enough time to recoil before Vallen ended him. Vallen turned and attacked the man to Young's right, defeating him with a single blow. Another two men dashed forward at me. I brought my knee up and pulled my dagger free from my boot. I rushed at the two men.

Ducking low, I slid into them, digging my dagger into the first one's knee. He howled and dropped to his good knee. I brought my sword up in time to defend against the short axe the other man was carrying, its wood handle snapping over my blade as they connected. The free blade of the axe head sliced through my tunic and cut across my skin before falling to the ground. Cursing, I turned quickly to defend against the man with the injured knee.

The sound of metal against metal rang in my ears as our swords met. The second thug, to his credit as a fighter, didn't give up now that he was missing the head of his axe. Instead he lunged at me, prepared to use the wood as a stake. I caught his movement out of the corner of my eye and brought my leg straight back in a kick that connected with his chest and knocked him back. His friend took advantage of my momentary lack of balance, tackling me and pulling me to the ground. He pounded my hand against a rock until I let go of my sword. Then, keeping my arm pinned, he pulled his own dagger.

In furious desperation I slammed my knee up into his groin, reached down with my free hand to his knee and pulled out the dagger that was still there. He screamed and swung wildly. I twisted beneath him and suffered only a light cut to the arm. Then I plunged my dagger into his chest and pushed him off of me. I reached for my sword as I quickly got back onto my feet just as the second man lunged for me. I thrust my sword deep and tore it free. The man's face showed his surprise as he crumpled.

When I looked up again Vallen had finished the rest of his opponents and Young was standing his ground as well. I watched with horror as the men from inside the building rushed out. Where had so many come from? I swear I had only seen two dozen or so.

I suddenly heard the sound of a horn blowing. My eyes darted in the direction of the noise. The man with the hidden face had his gaze narrowed on me as he called for a retreat. I started to give chase, but a nearby wolf howl stopped me. I turned towards the howl and pushed my legs to carry me into the woods. I could hear Young call something out behind me, but I didn't stop to listen.

The howl came again, this time followed by a painful yelp. "Heather!" I cried out. Movement to my left caught my attention and I changed course. A few steps later I found two men wrestling with a large wolf. One had a rope around its neck and the other was trying to stab it with a dagger.

"Calm yourself, you gnarly beast. You'll be done with soon enough," said the man pulling the rope.

"Hurry up, Cory, lets string him up and get this over with." The wolf growled at the man with the dagger.

I cleared my throat loudly. The two men and the wolf all stopped their struggles to turn and look at me. "Gentlemen, let the wolf go."

The one with the dagger stood up. He grinned, revealing that he was missing more than a few teeth. "Well look at what we got here." He pointed the dagger at me. "You got a soft spot for Were-mutts, little girl?"

The wolf behind him growled and pulled against the rope that held him. I looked back at the man with the dagger and quirked a brow as I lifted my sword. "Really? You want to do this the hard way?" I asked.

He lunged at me, forcing me to dive out of the way to avoid injury. I maneuvered quickly to his side and dragged the sword through him. I didn't need to look back to know he collapsed on the ground. Cory looked at me with panic in his eyes as I stepped closer. "Miss, you don't want to get involved. I work for some very powerful people. You d-don't want them as enemies," he stammered.

I felt the side of my mouth turn up in a grin. "No, it's them who don't want me as an enemy." I swung my sword, severing the rope from his hand. "Now run along home and tell Avery and all her little minions I am coming for them." With a foot stomp and mock lunge in his direction the man turned and ran.

I sank to the ground and untied the rope around the wolf. I watched with amazement as the wolf transformed into a man before me. His skin was black as night and his eyes were a deep charcoal grey. White tribal tattoos covered both his arms. He breathed heavily, looking up at me. "Thank you!" he exclaimed. He sniffed the air. "You've met my sister, Heather?"

"I have, she's been traveling with me. You are?" I inquired, offering him a hand up and doing my best to ignore his nudity.

"Uther," he said, taking my hand and climbing to his feet. He took a step towards me and winced, and I noticed his leg was injured.

Stepping forward, I wrapped his arm around my shoulders. "C'mon, let's get out of here and find the others." He leaned into me and limped along. When we arrived back at the hideout, Young had gathered the horses and Heather stood in all her naked glory speaking with the Dragons.

When they all turned at my approach, Heather's face lit up and she pushed past Vallen and Young and rushed in my direction. "Uther, you're alive!" she cried, wrapping her arms around the tall man beside me. Tears streamed down her cheeks.

Young approached, with Vallen hobbling along behind him. Vallen had a rather stoic look on his face. "We should leave here before they return with more friends," he said.

I nodded. "Uther, can you ride?" When he nodded, I motioned in the direction of Dabble. "Mount up. Heather, you can ride with me." Careful of Uther's leg, Young and I helped him and Vallen into their saddles before climbing onto our own. Heather sat behind me pressed tightly to my back. I was happy to see her dressed once more.

Chapter Fourteen

"Well, how was I supposed to know that Sir Sexy Dragon was off his rocker and he was just going to walk up to the front door of the mill?" Heather argued.

"That was *the* mill?" I asked.

"Yes, that was the mill the drunk guy was talking about at the inn. You're lucky you got out of there alive," she retorted. After our day of adventure, we were headed back towards the portal Young and Vallen had come through.

"Well that would have been damn handy to know before you ran away," I pointed out.

There was a loud *thunk* behind us. I pulled Slayer to a halt and prepared to draw my sword. When I turned it was to find Vallen lying face down on the ground. "Vallen!" Young and I yelled at the same time. I dismounted quickly, leaving Heather to try and control Slayer.

I dropped to a knee beside the Dragon, for the first time realizing just how large and heavy he was. Funny how you notice these things when you are suddenly faced with moving someone of his stature. I reached out and touched his face. "Vallen, can you hear me?" I asked.

He opened his eyes slightly and met my gaze. "Yes," he said on a pained breath.

Young took his hand in his own and squeezed it. "Come on, brother, we just need to get you back to Drakemoore so you can heal."

I looked at Young. "He can't ride like this. Go find me two long branches that are about the width of my arm." He nodded and disappeared off into the woods. I cast my attention up to Heather, who was trying to slide off of Slayer's back. "Find me blankets and rope," I told her. She nodded and began digging through our bags and theirs.

"I'll be all right. Just help me back on to my horse," he insisted, struggling to sit up. I pushed his shoulders down.

"Shhhh. You *will* be all right once we get you to the portal and patched up. For now you need to save your strength." He started to protest but stopped when I pressed my hand to his mouth.

Half an hour later I had managed to rig a sling between Slayer and Vallen's horse. We played a game of musical horses getting everyone mounted, with Vallen in the sling and Young and I riding the horses bearing it. Heather and Uther rode behind us as we set the pace. We had to ride slower, but by nightfall we had reached the sacred circle.

We guided everyone in and Young went to the stone at the center. I watched carefully as he recited the old magical rite that would allow us to cross the barrier between our realms. The circle shimmered to life around us and the world seemed to shift under our feet. I felt as if I were falling or tumbling down a hill with no end when all of a sudden reality reached back up to grab me.

The world shifted back into view around us and the smell of the ocean hit my senses. Breathing deep through my nose and out through my mouth, I let the sensation wash over me. "Ok, where is a safe place for us, Young? This is your home - you lead the way."

Young shot me a look that I didn't understand nor did I have time to contemplate. He looked around to get his bearings then pointed to the southwest. "That way. There is a cave on the shore that we have camped in many a time on holiday."

I waited for him to remount and we made our way across the sandy soil in the dark. After a short time, we hit the water's edge and turned due west, headed for a series of black cliffs I could just make out in the darkness. At the top of one was a large light that spun overhead, illuminating the rocks below.

"What's that?" I asked, pointing to the tower of light.

"It's a lighthouse. It's there so that ships can safely make their way into the cove just past that cliff." He pointed ahead.

We rode for another two hours in the darkness. When we finally reached the cliff wall, Young reached over and dug through his bag, pulling free a torch. With a few flicks of his wrist he was able to get it lit and he led us up a steep ledge. It was a nerve-wracking ascent as he and I were riding side by side with Vallen suspended between us. Finally he pointed to a cavern opening hidden by some vines. He dismounted and moved the vines aside and guided us all in.

I was surprised when he placed his hand on the wall and a series of lights began to glow. "We can secure the horses here and go down into the lair," he explained. I dismounted and watched as he turned a lever that filled a stone-like trough with water.

We carefully untied and lowered Vallen to the ground, then secured the horses. Young looked at me. "Lady Morgan, will you be able to handle lifting the other end of my brother's sling to carry him?" I nodded, seeing that Heather had helped Uther off her horse and was now helping him walk about the cavern.

We made our way through a narrow stone door at the back of the cavern, then down a series of ramps. When we finally reached flat ground, Young continued to lead us through twists and turns. Finally, he nudged a door open with his foot and led us all into a darkened room. "Just over here, Lady Morgan, we can put him on the bed." Sure enough my knee collided with a soft surface and I lowered Vallen down onto the bed.

I heard Young walk across the floor and watched again with amazement as the chamber lit up. It was larger than I expected. It had room for a large bed, a wingback chair, and shelf that now sat empty. Young motioned to Heather and Uther, leading them out of the room and back into the hallway. I wanted nothing more than to follow and see where he had brought us, but I focused on what needed to be done first.

With a room full of light I was able to better see Vallen. His skin looked almost white and was cold to the touch. The light made him shimmer as it caught the faint pattern of scales. His tunic and leggings were soaked in blood and I was unable to make out what was his and what belonged to others. "I'm sorry," I whispered in apology, and reached for my dagger.

As carefully as possible, I cut and ripped away his tunic, removing the blood-soaked bits of fabric. With a deep breath and a grimace, I started cutting away his leggings. Soon he lay completely bare before me. I pulled out a bottle of water and a clean rag from my bag and started the process of cleaning away the blood so I could see the full extent of damage.

I began with his shoulder, confirming my fear that he had ripped out all his stitches. I continued cleaning and found two new gashes across his chest, another on his arm that would require stitches, a nasty jagged wound that started deeply at his ribs and slashed across his abdomen where it wasn't as serious, an arrow wound to his thigh that *wasn't* my fault, and enough bruises to make his skin look blue even in Human form. Just as I let out a deep sigh, the door opened behind me again and Young came in with a large pot of steaming water and a pack full of fresh bandages. He sat them down next to me and started building a fire in the small fireplace.

With more water at my disposal I cleaned him up properly, then set to work closing his wounds. It seemed to take hours and Young, to his credit, was a wonderful nurse. He took orders, followed directions, and overall was an amazing help. When everything was done, Young looked at me with a smile. "Thank you, Lady Morgan. Heather has asked that you come take a look at Uther's injury when you finish here. I can also show you the bathroom, the kitchen, though it is empty, and the third bed chamber."

I blinked at him. "What is this place? It's not what I would call a cave."

He grinned at me. "It's a Dragon's Lair. One of my brother's closest friends is Lord Geren. This was his family's lair until they moved into the main nest about twenty years ago. Now this has become our secret little Dragon's nest by the sea. It's safe, warded, and a far better place than the dank and dirty woods to stay while we heal and regroup."

I nodded in agreement. "Please show me the way."

Young led me out of the room and down a short hall. The next door down was the bathroom, a large chamber with an equally large tub, a toilet, and two basins with running water. The two doors across the hall led to two more bed chambers. The door on the right was open, and inside I could see Heather sitting in a chair with her legs crossed. Uther sat on the bed with his foot hanging off the edge.

Heather looked up at me. "I think he needs stitches and possibly a bone reset." I nodded and all but staggered over to kneel at the side of the bed.

I looked at the wound carefully before meeting Uther's gaze. "If I set the bone and dress it in Human form, you will have to stay in that form until it is healed enough to remove the stitches and go without a splint."

He considered what I was saying. "I can shift if it would be easier to treat me that way," he offered.

I shook my head. "It doesn't matter which form you choose, you're just stuck in it until you're mostly healed."

Uther nodded. "Then it is better I stay as I am. I won't be able to communicate otherwise."

With Young and Heather's help I was able to clean the wound, set the bone, splint it, and close him up. When I finally climbed to my feet I was exhausted and sore. I bid the siblings good night and made my way to the door. Outside, Young caught me by the arm. "If you want to get washed up first I will see if I can find you a clean change of clothes."

I mumbled my appreciation and dragged myself into the bathroom. In moments I lowered myself into a tub filled with hot, steaming water. I began working the soap over my skin and washing away the smell of death. When I finally stood to climb out of the tub, the water was a dark muddy color that caused me to shudder.

Wrapping a towel around myself, I stepped out into the cool air in the hall. Being so deep underground chilled me to the bone. I peeked into the room that Young had said I could use, but found it dark and empty. I decided that before I turned in I would see if he had found something I could change into.

When I stepped into the chamber the Dragons were occupying, I saw that Young had covered his brother in blankets and he himself sat asleep in the high back chair, shirtless, with his arm half wrapped. Bandages lay limply in his other hand. I sighed and finished bandaging his injuries. I pulled the last unused blanket from its resting place at the foot of the bed and draped it over the young squire.

I started to leave, but something kept hold of me. I wanted to check on Vallen one last time before I went to rest myself. When I reached his side, I found that instead of being icy cold to the touch, his body was on fire with fever. Concern flooded me.

Exhaustion forgotten, I rushed back to the bathroom to fill the basin with clean, cool water. When I returned, I ripped a piece of cloth from the bottom of my towel and dipped it into the water. I used it to wipe his brow and neck. His whole body was covered in a cool sheen of sweat. I swore under my breath and prepared myself for a long night.

The hours passed slowly with me changing the water, caring for his fever, and changing the bandages. At one point during the night I thought I heard Young say something, but when I looked up he was still fast asleep. The fire dwindled and died without anyone to add wood to it. If I had known where to get more perhaps I might have seen to it amongst the other duties I had taken on.

When his fever finally broke, the room as was cold as ice and my limbs felt too heavy for me to move far. I looked at Young, who seemed perfectly content to sleep as he was. The bed was here and soft, so I pushed aside the blankets and slid under them. I tugged them back up over my head, thankful that there was enough room on the bed to sleep five comfortably, let alone two. Vallen would be able to sleep peacefully without me disturbing him.

I closed my eyes and drifted off to the sound of Vallen's steady breathing. Surely I would be less tired come morning.

Chapter Fifteen

I awoke slowly, which was unusual for me. I felt like I had been dead to the world for possibly years. You don't realize how tired you are until you haven't had a safe place to sleep in a few days. I snuggled deeper into my pillows and blankets, wrapping my arms around them and giving a good squeeze. I felt them wince as if in pain, tightening their own hold on me and then loosening just slightly.

My eyes flew open as a hand smoothed over my hair then returned to rest on my hip as if it had been soothing me. It was dark but I could make out that my head rested on Vallen's shoulder. Both of his arms were around me, holding me tightly. My breasts were pressed firmly against his side and chest, where I lay half draped over him, my leg thrown across his hips.

My head was covered by the blankets, which was good, because I was fairly certain that *I* was covered in a blush from my head to my toes. And that was all I was wearing, having lost my towel at some point in the night. I lay perfectly still, trying to ignore the feeling of bare skin on bare skin.

The muffled sounds of an argument continued in the hall until the door burst open and sound crashed into the room.

"I'm telling you, she isn't in here," Young insisted.

"I've looked everywhere, all day, and I haven't been able to find her. I'm getting worried something has happened to Lady Morgan." Heather snorted. "Her scent is very strong in this room. I don't think she would have left and not told us where she went."

"Are you calling me a liar?" Young spat angrily.

"I'm just saying that Lady Morgan would *never* abandon us without a reason. Did you do something to her? Like make her a midnight snack?"

"You're crazy!" exclaimed Young. "I was here all night caring for my brother. He's stabilized now but I am still concerned. Rather than point fingers, why don't you come with me to look for her?"

"You would love that, wouldn't you, Dragon? Get me alone so you can eat me next." Heather's accusation was almost too humorous to bear.

"Ha! Like I would eat you." Young's tone had turned almost condescending. "My brother and I are sworn to a code of honor. Even without all that she has done for my brother, I would defend her, not eat her."

"Then what is your explanation?" Heather demanded.

Vallen cleared his throat. The sound rumbled deep in his chest and when he spoke he sounded tired. "Would the two of you quiet down? I am trying to rest. Lady Morgan was also injured yesterday and is no doubt running on very little sleep from the sound of things. I'm sure wherever she is, she is safe and recovering. Maybe she just needed a break."

I heard heavy footsteps draw closer. "Brother, you should be resting," Young said, concerned.

"I will. Leave Lady Morgan in peace. I'm sure she will show up when she is good and ready. In the meantime – Young, go find some food for dinner. Heather, why don't you go find some firewood for the bedchambers and main room." Despite the weakness in his voice, Vallen spoke with a tone of so much authority there was no disagreeing. Both responded, "Yes, sir," before I heard their footsteps leave the room and the door close behind them.

I lay there cradled in Vallen's arms, unmoving and hardly breathing for what seemed like an eternity. Finally, he removed a hand long enough to fold back the blankets from my head. I stared up at him dreamily. The color had returned to his body, and his blue eyes flickered with a note of humor. Reading the question on my face, he smiled. "I know not the story of how you came to be in my bed naked, but I highly doubted you wanted me to throw off the covers and expose you to the world."

I felt myself blush again. "I'm sorry," I said, and started to shift. A sharp, burning pain at my side stopped me. Vallen's hands stilled me against him once again.

"Slow down. When I woke up and found you tossing and turning and bleeding out, I did my best to patch you up in my limited state." I reached down and touched my ribs. Heavy linen bandages were wrapped around my breasts, my hand, and my upper arm. I carefully touched each bandage, trying to remember what had been the cause of each wound.

I looked back up at Vallen. "Thank you." I carefully tried to move again, and this time he helped by pulling me up slightly along his body. I could feel my cheeks burning red under his stare. "I'm sorry to have been trouble." His grip on me tightened when I started to move away.

"Lady Morgan, look at me." I couldn't help but look up. When I met his eyes again they were soft and warmer than I had seen them before. "It is I who should be begging your forgiveness at being a bother. You have gone above and beyond to care for me, and I truly appreciate that."

"You're welcome," I said, absently resting my hand on his chest. He reached down and tugged the covers back up under my chin. I started to disagree, but I stopped when I realized how tired I was.

"Rest, Lady Morgan, get well and rest," he said in a soothing tone.

I was so warm and comfortable. I hadn't been cradled in someone's arms since I was a child. There was something so soothing about it. I made one last argument. "It's inappropriate for me to be in bed with you. Like this," I added.

Vallen chuckled in a manner I didn't think he was capable of. "Rest well and know your virtue is safe from me. As for it being inappropriate, is that your personal code or someone else's?"

I thought about the question. Fairies were normally very open about their coupling. What we were doing wasn't coupling, though. He wasn't touching me in a way that was meant as more, nor was he trying to seduce me. I studied his twinkling blue eyes. At least, I didn't *think* he was trying to seduce me. "This feels very intimate," I explained, "Far more intimate than I have been with anyone as an adult."

He nodded. "I understand. If you are uncomfortable I can stop." He started to pull away.

"No, it's all right." I leaned my head back against his shoulder. "It's nice. Today is the first time in a long time I woke up feeling safe."

His grip tightened for just a moment. "I will endeavor that, for as long as we are in each other's company, I will do all in my power to ensure that you continue to feel safe."

I smiled as I closed my eyes. I did my best to burn this feeling into my mind so I would remember it always.

When next I awoke, it was to a discussion about why Vallen hadn't mentioned I was in the bed. He was doing his best to calm down Young, who had been truly concerned about me. I cracked one eye to look at the room. The fire had been relit and Young stood holding a tray with bowls and mugs on it.

When he noticed I was awake he lowered his eyes. "I'm sorry to have woken you, Lady Morgan."

I lifted my head, blinking a few times. "No, it's fine; I'm sorry to have worried you all day."

Young lifted his gaze to meet mine. "I feel like a total fool for not knowing you were here." He paused. "In fairness though, there are a lot of blankets and furs on the bed."

I smiled. "If it makes you feel better, it wasn't my intention. When I came in you had fallen asleep bandaging your own wounds and Vallen had a fever that needed to be brought down. I didn't know if you had found clothing and the room across the hall didn't have a fire and it was cold…" I trailed off.

"I'm sorry, My Lady." Young seemed to be searching for words. "I will do my best not to fail you again."

Young truly looked dejected and hurt. "Young?" I fought to sit up and was thankful when Vallen gave me a gentle nudge. I clutched the blankets tightly to my chest. Young looked up at me. "I am very sorry I worried you. Please don't feel guilty. You did nothing wrong. We were all so exhausted last night. You were an amazing help and I couldn't have cared for everyone without you."

He studied my face. "My Lady, the point is, you shouldn't have had to care for all of us. I should have been able to take care of my brother and myself. I should have followed through with what I said I was going to do. I should have noticed you were also injured." He breathed out heavily. "Your words are kind and I know you mean them, but if I don't hold myself to knightly standards then I may never reach the greatness I was born for." Young sat the tray down on Vallen's lap and left the room, closing the door when he went.

I stared at the door for a long moment before looking back at Vallen. "Is there anything I could have said that would have prevented that?"

He shook his head. "Young is sensitive. He was born with a prophecy hanging over his head so he is forever hopping between trying to convince me I should let him be a bard, and feeling like he must bear the weight of the world."

"What sort of prophecy?" I couldn't help but ask.

"You know, the mumbo-jumbo that elders inflict on us to encourage us to do better and try harder. Young believes he must carry on the family legacy because I no longer have my Dragon Fire." He reached down and picked up a spoon, handing it to me. "We should eat while it's still warm."

I accepted the spoon. "What do you mean, you don't have your Dragon Fire anymore? Isn't that part of being a Dragon?" I dipped the spoon into the hot stew and took a big bite. My mouth swam with flavors.

"I had Dragon Fire, but I traded it to a Mage to make sure someone I cared for was reincarnated." I took a few bites then reached for the tea.

"You can do that?" I asked, a bit louder than I planned.

He chuckled uncomfortably. "Yes, it would seem you can." I continued to stare at him expectantly. He didn't budge.

"You aren't going to tell me about her, are you?" I asked, prying.

His eyebrows rose at my question. "I'm not sure we are…" he stopped and looked at my face, then shook his head in answer to some inner question. "Someday. I'm still not ready to talk about it."

"I like awkward conversations," I told him with a grin, before shoveling more food into my mouth. "Well, awkward for others, not so much for me. Did your brother make this?" I gulped more down as I started to realize just how hungry I was. I suddenly found myself trying to remember the last time I had a real meal.

"What about your wings?" he asked. "Or is that too personal?"

I stopped eating and thought about it for a moment. "I'm not used to being asked about them. I think the last person to see the scars before you was a doctor."

He finished his soup. "If you don't wish to talk about it…"

I cut him off. "It's not that. People just don't know." I shook my head. "The buds grew in but the wings never did. After a number of years, the doctors concluded that my Human half was preventing their growth. The buds were painful and often got in the way, so we had them removed."

"We?" he asked softly.

"My parents and I." I took a few more bites of food. "My mother was heartbroken, I think because I wouldn't be able to fly."

"I'm sorry, Lady Morgan. When we saved you back at the Troll's home you mentioned you no longer had family. May I ask what happened?"

"A freak pickle fire," I answered flatly.

He blinked in surprise. "A what?"

I sighed. "My mother had this recipe she had been working on for years. It was to make magic pickles. She was part of the Human Acquisition Department, I'm sorry, I mean Vesaria's Tourist Board. She realized a number of years ago that Humans liked to picnic in Fairy Circles. She thought that if she could develop a magical picnic food that would cause Humans to obey the Fae without thought, it may help things. Pickles seemed like a logical choice since they can be canned and stored for many years."

I could see him trying not to grin. I also had to try not to grin because even though the story was tragic, it really was such a harebrained scheme that it was hard not to laugh. "Please go on."

I nodded. "Well… a number of years ago my mother was working on a new formula since the last one just seemed to make Humans horny and resulted in one following her through the portal and insisting she marry him. Dad was sort of old fashioned like that." I smiled.

"That's how your parents met?" he blurted out in surprise, then looked ashamed of himself.

I finally cracked a laugh. "Yup, after a year she gave in and married him. Ten months later, poof, I enter the picture." Shaking my head, I finished the stew. "Anyway, so she was working on a new batch and the house caught on fire or something and due to all the magic in use I lost them both."

Vallen opened his mouth to say something then shut it again. "I'm really sorry."

"Ok, so I told you my tragic back stories of my dead parents and fiancé. Your turn to give me something, or else I'm going to feel like fate dumped on me." I placed my spoon in the empty bowl then watched as he carefully lowered the tray to the floor.

"Ok," he said, then sank back down into the pillows, pulling me with him and wrapping his arms around me. "I'm sort of responsible for Young, but I didn't raise him. I was off being selfish when all of it happened. As you know, there is a bit of an age gap between us. It won't mean much in a few centuries, but right now it is huge."

"How much of an age gap are we talking? Ten or fifteen years?" I knew Dragons aged differently than Humans and Fae.

"About two hundred years or so," he answered with a shrug. I tried hard not to be shocked. My own mother had been nearly six hundred when she had me.

"Oh, I see," I told him.

"I'm still young by Dragon standards, but that's another story. To continue the story. While I was away for a number of years on a mission for my King, my parents had Young. There was evidently some problem involving an Archmage and they were killed. My little brother, who was less than a year old, was sent to live with our grandmother."

I could feel his regret for being away from home. "Did you ever find the Archmage responsible?"

He nodded. "Yes."

"Good," I said, tightening my grip on him. Somehow it comforted me to comfort him.

"And like you, I lost the love of my life." He reached up and absently stroked my hair down my back.

"Does it get easier and hurt less with time?" I asked.

"Yes, but it can take a very long time." I closed my eyes at his words. I could picture Simon's smiling face, his red hair falling free of its pony tail so that strands fell in his face. His eyes were so dark they were almost black, but they sparkled so when he smiled. A tear ran down my cheek. Vallen moved his hand and reached up to wipe it away. "I promise there will be justice for what Avery has done to you."

I tried to smile, knowing he meant it. Right now, though, I didn't want to think about Avery. "Thank you," I whispered.

There was a knock on the door and then Young opened it without waiting for any word from us. He took one look at the two of us wrapped in each other's arms and blushed clear through his scalp. He averted his gaze and walked close enough to set the clothes down on the chair. "I'm sorry, I didn't expect... You and the Lady... and I'm leaving." He grabbed the tray and disappeared back out the door before we could correct his misconception.

Vallen growled and lowered his arms from around me. "I'm sorry. He has the wrong idea and it's my fault. I'll go find him and explain." He shifted and winced.

"Wait. You shouldn't be up yet. I can go," I offered.

He shook his head. "This is my fault." With a deep breath he pushed himself out of bed and groaned in pain.

Without meaning to I raked my eyes over him. Every inch of his body was covered in thick muscle. He wasn't bulging, but just looking at him you knew he was powerful. His body was covered in scars and bandages that told the tales of a life lived in the service of others. His dark hair had blue streaks in it, reminding me of a Fairy. His backside was like no backside I had ever seen in person. It looked like it should be made of stone and attached to a statue in Queen Mab's palace. He turned, giving me full view of his manhood. I had always heard they grew when excited, but with his there in plain view I couldn't imagine it growing larger, as it was already more than I would have ever known what to do with. He cleared his throat and my eyes flew up to meet his gaze. "My Lady, I believe my eyes are up here."

I blushed and tugged the blankets over my head, wanting in that very moment to die after being caught staring. He must have finished dressing because I heard him cross the room, followed by the sounds of the door opening and closing. Only after my breathing had returned to normal did I push the blankets off of my head and struggle to the side of the bed.

I let out a little cry as I climbed out of the bed. I hadn't realized the injury I'd sustained was anything more than a deep scratch. I reached the chair and lifted what appeared to be a short dress or a long top. I tugged it on over my head and sighed when it barely made it to mid-thigh. "Who wears stuff like this?" I said, glancing down at myself. The neckline was deep and showed far more than I was comfortable with and the back was even worse.

I walked slowly to the door and pulled it open. The hallway was brightly lit by sconces along the walls. I made a quick stop at the bathroom, then went to check on Heather and Uther.

When I entered their room, Uther struggled to his feet despite my encouragement to stay sitting and off his injury. Without warning he ran his hands over my arms, then wrapped me in a bear hug. I struggled to breathe between its constriction and the pain in my side. "Uther... stop... can't... breathe," I bit out.

He loosened his grip on me as I gasped for air. "I'm sorry, Lady Morgan. I have only today learned of everything you have done for Heather, and I am so grateful."

I patted his back and stepped away. "You're welcome, but we have only begun. I will stop Avery."

He looked at me with awe. "I saw how many of her men you dispatched yesterday. You made a large dent in her forces. She will no doubt need to do some heavy recruiting before she makes her move on Maht."

"How many does she have now?" I asked.

Uther thought for a moment. "You three took out nearly four dozen. She probably has another fifty. Maht is more of a city then a town, and as such has strong defenses. She'll need at least a hundred if she is going to capture it."

"How long did it take her to build her numbers last time?" I pressed him for as much information as possible.

"It took her about two months to build her group to that size, but she has a reputation now. Most likely it will take her about a week or so to recover." He sat back down on the bed. He leaned back and looked at me from head to toe. "You know, My Lady, I would be happy to give you a personal thank you for all you have done." Reaching out, he took my hand and kissed it.

Heather growled at him and he released me. "Ignore him. He is a terrible flirt and you're his favorite type. Confident and naive." She glared at him and he returned it.

I smiled and slowly started making my way towards the door. "Thank you for all the info, Uther." He nodded at me. "I'm still tired from my own injuries so I'm going to go get some rest."

Heather and Uther's brows both shot up. "You were injured?" Heather asked.

"Yes, but I'm sure I am on the mend," I tried to reassure them.

"Well, my sweet lady, I will come next door tonight and do my best to sooth all your aches and pains." Uther wiggled his eyebrows at me.

"That won't be necessary. I'll probably stay with Vallen and Young again. Vallen's injuries were rather serious and I want to keep an eye on him." I was relieved when Uther nodded in understanding and support.

"Rest well," he called after me, as I slid out of the room and pulled the door shut behind me.

I leaned against the wall beside the door and let out a breath. "Are you well, Lady Morgan?" My head snapped around to face Young.

"I am. I think I am ready to retire." I turned down the hall and headed back towards the room he and Vallen were staying in.

"My Lady, I have prepared your own room for the night," he said, motioning toward the door across the hall.

"Oh." I tried not to let the disappointment reach my face.

"Is something wrong?" he asked softly.

"No, I just have something to talk to Vallen about before I sleep," I told him.

"I see. All right then, let's go talk to my brother." Young led the way and opened the door for me.

Once inside, I sat down in the large chair near the bed. Vallen looked up from a book he was reading and tucked it away under the blankets. "Lady Morgan?" he asked.

"I spoke with Uther and Heather. It would seem that we, and by we I mainly mean you two, dispatched about half of Avery's men yesterday. Uther believes it will take her a week to rebuild her numbers even though it took nearly two months to build them the first time." I curled my legs up into the chair so my feet would no longer have to rest on the cold stone floor.

Vallen nodded, taking in the information. "You and I should rest a few more days. Tomorrow we will send Young and Heather to Maht with a message to start preparing the city defenses." Young started to interrupt, but thought better of it when he saw his brother's look. "We will join them within the next few days, once everyone is well enough to ride on."

The chill of the air sent a shiver through me, though I tried to stop it. Vallen looked at me, then at Young. "Are you all right, Lady Morgan?"

I nodded. "I'm fine," I assured them both.

"Young, would you mind making some hot tea for Lady Morgan and me?" Vallen asked his brother with a nod. Young's gaze narrowed for a moment, but he agreed and disappeared out of the room. "Now, tell me what is bothering you? You are far too skilled a warrior to need council on this."

"This is going to sound ridiculous but, can I?" I paused and really thought about if I should ask such a thing. "I mean, I don't…"

"Go ahead. If I can help in anyway, I will." He did his best to sound reassuring.

"I feel like a child asking this." I took a deep breath and lowered my head, unable to make eye contact. "May I sleep in here?"

"Oh," he said, then started to slide out of bed. "We can trade rooms for the night. That's fine."

"No, I mean can I stay here with you?" I clarified. I winced just asking it.

He breathed out slowly. "Are you sure that is what you want?"

"Yes. Right now I want to feel safe and whole. I feel that when I'm with you."

"I see." A complex display of emotions danced across his face. "My Lady, you are welcome here. If there is any comfort I can give, I am happy to do so." He held out his hand to me. I stood and walked around the bed to once again be on the side opposite his injured shoulder and slid under the blankets.

I had just slid under the covers when Young re-entered the room. His eyes went from the chair to the bed where I now sat. He brought the tea over and handed it to us. "If you're going to stay in here, may I use the bed in the room I prepared for you? Not that the chair isn't entirely comfortable."

"That would be totally fine, Young," I said, wrapping my fingers around the warm mug.

He clapped his hands together in front of him. "Then I will tend your fire and see you both in the morning." Moments later he banked the fire and left.

Chapter Sixteen

I sat in the bed stiff as a plank. While I had crawled under the covers, I hadn't made it as far as snuggling into his arms. It was one thing to find myself there by accident; it was another thing entirely when I asked to be there. *Did he think I wanted more? Did he expect more?*

I sat there too nervous to move. Beside me, Vallen did his best to arrange his pillows so he could lay down. I looked over at him, hesitant, as he slid deeper under the covers. I started to say something, but he derailed my thoughts by speaking first. "Lady Morgan, may I extinguish the light, or do you still need it?"

My mind raced. *I was going to be in the dark with him. In bed with him. ALONE with him.* My heart started to race. I watched as he reached for the flat disc on the wall. "No, wait. I'm not ready!" I begged.

He smiled. "All right. When you're ready, put your hand flat on this disc and rotate it to the right a quarter turn." He demonstrated, then returned the light to normal before nestling under the blankets and closing his eyes.

I sat there staring at him for a long time. He seemed perfectly content to just sleep. *Maybe he really didn't expect anything? Maybe I built this all up in my head?* I did my best to reason it out. Finally, holding my breath, I reached up and turned out the light. As soon as the room went dark my heart started to race again.

I watched his sleeping form across the bed. His chest rose and fell with steady breaths. He rested one arm on his chest and the other outstretched towards me. I lowered my head to the pillow, my eyes never leaving him. "Pssss, Vallen are you awake?" I asked in a hushed whisper. When I got no answer I did my best to move a little closer. "Pssss, Vallen are you awake?"

As if in response to my question he let out a snort followed by a soft snore. I huffed and reached out, sliding my hand into his outstretched palm. His fingers twitched, closing around mine, and his thumb gently stroked the back of my hand. "Vallen?" I asked again, this time in more than a whisper.

"Hmmm?" I got in a groggy voice.

"You didn't think we were going to do more than sleep, did you?" I asked.

He shifted his hand so that his thumb was rubbing the inside of my wrist. The touch sent little shock waves through my system. "No," he answered, shaking his head. I felt him shift closer to me on the bed and turn onto his side. His other hand came down to rest on top of mine, sandwiching my palm between his. "Lady Morgan, I surmise that you have largely interacted with countless curs, but I am going to tell you something here and now, and swear by it on my life when I do. As a man, I am perfectly capable of holding, caressing, and doing many other things with a woman, not crossing any lines she has given me, and always stopping when asked. Any male who tells you otherwise is lying."

"Oh. I mean, I realize that, but I also thought that my actions may have implied something else and was afraid that perhaps I had given you the wrong impression." I felt like a teenage girl trying to explain herself.

"I thought, when you asked, that you found comfort in the company of another soul. That being with another person you didn't have to protect allowed you to lower your guard and relax. I also thought that this old lair is VERY cold and that you enjoyed the extra warmth of a second body. If you have changed your mind for any reason, I can go share the other room with Young, or I can wake him and you can have the room. You don't need to be in my arms to share this bed. We did so the night in the woods because the pallet was very small, but that isn't the case here."

I let out a sigh of relief and moved closer, pulling my hand free. Vallen lay back on the pillows and I snuggled into his side. His arms closed around me and I felt like I was hidden away from the world. I ran my hand over his chest until it rested over his heart. Our legs tangled and I became aware he was nude. "Do you always sleep naked?" I asked.

"Typically, yes," he answered. His voice was husky and sounded tired.

"Oh. Should I sleep that way too?" I had never really thought about what to wear or not wear sleeping.

He shook his head. "Sleep however you are comfortable." I started tugging off the awkwardly small dress, and found it difficult. "What are you doing?" he asked.

"Taking off this flimsy piece of lace," I explained. He chuckled at me. "Hey, rather than laughing at me, how about giving me a hand?" I was startled when his hands moved to my hips, sliding under the dress and then up along my sides and shoulders until he tugged it off over my head and handed it to me. "You are strangely good at that," I said, eyeing his dark form.

"Yes, well, I can honestly say that most of the women who find their way to my bed aren't looking for merely the security and companionship I offer." He paused and shook his head. "That sounded lewd. My apologies." I laughed, and the more shocked he seemed the harder I laughed. Finally he reached up and just barely added enough light to the room to allow me to see his features. "May I ask what is so funny?"

"I have spent years surrounded by men, fighting at their sides. I have heard about bending ladies over a fence, why sheep are preferable to women, how to bed Elves, Dwarves, and a number of other races… in detail. You are the first man I have ever had apologize for implying that you have had sexual partners." I giggled again in spite of myself.

He breathed deep and his eyes flared. "You are a very different kind of woman, Lady Morgan. Did you know that?" he asked, with a boyish grin that made my arms feel heavy and my heart beat faster.

"I've heard that before," I said, trying to gulp in air.

Vallen cupped my face in his hand, stroking my cheek with his thumb. "Are you all right? Does your side hurt?" His voice shifted to a tone of concern.

"I'm all right," I said in a shaky voice.

He tugged the blankets up tighter around me and pulled me closer to his body. He turned the light out again and ran his hands over me in an effort to warm my skin. "Is that better?" he asked.

My body felt like fire pressed against his and I still felt as if I were shaking. "Yes, that's better," I told him. I stared up at the shadows of his face and focused on the feeling of his hands resting against my body. "Vallen?"

"Hmmm," he answered, groggily again.

"I trust you." His breath seemed to catch in his chest and he didn't exhale for a long moment.

"Thank you," he finally said.

"If I were to tell you, you could kiss me... would you?" I felt so strange asking the question.

I felt him shake his head. "I am perfectly capable of kissing you, but there is a difference between being able to do something and being welcomed to do something."

"What if I asked you to kiss me?" I had been denied kisses by Simon in the past, saying he wanted to wait until the moment was perfect.

"Have you been kissed before?" he asked hesitantly.

"Well, not romantically. I've had affectionate kisses like the kinds given between family and friends." I paused for a moment. "I once kissed Billy when I was sixteen and even that was chaste. Does it really matter?"

He swallowed hard. "Are you asking me to kiss you?" he finally asked.

"Yes, but only if you want to," I answered.

"Might I ask why?" His grip on me was unchanging.

"Because you are an honorable man. Because I know you are undoubtedly experienced. Because you are handsome in a way that seems almost unfair to the rest of the world. Because I almost died several times in the last six months and would have done so never having been really kissed." I shook my head. "I may never share my body with a man, but I want to know what it is like to feel cherished as a woman."

Vallen reached up and brushed the hair out of my face. "If the man in your life can not make you feel cherished without physical intimacies than he is not much of a man. Loving and caring for a person are in our base instincts. It doesn't require sex to do that. If someone is unable to do so without any promise of more, then they are selfish and undeserving of you and your body."

What he said sounded true. I didn't like it because it made me question my entire relationship with Simon. He had been fine with waiting, but refused to kiss me or hardly touch me because he said he doubted his ability to stop once he started. I'd heard whispers in the villages from many of the women that he was bedding others, but not me. "Am I unattractive because I'm mixed?"

Vallen laughed and rolled over to face me again. "Where did that nonsense even come from?" I was glad he couldn't see me in the dark because I was blushing again. I lowered my head. He reached out of the dark and lifted my chin. "Contrary to what you may think, I *can* see you."

"Simon…" I started then stopped. "When the people who proclaim to love you show little interest, you develop self-doubt."

He seemed to pause and consider my words. "Was Simon deeply religious? Or was he old fashioned?"

I shook my head. "No. I know it wasn't like that. I have reason to believe he was sharing himself with many."

"Why would you stay with someone like that?" he asked, frustration clear in his voice. He took a deep breath and sighed. "I'm sorry, I don't know the full story, and its shows poor character to speak ill of the dead, but he sounds like a selfish little prick. May I ask you something personal?"

"Of course," I answered.

"Did he ever ask you to mate with him?" He paused. "Not to be his mate, but to just sleep with him?"

"Yes, early on in our courtship. I wasn't sure, so I told him I wasn't ready." I closed my eyes, remembering the night. "We fought about it. He reminded me how lucky I was to have an Elf willing to take me as a lover since I was half Human."

"This was obviously before Prince Tallyn took Lady Lily as his mate," Vallen sighed.

I nodded. "Time passed and I told him I was ready. He gave me a quick kiss on the cheek and said that he didn't wish to mar my perfection until we had joined as mates."

"Years passed and it got pushed to the back burner," Vallen finished. "Then, when he's on his death bed, he tells you to join him on the other side."

"Yes." Talking about all this brought back a flood of memories both good and bad. When a person is gone, it is too easy to forget the bad.

"Lady Morgan, I believe that one's first kiss should be meaningful and beautiful. I think you should choose someone who is worthy of it, and not allow opportunity to choose for you. I am humbled you would even consider me." Vallen lay back onto his pillows and pulled me across his chest, resting his chin atop my head.

I lay there listening to his heartbeat and his breathing slow. Ignoring the ache in my side, I lifted my head and pressed my lips to the hollow of his throat. His body became rigid under me. His arms locked into place, his breathing shallow, his lips parted as if he were going to say something. "I want you to kiss me, Lord Vallen. I want my memory to be that of an honorable warrior who protected me even from myself."

His grip on my sides tightened in an effort to slow my progress. I lowered my lips to his and there was… nothing. He didn't respond. I lifted my head and looked down at his shadowed face. He pushed himself up into a sitting position, causing me to sit back onto my knees. "Do you understand that a kiss can't be taken back? They can be given in lust, in laughter, and many other ways, but once a kiss is given it can't be undone. For some, kisses are meaningless, and for others they mean the world. Which will this be to you?"

I didn't understand what he was asking, but as I thought about it I realized he wanted to know if I was just using him as a means to an end or if I was choosing him because I really wanted to kiss him. "This will be the kiss I remember for a lifetime. The one I will judge all others by in the future. You will be the one I judge all others by in the future."

"Then I pray, Lady Morgan, that I do this well and set the bar high." Slowly he slid his hand from my hip up to the back of my neck. The other, resting at the small of my back, pulled me closer to him. My hands were splayed on his chest as he lowered his mouth to mine.

His lips were gentle but felt like absolute fire. My lips parted in an effort to cool them, but as they did his tongue joined the dance, slipping in to taste me and drink me in. It darted over my own, inviting me to come play with him. He tilted my head back, giving him further access to my mouth, deepening the kiss more. I moaned into his mouth and slid my arms around his neck, pressing my chest to his. He twisted slightly, pulling me across his lap and laying my head into the pillow behind me. He stretched out to his full length, pressing my body into the mattress with his own. I thrust my tongue in response to the movements of his tongue, tasting him as he had me. I buried a hand into his hair, running a hand down his bare back and accidentally dragging my nails as I went. He moaned against my mouth, letting his hands casually caress the base of my back and nape of my neck. I almost screamed in frustration when he lifted his head and broke this kiss.

"We should stop here," he gasped. He lowered his head and pressed a feather light kiss to my shoulder. I became aware of the rock-hard bulge pressed against my hip bone. He rolled away and sat on the edge of the bed. He let out a few shaky breaths before announcing he would return shortly. Then he stood and left the room.

I wanted to call after him and beg him to stay. I wanted to tell him virtue be damned, but I did none of those things. Instead I lay alone in the large bed, wondering if I had done something very wrong or something very right to cause such a reaction.

When he returned a short time later, his hair and body were damp and cool, as if he had just crawled out of a cold stream. He snuggled close to me and fell asleep. At first I thought about waking him to talk about our kiss, but I decided it was better left for another time.

Chapter Seventeen

I woke up to the sound of tapping on the door. Vallen was still sound asleep, so I softly called out for them to enter. Heather poked her head around the door to look around the room. I waved her in. She stared, mouth open, for a moment, then grinned widely. "Lady Morgan, you little minx." Her eyes went to Vallen. "Good for you. He looks like a gentle giant." She winked.

"Can I help you?" I asked, getting past my embarrassment.

"Yes, I brought you a clean change of clothes. I washed them for you yesterday. Also, I am riding out with Young this morning for Maht. Is there anything I should pick up?" She stood there, just grinning at me.

I pointed at my bag, which sat on the floor by the chair. "Take the small pouch. It should have about twenty gold in it. Restock our first aid supplies, get some bread, another set of blankets to replace mine, and more tea."

She nodded, collected the small pouch, and slid out of the room. I leaned my head back down, resting it on Vallen's shoulder. Were the others under the impression we were sleeping together? I wondered if it mattered that we weren't. I slid my hand over his chest, absentmindedly tracing circles with my fingertips. His hand shifted and stroked my hair. I turned my face up to look at him. He was staring at my fingers as they caressed his chest. "Good morning," he choked out.

"Good morning," I said, stilling my hand and resting it where it stopped. I suddenly noticed a change in his appearance. "Where are your bandages?" I asked.

"I removed them to bathe last night. My wounds are closed, though they are still quite tender. If you would be so kind today, perhaps you could remove my stitches?" I gently traced the raised scars that covered his body.

"I can do that. Do you think Uther's are healed as well?" I asked.

"Possibly, though he did break a bone." He sat up, pulling me up along with him. "Shall we go find some food?" he asked, as his stomach protested loudly. I looked down at it. He blushed. Standing up, he moved to his and Young's bags and rummaged through them. He tugged on a long blue tunic then pulled on dark grey leather leggings. I couldn't help but watch as he moved. There was something predatory about him even when he was doing the most mundane tasks.

He walked ahead to the door, giving me privacy to get dressed. As I stood, the world seemed to roll around me and a sharp pain cut into my side. I sucked in air. Vallen didn't turn around, but he called over his shoulder. "Are you all right?" he asked.

"Yeah," I bit out, and quickly tugged on the clean clothes Heather had left for me, thankful I wouldn't have to walk around in the overly-revealing dress. Catching my breath, I followed along behind Vallen as he led me down the hallway, past the bathroom, through a large den where a fire burned, and into an annex-type room that housed a kitchen.

"If you have a seat, I will see what I can come up with for breakfast. I believe we have tea, maybe some fruit and cheese. If you like, I can go see if I can find something meat-wise?" He looked down at me with a grin.

I sank onto the hard wooden chair, already feeling exhausted. I pressed my hand to my side, hoping to relieve some of the pressure and ache there. When Vallen turned back around it was to set down a plate covered in cheese, apple, and pear slices. He also sat down a kettle of tea. I smiled up at him, forgetting about the pain. "Thank you."

He sank down onto the chair next to me and we ate in total silence. I felt like if I said anything I might destroy the magic of the kiss last night.
Remembering the taste of him on my lips caused me to blush all over again. "Stop thinking about it," he said in a whisper. A mischievous grin turned up the corner of his lips.

I blinked at him innocently. "I don't know what you're talking about," I chirped.

"Remind me not to let you ever play poker with my money," he mumbled.

"What's poker?" I asked.

"It's a game that Humans in this realm and a few others enjoy playing." His words were relaxed. He seemed happy to change subjects.

"Is it a game of chance or a game of skill?" I was fascinated. Most Fairies enjoyed games and were naturally drawn to them and I was no exception.

"A little bit of luck and a whole lot of skill," he explained.

"Really?!" I was so excited at the prospect of learning a new game I forgot all about the food.

Vallen started explaining the rules of the game as we sat there. When he noticed I wasn't eating he held up bites of fruit and cheese to my mouth until I took them. Before long, I thought I understood this new game and was sure I could master it quickly. We had also consumed all the food. Vallen moved away from the table with the plate and mugs. I watched carefully as he washed them and left them to dry.

"Shall we go check on Uther?" he asked as he turned around.

I nodded and stood up. Pain shot through me, causing me to stumble. Before I could hit the ground Vallen caught me in his arms and pulled me against his chest. "Thanks," I mumbled.

He eyed me carefully. "Are you sure you are feeling all right?"

"Yeah, yeah," I assured him. "I'm just not healing as quickly as you. I'm really sore." I made sure I was stable on my feet before letting go, and took a step back as if to prove my point. "See? Just fine." I added a smile for an extra measure.

After a moment of studying my face carefully he nodded. "Ok. Let's go see how Uther is doing, shall we?"

When we arrived at Uther and Heather's room, we were in for a surprise. Where there should have been a tall, black Werewolf warrior was a grey and brown wolf sleeping in a perfect fur bundle. "I told you not to shift!" I snapped loudly at him.

The wolf jumped to his feet, growling. Vallen protectively stepped in front of me. It was a gesture I had never been on the receiving end of, because I was always the guardian. When Uther saw it was us he sat down and shifted back into Human form.

"You startled me!" he said defensively.

"I told you no shifting until you were healed," I said sternly, stepping out from behind Vallen.

"I have healed." He pointed to his ankle.

I leaned down close to look at it. The stitches were gone, it looked like there was no sign of the break, and all that was left was a raised, welt-like scar where the injury had been two nights before. "Wow, that was fast," I commented.

He stood up and walked around to prove his point. "I told you," he said with an arrogant grin.

"What happened to your stitches?" I asked, narrowing my eyes on him.

He stopped walking and sat down on the bed. "I, ummm, cut them, then shifted and chewed them out."

I grimaced. "Yuck, that sounds unhygienic."

"Un-what?" he asked.

"Unhygienic. It means that it could have spread infection." He still looked confused by my explanation.

"I am not my little sister. I'll have you know I bathe regularly when I am in Human form." His lips split into a wide grin. "The ladies like it better that way."

I snorted and bit back laughter. Vallen rolled his eyes and asked, "You're what? Early twenties?"

"Twenty-one," Uther answered, still wearing his smug grin.

"Yup, you and Young are cut from the same cloth, Werewolf," Vallen said, shaking his head.

"I'll take that as a compliment, Sir Vallen. Young is a very remarkable young man. You should be proud of him." Uther's demeanor completely changed as he said this.

Vallen's features softened and he smiled, nodding his head. "I am proud of him. Every day he does something that makes me question how I live my own life."

Uther came over to me one last time and took my hand in his, bringing it to rest against his chest over his heart. "Lady Morgan, my sister and I are in your debt."

I pulled my hand free and waved away the comment. "No you're not, Uther."

He bowed slightly as I withdrew and I turned back to face Vallen. "Is it my turn to check on you, sir? I'll remove your stitches since everyone here seems to heal faster than I do."

Vallen nodded, opening the door for me so I could step through before him. We re-entered the chambers we seemed to be sharing and I smiled as he dragged off his tunic and then his leggings. I tried not to stare at his anatomy. "Is it better if I stand, sit, or lay down?" he asked.

I thought about it for a moment. "Sit on the edge of the bed. That way I can have you lie back if needed." He did as I directed. I dug through my bag until I located a small thin knife, tweezers, and a clean cloth before I moved to kneel behind him. Quickly, I removed the few stitches, then noticed the claw marks down his back. Blushing brightly, I sat dreamily remembering that I was the one who had put them there. Now they were little more than soft pink lines.

I carefully climbed off the bed, thankful for the moment he reached out to steady me. He kept his arm around my waist as I removed the stitches from his shoulder and arm. Placing my hand on the center of his chest, I urged him to lean back so I could see to his side and abdomen. He winced as I pulled a few of the stitches free, but soon they were all removed and all that was left was his thigh. I hadn't given much thought to it the night I did the stitches, but now I realized I would be working dangerously close to a part of his anatomy I wasn't yet sure I was comfortable with. Clearing my throat in hopes of sounding more confident, I met his gaze. "Can you move further back on the bed?"

He smiled and complied with my request. His eyes never left me. If I didn't know better, I would swear he was finding humor it what I was sure had to be my obvious discomfort with the situation. "Wait, before you begin. So I may preserve a little of my modesty," he explained as he positioned the tunic over his groin. The small gesture did a lot to relieve my nerves.

With a shaky hand I carefully removed the six stitches I had used to close the worst part of the injury. When I finished, I patted his leg. "You're all set." I moved to sit on the bed beside him.

"Thank you, Lady Morgan. Once I dress I will return the favor." I didn't process his words until he had landed back on the bed beside me.

"Wait, what?" I said, turning to face him.

He pointed at my side. "You've been babying it all day and it looks like you have bled through your bandages. Please let me see to your injury. If it is serious, I am capable of stitches or getting you to someone more capable than I." I groaned, knowing he was right. "You are welcome to leave your tunic on and just remove your injured arm and lift the side if it makes you more comfortable."

I eyed him closely. His mouth was smiling but his eyes held genuine concern. Here was a man that had seen my breasts several times. He'd had many chances to touch them inappropriately, and now I was worried about exposing them for medical attention? With a deep breath I struggled to pull my tunic off.

He started with my hand and wrist, unwrapping them carefully. The knuckles had mostly healed, but they were still swollen. Then he moved to the cut on my upper arm. When the bandage was removed, all that remained was a thin, raised welt. I took a deep breath as he reached for the bandages around my ribs.

His hand stopped and his eyes grew large and round. He leaned close to the wound, smelling it. With a startled look on his face he looked up at me. "What were you cut with?"

"An axe head. I defended against it and it broke free of its handle. I could have sworn it was hardly more than a nick." The more I looked at his face the more I saw panic spreading across it.

"I swear I will do whatever it takes to fix this." He grabbed my tunic and pulled it on over my head. He left me sitting on the bed as he rushed to the door and bellowed for Uther.

The sound of four legs pounding down the hall stopped short at the door as Uther transformed. "Yes, Sir Vallen?" the Werewolf gasped.

"How long were you in Avery's custody?" Vallen asked.

"About a month," Uther answered.

"Did you see any of the men treating their weapons with Dragon's blood?" Vallen's words washed over me as I started to realize what was happening.

Uther was silent a moment while he looked at me, then back to Vallen, nodding. Vallen swore loudly, then rushed to his bag, pulling out a stone talisman. He looked back at Uther. "Tell Young when he returns that Lady Morgan has been poisoned with Dragon's blood. I had to take the talisman to get her to Lady Jura immediately."

Uther nodded acknowledgement as Vallen drew a dagger through his hand, opening his palm. He closed his hand around the small rectangular stone, then bent down, capturing me in his arms and cradling me against his chest. He chanted just for a moment as the entire world went black around us. "Don't be afraid," he whispered, just before I lost consciousness.

Chapter Eighteen

When I awoke, it was to the hushed sounds of people talking nearby. I was in a dark place I didn't recognize, but the surroundings smelled like Vallen: a mixture of earth, spice and smoke that made me think of bonfires in the fall. I started to move, but realized my whole body felt heavy. Panic flooded my senses. "Vallen?" I cried out.

I heard the hushed speaking stop and the sound of quickly moving feet. He appeared at my side, sinking down onto the bed next to me. He took my hand in his. "Shhh, I'm here."

"What's going on?" I asked him.

He met my eyes with a sadness nobody ever wishes to see. "Some of the men we were fighting used Dragon's blood on their blades. Young and I are immune for obvious reasons. However, on Fae it can be quite dangerous, and on Humans it is lethal."

I took a deep breath, knowing in that moment the outcome wouldn't be good. "How long do I have?"

He tried to smile and failed. "I don't know. It could be a few days, or it could be a few weeks. Lady Jura has treated you with the anti-toxin the Fae and Elves normally use, but it's been in your system for over forty-eight hours now."

I took a deep breath and let it out slowly. "What's going to happen?" He shook his head, but I pushed again. "I need to know, for my own peace."

Finally, he nodded, gathering me up against him. "First, the toxin will spread through your blood and the wound it entered through will not close and heal. The area around it will blacken and begin to decay into ash, like it's being burned away. It will be very painful, and eventually the wound will be so far gone it will cause death. Your wound was very small to begin with, so it will take some time."

A tall woman with long, dark waves of hair stepped into sight. Her eyes were the color of amethysts and looked sad. "How are you feeling, Lady Morgan?" She took a seat on the other side of the bed.

I huffed at the humor of asking a dying woman how she was. "I've had better days," I told her.

She smiled. "I'm Lady Jura. Your stubbornness will get you through this tough time. I've given you a sedative to help with the pain, but it may make you a bit drowsy as well. If the pain returns, please let me know. There is no point in making you suffer when we have ways of helping."

"Is that why my body feels so heavy?" I asked.

"Most likely," he nodded. "Would it be all right if I borrowed Lord Vallen for a bit? I need to speak with him." She looked across me to Vallen, who nodded at her and looked down.

"Will you be all right for a few minutes on your own?" he asked in a voice so soft it didn't seem quite real.

A door burst open somewhere across the chamber and I heard panting. "How is she?" Young demanded. Someone muttered something and he rushed across the room, almost colliding with Vallen. "Lady Morgan, I flew all night so that I could get here."

I smiled at him. "That wasn't necessary. You could have come in your own time," I told him.

"No, if Vallen or I had protected you better, none of this would have happened." His eyes were filled with unspent tears.

He took the hand that Vallen wasn't holding and squeezed it, and I squeezed it back. "Young, you had no way of knowing, and neither did Vallen. I've been in a thousand battles and been injured on some level countless times. Even knowing what we know now, I still would have rushed in to help you two. The end comes for us all someday. I only know that I am proud that mine was a result of fighting alongside the two of you."

"You can't think that way, Lady Morgan. We will find a way to save you." Tears started rolling down Young's face. Lady Jura tapped him on the shoulder and both he and Vallen walked with her. I lowered my head and closed my eyes, making a mental note to refuse any more sedatives. I would prefer pain to not being able to live my last days.

When I awoke again, it was to the sounds of yelling. "If she can be convinced, I will take on the responsibility," Vallen insisted firmly.

Young argued. "What about Melody? What about Dani? You sacrificed your Dragon's Fire to have her reincarnated because you loved her. You love Dani!"

"I made that sacrifice because I loved Melody. If Dani is her reincarnation, then I am beyond happy because it means she gets a second chance at life. No matter what the case is, Dani and Melody are not the same person. Dani is entitled to her own happiness." There was a long pause from Vallen. I could hear him breathing heavily. "And what about you? You are barely out of your childhood. You deserve happiness. If you truly believe in the prophecy surrounding you, then you have to believe there is a Soul Mate out there for you. Give yourself a chance," Vallen insisted.

"How can I when Lady Morgan is in there creeping towards death? I want to do this for both of you," Young said firmly.

Vallen's voice lowered. "I care for this girl, Young. If it is in my power to save her, please let me."

Lady Jura spoke up. "There are other males in this nest that would take on this honor. Why not let the Lady decide for herself?"

"Fine," snapped Young.

Vallen grumbled something that made the other two gasp. Then I heard all three move in my direction. Vallen sat at my side and helped me slide up into a seated position. When I tried to make eye contact with him, he looked away. Lady Jura was the one to break the silence. "Lady Morgan, I think we can save you, but you may not like the price it comes with. As a woman, I will understand if you choose not to embrace this plan. As a mother of a young woman around your age, I will encourage you to truly consider this option. If you were my daughter, I would want you to live a long and happy life."

I shook my head, not understanding. "I'm sorry, I'm still a bit groggy. I thought I was dying?"

"You are," she confirmed sadly. "We have a solution, however. A cure, as it were."

"Great!" I said, more than a little relieved.

"Hear the whole plan first," said Young flatly.

"If you were to choose a Dragon for a mate and bind with him or her, you would both take on some of the strongest traits of each other. You would gain their immunity to Dragon's blood, because as a mate it would be necessary. Since you are half Human, chances are your life expectancy would also increase to better match theirs."

I nodded, processing the information. "This is my only option?" I asked slowly.

She squeezed her eyes shut with regret. "I'm sorry."

"And who is it I am supposed to bind myself to for a lifetime?" Vallen gave my hand a gentle squeeze.

But it was Young who stepped forward. "We would let the Lady decide."

"Oh, so kind of you," I said with sarcasm. The young Dragon looked wounded.

Jura continued. "There are a number of eligible Dragons in our nest. Several have spoken up and said they would gladly take on the honor…"

"You mean duty." I cut her off angrily.

"Enough, Lady Jura. Leave her to consider things for a while. We are asking her to give up much either way and it is a heavy burden to carry." Vallen let go of my hand and walked them both to the door.

When the door clicked shut I heard the unmistakable sound of a lock turning. I watched as Vallen slowly approached. "I'm sure you want to discuss this with me as well. About why I should just marry and bind with a Dragon. How it won't be so bad."

"You're right. I do want to discuss it, but I'm not going to tell you should choose any Dragon. I'm not going to argue with you about why you should choose life." He sat down and took both my hands in his.

"Well that's good to hear," I told him.

"I'm going to insist you choose me." I blinked at him in shock.

"You can't be serious?" I said, pulling my hands free.

He grasped my hands again. "Hear me out. If our last few days have meant anything to you, hear me out."

I narrowed my eyes at him. "I can give you the speech about how you'll want for nothing because I will be an excellent provider, as I am landed and established. What I would rather tell you is that I will not take your virtue. There are ways around the claiming. I will give you my blood, I will give you my name, I will give you my protection, and most of all I will give you your freedom from me if that is what you desire. I will not take you to my bed unless it is what you wish. I will not require you stay here with me unless it is what you wish. I will return your life to you and all you have to do is wear my mark."

"And what of you?" I asked. "You would be giving up on this girl Young says you love. You will bear my mark the rest of your days as well. It's not just I who would be making a sacrifice."

"The woman I loved died over a century ago. Her reincarnation, if it is her, is a dear friend. Do I care for her? Yes, and always will, but I know our destiny is not meant to be." He raised my hand to his lips and pressed a kiss to it.

"I will meet with all possible mates and will choose from the group. You deserve a chance at your own happiness, Vallen. Please understand I am saying this because the last few days have meant so much to me." I patted his hand. "Can you help me dress so that I might meet my potential suitors?"

He nodded and reluctantly released my hand. Thirty minutes later there was a parade of potential mates for me to sit and speak with. During the process Vallen was nowhere to be found. I was unsure if he was sulking or happy to have escaped the fate of being saddled with me for a lifetime. At the end of the line was Young.

Young approached the table, taking a seat beside me rather than across from me. "Lady Morgan, stop looking through the crowd and accept my offer. I know I am young, untitled, and unlanded, but I swear I will provide for you. I will not stop you from having the adventures your soul longs for. I will be by your side always. I will never stray from our bed and I would gladly die to protect you."

I took Young's hand in my own and squeezed it affectionately. "Young, I adore you and think that if I were to have a brother, I would want him to be just like you. You're kind to a fault. Brave when the moment calls for it. Honorable until the end. You are not meant for this destiny, and I hope you see it with all the love I intend when I tell you that."

He looked sadly at me. "You've made your decision, then?"

"I have," I said.

I stood and looked around the room. All eyes seemed to turn towards me. "Your kindness bewilders me. I am not sure what I have ever done to be treated with so much honor and selflessness. All of you amaze me, and there are no words that will ever express the depths of my gratitude. This decision is difficult, because while it grants me my life, it dooms one of you to enduring me for a lifetime. It means one of you will forgo the chance to find your one true love because you chose to save me. I know what a sacrifice this is."

Lady Jura stepped forward. I scanned the room, looking for my victim. My eyes settled on his hunched form pouring over a book in the corner. "Lady Morgan, have you made your decision?"

I nodded. "Lord Vallen, you made me an offer that I will accept. If you will still have me?" I watched as he lowered his book slowly and turned to meet my gaze. There was a spark of shock and surprise in his eyes. I immediately regretted what I was forcing him into.

He rose from his seat and nodded. "My Lady, I would be honored. We will see to the binding posthaste. Once you are recovered, if it is to your liking, we will make an announcement and hold a celebration."

I did my best to smile. "Thank you."

Lady Jura took hold of my wrist and ushered me out of the room and down a narrow corridor. "Keep up, child, there is much to do."

We passed through two doors and went up a small flight of stairs into a room that was grey. It felt like the sunlight was shining through the stone. Air particles were almost visible and it felt like being in a cloud. Vallen entered behind me with Young on his heels. The door closed behind them with a grinding sound that made the moment all the more finite.

Vallen took my hand in his and turned to face Lady Jura. Young stood behind us with his hands folded in front of him, in total silence. Lady Jura held a knife in her hands and lifted it heavenward. "Spirits of our ancestors, bear witness to those who come to you in this hour. Cast your blessings upon these two souls who wish to be bound together by our sacred rittes."

I watched with curiosity as Lady Jura cast a circle around us, calling on each of the elements. I knew the binding ritual for the Elves, Fae, and Dwarves, as I had seen more than my share over the years, but I had never witnessed any of the Darkling rituals. My stomach felt uneasy because I was binding myself to the Dragon for a lifetime. I looked up at Vallen; his face was unreadable.

"Goddess of the moon, bear witness to these children and guide them on their path. Protect them from harm and make them one. Who comes this day to the sacred ground to bind themselves to one another?" Jura's voice seemed to float on the air around us.

"I, Lord Vallen of Loch Omniglot, Knight of the Order of the Original Dragon, Dragon Lord of Drakemoore, come this day to be bound before the ancestors and ancient gods to this woman. I come willingly and with honor." His voice didn't even shake when he spoke.

I could feel my own hands shaking and took a breath to calm my nerves. "I, Lady Morgan Reulalainn, Dame of the Fae court of Vesaria, come this day to be bound before the ancestors and ancient gods to this man. I come willingly and with honor." Though my voice shook as I spoke, I managed to get the words out. I felt Vallen tighten his grip on my hand, though I was unsure if it was for comfort or for fear that I may make a run for it.

"It is our blood that gives us life and it is through our blood we will be forever tied to one another." I was fairly familiar with this part of the ceremony. As Jura spoke of the ancient rights of the blood, Vallen released my hand so he could offer both of his to

Jura. On his left hand she made a cut across the top of his palm, and in his right palm she cut an X. She then dipped the blade in holy water and turned towards me. I held my hands out in offering as Vallen had done. She made quick work with a slit on my left palm and an X on the right.

"Place your left hands together and lock wrists." We linked wrists and as our blood touched, it hissed and sizzled on the skin. Lady Jura held up a long piece of linen and began wrapping it around our wrists, binding them together. "Once for a life bound by love. Twice for a life bound in trust. Thrice for a life bound together by the gods." My wrist felt like it was on fire but I was unable to let go. "Speak your promises before our ancestors and gods so they may bless your union."

Vallen met my gaze, and there was a softness in his eyes that hadn't there before. "I swear to you that from this day forward you are forever *My* Lady first. I will protect you with my life, guard your heart as if it were my own, and stand by you as long as you would have me there."

The linen around our wrists seemed to tighten and glow a soft silver. I looked down at it and back up at him. "I promise from this day forward I will do my best not to complicate your life, protect you from those who mean you harm with all that I am, and do my best to make our years happy and long." I felt as if my life was spreading into the linen at our wrists and it now glowed with a soft gold light as well. The pain in my wrist began to fade away.

Vallen looked down at the linen binding us and back up at me with an approving smile. He lifted his right hand to me. "As we are bound by the gods, so are we bound forever by blood." Pooled in the cup of his hand was a spoon-sized amount of his blood. Leaning forward, I sipped it dry, running my tongue over his already closed wound. It burned like fire down the back of my throat.

I extended my own hand to him and repeated, "As we are bound by the gods, so are we bound forever by blood." He took my hand in his and lifted it to his lips. When he finished consuming my life's blood he kissed the palm of my hand before releasing it.

Jura rested her hands on our bound wrists. "As a priestess of the ancients I see that the gods show your binding favor. Who will bear witness to this blessing?"

Young stepped forward and gave me a wink, placing his hand on top of Jura's. "I bear witness to this blessing," he said in a clear voice.

"If it be the will of our ancestors and gods to bind these two forever, may they be bound in fire." Before my eyes the linen that bound us together was consumed in flames, and yet I wasn't burned.

Jura smiled. "It is done."

I looked at Vallen, who stared at our wrists where we still clutched each other in shock. Then in a fluid motion that I wasn't prepared for, he tugged me forward, wrapped an arm around me, and pressed his lips to mine. I melted against him and was glad when he held me close, because I wasn't sure if my legs would have held.

Sweeping me up into his arms, he cradled me against his chest, then followed Young back out into the nest. As we walked through the great hall where so many were gathered, everyone seemed to hold their breath until we passed through. There was a great cheer as we headed back down the hall and returned to Vallen's chamber.

Once inside, Vallen set me on the bed and allowed Jura and Young to enter. Jura winked at me with a sparkle in her eye I didn't approve of. She sat in the chair nearest me and leaned close. "I understand you're a virgin. I just wanted to talk to you beforehand and see if I could answer any questions you may have. Woman to woman."

I shifted uncomfortably where I sat. "Lady Jura, I understand that you are trying to be helpful, but it's actually making me a bit more nervous."

She looked at me, startled. "I'm sorry. I just wanted to make sure you knew how everything worked."

I paused for a moment. "In Fae culture, the brands are administered at the peak of pleasure so that neither party must endure the pain. Is it the same here?"

She nodded. "Yes, we will do our best not to disturb you. Normally you would have decided on your branding beforehand, and the ancestors and I apply them with magic."

"Right, can we try doing this a different way?" I asked. "Can we apply the brands before we consummate the marriage?"

She looked at me as she thought about what I said. "I don't think you realize how painful the branding is," she began.

"I do, sort of. If Vallen were to agree, though, I would like to be branded before we consummate. As a virgin Fae I'm told it can be quite difficult to climax and I'm going to have the extra challenge of nerves if I know people are watching." I hoped her experience with Fae virgins was limited.

"It's rather unheard of, but if Vallen agrees, we can do it that way. We will still need to know that the binding was consummated before we can fully close the book." She looked at Vallen and he nodded.

"Thank you," I whispered.

"I must still insist that you both lie down for this. I'm not sure if the pain will overwhelm you or not." She pointed to the bed.

Vallen and I peeled off our clothing and slid into bed together. I laid on my side and Vallen pulled me back into his body. He molded to my every curve, his hand resting on top of my arm. "I'm right here with you," he whispered in my ear. "We're in this together. Don't laugh if I cry like a small child, okay?"

I laughed at his joke. "Only if you agree to ignore my screams of pain and anguish."

He nodded, pressing kisses to my shoulder. I didn't remember giving him permission to do that, but the distraction was nice. At first the branding magic felt like someone was running a piece of ice over my skin. I heard Lady Jura chanting in the background, but she seemed so far away.

Vallen's grip tightened on me and his breath caught in his chest. Just then, I felt it - it was like someone had taken a knife from the fire and was carving into my skin. My skin cracked, smoked, and hissed as the branding was burned in. I heard Vallen moaning in pain behind me and I squeezed my eyes shut tighter. I grabbed his hand with both of mine, holding on tightly. The pain moved from the side of my breast, down along my ribs, and seemed to curl around over my hip bone. Then, when I thought it might be done, there was a flash of light and a feeling of frozen salt seemed to blast against my newly damaged skin. Despite my efforts I cried out in agony.

When it was done, Vallen smoothed the hair from my face and whispered sweet reassurances in my ear. The best of the reassurances was that the worst of it was over.

Young and Jura appeared at our bedside. Young seemed in awe of the branding. "It's beautiful," he whispered.

Jura carefully poked at both of them. "Amazing. They are a perfect match." She whispered too.

Vallen stilled, his hand resting on my head. "Perfect?"

"As far as I can see," Jura said. I began processing the information as well. "That can't be," I told her.

She shook her head and motioned for Young to bring over a mirror. I watched with a combination of fascination and horror as she pointed out each spot where there could have or should have been a slight difference. Our brands were a perfectly matching set of knots and stars reflecting on a wavy pool.

Vallen looked at the brands with an eagle eye, then back to Jura and Young. "I don't have a Soul Mate. We would know if we were, right?"

Jura shrugged. "I've heard that that some of us are lucky enough to find one person that is such a perfect match that it can only be the result of love so pure that even the stars are left in awe. They may not be Soul Mates, cut from the same soul, but rather two that fit in perfect harmony together. Maybe instead of Soul Mates you have found your one true love. Even if you don't know it yet."

She began packing up her bag and turned to leave. "Wait!" I called after her. "What now? What else do I need to do to make sure I heal?"

She smiled. "Take a look. You should find your wound is already looking better. The Lake Dragons have some mighty powerful magic."

Young gave a shrug. "Welcome to the family," he smiled. "I now get to go wait outside until you come tell me you've done the deed and consummated the binding."

Vallen tossed a pillow at his back, glaring in the direction of the door. It closed before the pillow made contact with it.

"Now what?" I asked.

Struggling to sit up despite the stinging pain in our sides, Vallen and I both leaned back against the wall at the head of the bed. "Well, first I want to look at your injury. Then I want to take a nap so Young misses dinner waiting on us. Then I want to make you scream and giggle in such a way they believe I showed you the best romp of your life." I glared at him. "Sorry, darling, I may not be taking your virtue, but there are still appearances to keep up."

When he said it like that I almost understood. It was true, they would expect a certain amount of noise to come from the room. "Do we have to take a nap?" I asked.

"Yes, it will help us both heal from the branding. Did you have something else in mind?" he asked, a mischievous twinkle in his eye.

"Well, how about a short nap and then you teach me how to play poker?" I smiled broadly.

He grinned and raised a brow. "What will we use as currency?" he asked. "Humans frequently use clothing, but we are already naked."

"As it is our binding day, might I recommend kisses?" I teased back.

"Our kisses may lead to other things," he said flatly.

"If they do, then they do. What does it matter at this point? We're mates." I was trying so hard to sound confident and blasé.

"Fine, but a nap first." He looked me over from head to toe where I hid behind the blankets and rolled his shoulders back with determination that he could make everything work out. "I do promise that I will not claim you until you are ready." He reached down, snagging the blankets. "Let's see that cut."

Chapter Nineteen

The Dragon's Nest left us in peace. Young knocked on the door once, then slid dinner on a tray into Vallen's chamber. Vallen walked across the room to collect it. I resisted the urge to peek at his cards. He sat the food on the bedside table then looked at me and chuckled.

"What?" I asked, pressing my cards to my chest.

"If you had asked me as recently as this morning what I thought I would be doing the night of my binding ceremony, I can promise you that it wouldn't have been this." His smile was genuine.

I quirked a brow at him. "Give me all your twos," I told him.

He sat down, snatching up his cards and handing me three of them. "You totally peeked didn't you?"

His mock outrage sent me into another fit of laughter. "I didn't," I insisted. "I thought about it, but I didn't."

"Oh, you thought about it?" His grin turned almost devilish. "You know what that means?"

"Ugh, really?" I tried pouting, but to no avail. With show, I threw down my cards and lifted my hands. I carefully balanced my hands on top of his, my eyes never leaving his gaze. Then in a split second I jumped back and snapped. "Ha! You didn't get me that time! I win that round of hot hands."

He laughed in a deep mellow tone. "Ok, grand master. Let's eat and then check your healing progress."

We curled up side by side and he lowered the tray down onto our laps. Two large bowls were filled with noodles, cheese, vegetables, potatoes, and meat. There was also a generous serving of some sort of tart, and fresh, hot bread. "If I eat all this I may double in size," I told Vallen.

He shrugged. "Eat up, you'll need your energy to heal and slay Avery."

"We're still going after her?" I asked.

"Yes, my mission isn't complete. I also get the distinct feeling I might lose a limb if I tried to go without you." I nodded my approval of his perceptiveness. I turned my attention back to the delicious looking food monstrosity in the bowl. Vallen leaned close to me. I could feel his breath on my ear as he spoke softly. "I promise it's delicious."

I eyed him cautiously. Narrowing his eyes on me, he scooped up a spoonful and brought it to his lips. He chewed and swallowed, reaching for another bite. This one he lifted to my lips for me to try. I opened my mouth and was shocked by the flavors that flooded my tongue. I chewed and grinned. "Oh, that's good. Really good," I said, nodding.

He turned his attention back to his own bowl. "I know," he said between bites.

"If I eat like this every day I will get quite plump," I told him, and was surprised when he just shrugged. "Wouldn't you mind having a chubby mate?"

He shook his head and swallowed. "Not really. You've seen the Dragons out there. Some are tall... okay, *most* are tall, but some are thin and others are round. Some of them are pale of skin and others are dark as night. None of that makes a difference, because they are all themselves."

I laughed. "Fae culture is a little different," I told him.

"Oh, I'm aware. Luckily for you, you are mated to a Dragon. Whether you wish to be chubby or thin, that's up to you. All that matters is that you're happy with your life. You will still be my mate, even if you are purple with green spots or sprout a mermaid tail." He shoveled the last of the food into his mouth.

"My father used to tell my mother that. As long as you are happy, what does it matter?" I grinned at the memory. I leaned over and poked his muscular stomach. "How do you stay so fit when you eat like this?"

He pulled off a chunk of bread, covered it in honey butter, then pushed it into his mouth and quickly swallowed it. "For now, I am very active and still quite young by Dragon standards. I realize I have a title and elder status, but that is simply because my father is no longer living. In all seriousness, I plan on someday getting chubby, staying home to read, and letting the younger generations fight the wrongs of the world."

I only partially believed him. He was too passionate about helping others to ever really stop being the hero. I grinned. "What if I tell you not to get chubby? Or I ask you not to go adventuring because it isn't safe and I'm worried about you?"

He put down the tart and looked at me. "Then I will eat less, run more, and find more books to keep me busy at home. However, in that scenario, you would still be with me. I don't necessarily expect you to stay with me after this, though. This binding was about saving you, as I swore to do."

"Oh, so you want me to leave?" I asked.

"No, I didn't say that. I just thought…" He was tripping over his words.

I wasn't sure why, but the knowledge that he expected me to leave after all was said and done hurt more than if he had physically attacked me. My eyes teared up. I handed back the bowl, rolled off the bed, and headed to the bathroom. "Excuse me, I need a moment," I called over my shoulder.

I heard the dishes rattle and he stormed after me. I turned on the shower over head without care to the water's temperature. I slammed the door shut and stepped under the water. It was so hot my skin turned pink in moments and the room quickly filled with steam. I sank to my knees and let myself cry. I cried because I was bound to a man that didn't love me and I had forced him into it. I cried because after this mission there was no place for me to return to, because all the people I once had were gone. I cried because for a split second, I had let myself believe that this entire situation wasn't as messed up as a circus side show.

"Morgan?" Vallen's voice called into the bathroom as he eased open the door. He saw me crumpled on the floor under the stream of burning water. He sank to the floor beside me, and despite my struggles, gathered me into his arms and pulled me to his chest where he held me. "I'm sorry," he said. "I was insensitive. I shouldn't have assumed you would run the first chance you got."

I sobbed and turned his words over in my mind. He thought I wanted to leave. His hand stroked my hair and back. "I don't know what I want," I told him.

"You don't have to decide right now," he told me.

"I feel like if I stay, I will ruin your world and your life. You only took me to save my life. Is it really fair for me to muck it up more than I have?"

He held out his hand and I eventually took it. He stroked the back of my hand with his thumb. "When I was a squire, my parents arranged a marriage for me because I was the firstborn son and that was my duty. I was still a child and only sixteen when it happened. What's more, she was a Pixie. My mother was Pixie and Dragon, and Melody was from her people."

"I thought Melody was your great lost love?" I asked.

Vallen smiled in a bittersweet way that spoke to me. "At first I rebelled and hated the idea. It was bad enough that *I* was mixed between the two worlds, but then our children would be mostly Fae." He let out a slow breath. "My father told me he and my mother believed that she would be a good match for me and to give it time. They even arranged for her to undergo part of her noble training at the court I was staying at. With time, we became friends, and from friends we became more."

I smiled, but he hugged me tighter and I knew I was going to hear the whole story he hadn't told me before. "When I was in my late twenties, I was knighted and sent off into a bloody battle between the Elves and Dwarves in your realm of Vesaria. Melody came to see me at the battlefront because she was worried about me. Someone confused her a combatant and she was killed. What was worse, I didn't even know it until that evening when I was assigned the job of helping count bodies and found her among the dead. I had just seen her the day before, so full of life. She had died from stab wounds with a blade tainted by Dragon's blood. A terrible but common tactic used by both sides to inflict more damage on one another. It's how I recognized it on you." His whole body was shaking and he rested his head against mine.

I turned on his lap and wrapped my arms around him. I hoped that I was offering some small comfort. "I'm sorry," I told him.

"No, I'm sorry," he bit out through a shaky voice. "You deserve a mate that isn't broken on the inside. I sacrificed my Dragon Fire so that she could be reincarnated. I am less of a Dragon because of it. I could have prevented you from ever needing to enter the battle to begin with if I had had it."

I laughed. I knew it seemed cold considering he had just poured his heart out to me, but I couldn't help it. "Vallen, did you ever take a close look at me?" To prove my point I held up my arm and pointed to a scar that ran halfway around my upper bicep. "This one almost took my arm clean off when I dropped my shield arm to get a better look down the battlefield. I grew up half-Human at a time when the Human realm was still sealed off from our world. I couldn't fly, my magic even now is a bit of a joke, and my parents were a bit of a trip. I was always getting into fights because children from any culture can be cruel to those who are different. As I grew up, I hated watching others being on the receiving end of bullying. So I stood up and said I wouldn't tolerate it. As an adult I hated it even more and devoted my life to protecting those who were not capable of defending themselves." I finished shifting so I sat straddling his lap.

Vallen rested his hands on my hips and studied my face. "I've seen dozens of arranged bindings bring happiness to the couples involved. When this is over, will you stay with me?"

I nodded. "Even if you get chubby from eating this ridiculously fattening but delicious food, I will stay and try to make this work."

"Then let's get out of this water, get some sleep, and go find Avery." He helped me to my feet, then climbed to his own. He wrapped me tightly in towels and led me to bed. I watched as he extinguished the light then slid under the covers next to me.

"Vallen, do you want to consummate our union?" I asked, more than a little nervous.

He was quiet for a long moment. "Truthfully, yes I do. Very much in fact. However, I am happy to wait until you feel the same."

"What if I am never ready?" I lay in the darkness, his arms around me.

"Then we won't. I will wait until you tell me you are ready." He ran his hands over my arm. "Now, if it is fear that is holding you back, we can discuss it, and I will do everything I can to put your mind at ease."

"What if I'm really bad at it?" I asked frankly.

"I highly doubt that. You kiss with so much passion I can't imagine you not being a wonderful partner." I could tell he was smiling.

"BUT what if I *am*?" Obviously this was weighing on my mind.

"Then we will practice a lot until you are so skilled you are teaching me things and giving me directions." I could tell there was a teasing element to his tone.

"Is that allowed?" I asked.

He laughed deeply. "Who have you been talking to? What lies have they told you? Yes, you should absolutely tell me what you like and don't like, and I will do the same. I swear it is so much better when you talk about it."

"I've heard that for Fae and Humans the first time can be quite painful. At least for the women." I felt ridiculous having this conversation at my age. I was nearly one hundred and I should know this stuff.

"It can be physically painful for females and emotionally painful for males." He groaned at the memory. "My first time I was so excited and had no clue what to do. All she did was touch me and it was over. It was messy and embarrassing. My squire brothers teased me about it for weeks, because of course the girl told *EVERYONE*." He sighed. "It took me three years before I was willing to try again, and in that time I read every book I could get my hands on concerning the subject. Then when the time came, I found out that the books did me no good and the best results came from honesty."

I smiled, knowing he could see it even in the darkness. "So often you say things and they come out almost perfect."

"I try, *My* Lady, I try." He squeezed me tightly one more time, kissed the top of my head and closed his eyes.

Chapter Twenty

"You just decided to be bound forever to a Dragon you've known less than two weeks?" Heather lectured me as we rode. She and Uther had camped out at a nearby village for the last few days, not wanting to disturb the Nest.

"Yes, but it's OK. It's my life," I told her.

"He must be amazing in the sack if you were willing to just … 'poof', like that." She snapped her fingers for emphasis.

"Why are you so upset about this?" I asked her.

"Because you were proof that females can be and do whatever they want. They don't need mates to complete their lives. For a brief time you were my hero." Her whole body, sitting atop Dabble, told me she was pouting.

"Look, Heather, I understand your feelings. A mate doesn't complete a person. You have to be whole on your own first," I explained.

"The sex was just that good," she said, shaking her head.

"Oh come off it. She's still a virgin. My brother wouldn't seduce her or force her. They even took their brandings without consummation." Young bit out. Both Vallen and I turned around and hissed at him.

Heather's eyes grew large and round. "You took the brandings without..." Her words trailed off. "I've changed my mind, you are totally my hero again. To have suffered *that* to keep your virtue intact? That's amazing."

I rolled my eyes and kept riding. Uther came pounding through the woods, shifting back into his Human form when he saw us. We slowed at his approach. "Wait up," he said, throwing his hands up.

"Is something wrong up ahead?" I asked.

"Maht has tightened their defenses as we advised, and there has been no sign of Avery yet, but something is coming." He sniffed the air to prove a point.

Heather, Young, and Vallen all did the same. Not wanting to be the odd man out, I closed my eyes and breathed in deeply. "Sulfur?" I said, opening my eyes.

Heather watched me as I met Vallen's eyes with concern. "They couldn't have brought the old Dwarven war machines through the portals? Portals are on sacred ground. No ill will, no harm done, isn't that the rule?"

Young looked confused as his head snapped back and forth between the two of us. Vallen shook his head. "How long ago was it that Avery was in Vesaria?"

"About six months ago," I filled in. I started processing information. "She was hoarding treasure on Fae land." My mind went over all the treasure she had recovered. "She was there to capture as many portal beads as she could," I said, letting out a bitter laugh. "Faking her death is a great way to disappear with the portal beads – she could have just stashed them in a pocket."

"Or to plummet to your doom," Young supplied. He still seemed bitter that she was such a coward as to fake her death.

"Why march all your men up to a portal?" asked Heather.

"Diversion," said Young, as he tugged on the reins to his horse.

"That way nobody would notice the Dwarven war machines being brought in," Heather said, sliding the puzzle pieces into place. "Maht is prepared for thugs in the form of an army. Not to hold their gates against machines built by the mountain men."

Uther shifted back into wolf form as we all pushed our mounts to breakneck speeds heading for the city. Our horses were exhausted by the time the city came into view. We finally slowed our pace on our approach to the gate.

Guards at the city gate stopped us as we arrived. "I'm sorry," one called. "We aren't permitted to allow anyone to enter without authorization."

"I authorize it," called Vallen. The guards leaned out to get a better look at him.

"Lord Vallen! Yes sir," the gatekeeper cried. The portcullis was lifted and we were allowed inside.

Vallen turned to the guard that rushed to approach him. "My Lord, we expected you sooner."

"My apologies, I was waylaid in my journey. My Lady was injured in battle and required medical attention." Vallen motioned to me.

The guard's eyes looked from Vallen to me. "My Lady, it is an honor to make your acquaintance even in such times. May I ask what brings one such as yourself to our fair lands?"

Vallen cleared his throat. "Perhaps I should clarify. Lady Morgan is *My* Lady, the new Lady of Loch Omniglot and Maht."

The guard's jaw dropped. "My Lord, you took a mate and we were not informed?"

"Please accept my humble apology - there was no time for fanfare, nor is there now. Provided we survive this ordeal, we will have the customary celebration." Vallen raised a brow, sending the clear message there was to be no more discussion on the matter. "Where is Lucius?"

"The captain is up in the tower preparing for battle." Vallen nodded, looking back at us.

"Young, take the ladies to the manor. Then meet me at the tower." I caught Vallen's arm as he turned to ride on.

"Really?" I asked, annoyed. "Young, could you please see that Heather and Uther are settled in?" I told the squire, before following Vallen.

We rode through the streets quickly, turning down alleys, cutting through yards, and maneuvering through the market on horseback. As we cut through the city, the large black tower that was silhouetted against the sky grew larger and larger. When we arrived I stared at the structure, wondering if it touched the sky.

I dismounted and hurried after Vallen as he pushed through the doors. Once inside, I stared wide-eyed at the number of stairs before us. Vallen stood at the center on a small platform, hand extended to me. "C'mon," he said, as I took his hand and stepped on the platform with him. He rang a bell to the right and a series of pulleys began lifting the platform through the center of the tower. I watched as the floors passed us by, taking us higher and higher. My heart pounded in my chest when I ventured a look over the edge. My head spun and I felt Vallen's hold on my hand tighten and pull me back.

"Let's not have you falling to your death today," he halfheartedly teased.

I nodded in agreement just as we reached the top. Carefully I stepped off the now-swinging platform and onto the observation deck of the tower. "My Lord, I was beginning to worry when you didn't arrive days ago." A short man with broad shoulders, light brown hair, and a square jaw stepped forward, locking arms with Vallen.

"I'm sorry for the delay, Lucius. My mate was injured in battle. I needed to see to her care." Vallen motioned in my direction.

Lucius studied me from my head to my toes. "The battlefield is no place for you, My Lady. I am glad to see you are well." Lucius turned his head to face Vallen once more. "When did you take a mate, My Lord? Why wasn't I welcome at your union?" He looked hurt.

Vallen stammered, unsure of how to handle this faux pas. I stepped up. "Captain Lucius, due to the state of my health at the time, the binding ceremony had to be pushed up. Young was the only one in attendance." I tried smiling. It did no good. "It wasn't our intention to exclude anyone."

"You seem well enough now, My Lady. Are you sure your ailment wasn't due to a need for commitment?" I could read it in his eyes - he thought I had forced Vallen into this union. Which I had, but not for the reasons he believed.

"I will keep that I mind when next I meet the wrong end of a weapon tainted with Dragon's blood. Or perhaps I should just leave Lord Vallen to battle nearly fifty armed men on his own with only his brother?" I rested my hands on my hips as I stared him down.

"I daresay he wouldn't have been in the situation if a pair of pretty blue eyes hadn't batted in his direction," he grumbled.

"Listen you grumpy Troll, I was knighted by Queen Mab herself. I defeated Avery once before and helped take out her goons on the way here. I have led my own troops into battle and I assure you I am a match for Lord Vallen even on his best days." I nearly snapped his head off.

"I'm a Dwarf," Lucius cut in. "I don't care who you are and how you got here. This is my operation."

As my eyes narrowed on him, Vallen stepped between us. "I don't think this is the time. Do either of you?"

I sighed heavily and nodded.

"Lord Vallen, you have always honored me and kept me in your employ because you trusted my decisions. I guard this city with my life. I must insist you remove *that* woman." The Dwarf thrust his thick finger in my direction.

I looked at Vallen. "Wait a minute," I said, holding up a hand. "This is your city?"

He shifted back and forth uncomfortably. "It was put into my care about one hundred years ago, give or take."

"You are Lord of *this* city? Meaning the Keep at the city center bears your seal?" I smiled wickedly at him and then the Dwarf. Vallen nodded. I turned on my heel to step past him and brought my face to within inches of Lucius'. "I am your Lady. I suggest if you want to survive this ordeal AND have a job when it's over, you shut up and do your job and let me do mine. If it makes things easier, just pretend I am a really pretty boy."

The Dwarf looked at Vallen and back to me. Finally he rolled his eyes, threw his hands in the air, and led us over to a table with a giant map of the area. He pointed to the portal. "There has been no sign of her coming through the portal."

I looked at the surrounding area. The woods would give excellent cover, but would be too hard to navigate the machines through. The shore line to the south would be easy to navigate, but give little to no cover. To the north were mountains and less friendly terrain. "How many villages lie to the north?" I asked.

"What distance, My Lady?" asked Lucius grumpily.

"Two day ride or less," I directed. I watched as he traced a circle on the map. Three towns lay within that distance. "Could any of those towns supply an extra hundred men or so?"

Lucius considered the options and pointed at a town called Brog that sat at the base of a mountain. "Brog has a thriving mining trade as well as the ability to house many travelers since it is the last town before you enter the mountain range."

"It would give her a place to hide the old Dwarven Iron Warriors," I offered Vallen.

The Dwarf's head snapped around. "What are you talking about, girl?"

"The old Dwarven war relics may be here and on their way to this city," I told him.

He paled and started sorting through his notes. "We don't have the manpower to defend against that and the group of thugs she has assembled," he told Vallen.

"I know," said the Dragon, already deep in thought.

"What is the closest Kingdom or Stronghold?" I asked.

"Drakebane castle. It's about two days' hard ride through the woods. Not that it would do us any good," said Lucius. "Maybe we could send someone back through the portal into Everbloom. Princess

Alizeyah is the King's sister. Perhaps he would be willing to hear our call for help."

"How far is it from here?" I asked.

"One day to the portal and another five on the other side," answered the grumpy Dwarf.

My head spun. I had been closer at the start of all this than I was now. "Why can't we appeal to Drakebane?"

"Lord Drakebane and I were squire brothers together. When he was given dominion here, he thought it was over the entire realm, including Maht, and not just his small part." I looked at him, shaking my head.

"Why does everyone want *this* freaking city?" I cried.

"Because it has a Fairy Circle in the basement of the keep," Vallen answered in flat annoyance.

"What, does it lead to the Forgotten Realm or something?" I said with a mocking smile.

"Yes."

"Wait, what? How did you get stuck with that duty? Why are you the gatekeeper?" I asked. I had learned far more about my mate that day than any new bride should in her first week.

"My grandmother is the Lady of the Lake." I blinked at him and everyone was silent.

"Great, the new in-laws are going to make things *so* much fun," I replied. I turned and stepped back onto the platform.

"Where are you going?" he asked with concern.

"To prepare for a trip to Drakebane Castle. We need help if we are going to protect that gate and these people." He stepped onto the platform just as I threw the lever that would take me back down to the ground.

"You can't go there alone," Vallen argued.

"Who said I was going alone? I'm taking Heather," I said with a grin.

"It's dangerous. Both the woods and Drakebane himself." He caught my hand as I stepped off the platform and back onto solid ground.

I turned on my heel to face him. "You can't go. You're needed here, as is Young. I've seen more combat then any of these men, and I'm a strong rider. I stand the best chance of getting through."

"I can't keep you safe if I'm not with you," he argued.

"If we are going to make this work, Vallen, you must trust in me as much as I trust in you." I sighed, but didn't fight when he tugged me into his arms.

"I've grown to be rather fond of you in the short time we've known each other." He pressed a kiss to my forehead. "It's nearly dusk. At least wait until morning to leave."

I nodded and went to gather Slayer from where I had hitched him. With the help of a guardsman I mounted up and followed Vallen back through the streets of Maht. All around me, people were going on with their lives as if the outside force threatening to ride in and crush them didn't exist. Bakers still baked. Merchant still sold their wares. On every other corner there was a pub filled to brim after another long day of work.

At the center of the city sat an ancient keep. It had been renovated to be warmer and more welcoming than its original builders intended. Its rough corners had been rounded out by master masons, transforming it into what Vallen lovingly referred to as "the Manor". I was sure given the right setting it could easily lend itself to stories of lost love and ghosts. A wall ran around the outer limits of the property. At the gate, a tall Ogre stepped out from behind the stones and offered to take our horses. I was greatly surprised by his gentle demeanor, since I had seen plenty of Ogres eat horses for dinner.

"You have quite the cast of characters in Maht, don't you?" I asked.

Vallen nodded and held out his elbow for me. "Many come here because it is a safe haven for all. I have worked hard to keep the peace amongst those who live here."

"It sounds like a worthwhile endeavor." I slipped my hand into the curve of his arm and allowed him to lead me into the manor. I did my best to keep my awe to a minimum as we walked through the doors.

The inside gleamed with white polished marble. Statues and pillars held up stairs leading to floors that looked as if they were floating. Green plants and ivy grew along the inner walls, curling into the windows and holding them in place. We passed through a hall that had walls made of waterfalls, leading to a river that ran beneath the floor.

"Where are we?" I asked in a whisper, as all other audible noises were reserved for marveling at the sights around me. "The only other place I have ever seen like this is Queen Mab's Palace. This place seems otherworldly, like it isn't quite real."

Vallen chuckled and led me up the stairs that wrapped around nothing. "Well, the Queen's palace also holds a circle that leads to the Forgotten Realm, as does one other place that I know of, but it is impressive for other reasons."

"Why don't you stay here all the time?" I asked, touching a butterfly that perched on a statue.

"All the Dragons of this realm came together to build the Nest. There is safety in numbers. Once upon a time, we were feared and held domains, but now there are many races that hunt us in hopes of claiming our treasure or secrets. Here, I would be out in the open instead of among my own kind." I understood his reasoning, but this place seemed too amazing to leave.

I stopped walking. "How can you claim this is a safe haven for all, and all are welcome, and all should live in peace, if you are unwilling to lead by example?"

"I'm not unwilling." He studied me and closed his eyes. "Now that I have a mate though, perhaps I should reconsider it." I nodded in agreement with him. "Then again, I do have another property that is my birthright. Perhaps I should take you there?"

"I would like to see your ancestral home."

"I had them prepare the guest room for you," he said, changing the subject and opening a door.

"Do you always stay in a guest room when you are here?" I asked.

"No I stay in the master…" he stopped himself. "I will have your things moved at once. If that is all right with you?"

"I think it's only right. Given the circumstances." I followed after him a few more doors down to the end of the hall where he pushed open a double set of arched white doors.

The whole room gleamed with decadence and magic. Two walls were a mixture of large windows and stained glass. Low-sitting bookshelves wrapped the walls beneath them. A large white marble fireplace glowed on the wall to our left. In front of it were two high-backed chairs that seemed to have been grown from twisted white birch. Each served as a frame for the pale blue and gold tapestry that made up the cushions. A matching table sat between them. A bed rested on a pedestal at the center of the room. It also looked as if it had been grown from twisted white trees. Its posts reached to the ceiling, where it continued to grow and decorate the room with its twists and turns. Hanging around it was Fairy silk the color of the sky that twinkled from all directions. It wrapped its way over the bed and mingled with the cushions that appeared to be made of clouds and spun gold.

Vallen pulled me into the room and directed my attention to two doors along the wall we entered on. "One leads to the bathroom and the other to a closet." I crossed the distance and pushed open the door to the bathroom.

The window above the sink basins would provide beautiful sunlight during the day and a view of the stars at night. They were in the shape of two large scalloped shells, surrounded by pearls the size of my fist. Water ran down the short wall below the window and into them with the turn of a few knobs. At the center of the room was a giant tub sunken into the white marble floor, also in the shape of a scalloped shell. Over it was a shower device that caused various speeds of rain to fall in the center. I had seen showers before, but nothing like this.

I left the bathroom to explore the closet because, after all, a closet was always of interest. I stepped inside and grinned. The "closet" was the size of two of my bedrooms in the house I had grown up in.

"Why are you grinning so big?" Vallen asked.

I shook my head. "You'll think it foolish."

He stepped close. "Tell me, please?"

I was still grinning. "Do you have any idea how many shoes I could fit in here?"

He burst out in rolling laughter. "And so it begins."

"Hey, just because I sweat with the boys doesn't mean I haven't dreamed of a shoe closet. This one closet is twice the size of the bedroom I grew up in." I paused. "Or it could be a rather nice nursery," I mumbled, then shook the idea from my head.

"A what?" Vallen asked.

"Nothing. Merely a random thought." I did one final spin with my arms open wide. "It's beautiful!" I cried.

"I'm glad you approve," he said finally.

Chapter Twenty-One

We ate a "modest" dinner with Young, Uther, and Heather. There was meat, soup, fresh bread, and fruit for dessert. Heather grinned happily as she ate to her heart's content, as did Uther. Vallen made it a point to make sure I tried a little of everything that was brought out.

"Can I ask why you are feeding me so much?" I finally said, exasperated.

"In the time I traveled with you, I watched you eat maybe twice. Three times if you count at the Nest. You worry about everyone else's stomach but your own. As your mate I am making it my personal responsibility to make sure you are as looked after as those you take care of." To emphasize his point, he added another spoon of honeyed apples to my plate.

I opened my mouth to complain but Young cut me off. "Lady Morgan, I have to agree. A steady diet of tea, jerky, and apples does not a warrior make."

I rolled my eyes when even Heather joined in. "You made sure I ate before you and you would hardly eat anything even when there was more than enough for both of us."

"You're still growing," I argued, throwing my hand in her direction. I looked at Young and Vallen. "You were our guests - it would be rude of me not to feed you."

Young quirked a brow. "Since when are people you meet traveling on the road 'guests'?"

I growled at him. He instantly quieted. Uther gulped down a glass of water. "Lady Morgan, I know you are Fae, but I worry about your strength fading because you are so thin."

"We are NOT doing this!" I argued. "My weight and size are fine as they are. Why do I need to gain or lose weight to be considered strong?"

Vallen captured my hand that now pointed a finger in the air and dragged it back down to the table. "Are you happy as you are?" he asked.

"Yes," I answered.

"Fine, then don't change a thing. I only want to make sure you eat regularly. I know for the next several days you are likely to once again not eat much." I saw the concern in his eyes.

"The next few days?" asked Heather.

"Oh, yeah. About that." I squirmed under her gaze. She knew what was coming even before I said it. "Tomorrow we're leaving for Castle Drakebane. I need you up, packed, and ready to go right after breakfast."

"But we just got here," she whined, crossing her arms over her chest.

"I know, but we are going to need aid, and the Lord of Drakebane may be able to spare the men needed to help protect the people here." I searched her eyes.

"Fine! I'll go pack." She threw up her arms and left the dining room.

"Lady Morgan, would it be all right if I accompanied you on the trip? I know my sister isn't the most helpful in a fight, and if it comes to that, I would feel better knowing you weren't on your own." Uther smiled and his white teeth gleamed. Normally I would gladly accept the company, but an uneasiness in my stomach slowed my response.

"I appreciate the offer, but the more of us that go, the more likely we are to draw attention. Two women look like they are frolicking. Add one male to the group and suddenly we are women of importance, because it looks like we brought a guard." I took a sip of the wine that had been poured for me.

Uther looked hurt by his exclusion and that certainly wasn't my intent. I smiled warmly at him and his mood appeared restored. "Then I wish you godspeed, My Lady."

"Thank you," I said, looking from him to Vallen and Young. "Now if you would all excuse me, I plan to take advantage of the hot bath tonight while I have access to it." As I stood to leave I caught Vallen's gaze and tried to subtly direct him with my eyes to the stairs.

Vallen nodded slightly and grinned. I was halfway up the stairs when I heard him say, "Gentlemen, if you would excuse me. I believe I will retire for the night as well."

I had no sooner closed the door to the bedroom then it reopened and Vallen stepped in. "Well that was fast."

"I thought you may need help with the bath," he replied.

"I'm sure I can figure it out," I told him with a smile. I entered the bathroom and began running the water.

"May I join you?" he asked. I was floored and didn't know how best to answer. "You can say no if you are uncomfortable with it."

I shook my head. "No, it's not that. I've just never bathed with a man before."

"Then you don't know what you're missing," he told me with a mischievous grin.

"I always worry when you look at me like that," I told him.

"Like what?" he asked. He took a step towards me and closed the distance between us so we were near enough I could feel his breath on my forehead. "Like this?" he said, lowering his face to mine, resting his nose against my nose. His features blurred together and I laughed.

"No, sometimes you give me this look that makes my knees go limp and promises me what I already know about you."

"And what is it you think you know?" His playfulness was something I felt very few ever saw, and I suddenly was thankful he showed it to me.

"I just know you're going to be trouble." I blushed and looked down.

"Shall I bathe alone tonight, or may I join you? I can wash your back, you can wash mine." In that moment I understood what he was asking me. And I felt my blush deepen even more. "Hey, it's too soon. That's okay. I'll take one after you," he said with a smile.

"No. I want you to," I brought my eyes up to meet his.

"Are you sure?" he asked again, hesitantly.

I nodded. "Yes, now get over here and help me with this tunic before I lose all my nerve."

He wasted no time in reaching out and tugging my tunic off over my head. I helped him with his and didn't resist when he insisted on assisting me with my leggings. His hands skimmed over my hips and legs as he dragged them down to the floor. Cautiously he wrapped his arms around me, kissed my stomach, and then hugged me close, resting his head against me. It felt natural to reach down and run my fingers through his hair. "I like that," he mumbled and it caused me to smile.

Standing back up, he waited for me to step in to the steaming tub. I sat down, sinking into water almost to my chin. I watched as he gracefully stepped in, then sat down in one of the rounded curves of the shell. He reached behind him and brought out what looked like a pink pearl. He dropped it into the water between us and I watched as it fizzed and frothed, causing the surface of the water to fill with iridescent bubbles.

Taking a deep breath, I sank beneath the water's surface. The currents in the giant tub swirled around me. When I reemerged, I pushed my hair from my face and gasped for air.

"It's violet," I heard Vallen say beside me. Reaching out, he captured my elbow gently and guided me to sit across his lap. He tucked the stray locks of my hair behind my ears and said it again. "Your hair, it just changed to violet."

I reached up and pulled the tips in front of me where I could see them. "So it did."

He lifted a cloth covered in sweet-smelling soap and began running it over my back. Each touch sent a series of small electric jolts through my body. I found myself leaning into it as he rubbed it over me.

He extended his reach to my arms and then down my sides. When he reached my breasts, his movements slowed to small circles. The cloth teased my nipples, causing them to harden. I hissed in air and felt my face turn red. He stopped and turned me to look at him. "Should I stop?" he asked.

Though I felt my face glow brightly I shook my head. "No. I like it," I explained, and he grinned again. I found myself thankful I was sitting on his lap, because surely my knees would have collapsed beneath me were I standing. His hands continued on, his soap-slicked fingers caressing my breasts and causing my heart to beat faster, causing me to breathe in shallow gasps, and then to my astonishment, I moaned and pressed myself against him.

He leaned close and whispered in my ear. "What would you like me to do?"

I shrugged, unsure I could form words. "Keep going," I told him. Taking hold of my hips, he encouraged me to turn from my side and place my back against his chest to straddle his lap. I watched as he added soap to the cloth, then once again continued his mission to wash me from head to toe. His hands slipped over my stomach, along my hips, down my legs, and finally, lifting my feet, he ran the cloth over my soles and between my toes. Despite the feeling of heat growing low in my stomach I tossed my head back and laughed, tickled by his action.

He sat the cloth aside and rested his hands on my hips. His chin rested on my shoulder and he pressed a kiss to the curve of my neck and then another just below my ear. Tremors of pleasure ran through my body. "Touch me lower," I begged.

Taking my hand and placing it on top of his, he whispered in my ear. "Show me where."

Once again I felt the blush cover me, but I wanted this and wouldn't be deterred. I slid his hand over my inner thigh and brought his fingers to rest at the apex of my core. "Please," I said as encouragement. His other hand slid up to cup my breast, sliding his thumb over my nipple, causing it to harden more. He spread his own legs, causing mine to open widely. I felt his manhood throb at my back and I couldn't help but wiggle against it, causing him to suck in deep breaths.

His hand moved slowly at first, tracing my inner lips with his fingertip, making me to roll my head back against his shoulder. He brought a fingertip to lie at the top of my slit, then began massaging the bead that rested there. My back arched and I gasped. The pressure increased, as did the speed, and I found myself panting with my eyes closed. "Should I continue?" he asked behind my ear.

"I swear I will run you through if you stop now," I answered between gasps. His hand on my breast slid below the water and began to massage the opening of my slit. I closed my eyes to the sensation. Then, carefully, he slid a fingertip inside me and the small penetration felt like heaven. He teased me with the small movement, never thrusting deeper, though my body craved it, and I could feel a pressure and burning building within me, spiking higher and higher the more he caressed that sensitive area. Soon I was gasping and moaning with each breath and all I wanted was to feel him inside me, but he wouldn't oblige. I found myself incapable of words.

"Relax and let it come," he whispered, and I wanted to tell him to shut up, to keep going, to never stop, and then it hit me. It was like jumping off a cliff into deep water for the first time. My whole body spasmed and felt like it was on fire. I screamed in release that echoed through the bathroom, and yet even as the waves settled and I felt intense pleasure, I wanted more.

Still gasping for air and shaky, I turned on his lap to face him. I had to see him. There was a mixture of smug male pride and concern on his face. When I opened my mouth the words tumbled out even before I meant to say them. "Take me to bed. I need to feel you and connect with you."

He cupped my face in his hand and brushed his thumb over my cheek. "Are you sure? I can wait however long until you are ready."

"I can't wait. I need this and I need you," I told him, then leaned forward and pressed my lips to his mouth. He clutched me tightly and took possession of the kiss. It was hungry, and for the first time reflected his own deep desire. A deep desire for me.

Shifting under me with a grace I had never seen from anyone else, he collected me against his chest and stood. With his elbow he nudged a lever and warm water rained down on us from above, rinsing away the last traces of bubbles. He stepped surefooted from the tub and carried me, still cradled against him, to the bed.

Our wet bodies sank deep into the feather-soft mattress. I felt the weight of his body on mine and moaned. He lifted his head and his eyes searched mine, checking for any sign that he had hurt me. I blushed and shook my head. With a nod he leaned close to my ear. "We must go slow so that you are prepared. I don't wish to hurt you, but your first time can be painful."

I heard his warning and it didn't seem to matter to me. Starting at my ear he kissed and nibbled at me. Each touch caused the fire within me to burn a little hotter. When he reached my breasts he took one taunt nipple into his mouth and suckled at it while he gently caressed the other. My back arched off the bed and I held his head there. "Okay, I'm putting that on the 'like' list," he mumbled, while all I could do was nod. He switched breasts, taking the other nipple between his lips, and sucked again. I moaned and parted my legs, moving my hips under him.

He moved off of me to lay beside me. He captured one of my thighs between his own, urging me to part my legs further. He slid a hand down between them. "If this hurts too much at any time, you MUST tell me." With one of my hands I urged him to continue. He slid a finger over my opening. He sighed in relief. "You are already so wet."

"That's good?" I asked.

He purred into my ear. "Yes, it means your body is preparing you for me to join you." With those words he slid a finger within me. I gasped as he thrust it gently in and out of my core. "Good?" he asked in a whisper, and I nodded. He added a second and while it was tighter, it still was not uncomfortable. He began rubbing that sensitive bead just above my opening while his fingers moved inside me.

I squeezed my eyes shut, feeling myself teetering on the edge again already. "Vallen?" I whispered. "Now, I need you NOW."

He moved carefully between my legs and pressed his throbbing manhood to my entry. He slid the tip inside and continued to massage the small pearl above my core until it felt like it would catch fire from the pleasure that was building there. "Slowly," he warned but I was unable to wait any longer and I thrust my hips up to meet his.

White-hot pain tore through me and I tried to retreat from it, but he allowed his weight to follow me back down into the mattress. He didn't move within me at all, but he lowered his head and kissed the tears on my cheeks. It felt so tight I thought I might rip in two. Slowly the muscles inside me began to relax and he started to move gently within me.

He leaned close to my ear again, whispering to me words I didn't understand, and the pain started to be replaced by a growing pleasure like nothing I had ever experienced. His hand slid down my side, capturing my hip with one hand and cradling the back of my neck with the other, and he increased his speed. I found myself wrapping my legs around his hips and encouraging him to continue.

Soon I was moaning in pleasure once more and I was left with a feeling of climbing. The deeper he reached inside me, the higher I came. Soon my gasps became full screams of pleasure and I felt myself teetering on the edge. Vallen whispered at my ear. "It's all right. Let it go." His words caused me to meet each of his thrusts with my own and soon his own moans joined mine, and in the instant I didn't think it could feel better I tipped over an edge and went rushing headlong into a fit of pleasure that left me unable to breathe. All I could do was watch colorful lights dance behind the darkness of my lids and feel myself tighten around him. Latching on to him so as to never let go.

I opened my eyes, wanting to share the joy of the moment with Vallen. With one last deep thrust he tossed his head back, gasping for air as he poured himself out deep within me. I felt fire flutter through my womb and my entire body tingled. When he finished, he gathered me to his chest, our bodies still joined, pulled a blanket over us, and buried his face in my hair. "Thank you," he whispered. "I will treasure you always."

I kissed his chin. "And I you," I told him, before closing my eyes and falling into a deep slumber.

Chapter Twenty-Two

The next morning came sooner than I would have liked. I snuggled closer to Vallen's warmth, where his arms still encircled me from the night before. I promised myself five more minutes, then I could focus on saving the world. He must have sensed I was awake because he brought his hand up to stroke my hair. "It's magenta," he whispered.

Sighing, I forced my eyes open and reached up to pull a strand of hair in front of me. Sure enough, my hair was a vibrant magenta color. "That will make it easy for me to blend in," I grumbled.

He shifted quickly, rolling on top of me and pinning me to the bed. I stared up into his dark blue eyes. There was a storm raging within him and I wasn't sure why. He lowered his head and pressed his lips tenderly to my own. "Then don't go," he whispered as he broke the kiss too soon. "Stay here and we will find a way to defend against Avery without the help of Lord Drakebane."

I shook my head. "No, we need his help if we are going to protect the people of Maht."

His eyes narrowed on me. "Not even here a full day and already behaving like the Lady of the Manor." His smirk told me he was kidding but there was also a healthy dose of respect in his tone.

I leaned up and pressed a kiss to his chin. "Yup, pretty much." I struggled and rolled out from under him. "You need to get moving as well, Lord Vallen."

He sighed and sat up on the bed, watching me move about the chamber, preparing for my trip. He didn't say anything as I dressed – he just watched every move I made. Having seen enough, he managed to convince himself to dress so that he could help me pack and see me off.

When I finally arrived downstairs, Heather was already dressed and had a large packed bag slung over her shoulder. She looked up at me with a knowing smirk, but said nothing. I nodded to her as I headed for the kitchen. I wasn't going anywhere without a cup of tea.

I was relieved to find a kettle of hot water already prepared and a scone on a plate. My eyes grew round as I bit into it only to discover it was still warm. I was so distracted by the confection I didn't notice when Heather entered the kitchen to join me. "I've packed enough food for five days."

I turned to look at her and nodded with my mouth still full. She grinned at me. "You know, Lady Morgan, for someone who seems to crave adventure, you don't seem like you are in your usual hurry to get on with it."

I swallowed hard. "I am. I'm just running a little behind this morning."

"Yes, well, spending the night in the arms of a lover will do that," she said matter-of-factly.

My eyes narrowed on her as I finished the last of my tea. "You, on the other hand, are not normally this excited to get going." I reached out and spun Heather around before she could leave the kitchen.

"The Dwarven war machines called Iron Warriors, are headed this direction. I don't know about you, but I really don't have a desire to be here when that happens." Her words were steady but I couldn't help but think there was more to it then all that. I shrugged and let it go, knowing that it was better to just get on our way.

Within the hour we were packed, mounted, and traveling at breakneck speed into the woods and across the kingdom. The sun wasn't even shining midmorning when we reached the tree line that would take us into the Darkwood, a forest so dense that even the brightest of days felt like night.

We reduced our speed once we crossed into the forest, knowing that it would only become darker and more treacherous the deeper we traveled. Soon the trees closed around us and the tree line where we had entered was no longer visible. Shortly thereafter, the road all but disappeared, leaving only a light path showing little wear winding through the trees.

Heather pushed Dabble to travel beside me, her gaze never faltering from our surroundings. "Lady

Morgan, I get the strangest feeling we are being watched and followed," she whispered.

"I'm unsure if it is our surroundings or an actual threat, but the hair on my neck is also standing up," I told her in my regular voice.

"Shhhh," she hushed me.

"Why are you whispering?" I asked.

She sat back for a moment and thought about it. "Because most of the time if you are out and about in the dark like we are, you are usually sneaking around."

I smiled. "But are we sneaking?"

She blinked a few times. "What about whatever might be watching or following us?"

"Ah, but they already know we are here," I told her, still speaking in my normal voice.

Heather looked deeply perplexed by this information. "What about new threats?" she whispered after a moment.

I gave her a wink, then whispered, "Then I guess we should be quiet." She fell back behind me so we were wandering through the dark growth in single file once more.

I found myself frequently shifting my weight back onto my tailbone. The hard saddle leather pressed tightly against my womanhood and caused me to ache from the prior night's exploits. Even now, thinking about my first coupling with Vallen, I felt my face grow hot. I was lost in my thoughts for what was no doubt hours when Heather once again interrupted the silence.

"What's that?" she asked from behind me.

I turned my head, looking for the source of the question. To our right, no more than two hundred paces away, was a strange blue light coming from within the woods. I pulled Slayer to a halt and examined the eerie glow. "I don't know, but I'm going to find out," I told her, before tugging on the reins and veering off course. I heard Heather curse under her breath and follow me.

As we grew closer, I realized it was a twisted white tree. It stood as an ancient relic to Fae guardians of the past. Its sheer size told tales of all it had seen. From its branches hung hundreds of small blue lanterns glowing against the darkness. My heart pounded as I looked at the tree.

"What is this place?" Heather asked once again.

"Those lanterns are Fairy lights, and this tree marks an ancient portal that leads to the Dreaming," I explained.

"What's the Dreaming?"

"It's a magical place that exists between the realms. Only a select few Fae can enter there. It's much like the Forgotten Realm in that it exists for a very special purpose." I breathed deeply through my nose and out through my mouth.

"And they just leave the gateway out where anyone can see it?" Heather was growing more uncomfortable the longer we stayed. "Or is it easier to find so that the Fae can more easily steal babies in the night?"

I whipped around to meet her gaze. I knew shock was all over my face, but this was the first time I had heard her say anything negative about the Fae. "We don't steal babies in the night." I paused, considering my words. "Changelings were outlawed over one hundred years ago." I crossed my arms over my chest.

"Yeah, but shouldn't it be harder to find?" She looked back at the tree with concern.

"It usually is, but my Fae blood stems from a portal Fairy. My mother was part of the Tourist Board." I smiled.

"So your mother was one of the Fairies that would steal people and trick travelers into crossing realms or into the Dreaming." I winced at her bluntness.

"When you say it like that you make it sound like a bad thing," I told her.

"It is," she snapped, before turning Dabble around and heading for the path we had been following. I rolled my eyes, giving up on making her see the truth, and followed behind her. We rode on for a short while in awkward silence. I couldn't tell if she was angry with me or if she was just as lost in thought as I was.

When my stomach finally growled, I knew it was time to stop and take a break. We were fortunate that the path we followed wound close to the stream that ran through the woods, so we were able to water the horses while we ate.

I watched as Heather removed bread and apples from her sack and handed them to me. It felt good to stand and get off my saddle. Heather was still uncharacteristically quiet. I eyed her carefully, but didn't want to force any conversations without knowing why she had reverted to such silent behavior.

When I finished my meal I told her I was going to go relieve myself and I would be back in a moment. She nodded to me, but said nothing. I slipped through the darkness, headed back for the tree and lights. I just wanted to touch it, but I wasn't sure why.

When I arrived, the air seemed alive with a buzz I hadn't felt since I was in my mother's workshop… I mean, kitchen. As I got closer to the tree, the buzz seemed to grow louder and beg me to touch it.

Fighting the urge to get any closer, I reached out and touched one of the blue lights with just a fingertip, and the buzzing abruptly stopped. The blue light grew brighter for a moment and pulsed. Then the trunk of the tree swirled and a door appeared.

I knew I should leave, but my curiosity got the better of me. I walked over to the trunk and pushed on the door. It swung open, revealing more soft blue light coming from the darkness within. My heart seemed to be pulled towards the entrance of the Dreaming, but I resisted, slowly stepping back. Knowing I would fall into temptation if I stayed, I turned and rushed back towards our encampment. I knew what I needed most at this moment was distance between me and that tree.

When I stumbled back into camp, I crashed over the fallen log that Heather was seated on. I stared up at her from my place on the ground. We exchanged looks of shock. Finally, she spoke first. "You went back to the tree, didn't you, My Lady?"

I felt my cheeks blush brightly at being caught so easily. "I can't help it. It just seemed to call to me." I accepted her hand and allowed her to help pull me to my feet. "Thank you," I said as I was once again righted.

She nodded quietly but began packing up. "Are we riding through the night?" she asked.

"That's my plan," I told her, eyeing the saddle, not quite ready to remount and face the discomfort again. Putting aside my own pain, I pulled myself up into the seat and sighed. My legs and body screamed angrily at me. "Let's keep going."

Hours passed. The problem with the Darkwood is you are never really sure if it is day or night while you are riding. When our limbs became too exhausted to keep us upright on the horses, I looked over at Heather. "Let's make camp and get some rest." Finding a nearby clump of trees and bushes that would give us some cover, we watered the horses, munched a bit more, then bedded down. We slept with daggers in hand.

When we awoke from an uneventful rest, I was happy to find the horses rested and even Heather in good spirits. About four hours into our ride we came across the road we were looking for. "Road" being a loose term, used for a dirt path with the occasional rock marker along the way. Nonetheless we rode on.

Pushing the end of the second day, we came across a sign that told us we were headed the right direction and the trees started to thin a little. "We're getting close," I told Heather as we pushed on. "If you don't mind riding hard, we can probably make it tonight."

She looked at our surroundings. "I would feel better if we camped for the night and rode the rest of the way in the morning. My nerves have been on high alert since we entered the woods. I thought getting closer to the end would make me feel better, but I've only been getting more anxious."

"What do you mean?" I asked.

"I can't prove anything, but I am sure someone is following us, and I get the feeling they are making sure we get to where we're going for a reason." The look of concern on her face spoke volumes.

"Hey, it will be all right. I know Vallen doesn't have the best record with this Lord, but I don't think he would harm us." I reached out to give her hand a reassuring squeeze.

"Please can we make camp off the road for the night and approach the castle during daylight?" Her pleading was all it took for me to nod in agreement and lead us off the road, deeper into the forest.

When I was confident we were far enough away from the road, I dropped off Slayer and began gathering kindling for a small fire. An hour later, the horses were fed and watered, camp was set up complete with a small fire for warmth, and our bellies were fed with cheese and wine from Maht's finest cheesemakers and wine cellars.

I extinguished the fire and sank into my bedding. Its warmth and comfort was calming to me after all the years I had spent camping under the stars. Still, it did little to make me feel the same warmth I felt pressed against Vallen. There was an easiness with him I had never planned on, but completely welcomed. Nothing felt forced with him.

My eyes drifted shut with thoughts of my Dragon. The dreams that entered my mind would no doubt make me blush if I were to revisit them during waking hours. He forced my hands behind my back and I felt rope encircle them. I blinked into sudden consciousness. Vallen would never do anything of that sort!

My eyes flew open and I looked into the wild eyes of a man holding a dagger against my throat. "Make one noise and we kill the girl," he said, stepping to the side so I could see. Heather was bound with her hands behind her back, bent forward over her knees with her chest pressed to the ground. A man stood over her with a boot firmly on her back and a sword tip pressed to the base of her spine just below her hair." Nod if you understand and agree."

Reluctantly, I nodded as I was yanked to my feet and made to march back in the direction of the road.

Chapter Twenty-Three

I awoke with a sharp, throbbing pain in my head. I opened one eye and then the other, realizing that the room was illuminated by torchlight. "Lady Morgan?" I heard Heather say.

I snapped the rest of the way into consciousness, sitting up and feeling a sudden wave of nausea as I did so. "Heather?" I said in a whisper, looking at where she sat huddled in a corner.

She quickly crawled over to me, wrapping her arms around me. "I'm so glad you're all right. I was worried when that man hit you, you went down so hard. I was afraid you were dead. You were hanging so lifeless over the back of the horse."

Memories started to flicker back to me. Our assailants had taken us along with our horses back to the main road. I had managed to wiggle my hands free and attack the man who was shoving me along. I had just finished climbing back onto my feet when I heard a rustle behind me, felt a sharp blow, and the world had gone dark.

"Are you okay?" I asked the young Wolf. She nodded. "Where are we?" I finally queried, surveying the cell we now inhabited.

"The dungeon in Drakehaven," she said. "They brought us in and had us sit before the Lord. You were out cold. He took one look at us and had us sent to the dungeon to rot. I tried to explain why we were there, but it was pointless."

I reached up and stroked her hair. "Shhhh, it's okay. I'll find a way to get us out of here."

She shook her head. "Do you know Lord Drakehaven?" she asked.

"No, why do you ask?"

"He seemed to know you. He leaned close to check your pulse and seemed to recognize you," she explained.

"He probably knows I am Vallen's mate and wanted to make sure I was out, and not dead. I get the feeling that he isn't one you would want for an enemy." I thought about my words. *What the hell is wrong with me? That doesn't sound right. Why would he hold us prisoner then?*

Pulling my arms free of Heather, I struggled to my feet and went to the door of our cell. I looked carefully at the hinges and realized there was no way for me to pop them. I turned my attention to the lock. If I could get my hands on something small I was sure I could pick it. I glanced around the cell and found a single nail, figuring it was better than nothing.

Heather watched with interest as I struggled with the lock. No matter how much I fumbled with it, I couldn't get it to release. Frustrated, I sank back down to the dirt floor. "Do you mind if I try?" she asked. Shrugging, I reached out and dropped the nail into her waiting hand.

She nudged me to move over and knelt on the floor beside the door. I watched as she pressed her ear to the backside of the lock and had to roll my eyes. Moments later there was a click and she grinned widely as the door swung open. My eyes narrowed on hers. "Do I even want to know?"

She grinned. "Cowards often make good thieves," she told me before pushing the door open. "Now, I got us out of the cell. It's your job to get us out of the castle."

I stood up and dusted myself off. "I think it is safe to say we probably won't find any help here if this was the greeting we received." We slid quietly from the cell and began moving down the small corridor along the row of cells. There appeared to be six in all, three on each side, but we were the dungeon's only current inhabitants.

At the end of the corridor was a large wooden door with a rectangular peephole in it. I looked through the opening, locating what looked to be the only guard. With nothing but my wits for a weapon, I thrust open the door with all my strength, knocking him off balance. I flung myself onto him, knocking us both to the ground, and with a few good blows subdued him quickly.

I found a nearby bit of rope and secured him to a chair, then used the sleeve of his shirt to gag him. I slid his sword into my belt and kept his dagger in hand. I motioned for Heather to follow as we both pressed ourselves against the wall and began to make our escape. As we rounded the last corner in what felt like an underground maze, I was relieved to find a set of stairs that led us up and out.

Once free of the dungeon and underground catacombs, I pulled Heather into a small passage between the buildings and the keep. We crept low to the ground, using hay bales, carts, and anything else as cover. I had the outer wall in sight when something caught my attention. Not so much something, as someone.

There in the courtyard, seated upon a large horse, was a man I knew well. His Elven features were completely unmarred, just as I remembered them. His long copper hair fell freely down his back. His eyes were so dark they looked almost black. His finely muscled body rippled under the light layers of silk that he wore.

"Morgan? What is it?" Heather asked in whisper.

"That man!" I said in disbelief.

"Lord Drakehaven?" she asked.

I blinked, misunderstanding her words. "No, that's Simon. My ex-fiancé."

She looked at the Elf seated on horseback, then back at me. "No, that's the Lord of the estate."

Before I could turn to get another look at him, someone caught hold of me from behind. I attempted to fight off the attackers, but soon there were more than I could handle. I tried to get one last look at the Lord of the castle before they overwhelmed me.

Kicking and screaming, I was dragged out into the open where we were surrounded by even more thugs. I drew my sword and lashed out at our nearest assailant. I managed to fight off four or five of them before I was driven to my knees, too overwhelmed by numbers to defend against them. I finally dropped my sword when I heard Heather cry out in pain.

I looked her direction just in time to watch as a man pistoned his fist into her stomach. "Stop!" I cried. "I'll surrender. Just let her go," I pleaded.

The man who had been attacking her lowered his fist and turned to face me with a wicked grin. "How do I know you can be trusted not to cause more trouble?" he asked, eyeing me closely. "What will you give me to assure your obedience if I let the mongrel go?"

"You can hold me for ransom. My mate will make sure you are well paid for my return. Please, just let the girl go?"

He considered my words for a moment. "I think the Lord will decide. My understanding is that your mate will be dead soon enough, and all that is his will be ours."

"What? Drakehaven aligned with Avery?" I asked, confused.

The man sneered. "Drakehaven is dead. This castle belongs to the Lady Avery."

My head spun with the knowledge that I was in the den of my enemy with no way to stop her.

"Take me to your commander," I demanded.

"How quickly you forget you can't make demands of us when *you* are the prisoner." He turned back to face Heather. He reached out and caressed her cheek before drawing back his hand and striking her. He grinned, satisfied, as he turned back to face me. "I will do with her as I please, but if you are foolish enough to ask to meet my master, I can't say I would be against watching him kill you." I made a mental note to kill this man before leaving if at all possible.

I was hauled to my feet none too gently, and a hand in my hair while two others secured me at the wrists assured I was led by my captors without incident. My eyes never left Heather, hoping I would see an opening to free her so she could get to safety. Perhaps she could get to Vallen and warn him.

The moment hadn't yet come when we were at last dragged into the great hall. Seated on the dais was the man in the mask I had seen weeks before in Everbloom. He watched me carefully, paying little attention to anyone else in the hall. He sat with a leg tossed over the arm of his chair, his chin resting in his palm.

"My Lord, the prisoners tried to escape," announced one of our captors.

"I'm surprised Lady Morgan took that long to try. I'm more surprised more of you aren't dead." He glanced over at Heather before looking back at me. "Although, she has always had the need to protect the weak and helpless." The last of his words seemed almost snarled.

I knew that voice. I knew that snarl. The man behind the mask was Simon. I wasn't sure how or why he was alive and here, but he was. The realization had me shaking my head, trying to knock reason into it.

"What's wrong, *Lady* Morgan? You always have something to say. Nothing smart-mouthed or threatening? Have you gone soft?" he taunted.

"Why aren't you dead, Simon?" was all that I could think to say.

It seemed like everyone in the hall held their breath at my words. Simon reached up and pulled the mask from his face and dropped it to the floor. "I was curious how long it would take for us to meet again."

I looked around the room and for the first time noticed a number of my men. Men I had trained were amongst his bandits. My heart sank. So many good men had been led astray. How had Avery done this? I shook my head. "Why would you betray your own people? Why would you betray me?" I asked.

He slid his leg off the chair and stood up. He motioned to the castle around us. "We would never have had all this. You were too good. Too pure. Too…. everything, to see what we had. We had an elite team that should have been rich, but you were willing to work for free if it meant we were doing the right thing."

I shook my head. "Tallyn trained you. Elves value honor above all else -" He cut me off.

"To hell with honor. Honor doesn't keep you warm at night. Honor doesn't feed your starving belly. Open your eyes, Morgan, this noble war of *good* you fight is for naught, because those with the most power have everything. Those without power have nothing. I'm tired of having none." He slammed his fist down on the arm of the chair.

"We had everything we needed," I argued.

"But not everything I *wanted*." His nostrils flared as his anger started to get the better of him. "Now answer my questions. Why are *you* alive?" he said, thrusting a finger in my direction. "Where is your honor? You swore to find me on the other side. I saw you that day in the clearing. The Dragon's blood should have killed you. How are you still here?"

I clenched my hands into fists and breathed deeply, trying to control my anger. "Considering you lied about your death, I don't think you have any right to know how or why I cheated mine." I struggled against my assailants, trying to pull my arms free. "Let me go!" I demanded.

Simon grinned in a way that used to make my knees weak. Now it just turned my stomach. Standing, he quickly strolled across the hall, coming to a stop before me. Reaching out, he caught the edge of my tunic and pulled it free of my belt despite my struggle, then lifted it. His eyes narrowed on my mate branding. "I see. Then it is true. The great Lady Knight took a mate, finally. Tell me, did you make him wait for the wedding night too?"

I growled at him and spat in his face. "I can't believe I ever loved you."

He pulled up the bottom of my tunic and wiped his cheek before releasing it and meeting my gaze again. "So unladylike. What would the Queen say?" he taunted me. "The feeling is mutual. You started as a conquest, one that proved too challenging even for me."

"I swear, when I free myself, I am going to take your heart back as a souvenir." I struggled one last time.

He tilted his head to the side. "There, *that* is a real Lady Morgan threat. For the first time ever though, I actually believe you." He turned and walked back to his seat on the dais. "Return the prisoners to their cell. This time I want guards inside and outside of the dungeon. If she escapes again before Avery returns, I will personally see to each of your punishments."

With that I was dragged from the hall kicking, screaming, and hurling insults at anyone I could. I was madder then I had ever been in my life. I didn't want just Avery's blood now. I wanted Simon's, the men who had betrayed me, and the asshat who kept tugging on my hair. More than anything though, I wanted to return to Vallen.

With a shove I was forced back into the cell we had been put in earlier. This time, though, a guard was posted inside the dungeon with us, and I had little doubt that Simon would make good on his threat if any of the men failed him. Unfortunately for them, I had no intention of staying put.

With little else to do but sit and plot, I sank to the floor and started planning our escape, because I knew they were too confident and confidence leads to mistakes. If I was patient, they would give me my opening, and this time I wouldn't be trying to find an escape route.

"Lady Morgan?" Heather asked.

"Yes, Heather?" I said, turning to face her.

"Lord Simon was your fiancé, right?" There was a bigger question there she wanted to ask.

"He was," I told her as I really thought through all that I had just learned. He had plotted to make me commit suicide so he didn't have to get his hands dirty. Why not just leave me? "Don't call him Lord. He was never elevated."

"Are you elevated when you choose a mate of higher status?" she asked.

"Yes, but that still doesn't make him a Lord…" It suddenly all clicked into place. "When they brought me in and introduced him to you…?" I couldn't finish the thought.

"They said that Lady Avery was his mate," she filled me in.

I felt as if I had been kicked in the gut. My head jerked back. I took a deep breath and let it out slowly to give the pain in my heart a chance to subside. "He never loved me," I said pathetically.

"Does that really matter now?" Heather asked.

I shook my head. "I guess not, but I trusted him with my life. I mourned him for months. I actually tried to die, all because he is an asshole."

"This is good," she said. "Channel that anger and figure out how to get us out of here." She pointed to the door.

I shook my head. "It's no use, really. Simon knows me. We trained together. He is a perfect match for me. He knows all my tricks."

"You can't give up. What about Vallen? What about all those people counting on us? What about Young?" I blinked at her last concern. She must have read the question on my face. "I mean, he's not the brightest lad and he's stubborn. They'll kill him."

"And you care?" I asked skeptically.

"No… maybe. He's nice, and doesn't deserve to die in a battle he can't win," she finally blurted out.

I was at a loss for words. A war raged deep inside me. On the one hand, I knew I was up against an opponent who knew me inside and out. He would know how to stop me. On the other hand, there were people counting on me and a Dragon I really would like to see again. "I just don't know if I can," I told her.

"You do realize that you have taken out entire camps of these clowns by yourself? What difference does one man make? You don't have to face him now. You just have to escape." She crossed her arms and flopped down to sit when I didn't respond.

"Well, if you two ladies are done with your talks about men, menstruation, flowers, and shoes, what do you say we get out of here?" Both of us turned to glare at Uther.

Chapter Twenty-Four

"Well that was rather sexist," I told him.

He grinned widely as he unlocked the door to the cell. "Yeah, I know. That's why I said it."

"Why are you here, Uther?" Heather demanded.

"I'm a Werewolf. I only take orders from my Lord. If you want me to do something, demand I do the opposite," he said with an eyebrow wiggle.

Heather and I both rolled our eyes but wasted no time in exiting the cell. "You were the presence following us in the woods," Heather accused as he urged us down the hallway.

"I was," he said simply.

"What about the guards, Uther?" I asked as we approached the door. I pulled him to a stop.

"They won't say anything. They know I'm in here," he told us.

"Wait, what?" I asked in confusion.

"Who do you think told them you were coming and where to find you in the woods?" he said proudly.

"Why would you betray us?" asked Heather with hurt in her eyes.

"To put me back in their good graces and to get you two through the doors without too much trouble," he explained.

I narrowed my eyes on him. "Why didn't you alert us to your plan?"

He sighed. "I didn't have time. When I found out what was going on, I knew I had to do something. Originally I thought I would just come along and offer back-up if needed."

"And how do we know we can trust you now if you are back in their good graces?"

He shrugged. "I guess you don't, but I do promise if you don't do something, a lot of good and innocent people are going to die."

"Ugh." I hated that he already had me so figured out.

When we opened the door, Uther grabbed me by the nape of the neck and gave me a shove. "Move faster, wench. I would hate to mar your pretty face before the Lord has had his chance with the two of you."

The two guards on either side of the door grinned knowingly. I pretended to struggle and threw around a few vile names for added affect. One of the guards stepped forward and took hold of Heather. "I'll give you a hand," he said, grinning at Uther. "Maybe when the Lord is done he'll share." My stomach turned as he winked.

We were led through the long corridor again, but this time Uther stopped us part way down. "Wait, we are to take them to his chamber." The guard ahead of us with Heather nodded, then grabbed hold of her hair and pressed her against the stone wall while he felt along a ledge. There was a click and a door swung open.

I suddenly understood what Uther had wanted me to see. This corridor was seemed long because it probably hid a network of tunnels that ran all through the keep. If we could gain access to them, then we could move with less chance of detection. Soon we were being shoved along an even darker corridor and then up stairs we didn't know were there. Heather was righted when she tripped by a strong hand yanking her back to her feet by the hair. Both Uther and I tensed at her pained yelp.

As we climbed, Uther lifted the back hem of my tunic and slid a dagger into the waistband of my leggings, then dropped the tunic back in place. He reached down and slid a longer one into the top of my boot. Then he gave my backside a soft pat. An offense I would make him pay for later, I swore.

Finally, there was the click of a door and we were shoved into a lavishly decorated room. The maids seemed startled as we stepped out from behind a wall hanging. They looked at us with disgust. "Good evening, ladies," Uther said in a sickeningly sweet voice. "The Lord has requested these two wenches for dessert."

The maids exchanged looks and almost sneered. "So what, he doesn't want us anymore?" the redhead asked angrily.

"Oh no, quite the contrary. He wishes for all four of you. You two were chosen to join in because I'm told your skills are beyond compare." Uther spun a web of lies that made the girls giggle. "You are to instruct these women in your arts, and I am told you will be rewarded handsomely for your efforts."

The women's eyes grew round and wild with greed. Their lips stretched into smiles and they shooed away the men, demanding the privacy they said they needed to prepare the two of us. When Uther and the other guard stepped through the main door that led out into the keep, the brunette woman followed him to request hot water and the tub.

Soon several lads bearing buckets of steaming water appeared and filled a wooden tub. When they were gone, the redhead pointed at the tub. "Both of you strip and get in. The Lord likes his women clean and smelling of oils."

Heather grumbled and moved to do as she was bid. I had been standing in such a way as to keep the dagger in my boot hidden. I sat on the floor and pulled it off, taking care that the dagger slid into the empty tube of the boot. I carefully removed the second dagger at my back and slid it into my other boot while the other women were fussing over Heather. By the time they looked back at me, I was naked and strolling towards the tub.

The redhead eyed my mate branding critically. "You have a mate."

"I do," I said flatly, sliding into the tub with Heather.

"And what will your mate think of you lying with another?" she asked.

"Hopefully he will understand I had no say in it." I began scrubbing myself with the cloth the brunette handed me.

The redhead put her hands on her hips and stared at me. "Our Lord is not a monster. He would never take a woman against her will."

"Your Lord and I used to be engaged. I assure you he sees it as taking what he believes to be his." I refused to admit it, but it felt wonderful to be washing away the smell of the dungeon. Everyone suddenly gasped. "What?"

"Your hair just changed to a dark color, almost black," Heather told me.

"Anya, do you think she is lying about the engagement?" asked the brunette.

The redhead shrugged. "It doesn't matter. I'm sure the Lord will handle her and her lies later. For now we should do as we are told."

Soon we were cleaned and dressed - if you could call what we were wearing 'dressed.' We wore Fairy silk that you could see right through, casting a shimmer over our skin but leaving nothing to the imagination. Our hair was pulled up into tight buns on top of our heads and the women began explaining the rules of the bedroom to us.

"What does the Lord's mate say about him having you girls?" I asked.

Anya smiled widely. "Sometimes she joins in. The Lord has particular tastes and the Lady doesn't always fancy them. In fact, Lady Avery brought me back as a gift for her mate. Torree was promoted when we took this castle. Until we came she was kitchen staff, but the Lord took a liking to her." The brunette smiled and bobbed her head.

"What sort of tastes?" Heather asked innocently.

"He likes to ravage us. He is an excellent lover, as most Elves are." Anya grinned. I resisted the urge to roll my eyes. She looked at me. "But then, if you were his fiancé, you would already know that."

I cleared my throat. "Actually, I was a virgin when I was bound to my mate." Both women exchanged looks and burst out laughing. "I don't see why it is funny. I think it is beautiful that my mate is the only lover I have known."

"Then we will hope that your mate was an excellent lover and taught you well, or you may find yourself bored tonight." Torree grinned.

"I've told you before, I am not here willingly." They just laughed harder. In some ways I could almost understand. Simon was a handsome man and even I had heard stories of him as a lover.

There was a double knock on the door. Anya looked up from our discussion. "Enter," she called and kitchen maids entered carrying platters of food. When they left she looked over the selection. "We should eat so we have our strength for the night."

Heather munched and chatted with the maids as I formulated a plan. Finally I rolled my eyes, feeling kind of guilty for what I was about to do. Forcing myself to try and smile, I sat down with the other three. "So the particular tastes of the Lord, what are they?"

The women giggled and give me a run down. I couldn't keep the shock from my face. "Doesn't that make you feel violated?" I asked. The two exchanged looks before looking back at me and shaking their heads no. "What if Heather and I tied you to the bed and blindfolded you? Then when the Lord arrived you would be all ready for him." I tried not to think about it.

"What would you and Heather do?" asked Torree.

"Assist, of course. I mean, after all, the two of you are his chosen favorites." They smiled and giggled again and started talking about how the Lord would react to such a surprise. Finally they agreed. Sighing heavily, I followed their directions and tied them up as they told me to. Then I blindfolded them and even gagged them for a good measure. Shaking my head, I crossed the room and redressed.

Heather stared at the girls on the bed and then back at me. She shrugged out of the silk and pulled her own clothes back on, watching as I secured my new daggers. As quietly as possible, I crossed the room to the secret corridor entrance and popped the latch. Heather and I both stepped into the darkness, leaving the two maids to giggle and test their bonds.

When the door was shut and latched in place again I breathed a sigh of relief.

The familiar voice of Uther piped up in an intense whisper. "Took you two long enough."

"I think I'm ready to leave now," I told him.

We all linked hands and I allowed him to lead the way. We walked deeper down the corridor until we hit a wall. Uther released my hand long enough to stoop near the floor and run his hand along the stones. There was a click and another door swung open. "How did you know that was there?" I asked.

He took my hand and led us into the next corridor. "Easy, I can see in the darkness and could smell the draft."

I turned my head towards Heather. "Can you do that too?"

"Of course," she said with a shrug I could feel more than see.

Time seemed warped as we traveled through the maze of tunnels and corridors. I found myself thankful to be in the company of two Werewolves that could see and smell their way through. We finally stopped after too many turns to remember. "Here," Uther said in a whisper.

"Where is here?" I asked.

"This is the armory where some of the Iron Warriors are being stored. I don't know where all of them are, but I figure if we can disable what is here then we may stand a chance against what they have left." Uther cracked the door and sniffed the air.

Heather leaned forward and did the same thing. "I smell at least six men," she whispered.

"I only smell four," he insisted.

I rolled my eyes. "With three of us we should be able to handle six."

Heather was silent, but Uther agreed softly. Urging the door open little by little until we could see in without alerting the guards, we slowly slid into the room and coaxed the hidden door shut again. To my surprise, both Uther and Heather slid behind barrels, hiding.

"Cowards," I muttered to myself, and started moving about the armory with as much stealth as possible. When I came upon the first guard I was thankful his back was turned. I snuck up on him and with a small measure of regret snapped his neck, knowing that regardless of who these men might have been once, they were no longer my friends and allies.

I looked up at the first Iron Warrior. It was massive and looked like a huge iron dwarf that stood twenty feet high. Cursing under my breath, I began climbing along it until I reached its controls three-quarters of the way up. Everything was made of metal and I didn't have the slightest clue how to stop it. If it had been wood, I could have set fire to it.

"I need Heather," I whispered to myself, and I knew to do that I would need to secure the armory. I used my higher vantage point to see who else was about. I counted five more men. Heather would be excited to learn she had been right.

With as much grace and stealth as I could manage, I slid from the cockpit and down the side I had climbed up. I snuck around the warehouse, diving between machines and working quietly to seize control of the building, knowing that if an alarm was raised we would be swarmed.

The next three were easily dispatched as they were all wandering about on their own, but the last two were out in the open at a small table, playing a hand of cards. They sat close to a door and it made me uneasy. I searched around the floor for a rock but found none. Of all the times for an evil hideout to be clean.

I looked up at the Iron Warrior I hid behind and noticed the tracks on it were held in place with bolts. Quietly I unscrewed a few bolts. I quickly tossed one towards the back of the building. It landed with the expected clatter. Both me looked up and exchanged looks. "What was that?" asked one of them. The other just shrugged.

I tossed another bolt in a different direction. They looked up again. "Should we check it out?" asked the first guy.

"Nah, we're on break. Let the others do it," said the second.

I wanted to scream for them to get off their lazy asses and go check, but that would have defeated the purpose. I had two bolts left and I chucked them at the same time as hard as I could. This time the sound was louder and there was a lot more clattering. I had managed to knock something over.

This time both men jumped to their feet and drew their weapons. "I swear, if it's a rat, I'll gut it and eat it for dinner," growled the second man. Both men stalked away in the direction of the sound. I crept along behind them until I was satisfied they were in an area where I could keep them from raising the alarm.

Both men stood over a broken jar, looking down at it in confusion. Its contents - what looked like hundreds of small metal balls - were scattered across the floor. The men grumbled but slid their weapons back into their belts and knelt to begin picking up the balls. I chose that moment to strike.

I charged forward and buried a dagger into the back of the nearest guard. He gasped, readying to scream, but I snapped his neck before he got it out. I pulled his sword free of his belt, bringing it up in time to defend against the other man's axe. I knew I only had a short time to defeat him so I pressed hard with my sword, driving him back so he had to focus on me and not on raising the alarm.

When he opened his mouth, I plunged my sword into his chest. He stopped and looked down at it, then back up at me with confusion. "My Lady?" he said, his eyes momentarily sparking with recognition before the light in them faded away.

I studied him carefully. "Goodbye, Charles. You chose the wrong side," I whispered, remembering him as among the men I had believed already dead. With a heavy sigh, I headed back to where my allies were hiding.

I looked at both of them. "I know why Heather hid, but what about you, Uther?"

Uther shifted uncomfortably on his feet. "If you failed to subdue them, I wanted to be able to claim you escaped and save Heather."

"Great, I get to babysit both of you." I rolled my eyes and looked at Heather. "You ready to earn your keep?" I asked her.

She looked at me, confused, but nodded and stepped out of her hiding place. "What do you need me to do?"

"I don't know how to disable these things so they can't run, but I get the feeling you do. Or at least you can." I smiled.

Her chest puffed with pride and she grinned. It was the moment she realized that I trusted her to be able to do something I wasn't able to. Pride drove her to pick up tools and enthusiastically set to work. I armed myself again and went to guard the door. I was sure at some point another shift would come to watch over the place.

Hours passed and I heard scraping and clanking noses from all over the building. Sure enough, another shift of six guards had come as I expected, but this time, with Uther's help, we were able to make short work of them.

Night fall had come and only torchlight and lanterns illuminated the building. Heather approached me where I stood by the door. "Five out of five destroyed," she told me. "If for some reason they *can* get them started, the mixture of sand, water, missing bolts, and ball bearings in the fuel tank will make sure they never reach Maht." Her smile told me she was confident and that was good enough for me.

I reached for a large bundle of rope that hung on the wall and draped it over my shoulder and across my body. "What do you say we escape now?" I said, looking at the two of them.

Heather nodded in full agreement with me. Uther seemed hesitant. He shook his head. "They are going to notice you missing soon enough. If we get you back to the cells we may have a better chance tomorrow."

I tried not to laugh. "I'm not going back into that cell willingly. You can choose to stay here if you don't wish to come with us, but we're going."

Uther stood his ground. "Then go on by yourself, Lady Morgan, but my sister and I are staying here."

Heather looked at him like he had worms growing from his ears. "I'm not staying," she corrected him.

Uther jerked back and glared at her. "I'm your older brother and you will do as I say."

"I'm the Lady's Squire. I'll put my fate in her hands as is only proper," she argued.

I said nothing, but the existence of my new squire was news to me. I watched as it played out. The two argued back and forth for a few more minutes before Uther threw his hands in the air and turned to face me. "The south wall has the least protection. Guard my sister with your life. I will do my best to help you if I can." With those words he turned and stormed towards the door.

"Are we going to leave him?" she asked.

"Think we can convince him to come with us?" I asked her.

She was silent for a moment, but shook her head. "I'll just have to pray he comes to his senses. Making Uther do something he doesn't want to do is near impossible."

I handed her a dagger, which she gladly accepted and slid into her boot. She also took a sword off one of the unfortunate guards who had met their end this night.

Silently we slipped out of the armory and began clinging to the shadows of the different buildings. I relied heavily on Heather's nose to alert us to oncoming danger. When we reached the south gate, I pointed to the stairs that would lead us to the top of the wall. "Why not the gate?" she whispered.

"They are less likely to notice us going down the wall than through the gate," I explained. She nodded in agreement and followed my lead up the stairs. At the top of the stairs was a single guard with his back turned to us. He was heavily armored and would not be easy to defeat with the light weapons we now carried.

I rushed forward, throwing all my strength into it, and managed to push him over the wall. He was taken so much by surprise that he barely yelped as he went over. I craned my neck over the side to see how big the drop was. "Over four stories," I remarked to Heather, who had moved to stand beside me. Sinking low, we maneuvered around the top of the wall until we found an area of reasonable shadow.

I pulled the rope from across my chest where it hung and secured it before dropping it over the side. Even with its length, there would be a ten-foot drop at the end. I encouraged Heather to go first. Scared, she nodded and slid over the wall and began her climb down. When I saw her drop to the ground, I began my own descent. I heard movement above and knew I would be discovered if I didn't move quickly.

Ignoring the burn in my hands, I slid down the rope as fast as gravity would allow and dropped to the ground in a crouch. Heather reached out to catch me. We pressed ourselves to the wall for as long as the shadows would conceal us as we made our way towards the forest. When the tree line was in sight, we waited patiently for the right moment and made a break for it.

Chapter Twenty-Five

I was delighted to find that Slayer had somehow escaped the men who took us. However, it meant we would be riding slower with two riders. Heather rested her head between my shoulder blades as we rushed through the woods. I did my best to navigate in the darkness, but I had no intention of sticking to the road.

We had made it back into the heart of the woods when a distant sound made my heart almost leap from my chest. "Riders," Heather whispered behind me. She sniffed at the air. "At least a dozen," she told me. I could feel her lean back and tug off her tunic. "We can travel faster if I'm in wolf form and you're the only rider."

I wanted to argue with her, but I knew the best chance for both of us was to separate. "They want me more than you. Meet me at the Fairy Tree. If I don't show up within an hour of your arrival, head for Maht and let Vallen know I've been captured."

She nodded understanding and slid off of Slayer, shifting into her Wolf form as she hit the ground. With Slayer's load now lightened, I pressed my body low over his neck and pushed him to a gallop, focusing heavily on the terrain so as to not maim him or send us over a cliff. I road fast and hard, pushing him as I had never pushed a horse before.

"If we survive all this, I promise you all the apples you can eat," I whispered in his ear. My animal connection with him stirred deep within me and I felt him push himself harder. After we crossed the stream, I slowed him a bit, knowing if I continued to ride him at this pace his heart would give out.

I closed my eyes and allowed the Dreaming to call to me. Sure enough, there was a pull. It felt like a rope was attached to my heart and drawing me through the forest. Soon I could see the soft glow of the Fairy Tree. The blue lights shone brightly. Slayer was not thrilled to approach, but he did as I directed.

I reached out and touched a lantern. It glowed brighter and seemed to pulsate. Soon all the lanterns on the tree were glowing. I realized that the rhythm matched that of my heartbeat. I adjusted my breathing and watched as the twinkle slowed along with my heart. "Please," I whispered. "Help me and my friend."

The lights stopped twinkling and started to glow a steady blue. I heard a nearby twig snap, and I looked over to see Heather standing naked in her Human form, watching me talk to the tree. "They will be here in half an hour," she panted. "We can't outrun them."

I looked back at the tree and bowed my head. "Great spirits of my ancestors. Help me now. If I am truly a child of the Dreaming, grant me the ability to walk there and keep us safe from harm."

The lights in the tree dimmed and the tree itself seemed to glow with a silvery light. The trunk shifted, revealing a door large enough to ride through. I turned and looked at Heather and held out my hand. "Let's go," I told her.

She looked at the tree and back at me, then shook her head. "I can't enter the Dreaming. I will be lost."

I waved my hand at her some more. "You don't have to trust the Dreaming or the Fae, you just have to trust me," I told her.

She considered me for a moment, then she took my hand hesitantly and allowed me to pull her up onto Slayer's back with me. "I'm afraid to do this," she admitted as I urged Slayer towards the hole in the tree trunk.

"I know. I am too. Just hold on and don't let go." Her arms encircled my waist tightly and once again she rested her head between my shoulders. The door behind us grew closed.

At first we were surrounded by darkness. It felt suffocating, like I could hardly breathe. The air felt thick and had a heavy, floral quality to it. I gagged a little at first, but pushed down the panic that so desperately wanted to take hold of me. Slowly the darkness filled with a soft light. It was like being in a dark tent with lights shining from the outside, only clearer. I could see everything in black, white, and grey. The Darkwood stretched out around us and I felt as if we were moving in slow motion.

I urged Slayer to trot forward, and sure enough there were no barriers to stop us. The world moved around us slowly in black and white. The riders that chased us arrived at the tree, led by hounds. Uther sat astride Dabble, and I understood now that he had set Slayer free so the horse wouldn't be captured.

The dogs circled the tree, sniffing. Simon sat angrily upon his horse and snarled. Uther stared hard at the tree as the riders rode on in the direction we were heading. Though we were moving at a slow, comfortable pace, we seemed to rush past them.

Heather lifted her head and looked around. "What is this place?" she asked.

"The Dreaming," I said.

"I thought it would be dark and scary. This is just.... strange," she said.

I didn't have to worry about trees or rocks in the way. Slayer seemed to be able to walk right through them. I remembered what my mother had always told me of the Dreaming. "There are the realms," I explained. "Between each realm there is a glue that connects it to other realms. That glue is called the Planes of Existence. There are three planes between each realm. One is the Dreaming, where we are now. Another is called the Meliah. It is a plane between the Forgotten Realm and all others. It's somewhere between life and death. The last plane is called the Hour. Time doesn't exist in any of these planes. Those who walk within them control the passage of time. Within the plane known as the Hour, magic controls time."

"Huh?" she said, confused.

"Only certain people can tap into each plane." I thought about how to explain it. "The Fae have access to the Dreaming. The Dark Elves control the access points to the Meliah. Mages control the Hour."

"So the people following us can't access the plane we are in right now?" she asked.

"Correct, unless one of them is a Fae with a bloodline connected to the Dreaming." I wanted her to feel safe.

"So wait, if these planes are between the realms, how do you pass from realm to realm if you're not one of those people?"

I smiled because for the first time ever, everything clicked into place and I understood. "Fairy Circles were the very first portals between Realms. Fairies who could walk in the Dreaming would create a path from one marker to another between the realms. That's why many of the very oldest Fairy Circles only go to one specific place in another Realm. Over the centuries, with better understanding and the help of the Dark Elves, we were able to develop Portals that gave us the ability to connect with any other Portal as long as there was a marker there. Finally the Mages were able to harness the magic within all three races and create stones that could take you anywhere in any of the realms. They were originally called Fae Tears, because usually the Fairies capable of making them were used as slaves in their creation. Now that their creation is regulated closely and is humane they have come to be known as Portal Beads. They allow the wearer to travel between realms as long as they have a connection with the place."

"That actually makes a lot of sense. If we have the power to make the beads now, why don't more people have them?" she asked.

I looked ahead at the edge of the forest. I hadn't realized how far we had traveled during our talk. "There are only a few Fae that know how to make the beads. To make them requires certain set of materials that are available in very limited supplies. Beads are only given to those who are in need of them."

"I see," she said, lost in her own thoughts. "How do we get out of the Dreaming?" she finally asked.

"We have to find another doorway," I said.

"Do you know where another doorway is?"

"I have a suspicion where one is," I told her.

"What if you're wrong?" Panic was creeping into her voice.

"Then I will find one. Relax. I told you to trust me." My words seemed to have the desired effect. Her grip on my waist seemed to lighten and she lifted her head to look around.

Ahead of us lay the outer walls of Maht. I urged Slayer to bear west around the walls of the city. "I thought we could walk through walls?" Heather asked.

"We can, but I'm looking for something," I told her and I could feel her nod. On the far side of the city sat a clump of bushes low to the ground with a blue light shining from them. I lined up Slayer with their glow and urged him forward. Sure enough, we soon sank into the ground and were riding below the city in a long-forgotten tunnel.

The tunnel shimmered with color, and I recognized the complex web of wards guarding it. With the incoming attack I would need to make sure the glyphs and wards were reinforced. We rode deeper under the city until we reached a thick stone wall. I tried to push Slayer through it, but it was no use. Glyphs and wards glowed to life even in the Dreaming, preventing us from passing through.

Sighing heavily, I turned Slayer and we followed the curve of the wall until we met a large wooden door. Glyphs and wards shone brightly across its surface. I turned Slayer to the side so I could try touching them. They glowed to life with bright blue fury and the mate brand on my side burned painfully for a moment, but it was quickly replaced by a cooling sensation. The door, glyphs, and wards all turned grey and faded into Drakemoore and out of the Dreaming.

Heather gasped behind me and tightened her grip again. "I trust you, I trust you," she chanted quietly under her breath. I urged Slayer forward, and this time we passed through the door and into a large stone room.

At the center of the room stood a deep blue pool with a high golden fence around it. The gate had a large lock in the floor before it. To the right of the pool stood the mighty white tree whose branches grew throughout the manor above.

When we approached the tree, I reached out and touched it. "Thank you for the safe passage," I told it, stroking its trunk. It glowed to life with a silvery light and the trunk opened up a door wide enough to ride through. Slayer obliged, and as if pulled into the tree, walked through and out the other side. The tree grew closed behind us and the world shone brightly with color once more.

Heather and I looked around, amazed. I slid off the horse, now faced with the task of getting him to climb stairs. Heather slid off as well and pulled her tunic and pants back on. Her boots had been lost in the ride. Taking the reins, I guided Slayer to the massive staircase the wrapped around in a tall winding spiral with no end in sight.

Twenty minutes later, gasping for air, we made it to the top of the stairs. I pushed the door open to the surprising location of our dining room, hidden behind a panel in the wall. Young, who had been eating, stared wide-eyed as Heather and I walked through the hidden doorway, pulling along my horse as we went.

"Where's Vallen?" I asked firmly.

Young blinked a few times, still in shock. "Try the kitchen," he squeaked out. I left him, Heather, and Slayer to keep each other company in the dining room and went to look for Vallen.

I quickly made my way out of the dining room, down the hall, and into the kitchen. Vallen stood with a cup of tea in one hand, staring down at a book in the other. Without looking up, he took a sip of the tea. "I didn't ask, but when do the Dwarves expect to arrive?"

I cleared my throat. "I'm not really sure, but we can't count on Lord Drakehaven for assistance."

He almost dropped the book and the tea when he looked up. Closing his eyes for a moment, he breathed a sigh of relief. He stood up and met me across the floor, folding his arms around me and burying his face in my hair. "You're home in one piece," he said, kissing my forehead.

"You doubted my abilities?" I asked as I slid my hands around his waist, pulling myself closer.

"No, but when left to its own devices, the mind always plants the seeds of worst-case scenarios." He leaned down and captured my mouth with his. His tongue felt like liquid fire on my lips. I opened to him and met his deep kiss with passion of my own.

When we finally broke the kiss we stood a long moment in silence enjoying the closeness of one another. "What's this about Dwarves?" I finally asked.

Releasing me but still keeping a hand at the small of my back, he guided me to one of the two stools that sat at the kitchen counter. "When you left, Uther went missing and we suspected he followed you. Young couldn't handle doing nothing, so he went to the Princess of Everbloom and asked for her assistance. She sent back a large portion of the guard and promised to have the Dwarves send more reinforcements."

"How did he get there so fast?" I asked.

"He flew," Vallen said with a shrug. "In places that don't really see Dragons very often we try not to take on our Dragon form, but this is an emergency."

"Is this the princess responsible for the pitiful protection of her people in Everbloom?" I was a little less than thrilled she had let her kingdom come to this point.

"No, that was more her brother. She was the one who actually raised a guard recently and has been training them. At the time security was lax, she was busy breaking Dragon law and raising a dead Soul Mate," he grumbled angrily. I made a mental note to come back to that sooner or later. "Now, how was your trip?"

"A disaster," I said simply. He blinked at me and nodded for me to continue. "Uther did follow us, then aided the enemy in capturing us because he felt it was the only way to safely get us in the keep. Lord Drakehaven is dead. Avery and Simon control Drakehaven and are using it as their base of operations."

"Simon?" he asked, confused.

I took a sip of his tea before meeting his eyes again. "Yes, my dead fiancé isn't dead. He and a number of my men faked their deaths to join Avery and her band of highwaymen." He locked his jaw in place, the red glow of anger creeping up his neck. "So yeah, he planned for me to kill myself, or at least highly encouraged it, and when I didn't, he made sure I faced men whose weapons carried a lethal dose of Dragon's blood. After all, he couldn't have me finding out that, not only had he betrayed me, but he had also mated with Avery."

The last words dropped Vallen's jaw. The red anger on his face disappeared and was replaced with confusion. "I don't understand," he said.

"What don't you understand? The betrayal part or the part where I'm a moron?" I said snidely.

He looked up at me. "You aren't daft for loving someone." His voice was soft. "Love is a beautiful thing. My regret is that you have to know more pain after what you went through mourning his loss." He took the tea mug from me and took another sip before handing it back. "No, what confuses me is Avery."

I shook my head, not understanding.

"I was under the impression she favored women. In fact, I thought she was also in love with Melody." He seemed very perplexed by the news she had taken Simon as a mate.

"You were both competing for the affection of the same woman?" I asked.

"I always thought we were," he said, with a shrug. "Maybe she doesn't have a preference. Maybe she just loves who she loves," he finished.

"I guess. Simon is handsome and can be charming when he wants to be, so I guess anything is possible." He reacted like I had hurt him with my description, and I immediately recognized the short-lived moment of jealousy as it clouded his eyes. I couldn't explain why, but for a moment my heart skipped a beat knowing he craved my affection and praise. "Of course, his features and charms pale when compared to yours." He grinned smugly and I knew I had mended the jealousy.

"How did you get back so quickly? You said Uther aided in your capture?" he asked.

"Yes, and then aided in our escape. I don't entirely understand the web he finds himself in and I am not sure where his loyalties lie. We should be careful. We shouldn't distrust him, but we shouldn't blindly follow him either." He nodded his agreement.

Just then Young came into the kitchen and looked at the two of us. "Morgan, I know we are family now, but keeping your horse in the dining room is just too weird. He needs to be returned to the stables." Young stomped his foot to make his point.

Heather stepped into the kitchen. "I'll take him out, My Lady." She snatched Slayer's reins, who had followed Young, and I heard him clop down the hallway.

Vallen narrowed his eyes in suspicion "How did you get the horse into the manor without me knowing?"

"She came through the secret door in the dining room," Young filled him in.

They both turned to stare at me. I felt like I was in trouble with the teacher and headmaster in school all over again. "To escape recapture, I slid Slayer, Heather, and I into the Dreaming. The tree in the basement was the first doorway I found out of it. You should be impressed I got my horse to climb all those stairs," I told them with a certain amount of pride.

"The chamber below should have been sealed even to the Dreaming," said Vallen.

"Oh, it was," I assured him. "I think the wards recognized my branding and allowed me to pass because of it. It burned and cooled before letting me pass through. That being said, you may want to check those wards and glyphs again. You may also want to check the ones on the outer wall as well, because I had no difficulty finding the corridor."

Young swore and Vallen nodded. The brothers' gazes met and Young bowed his head. "On it now," he said, disappearing out of the kitchen.

Vallen looked back down at me. "Well it sounds like you've had an exciting four days. Are you hungry?"

The man could read me like a book. I smiled and nodded, settling back onto one of the stools to watch him cook. Soon I was looking down at a plate with two eggs, some sausage, and some fried potato slices with fruit. I gobbled the food up greedily and didn't argue when he slid more on my plate.

When Heather returned, she looked wide-eyed at the food and Vallen smiled before loading up a plate for her as well. Having finished my food, I sipped on a cup of tea and filled him in on more details about the Iron Warriors, number of Avery's men, and the defenses of Drakehaven.

"Well, it sounds like you two did a good job at hopefully slowing them down. Since Uther didn't return with you, he is unaware of the reinforcements being sent." Vallen looked at Heather and sighed with a heavy heart. "I know he is your brother, but if he has betrayed us I can't allow him to go unpunished."

Heather looked at me and then back to Vallen. "All I ask is that you give him a fair chance. If he has truly betrayed us, then he is a fool and deserves the punishment he will get, but at least give him the chance to defend himself."

Vallen and I exchanged our own looks but agreed. I reached out and took her hand. "We really do hope he is still with us."

Chapter Twenty-Six

The air was unseasonably cool when I awoke the next morning. I had had every intention when I went to bed last night to enjoy my new mate and his welcoming arms. Unfortunately, those arms were my undoing. They offered me a place where I felt safe and secure. I fell asleep within moments.

Now I was in bed alone, looking out a window that shone brightly with midmorning sun. I slid from the blankets and marched into the closet. I had no clean clothes, but I wasn't about to let that stop me. I tugged on one of Vallen's overly-long tunics that came down almost to my ankles. I wrapped my long belt around my waist twice and pulled on a pair of sandals I usually used when bathing while I traveled.

I reflected on the day before. We had seen to the defenses along the walls, checked in on our small army, and prepared both offensive and defensive battle strategies. We were as ready as we could be without the Dwarves.

I descended the stairs as fast as I could and went to the kitchen. Nobody was there. I looked in all the common rooms and even went to check both Young's and Heather's chambers. "Where is everybody?" I thought out loud. Finally I gave up and decided to be productive in some way. I returned to my and Vallen's chamber, made the bed, washed my face, fixed my hair, and prepared a small purse with coin.

When I headed out into the city, I was on a mission to find more clothing. Two changes of clothes were not enough for me or Heather. I went from vendor to vendor looking for daily basics. A short while later, I had a mix of leggings, tunics, work dresses, day dresses, shoes, and womanly goods to keep us for a while. I had never really had the chance to enjoy shopping before, and even though I knew a battle was coming there was a strange comfort in doing something so mundane.

I passed a vendor that caught my eye. In his shop he had a number of pretty trinkets. I had never really been one for jewelry, but there was a tradition my father had carried over from his Human side. I ran my fingers over a collection of rings and found two silver bands. Each was inlaid with blue stones. They looked like waves in the ocean. I picked them both up and bartered with the merchant, then slid them into my purse for safekeeping and headed back to the manor.

When I arrived I was greeted by a household maid that seemed too happy to relieve me of the packages. I told her what was mine and what was Heather's and sent her on her way to see them all put in their proper places. I then proceeded to the kitchen to make a cup of tea and find something to eat. I was surprised to find Young sitting there eating lunch.

He looked up with a grin. "Good afternoon, sleepy head." His teasing was brotherly.

"Actually, I have been up and out of the house for a while now. I just returned." I plucked a slice of apple off his plate and plopped it in my mouth.

"Shopping?" he asked with a smirk. I ignored him and poured a mug of tea to sip on. "Get anything good?"

"Just basics. Heather and I had two sets of clothing each, so I just made sure we had enough to serve us a bit longer. I replaced the stuff that was in the packs we lost when we were captured and taken to Drakehaven." I thought of the rings. "I did buy something for Vallen though."

His eyes lit up. "Did you?"

I removed the small pouch from my purse and pulled the rings out to show him. "My parents followed the old Human tradition of wearing a ring to signify the binding between two mates."

Young gently picked the rings up and studied them. "So you accept my brother not only as your mate, but also your husband?" He turned the rings over in his hands. "The bands are very simple, but they are pretty."

I frowned a bit. *Would Vallen prefer something more ornate?* I wondered. Young must have read my face because he quickly amended his statement. "My brother's taste runs to simple elegance. I'm sure he will love the design. I couldn't have chosen better myself."

I let out the breath I had been holding and relaxed. "Where is Vallen?" I finally asked.

"He left about the same time I did. He mentioned checking on you and getting cleaned up. We were up early adding more wards to the existing barriers. We tried to do it before the staff arrived." He leaned down and took another bite of his food.

"Thanks, Young!" I said, turning towards the door. I tucked the rings back into their pouch and headed for the stairs. I mounted them two at a time, in a hurry to find Vallen. When I arrived at our chamber I found him brushing his damp hair. He sat bare-chested on the side of the bed.

Vallen smiled at me when I entered the chamber. He looked tired but otherwise in a good mood. "Good morning," he said. "You didn't have to make the bed. There are maids that do that."

I shrugged. "My father raised me to do those things for myself."

He motioned towards the closet. "I see you did a little shopping this morning." There was a strange grin on his face.

"What?" I asked playfully. "I only purchased basics."

He held up his hands. "Dragons collect treasure. Dragon women are known for their shopping prowess. I didn't know what to expect since I have seen my share of elaborate and ornately-dressed Fae. When I watched the maid put the items away I was surprised by your modest purchases."

I blinked, realizing that Young had no doubt thought the same thing. "Does it disappoint you that I made modest purchases? I think a simple life is best. Material items are nice, but they aren't what brings happiness."

Vallen's grin widened. "I'm not complaining. If you are happy with modest, then so am I. If you wish to be showered with trinkets and treasures, I will oblige." He held out his hand, inviting me to come sit with him. I accepted it and didn't fight when he drew me down to sit on his lap.

"I bought you something too," I told him, suddenly nervous. I pulled the pouch from my purse and handed it to him. "My father was Human, and so he and my mother observed the Human tradition of wedding rings."

Vallen's smile didn't fade as he reached into the small pouch and pulled out the bands. He looked at them carefully. "They are beautiful and I will proudly wear it. Are you saying that you wish me to be your husband as well as your mate?"

I bit my lower lip. "To me they are always one and the same. I would have us know peace, trust, and maybe someday love."

He slid a ring onto my finger then handed me his to do the same. "I would very much like that too."

In a motion so fluid I was taken by surprise, Vallen turned, rolling me on the bed and tucking me beneath him. I shoved at him, trying to slide him off. "I can't breathe," I gasped, giving him a nudge.

"Yes, but I am so comfortable here. I think I'm going to take a nap right here on top of you." I laughed, pushing on his shoulders as he pretended to snore.

Finally I gave up and wrapped my arms around him as best I could. "What is it with you and naps?" I asked.

"They are code for 'let's get Morgan in bed.' " He grinned, leaning down he to capture my lower lip between his teeth playfully.

"We could play Go Fish again. Or I could fail at Poker again," I offered.

He bit my lip harder. "Or, you could let me strip you down and make love to you before the city is consumed in fire, mayhem, and chaos."

"Or we could go do stuff to prevent it," I pointed out.

"We are as ready as we can be. The Dwarves and the rest of Everbloom's Royal Guard arrived this morning." He reached for the buckle on my belt, swiftly undoing it. He tugged the belt free, letting it fall over the side of the bed along with my purse.

"You look so tired. Maybe I should let you get that nap." I tried to slide away.

His hand slid up under the tunic and caressed my thigh. "Tell me to stop or that you don't want this, and I will roll over and take a nap now. Allow me to make love to you, and we can take that nap in each other's arms. Or tell me you want to just take a nap with me. Tell me what you want."

I breathed out. "I just want to make you happy," I told him as I struggled with a bit of embarrassment. It was hard to tell him what I wanted. Everything was so new I didn't really know.

"Yeah, like you are getting off that easy. I'm already happy." He moved to the side, shifting his weight off of me. "I want to please you and worship you as you deserve. I know you are feeling embarrassed because it's new and you aren't really sure about things."

I lowered my eyes. "I just don't want to be bad at it or disappoint you," I explained, my pride taking a backseat.

"You can't disappoint me by telling me what you want. Part of trust is believing that it's all right for you to confide in me," he murmured. "Start small."

I thought about what he said. "Kiss me," I said timidly.

"Where?" Vallen prompted.

At first I was going to say my lips but at the last moment I turned my head and ran my finger down my neck. "Here."

His hands stayed still, one resting on my thigh and the other on the bed. He lowered his head and pressed his lips to the tender flesh of my neck. He kissed, and lapped, and even bit lightly at the delicate skin. His mouth sent a shiver through my body.

"What else?" he prompted with a whisper just below my ear.

"Hold me," I said in a breathy voice.

"How?" he prompted once again. I guided his hands over me. I slid his hand on my thigh up to my hip and moved the other to the small of my back.

"Like that," I encouraged.

His hands slid over me and pulled me along the hard lines of his body. His fingers caressed and stroked me. I turned my head and offered him the other side of my neck. He lowered his head and ran kisses and nibbles along the skin. My breathing was becoming more shallow with each kiss. I reached up and pointed at the base of my throat and along my collarbones, which disappeared under the tunic.

Vallen moved with expert precision over the exposed skin. I pressed my body closer to his, encouraging him to go further but he didn't. I looked up into his eyes and realized he was waiting for me to direct him more. "Help me take off this tunic, please."

His grin revealed he was quite happy with this request. When he sat up, he grabbed the hem of the tunic and pulled it up over my head. He was surprised to find there was nothing beneath it. "Temptress," he mumbled, but waited for me to give the next direction.

"Caress me," I said, feeling the heat of my embarrassment cause my skin to glow.

"Where?" he asked, his grin growing wider.

"Wherever you like?" I said innocently, but he shook his head no. I pursed my lips together, feeling the color in my cheeks glow even brighter. Cupping my breasts I said, "Here." Then I ran my hands down my sides and over my hips and thighs. "And here."

Reaching out, he ran his fingertips lightly over my nipples. They tightened under his touch, causing me to suck in my breath. He caressed one and then the other as he slid his hand lower to massage and cup my hips and buttocks. I ran my fingers through his hair and urged his mouth down to my breasts. "Kiss here too." I was almost pleading.

He was excellent at taking orders. He ran his tongue through the valley between my breasts, then kissed his way to one pert peak, capturing it in his mouth. My fingers still held tightly to his scalp as my head fell back and I moaned at the sensation of him gently rolling my nipple between his teeth. "Vallen…" I whimpered.

He raised his eyes to look at me expectantly, my wet peak still clasped between his lips. "Yes, love?" he mumbled against my breast.

"More please… please…" I said, unable to put coherent thoughts together.

"Like this?" he asked. He leaned over and took my other peak between his lips, rolling it gently between his teeth. I moaned again, this time feeling myself pant.

I nodded yes, then shook my head no. I wanted more. He slowed down his pace and I almost cried out. "Don't stop," I pleaded.

"Words," he prompted. "Tell me and I will do it."

Frustrated, that I had to think, I released his head and ran a hand down my chest, down my abdomen and then touched myself at my core. I panted harder feeling even just my own touch. "Here, touch me here," I begged.

I started to pull my hand away but he caught my wrist and held it there. "What do you feel when you touch yourself here?" he asked. To illustrate his point he reached between my legs and ran a finger between my lips. I arched into his touch but he pulled away his hand and urged my own between my thighs. "Here, sit back."

He urged me to sit rather than kneeling as I had been. He then moved my hand between my spread legs. "Touch yourself so you can tell me how you want to be touched. Show me," he directed.

I ran my fingers over myself as he had done before. I could feel the heat radiating off of me, whether from desire or embarrassment, I didn't care anymore. I allowed my fingers to wander until they found my slit, which quivered under my own touch. Its heat was almost scalding and its wetness all but dripping. I ached to feel him touch me here and to fill me. I moaned as I slid a single finger inside. I was amazed at the feeling of my muscles tightening around me. I withdrew my finger and moved it to the bundle of nerves just above my opening and circled it with my finger. It caused a pleasant ache to shoot through me and I found myself moaning despite the fact Vallen wasn't the one touching me. "Here," I said in a breathy voice, spreading my legs wider so he could see. I circled my nub again, bucking against my own hand.

I looked up into his eyes and saw how he watched me. I could see the desire in his eyes and knew how much he wanted me. I lowered my hand again and slid a finger inside myself again, only this time I watched as the breath caught in his throat. Reaching between my legs he captured my wrist and pulled my hand away. He captured my other hand as well and pushed them above my head where he pinned them.

Then with his free hand he touched that area between my legs, and it burned like a fire so intense it was pleasurable. He caressed the nub above my entrance in maddening circles like I had done. I struggled against his grip, watching him as he pleasured me. I bucked against his hands and felt an intense burning growing hotter and deeper within me. I was gasping for air between movements, praying he would push me over the edge because words seemed like a distant memory.

Then the first hard wave of pleasure rocked me and I strained against where he held my wrists. I cried out in release but he continued the maddening circles until I couldn't breathe and was quickly swept overboard with another rush. I closed my eyes to the sensations. "Look at me," he urged, and my eyes flew open to meet his. As I met his gaze he pushed a finger deep into me. "So wet and ready." I moved against his invasion, mewing like a cat in heat, begging him with my eyes to continue. "Do you know why you feel so hot? Why your body is so wet right now?" he asked me.

I shook my head and found I struggled to speak. He slowed his pace and I wanted to cry out. I would need to answer if I wanted him to continue. "I don't know," I was finally able to respond.

His grin turned to one of almost wicked proportions. "Your body is telling you it is ready for me. It wants to accommodate me. It wants for us to come together." As he explained he began to stroke me with his fingers and the feeling of growing heat returned. He increased the speed of his hand's thrust until I no longer had time for breaths between. I tried to hold off and let the feeling grow. "Let me see and hear you release. You can find that with me." His gentle words were all the coaxing I needed and I cried out, feeling my muscles tighten around his fingers, but they kept moving and I found myself continuing to ache and grow hotter even in the throes of passion. "Tell me what you want," he prompted again.

Looking him in the eyes I could hardly believe my words. They were said with no embarrassment or fear. "I want to feel you inside me. I need you."

He smiled and released my wrists. When he withdrew his hand I almost moaned, until I saw him return moments later bared, enlarged, and standing at attention. He captured one of my hands and brought it to rest on his manhood. In a husky voice he held my hand against him. "This is how you know my body wants and aches for you. I desire you more than I ever thought possible."

He wasted time no longer, laying me back on the bed. He positioned himself between my legs and I moaned as he entered me deliberately, with control. I wanted to feel all of him right then, but he knew better, sinking slowly into me.

When he began to move in me it was leisurely and with purpose. As my moans and breathing became more erratic, his speed and force increased. I begged him for more. I wanted faster and deeper. I wanted to not only be pushed over the edge but dragged under and away. He gathered my legs against his chest so that my feet rested near his ears. Grabbing my hips he delivered just what I begged for.

I screamed in ecstasy, praying that it would never end and at the same time praying I found release soon, because I wasn't sure I would manage to stay conscious from the overload of pleasure. Just when I found I was unable to take another breath, I washed over. My body exploded with sensations and I felt like fire rushed over my skin as I screamed with a raw voice, announcing my release. Vallen's grip tightened and his speed increased. I opened my eyes so that I could enjoy his release. Blue flames washed over us as he tossed his head back and cried out with his own climax, spilling his seed deep within me.

He fell limply forward, gathering me into his arms and raining kisses down upon my face. "Thank you," he whispered into my ear as he struggled to regain his breath. "Thank you, my love." He stroked the hair from my face and tucked me under his chin.

I fell asleep listening to those simple words and finally accepting something I hadn't felt in years. I was finally home where I belonged.

Chapter Twenty-Seven

"I'm not saying the two of you can't enjoy your coupling. I'm saying you shouldn't do it loudly enough as to make your brother-in-law think something terrible is happening upstairs," Young argued.

"You could have knocked before barging in with your sword drawn. If you enter a bedroom without knocking you should be prepared for what you see," I snapped back.

"I only entered because I heard you and Vallen screaming," he countered.

Vallen and Heather quietly munched on dinner as Young and I continued our battle of words. "Pass the bread please," Heather said to Vallen.

He politely handed her the basket of dinner rolls. "Here you go."

"What did you think we were doing?" I asked Young, loudly.

Young shrugged. "We have enemies. For all I knew, an assassin had snuck in to kill you and my brother. I was protecting my family."

"Please! As if Vallen and I couldn't handle one little assassin," I spit out.

"Point taken but… I'm jumpy. Okay? We are just waiting around for an attack, that may never come at this rate," he growled.

I understood his annoyance because it matched my own. "Still, *I* was a virgin until recently, and even I knew the difference between giggles and squeaks from pleasure and full-out screams."

"YOU WERE SCREAMING!!" he yelled across the table.

Heather cleared her throat. "Will you two be quiet? I'm sure there is nobody at this table that hasn't walked in on someone during the act. Can we just drop it?"

I blinked at her and felt my nerves cool. "Fine," I grumbled and tore apart a dinner roll, stuffing it in my mouth.

"You started it!" snapped Young.

I shot up and motioned with my hand at him, looking towards Vallen and Heather. "See?!"

Vallen urged me to sit down. "I'll handle this," he said. Vallen looked across the table at Young. "Remember that time I came home for a vacation and caught you pleasuring yourself to pictures in some of Lady Jura's religious books?"

I choked on the bread as I tried to laugh and swallow at the same time. Young glared at me and his brother.

"Yes, you should have damn well knocked before entering."

"I will point out that at the time we still shared a room at the nest. Also, you were grunting and moaning. I thought you were sick or injured. I rushed in to help you and I caught you with your pants down, handling yourself." Vallen took a sip of wine as Young turned a brighter shade of red and sunk down lower on his chair.

"Yes, I remember. Can we drop it now?" Young asked.

"Nope." Vallen went on. "What about the time you decided to barge into my tent on the camping trip?"

Young rolled his eyes. "Ok, fine, yes we all make mistakes." Young turned to look at Heather. "Good luck with them when I return to my training."

She blinked at him in surprise. "What do you mean?" she asked between bites.

"I'm in what I hope will be my final year of training as a squire. Soon I will be a knight. Until that time, I train in another realm under Sir Leon, the knight that trained Vallen." Young pointed across the table.

"There's training to be a squire?" she asked.

Young almost choked on his wine. "Yes, there is training. Being a squire *is* the training to become a knight."

Heather looked at me. "Lady Morgan, you're a knight, right?"

I blinked and nodded. "Yes, I'm a knight. In the Fae court we use the term Dame for a female, but it is the same rank."

"Were you a squire?" she asked.

"Sort of. I trained under Prince Tallyn directly, but I wouldn't say I was his squire," I told her.

"What if I want to be a squire and not a knight?" she continued.

"I guess that is possible. Why would you want to be a squire and not a knight?" I was intrigued by her line of questioning. Especially since a few days prior she had declared herself my squire.

"Knights always have to be brave and strong. I don't think I can be brave and strong all the time, but I think I can learn to be most of the time. I am a good sidekick and squires are good sidekicks," she explained.

Young rolled his eyes. "I'm no sidekick," he corrected. "I am a hero. I just happen to be in training."

I laughed at his response because it was just so... squire-like. "Oh, Young," I sighed, before looking at Heather. "You can't be a squire. You don't kiss ass or do windows," I teased.

I swear I saw smoke come out of both Vallen and Young's ears. "Now wait a minute," Vallen cut in. "There is a lot that goes into being a squire and kissing ass is only a tiny part of it. The window part was never a factor for me, but I can't speak for Young."

Young growled at us both. "I don't do windows and I don't kiss ass."

"If you don't kiss ass then you have more than another year of training ahead of you, my boy." I looked at Heather. "I wouldn't count on him being knighted anytime soon."

She looked at me, very confused. We all bickered back and forth for a bit. Finally Heather stood up and slammed her hands down. "I'm not joking! I want to be a squire. More to the point, My Lady, I want to be *your* squire."

I blinked. "All right, can you explain why you want to be my squire?" When Young laughed I shot him a look that had him sinking in his chair again.

Heather paused for a moment. "Before you, I thought I always had to be weak and a coward. I thought I needed to run away from everything, but then I met you. Nothing scares you. Even when you don't know what to do, you just handle it."

"I'm scared most of the time," I said flatly, and she looked at me with shock. "I just learned that fear can't be something that stops me."

Heather breathed. "I want to be good. I want to do what is right," she said. Young started to say something, but Vallen held up a hand to stop him. "I think you can teach me to be a hero. I think you already inspire me to be a better person than I am. You believe in me when nobody else did or does. I may be a very bad squire, but I swear I will try harder than anyone else to be whatever you think I should be. Please, teach me."

I looked at Vallen and he nodded. "She sounds serious to me."

I looked back at Heather. She stood up and walked with purpose around the table to kneel before me. She took my hands in hers. "Lady Morgan, I pledge my life to you. I will be at your command. Teach me, train me, and I swear I will always be your sister."

Young rolled his eyes. "You're doing it wrong," he said. He stood and joined Heather, kneeling beside her. He drew his sword from its resting place on the chair back and placed it in front of her, reaching around and placing her hands on its hilt. I rested my hand over hers. "Repeat after me, Wolfgirl," Young directed.

Heather nodded.

"I, Heather, swear on my life's blood to honor your words and training. I will live by your commands. Defend as you defend. Live as you live and die as you die." Young nodded at Heather and she repeated the words, her eyes locked on mine.

Young continued. "I swear to uphold the teachings of chivalry. I will be kind, honorable, truthful, brave, and faithful. I will be faithful to my Gods, my king, my family, and to you. My blood is yours to spill if I should ever fail you." Heather swallowed hard, but nodded as she repeated the words. I could see she meant every last one of them as she spoke.

I smiled down at her and sighed. "I, Lady Morgan, Dame of the Fae court and Guard to Queen Mab, proudly accept your oath of fealty. I will take you as my ward and keep you safe. I will train you to be your best and push you harder than you have ever known. From this day forward, my name and house will protect you in fealty, honor, and by the sword. This I swear."

"Now lean forward and kiss the sword," Young whispered. Heather took a moment to respond but did as directed.

"Am I your squire now?" she asked, so innocently.

"I would say you are." I smiled at her.

Young sheathed his sword and held out a hand to help Heather to her feet. "Now what?" she asked.

"Now we finish dinner," I told her.

She sat down and reached for another roll in silence. I had just started to eat my bird when there was a

Dragon's Guide to Slaying Virgins

knock. A small maid opened the door and stepped inside. I resisted the urge to point out to Young that *that* was how you knocked on a door.

"My Lord and Lady, Captain Lucius is here to see you," I exchanged glances with Vallen and immediately all four of us were on our feet as the loud, broad-shouldered man entered the room.

"My Lord," he said, glancing at Vallen. "My Lady," he mumbled quickly. "An army has been seen approaching from the west. There are no signs of the Iron Warriors yet, but it wouldn't surprise me if they mounted their attack later in the battle once they have worn us down."

I thought about what he'd said for a moment. "No, Simon will lead half the charge and Avery will lead the other half." The captain turned to look at me.

"Who is this Simon?" he asked gruffly.

"Avery's mate. Before he was her mate, though, he was my fiancé and second in command." I looked at Vallen to see what he was thinking.

Vallen nodded. "That would match Avery's style of warfare as well."

The Dwarf looked back and forth between us. "Then what would you have me do?"

"Captain, take your men and part of the Guard from Everbloom to defend the west wall. Send the Dwarves and the rest of the Guard to the south wall.

They will attack there second because it is the weakest point of defense. Vallen, you should lead the battle to the south wall and gate. I need approximately four men to help me hold the east wall. Because of the mountains they won't come at us from the north, but some of the men in their team are trained at infiltration and taking a lot of people out quickly."

The captain started to ask how I knew and stopped. "Some of these men used to be yours?" I nodded. His face softened just a little, realizing that I was going to kill men that I once called friends in order to defend his city. "They turned for the money, My Lady. They were never your men if they could be bought so easily." It was the first time he had addressed me like he meant it.

"I know." I looked at Young and Heather. "Heather is with me. Young, are you going with your brother, the captain, or me?" I asked.

"You're asking me?" He seemed shocked.

"You're a hero, right? I think it's time we heard what you have to say," I told him.

"These two don't need me there, but you may need my sword and fire. I will have your back." I smiled at the Dragon. It was refreshing to know that we could yell at each other one moment and be family the next.

"I need at least two more," I told them. "They need to be light on their feet and preferably at least one of them a decent shot."

Captain Lucius nodded. "I have just the lads. I'll have them meet you here in ten minutes." I nodded and watched as he turned with his orders.

I looked at Vallen and threw my arms around him. "Kiss me," I whispered, and he dropped his head and claimed my mouth obediently. "Come back to me, Lord Dragon. I've grown far too attached to you to lose you now."

"Be careful with my heart, trickster Fae." He smiled before turning and leaving as well.

"Young, I think I need to visit the armory," I said, not willing to waste any more time. He snapped to it, directing us out of the house and into a nearby building.

"I'm sorry, I'm not sure what we have for armor," he said as he opened the door.

I quickly found some light leather leaf armor, which the Dragon scoffed at. I pulled the chest piece on and Heather began lacing it closed as I secured the shoulders. Next, I tugged on some bracers before buckling a quiver to my hip. I handed one to Heather as well and helped her quickly secure it. I slid a sword into my belt and a dagger into my boot. Grabbing a couple bows, we made our way out the door and back to the meeting place in time to catch the two men the captain had sent.

"Everyone follow me," I said, leading them towards the stairs that would take us atop the east wall. We climbed quickly, and when we reached the top I realized Young was in full armor. I needed to remember to ask him about that. I would love to be able to don armor so quickly.

"My Lady?" asked the boy with the bow.

"You, I, and Heather will spread out the length of the east wall. There will be a team of mercenaries coming, between eight and twelve in size. Start shooting and send up the alarm. If they make it over the wall, many will die. These aren't your typical highwaymen, these are trained killers."

"You're sure, My Lady?" he asked.

"Yes, because I trained them myself." He paled, no doubt from the tales spun by my new squire.

We spread out along the wall, with Young and the other lad standing between us archers. We stayed low and avoided moving as much as possible. Across the city we could hear the cry of attack. I sent up silent prayers, hoping that Vallen would be safe.

We were still sitting in silence when twenty minutes later, the sounds from the south side of the city carried to us and I knew Vallen now had his hands full. "Be safe, Dragon," I whispered again.

"My Lady?" I heard the lad who wasn't an archer ask. "Are you sure?"

"I'm sure," I told him. Just then my eyes caught movement along the tree line. I motioned to the others. We all peeked through the slots. Sure enough, there were men advancing slowly on the wall. I had been wrong about the number, however. We faced easily two dozen mercenaries.

"When they get in range, focus on the archers first. Swordsmen, any hooks that come over the wall, sever the rope. We are far more outnumbered that I would like, but we will do this. Failure is not an option. If we fail, our families and loved ones die."

Everyone nodded. I nocked my first arrow and took a deep breath. Quickly popping up, I let it fly for the first man I saw with a bow. I was rewarded with the familiar cry of pain as it lodged in his chest. Ducking quickly, I watched as three arrows came over the wall. I grabbed them from where they landed, spacing them between my fingers, and returned them. My first arrow missed, my second caught an archer in the shoulder, and the third went through the throat of the closest ropeman. I ducked as two more arrows came over the wall, one just missing Young's shoulder by an inch.

I looked down the wall as Heather bobbed different directions to take her shots before dropping down. The other young bowman did the same, but spent far more time huddled low. By the time the first hook came sailing over the wall, we had successfully downed ten of the men, most of whom were archers.

I called down the line. "Focus on the ropemen now. I will clean up the last of the archers." Taking a deep breath, I rose and took a shot, taking out one of the remaining archers. As I did I heard an arrow cut through the air towards me. I turned just in time for it to catch me in the shoulder and not the head. It pierced the heavy leather armor and my skin, but only barely. It wouldn't even require stitches. I dropped to one knee, pulled the arrow free, ignored the concerned look on Young's face, then hopped back up to return the arrow to its owner. It caught him in the arm. I drew my own arrow and this one found his chest.

I turned my attention to a ropeman to the left of Heather. I buried three arrows into his hide armor before getting one of use. "Young, pick up that hook!" I commanded.

He saw the rope I referred to and ran at it, slicing the rope as the man was within feet of the top. He fell several stories to the ground below. Down the line I heard a gut-wrenching cry from the young swordsman as he tried to defend the archer. I looked at Young. "Protect Heather!" I commanded, and ran down the length of the wall, drawing an arrow as I went. The young archer huddled with his hands over his head. His friend lay dead beside him. I let the arrow fly into the back of the man who had just come over the wall.

The man jerked and yelled in pain, spinning around to face me. I released another arrow that plunged deep into his chest. He looked down at it and snapped it off, appearing to be unaffected by the wound. Tossing my bow down, I drew my sword, aware another man was coming up behind him.

He lunged forward at me, swinging his sword. I brought mine up confidently to meet him and watched as he was knocked back a step. Pushing forward, I continued to press him until he blocked the path of the man behind him. I looked for my opening and found it. I stepped in close, using my speed, and pulled my sword through his weapon arm. The arm and sword hit the wooden slats of the top of the wall. I then threw all my weight into him, knocking him over the wall. His friend behind him tumbled backwards and managed to get a hand on top of the wall, preventing his fall.

Our eyes met just for a moment and there was the recognition of someone I had fought beside. "You're alive?" he whispered, just before I severed the rest of him from the hand that saved him. He fell to his death below. In the next swing I cut the rope that hung from the hook. The man climbing it fell, but not far enough to hurt him.

I turned and looked at the archer. "Either man up or get off the wall. You are too much of a liability."

The lad sniffled. "My friend is dead," he said, and burst into tears.

"Mourn him later, but for now don't let his sacrifice be in vain. Seek vengeance for this moment." I turned, running down the walkway to where another hook had come over the wall. I sliced through it in time to look up and see Young taking on two men. Another was within feet of Heather.

I ran down the wall again, swinging my sword with deadly strength as a man reached the top of the wall. I sliced through his neck, sending his head, followed by his body, to the ground below. I then swung my sword, cutting the rope and watching the man that was behind him also take a deadly fall.

"I'm out of ammo," Heather said, releasing her last arrow. I reached into my quiver and pulled out the handful I had left and handed them to her.

"Just keep going," I told her, as I turned and kicked the assailant on Young's left. The man stumbled back, and quickly realized I was the more serious threat. I met his next two blows as he brought them down on my sword. I heard the familiar sound of a downed opponent beside me, catching sight of Young as he pulled his sword free. He turned and plunged it into the ribs of the man challenging me.

There was a gurgle of pain and my assailant dropped. I looked at Young and sighed. We nodded the wordless message of, "I'm okay," before darting around to take care of the next batch of hooks. There were already two more men on top of the wall by the time I got to the newest hook. One threatened the other archer, who was once again huddled on the ground, and the other was behind me. I heard Heather scream but saw Young step in to engage the man who threatened her. I rushed the man in front of me, slamming him into the nearby torch post.

He grunted in pain and staggered backwards, turning to face me. I cut the nearby rope, not bothering to see if anyone was on it. I looked at the archer. "Run!" I commanded, and watched as he followed the order. The man I now faced was almost twice my size. He had to be half Orc.

He swung a heavy axe in my direction and I dove out of the way, rolling to safety. The axe buried itself deeply into the wooden slats as it missed. I took advantage of the moment and brought my sword down hard on the axe's handle, splintering it. The monster of a man swung around, angrily batting at me. I ducked under his arms, trying dodge past him. He captured my waist and lifted me off the ground.

Over his shoulder I could see where another two men were about to hit the top of the wall. I pointed my sword towards the heavens, gripped it with both hands, and with all my strength struck the man in the top of the head with the pommel of my sword. His skull crunched under the blow and blood splattered the air, blurring my vision. The man released me and staggered before tumbling backwards off the wall.

I rushed forward, plunging my sword deep into the back of the man nearest Heather, ignoring the man behind me. As I did I felt the familiar whoosh of an arrow flying by me. Both men fell dead at the same moment. I looked up to see I looked up to see Heather standing with her hand still raised from the arrow's release. When I looked over my shoulder, an arrow stood straight and proud from the man's skull. I looked back at her. "Good girl!"

Young's grunts reminded us we were still engaged in battle. Heather drew her dagger and rushed forward, burying it deeply under t arm of Young's assailant and drawing it down his side. He turned on her, swinging wildly and screaming in pain. Heather shifted and lunged at him, knocking him to the ground and going for his throat. I turned in time to see the last of the men coming over the wall. I raised my sword to meet him.

"Hello, Uther!" I said with an edge of anger. The Werewolf stopped when he saw his sister in Wolf form and covered in the blood of an enemy. She growled at him. He tossed his sword to the ground and held his hands up. Heather shifted back and picked up his sword.

"Friend or foe, brother?" she asked with menace.

He looked confused. "I'm a friend?" he answered, sounding unsure.

"I don't have time for this," I said, and clocked him hard in the jaw. My hand screamed in pain but it had the desired effect. He slumped to the ground unconscious. "Search him and secure him," I said quickly, glancing over the wall to make sure the coast was, in fact, all clear.

When I looked back, Young had tied him to a post in a sitting position. "That should keep him out of trouble for now," he said. "Now what?"

I turned and surveyed the city. "I'll take Heather to get more ammo and then head to the south gate. You head over and help the captain."

He nodded and the three of us tore down the stairs off the wall, headed for our targets. After refilling our quivers and picking up another bow for myself, we headed to the south wall. I only hoped Vallen was still alive and holding strong when I arrived.

Chapter Twenty-Eight

When we arrived at the front gate we came to a screeching halt. Two Iron Warriors did battle on top of the rubble that was once a gate house. Soldiers, citizens, and bandits crowded the streets in a clash of arms with one another. I looked for the thickest pocket of the enemy and figured my mate was probably at the center of it.

My intuition had not led me astray. I found a heavy cluster of bandits gathered into a circle, cheering. "This can't be good," I mumbled. I looked at Heather. "Stay close, we're going in." Reaching for my sword I drew it and took a deep breath. I kicked the closest bandit in the arse and gave a battle cry. He and three of his mates whirled around to face me with a growl.

He looked at Heather and drew his dagger. "Why did you have to go and do that, doll? Now we just have to rough you up before we go back to watching the sport."

"You can try," I taunted.

He pounced at me and I shook my head. After the men we had just faced, this seemed almost too easy. I snapped my sword at him, knocking his dagger to the ground. His friend charged me and I drove my blade deep into his belly. Pulling it free, I countered the next man's attack, leaning out of the way as

Heather let an arrow fly the short distance into his heart. The first man recovered his dagger, swinging it at me from where he was on the ground. I sidestepped his attack and connected my knee with the back of his head. He tumbled forward and I stepped on him to avoid Heather's next mark, which was the fourth man. He yelped as the arrow buried itself into his groin just before I removed the hand carrying his sword.

At this point the crowd that had gathered had split their attention between what was happening at the center of their circle and the wrecking ball busting through them. We continued to push our way through half the circle until it finally parted. While we were still under attack, I was at least able to see what was going on.

Vallen, Geren, and two Elven Guards stood at the center, defending against at least a dozen attackers. "Idiots," I sighed, disemboweling the next thug who was foolish enough to approach me with a weapon. Heather and I continued our push through the crowd, clearing away much of the circle. When we reached the inner group of thus, they were bloody, injured, and only standing because of luck and adrenaline. Meanwhile the Dragons and Elves looked no worse for the wear.

I spun an assailant around to face me instead of Geren. He sloppily took a swing at me and it was hardly worth the effort of killing him. I looked at the four foolishly fighting. "Will you four stop playing with your food and end this?" I snapped angrily.

All four of the trained warriors glanced around at the trail of bodies that seemed to follow me, then finished their fights. Vallen stepped forward to look at me, scanning for any possible injuries. He zeroed in on my shoulder. I held up a hand. "It won't even need stitches."

"The east wall?" he asked.

"Has been secured," I told him.

"Young?" The question in his eyes was mixed with fear.

"At the west wall now, helping the captain hold ranks. The east wall had more men attacking then I expected, but we held it without fail." I turned and looked at the Iron Warriors. "What's going on there?" I asked.

"The enemy had three Iron Warriors they were able to get here. One of the Dwarves scaled the side of one of them and took control. We've been trying to do the same with the others, but since they are engaged in battle it's been too difficult for anyone else to make the climb."

I looked at the machine carefully. "Can you guys clear the ground around it?"

"Of course." He yelled orders for a group of Dwarves to take the area around it. They charged in with a fierce battle cry, causing several of the bandits to drop their weapons and run.

"Good! Have a pilot ready to take control of it so we can take it around to the west wall." He looked me in question. I looked back at Heather. "Follow me and give me cover while I climb."

We pushed our way through the crowds of people, taking out enemies as we needed to. When we arrived at the base of the machine, I pulled the remaining arrows out of my quiver and handed them to Heather before unclipping it and the bow. Sliding my sword into my belt, I looked back at Heather one last time. "I am more proud of you than I have been of anyone in my life. Keep your elbow even and both eyes open."

She called after me, wishing me luck. I charged at the machine, jumping up and grabbing hold of its moving parts. I moved as quickly as I could, searching for handholds that wouldn't cost me my fingers. A few times the machines clashed and I fell part of the way down, causing me to scramble for any hold that would save me. Now that they were operational they stood at their full heights and towered above the city walls. I finally caught hold of the bottom edge of the cockpit and pulled myself up.

The pilot was too deeply engrossed in battle to notice I was in the cockpit with him until it was too late. I shoved him away from the controls, hard. Grabbing the bars above me, I swung my feet and kicked him. He almost tumbled out the other side of the cockpit. With my feet under me, I drew my sword and swung. I narrowly missed him as he pivoted out the door and onto the face of the machine to avoid my thrust. Before he could recover I thrust through the window and pierced him deeply with my sword. He tried to retreat, but threw himself backwards into the air, where he fell to his death before being crushed by the other machine.

The pilot in the other Iron Warrior pointed to my left side where a Dwarf quickly joined me and took over the controls. "Are you staying up here for the ride, My Lady, or do you want down first?" I pointed to the west wall and held on tight as the machine lurched forward, following the other Dwarf-controlled Iron Warrior across the city, crushing enemies underfoot as we went.

When we arrived I could see the panic on the faces of the guards who were doing their best to defend the city. Their fear turned to cheers of support when they realized the two machines that had arrived were there to pound on the third. I looked at the pilot who drove the machine I was on. "How close can you get me?"

He blinked. "You can't be serious?"

I grinned at him. "As serious as they get. I can make the jump. Trust me."

"My Lady, if something happens to you…" he tried to argue.

"Then I died fighting the good fight and defending people who needed my protection. Tell my Dragon I think I loved him." I turned and used the same handhold the earlier pilot had used before I killed him. I got my feet under me and climbed higher, to almost the top of the machine. It jerked wildly under me, but I crouched low and held tight, waiting for my chance.

It came just seconds later. The other Dwarf-controlled machine plowed into the machine we were attacking, knocking it closer. With only three steps for momentum, I pushed off the cold metal surface. I focused on pushing away from the ground and feeling weightless. I stretched my body out as far as it would go and pictured my hands catching the other machine.

When my fingers met the cold metal they tightened in a death grip and I started pulling myself along the cold surface. I felt the familiar sting of an arrow as it dug into my thigh, but I was too close to let it stop me. I climbed into the cockpit and didn't even give the pilot a chance to see me. I grabbed my sword and ran him through until he fell, sword and all, out the other side.

I looked at the controls in front of me and after a few moments figured out how to at least move it in a general direction. Cheers from the wall and the other machines went up as a horn sounded and the bandits began a hasty retreat. I led the charge with the Iron Warriors and followed them. Behind me our own troops regrouped and also decided to give chase.

Across the open expanse of land we chased down those who retreated. On the edge of the field I saw a tower that had been erected and I knew that was where they were headed. Suddenly out of nowhere, a boulder came flying at me. It hit the machine I was in, rocking it side to side, but I managed to keep it upright. I began moving it side to side in a zig-zag pattern, hoping that it work for boulders like it did for arrows. I managed to glance behind me and noticed the other machines were doing the same thing.

The next boulder missed me altogether but a third followed close behind, clipping the left arm of my machine and knocking it loose. The whole machine rocked again and I did my best to keep it upright. Luck was surely with me, because it lurched forward, still moving steadily. The boulders changed targets, focusing on the machines behind me. I pushed all the levers forward and the machine sped up. I intended to ram the tower and bring it down.

As I got closer, I left the machine running and began climbing down it, doing my best to get secure hand and footholds as it moved at full speed. At about two stories up I pushed off and hit the ground rolling. I stopped just in time to watch the tower crumble to rubble under the momentum of the Iron Warrior.

All around me people swarmed into battle. The Dwarves were fierce warriors and seemed to bowl over all who opposed them with little resistance. I watched as men and women were rounded up and captured or slain based on their response to being surrounded. When the last of the battle seemed to die down, I sank to the ground, snapped the arrow in my thigh and waited. I knew it wouldn't take long for one of the Dragon boys to find me.

Sure enough, Young showed up and dropped onto the ground beside me, holding out a canteen of water. "Thirsty?" he asked.

I accepted the canteen, taking a long swallow. The water helped me clear my throat and find my voice. I took another drink, wondering if I had ever had water that tasted as refreshing. Finally I handed it back to him. "Thank you."

He took a sip and was silent for a moment. After a while he spoke. "I have never met anyone like you, Lady Morgan. At first I thought you were insane in the Troll's home, and then I thought you were brave, but now I know you're just insane."

I smirked. "Was it the leap of faith or climbing off the fighting machine that convinced you of that?"

"Actually, I think it was when you took out the Orc with the pommel of your sword that convinced me.

Watching you jump from one machine to the other just confirmed it. I haven't even seen Elves make jumps like that, and they're known for being crazy." He patted me on the back.

"Do you think your brother saw it?" I asked, wincing at his pat. I was starting to realize just how bruised and beaten I was.

"If he didn't, I'm sure he has heard about it." He sighed and leaned back in the grass.

Soon Heather found us sitting on the grass and collapsed on the ground between us. "I am so tired."

Young reached out and pulled her close so she could rest her head on his shoulder. I grinned knowing the two had developed a fondness for one another.

Geren and Vallen soon appeared, staring down at us. "Lazy bums, the lot of you," teased Geren.

"Lord Geren, I wasn't aware you were going to come join the battle?" I had only known the Dragon a short time, but he had been kind and almost brotherly from the first moment I met him.

"I couldn't let you have all the fun. Besides, you couldn't have paid me to miss seeing the Lady Fae Knight in action. I think you may even be able to take on Vallen or Princess Alizeyah." He chuckled.

I didn't know much about this mysterious Princess except that there was angry outrage as well as deep respect for her. Either way, I was sure in time we would eventually meet. I turned my attention to Vallen. "Did we get them?"

He smiled. "The city is safe. Very few citizens were actually lost in the battle. Avery, Simon, and a few men did escape, but now it is just the work of hunting them down and serving out justice."

I was annoyed that Avery had slipped away again, but had no doubt that her and Simon's days were numbered. Vallen held out his hand to me. I accepted it and winced, sucking in air as he pulled me to my feet.

"I thought you said it was a mild injury?" he asked, looking at my shoulder.

"That is," I assured him. Then I pointed to my thigh. "This, however, is a bit deeper."

He looked down, alarmed. Gathering me up into his arms, he slipped an arm under my knees and carried me over to a nearby horse. He lifted me to sit on its back before mounting behind me. He spoke briefly to the captain, who beamed at me with pride as we rode by. "I think I liked it better when he hated me," I mumbled.

"Who?" Vallen asked.

"The captain. I don't really know what to say when he's being nice. I handle rude and surly better than I handle polite and respectful from men like him. Now

I'm going to feel obligated to get to know him." I sighed heavily.

Vallen chuckled and held me close to his body as we rode. Soon we were back in the city. Citizens were already working on repairing buildings and the walls, clearing the rubble, and cleaning up. Many waved and thanked us as we passed by. When we arrived at the manor, he lifted me off the horse and carried me inside.

"We're home," I whispered, not even trying to hide my pleasure.

"Do you really like it here?" he asked cautiously.

I shrugged, looking around. "It's nice, but I'll be happy anywhere. We can stay here, go back to the Nest, or find a little cottage in the realm near where Young trains. It doesn't matter. I haven't really had a home since my parents passed away."

He looked down at me. "It really doesn't matter to you?" There was something that almost looked like hurt in his eyes and I thought I understood.

"As long as we are together, I *am* home." He paused, looking down at me. "So you really want to stay with me?"

"Of course. You're my mate and husband. Why wouldn't I want to stay with you? I've become rather fond of your snoring. I'm not sure I can sleep without it," I teased.

Night gave way to morning. Vallen helped me bathe and get bandaged up. The shoulder wound, as I expected, was hardly anything. It had already closed by the time we got me undressed. The thigh injury did take a few stitches, but even that was not too bad.

We heard Heather and Young come in, but both of us were too tired to actually go downstairs. Since neither seemed to be on their death beds when we left them, we assumed they would survive until all of us had gotten some well-deserved sleep.

Chapter Twenty-Nine

Our minor injuries healed quickly. After a few days' rest and the expert care of the healers in Maht, I could comfortably say none of us were suffering any long-term effects.

The captain's entire attitude had changed towards me. He now not only recognized me as an equal, but came to me with questions that he used to ask Vallen. When he recounted the battle, he told others about my selflessness, courage, and "Dwarven" spirit. I always blushed at his praise and thanked him for his kind words.

I spent my mornings working with Young and Heather in the courtyard. The two had become almost joined at the hip since we had first arrived in Maht. Young still needed a lot of work for his squire training, and Heather needed even more. Young was skilled with a sword and decent with a bow, but he needed improvement with both. Heather had been a surprisingly good shot from the moment she first picked up the bow, but was more of a danger to herself with a sword than to others. Then there was the little issue of both of them on horseback. I shook my head. We had a great deal of work to do.

My afternoons were spent running errands, running a household, and running a city. Vallen had left on some mission right after the battle without much of an explanation other than he would be back soon. He had promised we would go after Simon and Avery together, but I doubted that more the longer he was gone.

Soon the day came when Everbloom's Guard and the Dwarven detachment finished helping us rebuild the city and wall. Vallen had been gone for nearly two weeks and I doubted he would be back to see them off. Never having been in a position where one would show thanks on behalf of an entire city, I was unsure of the customs or traditions. I paid the Everbloom Royal Guard wages for their fight and sent home a shipment of Fairy silk, Maht cheese, and a personally written note of thanks to the royals who had kindly loaned us their aid.

The Dwarves refused payment, saying it had been their duty to resolve the issue of the Iron Warriors and that they had learned a valuable lesson from the experience. *Fae are crazier than Elves, never go to war with Queen Mab.* They did, however, accept a cart of locally brewed ale and wine from the North to take home with them. They promised to drink it and sing praises of the Fae Lady Knight who fought like a Dwarf, moved like an Elf, and was beautiful enough to be one of Queen Mab's handmaids.

After a rather long and late-running celebration to send off our heroes, I retired to the chambers Vallen and I shared. I had taken to reading at night. The books that Vallen kept told stories from every race imaginable. I learned about Dragon, Elf, and Fae origins. I studied the teachings of Arcane magic as written by Mages. I learned about Human realms where the technology was so advanced that the need for magic had died from the world.

Every night was the same, though. I would fall asleep hoping and praying he would return, and every morning I awoke alone in the large bed. I leaned my head back against the headboard and ignored the swimming feeling. I had consumed too much wine at the party and would no doubt pay the price tomorrow. All I wanted in this moment was for him to come home. I had almost dozed off when there was a knock on the door.

"Enter!" I called out. I expected it to be Heather or one of the maids. Instead, Young entered my room and came to stand by the bed.

"Lady Morgan?" He looked concerned. "Have you had any word from my brother?"

"No. I was told he had a mission to attend to and that he would be back as soon as possible." I recapped the little bit of information I had been provided, trying not to take out my irritation on the little brother.

He nodded. "He had told me he would be back in a week's time. It's been over two. When I saw you going about things normally, I just assumed you'd had word that he had been detained."

I pursed my lips. My stomach was feeling more and more unsettled. "Has the captain had any word?"

"None that I know of, but we have also had a recent report of Avery and Simon being spotted in the mountains to the north of here." He was clearly hesitant to tell me this information.

"Do you know where your brother has gone?" I asked.

"After the battle my brother mentioned something about possibly regaining his Dragon Fire. It was a gift he traded away to…" He trailed off, afraid he had said too much.

"Yes, so that Melody's soul had another chance at life. Do you think he went to check on Dani?" I asked.

"I don't know. I do know that Princess Alizeyah is very protective of her and the two are the best of friends. If she is safe with anyone, it would be with the Princess," he said with a shrug.

"Tell me about the Princess. Everyone talks about her, but all I have heard is that she is the Princess of Everbloom. I must admit I am a bit confused." I reached out and urged him to take a seat in the chair near the bed.

He took a deep breath and thought hard for a moment. "Princess Alizeyah was a Changeling left in the Human realm of Tarell for her own protection.

She is the daughter of Lady Jura and the Elven King Leonide. Being both Elven and Dragon means she is a unique balance of both Darkness and Light. She is also the Soul Mate of Lord Hudraer. He's sort of the unofficial Dragon Prince."

I could tell he was trying to simplify what seemed to be a complicated story. I urged him to continue. "Why does Vallen have such mixed feelings about her?"

Young nodded, finally understanding what I was asking. "You know the lake under the Manor?" I nodded. "It's a gateway to the Forgotten Realm. It's connected to the Great Lake that leads to the afterlife. Part of our bloodline's heritage is to protect the lake. Once you're dead, you're supposed to stay dead." He cleared his throat. "Lord Hudraer was killed protecting Alizeyah. Most Soul Mates go mad and die without their other half. Alizeyah walked that thin line between madness and sanity. She broke Dragon law, used the gateway here in Maht, and retrieved Hudraer from the afterlife."

"Wow, isn't that impossible?" I asked. I had heard legends of those who had tried.

"It should have been. Vallen carries a grudge and even I do, a little. We have mixed feelings on the topic. We are the first Dragons of our bloodline to fail at preventing such an act from happening. On the other hand, Hudraer was like a brother to us and Geren. His return to our world has been joyous as well. Very few have seen him since his return the world of the living." Young shook his head and smiled. "For as angry as I am that she would break our laws and customs, I think I respect her a little more for what she did."

I thought about Vallen and the anger and longing his eyes always held when he talked about the infamous Princess. Based on what I now knew, I still couldn't form an opinion of her. I would just have to wait until I could meet her face to face.

I changed my focus and went back to thinking about Simon and Avery. "Young, can you give orders to have our horses saddled, bags packed, and provisions ready for morning?"

Young blinked a few times, processing what I was saying. "Are you going to go meet the Princess?"

I shook my head. "No, we are going to go after Avery and Simon."

"Shouldn't we wait for Vallen to return?" he asked.

"We have a lead on them and right now we have no information on where to find Vallen. I need to give the people of Maht peace of mind knowing it's over." I clasped my hands together in my lap.

"Do you really believe that we are a match for the two of them?" Young seemed unconvinced.

"I'm not sure, but I know I can't live with the constant need to look over my shoulder."

Young nodded. "All right then. I will send word to the captain tonight. I want us riding with at least a few guards. I will let Heather know we leave in the morning and see that preparations are made." I watched as Young stood and left the room with a little bow.

I left the bed and went to Vallen's desk. Rummaging about I found a quill, ink, paper, and his seal. I sat down and began to pen him a letter.

My Dearest Vallen,

If you have found this letter you know I am not in Maht at this time. Avery and Simon have been seen to the north, fleeing into the mountains. You've been gone so long that I fear the worst, but I will make sure the people of Maht are safe and the gateway here stays protected.

If for some reason I shouldn't make it back from this adventure, I want you to know that the times I have spent with you are some of my most treasured memories. I know your heart lies with another, but also know that my heart will forever lie with you. Perhaps the real reason nothing ever happened with Simon was because my heart always knew it was waiting for you.

Though it happened too fast and I thought it was anger at the time, I believe I may have loved you from the first moment we argued in Agshi's house. Thank you for all that you have done.

All my love always, Morgan

I stared down at the letter for a moment before folding it and sealing it with wax. I returned to bed and left the letter on top of his pillow before closing my eyes and trying to get my last good night of sleep for a while.

My dreams were fitful, showing me visions of things I never wanted to see. Vallen lay broken, bloody, and dead at the feet of Avery with his heart grasped in her blood-soaked claw. I flew up to a sitting position, gasping for air and taking in the knowledge I was in bed within the Manor. I went to the kitchen and had a cup of warm water and honey, trying to calm my nerves.

Once I finished the warm drink and my hands were no longer shaking, I returned upstairs to my bed. I pulled the covers up tightly around me and closed my eyes. I tried to focus on happy thoughts that would allow me to sleep easier, but the dream had unsettled me enough I realized that any sleep I got the rest of the night wouldn't be peaceful.

Sure enough when I awoke the next morning, I had been correct in my assessment. I had consumed far too much wine the night before and was paying for it. My stomach did flips and my head swam. I picked at breakfast, eventually settling on some toast and tea, hoping the combination would settle my stomach.

Young, Heather, and I ate in silence, reflecting on the mission we would set out on. When halfway through the meal there was a knock on the front door

I excused myself, expecting it to be those traveling with us. What I found instead was the captain holding Uther by the arm with his hands bound in front of him. "Good morning, captain. I can see by the present you bring me this is not a social call."

Captain Lucius rolled his eyes skyward and shoved Uther into the foyer ahead of him. "We caught this one stealing from a vendor last night and trying to sneak out of the city. Normally he would be put in the stocks for a few days then made to work off his debt, but knowing he was your squire's brother I thought I would bring him here first and see what you want done."

"Heather? Can you come in here?" I called for the girl. Heather and Young both came out to meet the captain and Uther. Young seemed shocked and Heather looked ready to kill him without even hearing what had happened.

"What did you *do*?" she snapped at him. Uther lowered his eyes to stare at the floor in shame.

Young patted her shoulder to calm her down. I looked at her and in a steady voice explained, "You brother was caught stealing last night, then tried to flee the city. Typically the punishment called for is the stocks and community service. The captain holds you in high regard and so thought it better to come here before doing anything."

Heather marched over the Uther and placed a finger under his chin, lifting it so he met her eyes. "Explain yourself, immediately. Why didn't you just come here if you were hungry or needed money? I would rather sell my possessions then have you return to a life of crime. When we released you after the battle you said these days were in your past." This was by far the angriest I had ever seen Heather.

"Everyone here still treats me like a child and a thief," he complained.

"Did you even try looking for a job? What about offering to just help out?" she asked.

Uther shrugged. "Jobs are boring. Why should I help out and not get paid for it?"

Heather reached up and smacked him on the top of the head. "Really? How are you five years older than me?" She took a deep breath to calm down. "If you help others out, the community will see you are trying to change. It would make it easier for them to trust you with a job."

"Why would I want a job?" he asked. "I don't want people telling me what to do all the time."

"And how is that different than being a thief? When you work in a band there will always be someone else calling the shots. If you are in charge, someone is always going to want to put a knife in your back. Take my advice, older brother. Work hard, learn a trade, and then open your own shop." Heather looked back at me and shrugged. "Is that unreasonable?"

Young cut in. "Not at all."

Heather looked at Uther and sighed. "Part of your problem, and it was part of mine too, is that we never had to face consequences for our actions. You need to learn people won't always bail you out." She faced the captain. "What is the normal amount of time in the stocks and the hours of community service?"

"Two days in the stocks and a number of hours equal to the cost of what was stolen," he said.

Heather pursed her lips. "An example needs to be made. First that this behavior isn't tolerated even by family, and second so that he will learn his lesson. Please put him in the stocks for three days and double his community service. I want him to always remember that there are consequences. Honest hard work seems like a good place to start."

The captain looked at me for approval. I nodded. He turned to leave after wishing us luck on our journey, but Heather stopped him and asked him to wait. She ran to her chamber and returned with a small purse. She pulled out two gold coins and handed them to the captain. "Please make sure he is fed, clothed, and provided for while we are away. I would hate to think he would try this again because he lacked the basic necessities of living."

I beamed with pride. My little Wolfy had learned some major life lessons over the last few months. It is a lot easier to stick to the right path when someone believes in you and you don't have to worry about where your next meal is coming from.

Uther was escorted out of the manor. His eyes were filled with shame but I had faith he would learn from this experience. I returned to the dining room, catching an exchange between Young and Heather. He pulled her into his arms and held her as she buried her face in his shoulder, teary-eyed over the decision she had made for her brother.

I rolled my eyes. I was not looking forward to Young's return to Sir Leon. I had a sneaky feeling that Heather would be near impossible to deal with for the first month. Already my head spun with plans to keep her busy and distracted.

"Morgan?" Young asked. His forwardness took me by surprise. I had given him permission to drop the title, but this was one of the few times he had actually done so. I looked back at him. "We'll be ready to leave within the hour."

I nodded. "Good. I'm as ready as I'll ever be," I told him. I decided to skip the rest of breakfast and return to my chamber. I just needed a piece of Vallen to take with me, I told myself. Something to feel connected to him.

I entered the closet and sifted through his belongings. I wasn't really trying to be nosy. I ended up finding the pack he had carried when we first met. Inside was the magic torch with its extra fuel supplies, a spare tunic, and the blanket we had shared. The pack was small enough it wouldn't add extra bulk, really. I added extra bandages, ointment, and needles before cinching it closed. I tossed it over my shoulder, happy with my discovery, and headed to the stable to make sure Slayer wasn't overly weighted down with the new armor Vallen had ordered for me before he left.

Slayer nuzzled my hand after chomping into the apple he found there. It was hard to believe that this gentle giant had once been a horse that frightened local farmers. Now he was a spoiled stallion with a mature palate for apples. He loved them all but clearly favored some over others. "You ready for another adventure, friend?" I asked him as I held up another apple for him to munch.

"He's going to get fat if you keep feeding him like that," Young said as he entered the stable. He turned to speak with the lad who had prepared the horses. He had acquired a new mount for Heather to replace Dabble, who we had lost on our trip to Drakehaven.

I led Slayer out into the cool morning air. I was all too aware that as the day went on it would grow hot. Summer was in full swing now and if we hadn't been heading into the mountains to track Avery and

Simon, I would most likely have taken my chances without the armor. I looked up at the sky and sighed heavily before pulling myself up into the saddle.

I watched as Young and Heather mounted up. Neither would be what I could ever call graceful, but Heather was no longer afraid of horses, so that was at least a start. I led the way out of the city, trying hard not to think about how I was going up against some of my most dangerous opponents with only two squires for backup. At the last minute I had decided against taking two rambunctious guards who looked like more trouble than the squires. "Where are you, Vallen?" I wondered quietly as we left the safety of the city walls.

Young rode slightly ahead, guiding us down a series of roads and paths that would lead us ultimately into the mountains and away from our comfortable existence. A large mountain range started about half a day's ride north of Maht. Its lower foothills actually rolled down to almost touch the north wall of the city. To avoid ending up being pushed into the Blott pass, we had to ride partially out and around the foothills to pick up a road that would lead us up into the mountains themselves.

"How much further?" Heather whined as we continued to push our horses up a steep incline.

Even as an accomplished rider I was feeling the strain of the day's ride on my body. We had stopped briefly in a foothill town for lunch before continuing on our way. I looked up at the sky, seeing that the sun wasn't yet ready to set. "Maybe another hour or two," I told her. "Then we will look for a place to break camp for the night."

Young pointed to a ridge at the top of the mountain we were steadily climbing. "If we can reach that ridge, there are a series of caves up there that would offer a safe place to stay for the night."

I glanced at Heather who huffed, blowing her hair out of her eyes. She looked at me and nodded. Looking back at Young, I smiled. "Sounds good. By then I will be ready to be off this horse."

Sure enough, it took us another two hours to reach the ridge, and when we did the sky was already turning shades of red and orange as it said good night to the sun. Young led us to a cave that was deep and cool. It had a place to tether the horses within and was tucked back behind a rock, obscuring it from view.

The only concerning part was the remnants of a recent fire, hoofprints, and other signs of use. I looked at the fire circle that remained. "It's no more than two or three days old. Someone was here recently. Let's hope if they come back, they're friendly."

Young and Heather disappeared briefly to find firewood while I unloaded and cared for the horses. While I waited for their return, I decided to take a closer look at our accommodations for the night. I pulled the magical torch from Vallen's bag and explored deeper into the cave.

The ceiling dropped lower and lower the deeper I ventured. I was about ready to turn around when I noticed a space small enough to crawl through at ground level. I would have left it be, but it looked like it had specifically been carved out.

I knelt low and listened for a moment. There didn't seem to be any sound coming from the hole, but there was an air current. Taking a deep breath, I crawled along the corridor for about ten feet. Reaching the end, I shone my light into a large cavern. Carved into the walls was a spiral walking path that wrapped up into the mountain and ran deeper below it. Deciding I would rather go up than down, I followed the path, trying not to look over the edge to the deep drop.

The path was steep and in areas a bit narrower than I was comfortable with, but something drew me onward. At the top, the path led out onto a flat surface where the sky shone brightly above. Stars twinkled overhead, and for a moment I felt almost overwhelmed with how tiny I was in the world. I was about to turn and return the way I came, but I saw something carved into the stone nearby.

I approached the stone, running my fingers over it and shining the light across it. I peeled back a bit of moss that had overgrown and exposed the carving.

"VALLEN" was carved into the surface in an old Draconic script. I wouldn't have recognized it had it not been for it being scribbled on the inside cover of all his books. I smiled as I touched it, feeling a connection to him. It seemed like a lifetime since we last saw each other.

A thought suddenly occurred to me. "*What if* the last person here was Vallen?" Young obviously knew of this place, and the rock proved that Vallen did as well. Perhaps he was only a few days ahead of us, also hunting for Avery and Simon? Hadn't he promised, though, that we would go after them together?

Realizing I had been gone longer than I wanted, I carefully made my way back down the narrow path to the carved corridor. I hurried back through and almost ran back out to the entrance of the cave. I was panting when I arrived to find Heather and Young cuddled up beside one another, cooking some of the supplies we had brought with us.

"Where did you come from?" asked Heather.

"You found my brother's thinking place, didn't you?" Young asked.

"What if the last person here was your brother?" I blurted out.

Young considered the words for a moment. "If it was him, then we need to leave by first light."

"Why?" I asked.

"After Melody was killed, he refused to come here anymore. It hurt too much," he explained. "Did you see the pathway that leads down into the cavern?" I nodded. "That's where he laid her ashes to rest."

"I'm suddenly glad that I chose to go up and not down," I told him.

Young shrugged. "This place has never bothered me. It has always felt peaceful to me."

I looked at Young. "Would your brother go after Avery and Simon without me?" I asked pointedly.

Young shifted around uncomfortably. "Do you want an honest answer or the one you want to hear?"

"I always want to hear honesty," I told him.

"When we started this mission together, yes. I have no doubt after he saw you hold your own he would have let you go with him. Then you almost died from the Dragon's blood and he had flashbacks of Melody. After that you had your binding ceremony and despite his efforts, he started falling hard for you." Young shook his head. "I fully believe that he had every intention of taking you right up until you proved how truly reckless you were with your stunts with the Iron Warriors. He didn't see you make those jumps and climbs like I did. Instead he had to hear about them and imagine them."

"That's not fair," I argued.

"Like how he wouldn't let you throw your life away to be Virgin Soup? Or that he willingly, and might I add happily, bound himself to you to prevent your death? Morgan, my brother doesn't care about what is fair, he cares about what is right. I guarantee you that he thinks it is wrong to let you take a risk like this." Young held out a mug of hot tea for me.

"Then why are you here?" I asked.

He thought about it for a moment. "I would have been just as willing to bind myself to you for a lifetime because I see the good in your heart. I don't know where my brother is, or if he is even after Avery and Simon right now. I do know he wouldn't let you do this alone, and since he isn't here I will guard you with my life, because he is my brother and I love him and he loves you."

"He doesn't love me," I said, pushing the theory away. "I believe he is very fond of me, but I don't think he loves me yet. Love takes a long time to build."

"Are you saying you don't love him?" Young countered. I couldn't maintain eye contact with him. I looked down at my hands. "That's what I thought," he said.

Heather had stayed unnaturally quiet through the entire discussion. I turned to look at her and she squirmed under my stare. "Tell me," I commanded.

She sighed heavily. "Vallen was here recently. I can still smell his scent."

"Can you tell how recently?" I asked.

She shook her head. "Not in this form, but I can tell you that I recognize other scents here as well - including Simon's."

"I'm going to kill him," I said flatly as I climbed to my feet.

Young jumped up to his feet preventing me from exiting the cave. "Where do you think you're going?" he exclaimed.

"To find your brother and give him a piece of my mind. He's going to wish he had left me to be Virgin Soup when I'm done with him." I attempted to push past Young but he wrapped his arms around me. "Let go, Young!"

"If you go out there now you could easily fall off the side of a mountain and die." He tightened his grip around me.

"Then he can put my ashes here and not visit me either," I argued, pulling against him again.

"And what if he is in trouble and you are the only person that can save him? Are you going to let him die because you couldn't control your temper?" I felt like he had struck me.

"Do you think he is in trouble?" I asked.

"Vallen told me he would be back almost a week ago. It can't be a good thing when something causes Sir Dragon Stick in the Mud to be late." Young loosened his grip on me and I sank to the ground, shaking.

"What if he is in trouble because I wasn't there to help? I should have been there and he shouldn't have gone without me." I pounded my fists against my thighs in frustration.

Young lowered himself to the floor in front of me, wrapped his arms around me in a hug, and let me sob out my anger, frustration, and fear.

Chapter Thirty

I awoke the next morning before either Heather or Young. Heather had shifted into wolf form and slept more on top of me than beside me. Young had an arm under my head and a protective hand on Heather's back. I stifled a laugh about how this would be the weirdest threesome ever.

I nudged Heather off of me towards Young, then carefully sat up, trying to avoid waking them. If I could get most of our belongings packed and the horses fed, it would mean an easier and quicker departure. Vallen was somewhere nearby and I had every intention of finding him as soon as possible. He could be upset with me for coming, but I would gladly face his disappointment if it meant I knew he was safe.

I marched over to the horses and filled their feedbags, strapping each one in place. I then ran a brush over their backs, checked their feet, and made a quick check that they were in a position to carry us up the side of mountains again. As I walked away, Slayer bumped me with his head. I paused long enough to give him a quick snuggle.

It only took me a few moments to gather and pack our belongings. All I needed now were the squires to be awake enough to ride and we could leave. I walked to the cave opening and peered out.

It was still dark and the stars were shining overhead. The closer to the horizon they were, though, the more faintly they glowed. The softest glow started to show behind a distant peak, causing the sky around it to turn a medium blue. The sun would be up in about an hour and I really did want to be out of here at dawn's first light.

I looked back over my shoulder and decided I would let them sleep just a little longer. I was past the point of being able to rest peacefully. I knew I wouldn't feel that again until Simon and Avery were no longer a threat and I was wrapped in Vallen's arms. I almost gagged myself with the romantic dribble. Its sweetness caused my jaw to tighten and ache. "Yep, I think it was the moment I saw you at Agshi's," I told myself. I looked down at my hands and stared at my ring.

Young stirred first. He clenched his fist open and closed, trying to regain feeling. He slid carefully out from under Heather so as not to awaken her and climbed to his feet. He scanned the cave, quickly finding me where I stood near the entrance. His hair stood out at odd angles as he approached me, eyes still heavy with sleep. "Why are you awake so early?" he asked.

I shrugged. "I just couldn't sleep."

"You're worried about him. I can see it in your eyes." He turned and looked out at the slowly lightening sky. "Give me a moment to go take care of things and I will start packing up and preparing the horses."

I smiled. "Go do what you need to. I've already handled the other stuff."

"You can wake up Heather while I step away," he offered.

I smiled mischievously. "Oh no! You're the hero. You get to awaken the furry beast."

He shot me a dirty look but stepped out of the cave and disappeared someplace nearby. While he was gone, fortune smiled and Heather woke up on her own. Not bothering to shift into her Human form, she padded past me out the cave entrance and also disappeared. She returned before Young and shifted as soon as she was safely hidden within the cave walls. "For the life of me I will never understand what takes men so long to get ready," she mumbled to herself as she dressed.

Within the hour we were mounted and riding steadily up and across the ridge. At the top of the first crest we found a bridge. A sign to its left warned about riding no more than two horses across at a time. For safety's sake we crossed one by one. The bridge felt solid underfoot, but why tempt fate?

Soon the sun was high in the mid-morning sky. Its heat beat down on us and even at the higher elevation I was sweating under its rays. When I looked at the others, Young seemed no worse for the

Isabelle Saint-Michael

wear but Heather was dark red and panting. At the
first patch of shade we found, I called for us to take
a break and water the horses as well as the Werewolf.

I poked Heather's shoulder and she hissed at me.
"Ouch, why did you do that?" she complained.

"You have a sunburn," I explained, pulling a small
jar of ointment out to smooth over her skin.

Young looked confused. "I didn't know someone as
darkly complexioned as you could burn."

She glared at him. "Of course I can burn. Uther
burns every summer, and he's even darker than I
am."

She breathed deep as I gently worked the ointment
into her damaged skin, then pulled my white tunic
off over my head. "Trade shirts with me," I told her.

She looked at me, confused, but pulled her top off.
Young looked away from both of us, blushing
brightly. "What good is this going to do?" she asked.

"The white cloth will reflect the light and the longer
sleeves will protect your skin," I told her, then
tugged her sleeveless purple tunic over my head.

"Then won't you end up sunburned as well?" she
asked.

"I'm less likely to burn than you since I'm half Fae.
The sun nourishes me and gives me strength. My

Human half burns, though. If need be I have another long-sleeve tunic with me I can pull out." I smiled at her as she lifted a canteen of water to her lips and drank deeply.

I looked over my shoulder at Young. "It's safe to look again. Our breasts are covered," I teased him.

"I don't see why respecting your bodies makes me a target for mockery," he complained.

"You're my little brother now. That alone makes you a target for teasing. I don't really need a reason." I gave him a wink before sitting down on the ground and also drinking some of the water.

When we and the horses were all properly hydrated and both Heather and Young had returned to more reasonable colors, I suggested we continue on our way. Young and I rode side by side on the wider sections of path and Heather seemed to be in her own little world, lagging behind.

Finally I turned and in hushed tones asked Young, "Are your intentions with my squire honorable?"

He jumped so high he almost slid off his horse. Casting a nasty glare in my direction, he looked over his shoulder at Heather. "She's just a kid," he scolded me.

"By Dragon standards, so are you," I pointed out.

Young shook his head. "It's not like that. She's like a little sister to me. Besides, I'm the second-born son.

Before I can even think of relationships, I need to finish my squire training and spend several years as a knight, building my reputation and Dragon vault."

I blinked. "I wasn't suggesting you take her home and complete a binding ceremony. I was just making sure you weren't going to toy with her heart."

Young rolled his eyes. "There are women who are looking for a short-term good time and there are those you wait for and build a relationship with. The first group is looking for sex and company. Heather is the second type, and until she gets older I can't even consider it one way or another."

"Werewolves, much like Humans, consider their children adults when they hit eighteen," I pointed out.

"Has she told you she fancies me?" he asked flatly. "Or is this my new sister-in-law playing matchmaker when she shouldn't be?" I gave him my best shocked look. He squinted in my direction and rolled his eyes. "You're a terrible actress."

It was my turn to huff and roll my eyes. "I can tell she likes you."

"You'll forgive me if I don't believe you. You couldn't even tell my brother loves you or that Simon was playing you. It may sting to hear, but I don't really consider you an expert in this field." Young sure was cranky.

"Fine, don't believe me. Just do me a favor. If you care nothing for her, make sure you aren't accidentally leading her on. I know firsthand how much it hurts." I nudged Slayer and passed Young, taking the lead.

As the sun started to sink into the sky, I noticed puffs of smoke in the distance. I pointed them out and Young confirmed that there was in fact a small mountain town ahead, but that we should also be careful because of the Orc tribes that lived in in this area. "They aren't exactly known for their hospitality," he explained.

"I see. Do you think we can make the village before dark?" I asked.

Young stared at the distance and looked back at me. "We can make it tonight, but we would be traveling after dark. Is that a chance you want to take?"

I took a slow breath. "If we break camp before dark, will we be out in the open at night?"

"Probably," he said.

It's amazing how your opinions of risk change when you are suddenly responsible for others. If it were me by myself, then I wouldn't worry about camping out in the open. Even if Vallen was here. Knowing that Young and Heather were my responsibilities somehow changed things. "I think it would be better if we got to the town tonight. We should push ourselves to use as much of the light as we have left."

"Are you afraid of being out here alone at night?" he asked.

"No, I'm afraid of being out here alone with the two of you," I explained.

Young was silent for a long moment. "You have seen me in battle. I'm not a child you need to protect. I can be responsible when I need to be."

I nodded. "I know, and I'm counting on you to be just that. If something goes wrong I want you to keep Heather and yourself safe and get out of there."

"I thought you wanted me to come as backup?" he asked.

"I do," I said. "I also want you to be a good knight and follow orders. Can you do that?"

It was his turn to be silent. He turned and looked at Heather, who seemed to still be a bit out of it. "I will protect her with my life. I swear this to you."

"That's all I ask. I plan on coming home from this adventure, but I always like to have a backup plan," I said.

"Was being eaten by the Troll a backup plan?" he teased.

"Yes. Yes it was. The plan before that was telling a bunch of Werewolves that their kilts were really pretty skirts," I said, grinning.

"And you survived that?" he said, wide eyed.

"Yup, with hardly a scratch." I beamed, remembering the brawl. It had been a good fight.

"Do me a favor. Next time you get a hankering to explore your death wishes, leave me out of them." He sighed. "Why you chose my boring and grumpy brother I will never know."

We crossed two more bridges before the sun began to set. If we could just make it up and over the next ridge. Then we would get to the town without mishap. Behind me Heather whined. "My butt hurts, are we there yet?"

"Sounds like a personal problem," I teased. "Maybe an hour after nightfall."

"Can we stop for a few minutes? I really need to get off this horse and take care of things." I almost made a lewd comment, but thought better of it. When we finally found a wider spot in the road, we each took turns dismounting and taking care of things. My things involved checking a map and pulling out a heavier tunic for warmth.

After a brief argument we convinced Heather to get back on her horse and continued the journey. The night brought a darkness that made it far more difficult to navigate some of the narrower parts of the road. We were forced to ride single file for the last hour or so. I took the lead and Young brought up the rear.

I was just beginning to question if Young really knew where he was going when I saw the lights of homes and buildings ahead. Resisting the temptation to push Slayer to ride faster than I knew was wise, I continued on with caution. Thoughts of a bath, bed, and a hot meal called my name. Soon the road widened as we entered the mountain town. A sign at the heart of the overgrown village read, "Torc."

"Towns and cities in this realm have some weird names," I mumbled as we rode through the gates of the inn. An Elven lad who looked no more than twelve summers rushed forward to take our horses and help us unpack. We each shouldered the bulk of our gear and walked into the noisy first floor of the inn, which doubled as a pub. Nobody really seemed to notice our arrival, so I walked to the bar and flagged down the bar keep.

A short Dwarven fellow with a thick brown beard and matching long hair approached. He regarded us for a moment. "Well, aren't you a ragtag bunch. Let me guess, you want a room too?"

"Too?" I asked.

"Yeah, another Dragon arrived just before nightfall wanting a room and a bath," he explained.

"That is wonderful news," I exclaimed, not hiding my excitement. I looked back at the others. "Two rooms please," I said.

The barkeep shook his head. "We only have one room left, but it is a large room," he said.

"We'll take it," declared Young, stepping in and paying the barkeep. "If you would be so kind as to arrange for a bath and hot food to be brought up, we would appreciate it."

The barkeep looked at the payment and smiled. "Absolutely, My Lord. You and the ladies will be comfortable, I'm sure." The barkeep turned and yelled over his shoulder. "Millicent, show these three up to the suite."

A small Fae woman appeared beside us. Her hair was a combination of green and pink that reminded me of a spring meadow. She smiled warmly and asked us to follow her. We climbed up two flights of stairs to find ourselves on the third floor. There was one other door in the hallway and it sat directly across from our room. "Is that the room the other Dragon is in?" I asked hopefully.

The maid looked confused for a moment, then looked at Young. "Oh, yes. Perhaps a friend of yours?" she said.

"That's right," I said cheerfully. Heather lingered in the hallway for a moment before joining us in the suite.

Isabelle Saint-Michael

Millicent showed us where a few of the necessities of the room were and then answered the door as three lads carrying buckets of steaming water entered. They filled the tub that sat behind a red silk screen and then excused themselves, only to return for a second time a few minutes later before leaving for good. "I will have dinner sent up to you immediately, and when you are done with the bath, let us know and we will have the water removed for you."

"Thank you for your hospitality," I told her as she left. I looked back at Heather and Young. "Would either of you like the first bath? I can wait until they can bring more water."

Young motioned towards the tub. "By all means, go first. I know you are dying to wander across the hall and talk to my brother."

"What about you, Heather? Fancy taking the first bath?" I looked over at the Wolf and she still seemed preoccupied. I reached out and touched her shoulder. She jumped and spun around to face me.

"No, go ahead. You know how I feel about baths," she told me.

Smiling widely, I grabbed soap and a towel and went to cleanse myself. I made short work of it once I heard the food delivered. Quickly rinsing away the remaining bubbles, I stood and wrapped the towel tightly around myself. "Hey, save me some," I told the others as I rounded the silk screen.

What I found chilled my blood to ice and caused my heart to almost stop. Standing less than ten feet away from me was Avery. Young was doubled over on the floor and Heather was pressed against the Dragon's body with a knife to her throat. "Well, look at this. I thought it was strange when the maid told me my friends had arrived and were staying across the hall. I thought she was talking about Simon and his pets."

"Let her go, Avery!" I commanded

"I thought when we lost the battle at Maht that my plans for revenge had all come to an end, but fate has smiled on me. I have both of the Lake Dragons *and* the witch that stole my eye." Her vile grin split her lips. "This one is just an added bonus. I can't kill her screw-up brother, but at least I can slit her worthless throat."

I held up my hands. "Leave the kids alone." I had caught the part where she mentioned having Vallen, but I didn't want to let her know we were mates just yet if she didn't already know.

"I don't think so. See, I learned last time that you don't give much regard for your own life, but others…. Your selflessness will be your undoing." Her words were filled with menace. "Boys!"

The three lads who filled the bathtub appeared once again. "They work for you?"

"Anyone can be bought if the price is high enough." She said to me, before turning to give them orders. "Tie her and the Dragon up. Make sure it's extra tight. She is a Fae, after all, and a trickster."

"Big words for a Dragon that fakes her own death and steals someone's fiancé," I taunted back.

She seemed amused. "Stole him? Is that what he told you?"

"Why else would he have turned his back on me and his people?" I winced as the ropes cut deeply into my wrists. As long as Heather or Young were in danger, I couldn't do anything rash.

"Oh, sweet girl." She cooed at me. "Simon and I had been promised to each other for over one hundred years. He played you in hopes that he could get in good with Prince Tallyn or Queen Mab. He wanted power and title before we were wed."

"I can see how well that worked out for you," I spit out. "He took advantage of a young girl's emotions and you are a traitor to one of the oldest orders of knighthood. You're both cowards and traitors who have no honor."

She rushed across the room, letting go of Heather. With a clawed hand she gripped my throat and slammed me against the back wall. "What do you know of honor? What do you know of sacrifice for an order that *never* gives back?"

"Everything!" I growled back. "I know everything about it, but I still choose the path of good, honor, and bravery."

She drew back her hand and with a snap of her arm and a sharp pain the world around me went dark. I fought to stay aware of what was around me but my consciousness faded away and all that was left was oblivion.

Chapter Thirty-One

"Wake up, My Lady." Cool hands pushed the hair from my face and carefully examined my jaw.

"Vallen?" I asked, as my vision attempted to return.

"No, common mistake. I'm the younger and more handsome brother." Young chuckled.

"Young?" I glanced around and found we were surrounded by stone walls and a heavily barred door. "Where are we?" I asked.

"Some old Dwarven keep be my best guess," he said. I accepted his hand to help me sit up. "How are you feeling?"

"Like I would have rather spent the night with the Orcs," I told him. "Where is she keeping Heather and Vallen?"

"Vallen?" he asked.

"Yeah, she said something after they knocked you out. Something about having both of the Lake Dragons." I struggled to my feet only to realize I was clothed only in a tattered towel. Young saw my concern and pulled off his tunic and handed it to me. "Thank you," I said as I tugged it over my head.

Young looked confused. "I don't know where either of them are. I haven't seen or heard anything that would make me think Heather is here at all."

A knot formed in the pit of my stomach. I felt all the blood drain from my head and my limbs felt heavy. "Oh no!"

"What's wrong?" he asked.

I looked at him with unmasked sorrow. "What if Avery…?"

"Don't think like that. We need to focus on getting out." Young grabbed me by the shoulders to steady me.

"Well, isn't this sweet?" I turned and glared at the door. Simon stood on the other side with a smug grin on his face. His eyes swept over my exposed legs and came to rest on my bosom. "You know, I think I liked you better in just the towel."

"Pervert!" I screamed.

"Oh Morgan, you and I both know I am far worse than that." His eyes darted to Young. "Has anyone ever told you that you look like your brother? You're both handsome men. Perhaps I could be persuaded to keep you around a little longer. I could always use another pet."

Young looked repulsed and I couldn't say I blamed him. "Where is Heather?" he demanded.

"Oh, the cute little Wolf girl?" Simon asked. He sighed heavily. "It would seem she was slowing down Avery's escape, so I believe she was dropped off the side of the mountain. Such a waste, if you ask me. She would have made a fine pet as well."

Young staggered back until he hit the wall of the cell and sank to the floor. My heart wrenched at the knowledge that I had failed to protect her.

"You monsters!" I spat angrily and rushed at the door, shoving my hands between the bars, dying to grab hold of him. I just wanted to hurt him like he had hurt the people I cared about. Simon taunted me by standing just close enough for the very tips of my fingers to brush the cloth of his tunic.

"Perhaps if you had been this eager to touch me while we were engaged, this situation would never have come to pass," he joked.

"Avery told me you were promised to her long before meeting me. Don't think you can play mind games on me now." I gave up trying to reach him through the bars and focused instead on killing him with my eyes.

"True, I would have still been bound to her, but she and I both have our own playthings. She doesn't always like the sort of games I play. I could have kept you, and you could have been one of us," he reasoned.

"I would never turn my back on my order, my people, or my honor. That's the difference between you and me, Simon. I've always been willing to work for it and you just wanted it handed to you." I pictured my hands around his throat.

"See, there you go again with your high morals. I have a fun game." He watched me carefully. "Give yourself to me and I will let you choose one of the Dragons to set free."

"Avery would never allow it." I felt my face twitch in a grotesque smile.

"She doesn't wear the pants in this union - I do," he declared. I heard Young move behind me.

"I have a different offer," Young said. "Let my brother and Morgan go and I'll stay as your pet."

Simon grinned widely. "I could let Morgan go, but if you're staying as a pet then your brother must die."

I turned and glared at Young. His face was hard and his emotions unreadable. "No, my brother must go free."

"I'm sorry, I can't make that deal," Simon said. He turned to walk away.

My voice cracked as I spoke. "Simon, let me see Vallen." He stopped and turned to face me.

"Why would I do that?" he asked.

"Because you owe me that much." I felt the tears slide over my cheeks. "My squire is dead, and you plan to kill Vallen and me both. I mourned you for six months. I tried everything I could think of to die an honorable death. I was even going to let a Troll eat me." He looked at my tears and I could see something inside him move. "All I'm asking is five minutes with my mate. You can be there, but I want to say goodbye."

His eyes narrowed on me. "You've never been a docile creature. How can I trust you?"

"I've never been in love before. Not like this," I told him.

He growled. "Put your wrists together." I followed his orders and he reached through the cell door and bound my hands. He looked at Young. "If you try anything I swear I will make you watch as I violate her." Young took a step back at his words, horrified.

When the cell door swung open I obediently stepped outside and allowed him to grab my elbow and force me through the halls. The keep had a simple enough layout. It was square and two stories tall, with an upper row of doors that looked down into a great hall. We descended to the lower floor and crossed the hall. Ducking through the kitchen, Simon threw open the door to what had probably served as the pantry.

With a shove, he propelled me through the door and slammed it closed behind me. A single torch illuminated the room. On a table on one side of the stone room lay Vallen, stretched out and secured.

His body was covered in bruises and welts where he had been beaten. I bit back the sob that threatened to surface.

"Vallen?" I said, in a voice little more than a whisper. At first I thought he was asleep, but then his head turned and I could see where his beautiful face had been bloodied. I rushed over to him, dropping to my knees and resting my head against the table.

"Morgan?" he coughed. "What are you doing here?"

"I could ask you the same thing." I shook my head. "I only have a few minutes. I don't want to spend them arguing."

"Young?" he asked.

"Is safe for now, but being held in a cell with me. Heather is…" I couldn't say it.

"Shhhh, it's ok. Do whatever it takes to get out of here. Don't worry about me. Just escape," he told me.

"I can't leave you," I told him.

"Morgan, they're going to kill me for revenge and for what is mine. Escape, save yourself. Once they have the gateway they will forget any little vendetta they have against you. They'll have won." He forced a smile. "It will be all right. Forget me."

"I can't forget you. I can't leave you." I tried to blink away tears. "I love you. I would rather die together today then spend hundreds of years without you."

He sniffled. "Didn't I save you once from throwing your life away over some guy?"

"You aren't some guy. You're my mate, my husband, my world now. Where you go, I do too." I bit my lip.

"Please, Morgan. Take our child and escape," he pleaded.

I blinked at him in astonishment. "Our child?"

"When last we lay together there was Dragon Fire. I gave mine up for Melody's soul. Our union created the babe that you now carry. It's why I couldn't bring you with me." His eyes were filled with a mixture of sorrow and pride. "I love you, *My* Lady Morgan."

As if on cue Simon swung the door open and smirked at us. "Time's up."

I was dragged back to my cell. I put up very little resistance. This new revelation weighed heavily on me. When the door closed behind me, the loud noise seemed to snap me back to reality.

"Lady Morgan, have you seen my brother? Is he all right?" Young asked.

I shook my head. "They've beaten him and weakened him. We need to escape and save him, Young."

"I'm open to any ideas you may have," he said, motioning to the door.

"You don't happen to have a nail or something I could use to pick the lock, do you?" I asked.

Young patted all of his pockets and then stopped. He reached down to his shoe and pulled out a tiny green pouch. When he opened it and shook its contents out onto his hand, I was surprised to see the same nail we had used to escape at Drakehaven. "Heather gave this to me the day of the battle at Maht. She said it was her new good luck charm and it had helped her before."

I smiled at it, then held out my hands to him. "Think you could untie me so I can get us out of here?"

Untied and frustrated, I struggled for almost an hour before I heard the lock click on the door. I retrieved the nail, handing it back to Young and making a mental note to tell him about where it had come from if we survived this new adventure. Taking a look around as best I could before opening the door, I gave it a gentle push, only opening it far enough for us to squeeze out.

"Where's Vallen?" he whispered near my ear.

"In the pantry, which is down the stairs, across the hall, and through the kitchen," I said.

"They sure didn't want to make this easy, did they?" he commented.

I shrugged and began sneaking through the corridor that would lead us to the stairs. We were unarmed and facing highly trained opponents. We also had no clue how many little lackeys may be running around the place. I started looking around for anything that could be used as a weapon.

At the top of the stairs, mounted on either side, we found a stone axe and a stone sword. I looked at Young, who picked up the axe as I lifted the sword from where it was mounted on the wall. It was far heavier than the swords I typically used, but the edge was sharp and it would no doubt do damage to the person who found themselves at the other end.

Crouching low in hopes of avoiding detection, we crept down the stairs into the hall, pausing at the bottom to see if we were alone. Instead of an empty hall we came face to face with a horrific scene. Stretched out on a wooden frame hung Vallen, his body slack and bare. Avery stood behind him, whip in hand, meting out vicious strikes.

With each crack Vallen's body jerked violently, but he refused to cry out. After a few more blows she stopped long enough to take a drink. "It didn't have to be like this, Vallen," she said. "If you had just returned my feelings, none of this would have happened."

"I didn't know," he whispered. "It wouldn't have changed things, but I would have tried not to hurt you."

"Ha! Like you could see beyond that little whore of yours!" Avery spat angrily.

I felt like that was a little cruel. After all, I had been a virgin until Vallen. I started to say something, but Young stopped me.

"Melody was your best friend. I thought you might have even been in love with her yourself," Vallen tried to explain. Pain was written on his face as he gasped for air.

"Melody? That useless little twit? She stood between me and you. Of course I pretended to be her friend. I played her little games. She knew how I felt about you." Avery growled, a puff of smoke escaping.

"Melody couldn't have known. She loved you. She talked about you like the sister she never had," he argued weakly.

Avery laughed. It was the sort of sound that sends chills down your spine. "She knew, because I told her. Right before she died."

"You saw her?" he asked, his eyes growing wide. "Why didn't you tell her to leave? She was an innocent, you should have protected her."

Avery stopped laughing. "There you go again with all that hero speak. When we were younger, that was a total turn-on for me. Now it just makes you sound like a tired song."

"You were a Knight of the Order. It was your duty." He looked angry but I don't think anything could have prepared any of us for what came next.

"I would have protected her from anyone else because her death was for my pleasure alone. The look on her face as I slipped the dagger covered in my own blood between her ribs was priceless. I have never felt so much joy in my life." She grinned maliciously. "Until now. You see, you are broken and beaten. Unable to protect your mate. I'm going to take great joy in making you watch as we use her, torture her, then kill her. Then, only after I have destroyed your precious heart, will I give you death."

Vallen jerked hard against his restraints. "No!" he screamed. "Kill me, take my birthright, but spare Morgan. Please. I beg you."

Avery tossed her head back with laughter. Raising her hand she snapped the whip across his chest, leaving a long, thin open gash. "I love hearing you beg, but it does no good."

"What do we have here?" came a voice from behind us. "Come now Morgan, I never pictured you for a voyeur."

Young and I whirled around to see Simon and three men standing behind us with swords drawn. I stepped up beside the Dragon squire and he turned, pushing me behind him. "What are you doing, Young?"

"Go help my brother. I can handle this." He gave me a little shove.

I turned, stumbling out into the hall, drawing both Vallen's and Avery's attention. "Oh, look at this!" Avery said, motioning to me. "She came here to watch me beat you." She turned to me. "You are just so thoughtful, Morgan."

I raised the sword in front of me, sinking back into a defensive stance. Up the stairs I could hear the clash of battle. "I took your eye last time. I've been working really hard at improving my aim. This time, I'm taking your entire head."

She growled at me and snapped the whip in my direction. I watched as she began shifting. Her entire body lengthened, her tail unrolled, her claws grew, and her wings spread themselves wide. Her scales shimmered gold and black and her remaining eye was red and angry.

She whipped her spiked tail at me before I really knew it was coming. I heard Vallen yell from across the room. "RUN!!"

My warrior instincts kicked in and I dove out of the way, avoiding the blow. The sword I carried was heavy and made maneuvering more difficult, but I worked my way in close to her body, making it harder for her tail to reach me but easier for her to snap her jaws and slash with her claws. I stepped back to avoid her next swipe, but as I did she brought her tail down towards me hard. I swung my sword up to meet it with all my strength and was amazed as the blade sliced through it like it was paper thin.

Avery threw her head back in a scream of pain as her tail fell lifeless to the cold stone floor. I looked up at her and fell back into a defensive stance. "It doesn't have to be like this, Avery. We can both walk out of here alive."

Her response was a loud roar. She reared back and I barely made it out of the direct path of her Dragon Fire. I cried out as the stone floor under my feet superheated, searing the skin on the soles of my feet. Wincing with each step, I held my ground, prepared for whatever would come next.

Avery didn't disappoint me. She slashed at me with her claws, catching me across the thigh with her second swing. Her gargled chuckle told me she thought she had won. It was hard to stay standing - my body was hurting and I was so tired. I glanced at Vallen where he struggled against his restraints, then back at Avery.

I had been backed into a corner when she reared her head back again. The sound of her fiery breath rumbled deep in her lungs. With one last burst of energy, I charged forward, kicking off the ground and imagining I was pushing the world away from me. I swung the sword with all the strength I had left, drawing it across my body. My left hand was caught in the fire, sending pain through my entire body like I had never experienced.

When I hit the floor, I collapsed to my knees, too overwhelmed with pain to hold myself up. I heard the sound of a heavy thump behind me. Looking over my shoulder, I saw the end of Avery. Her head lay detached from the rest of her body on the stone floor. I managed to look up at Vallen in weary acknowledgement.

I somehow found the strength to climb to my feet, and with the sword that slew Avery I cut Vallen free. We both slumped to the ground as I collapsed against him. I felt Vallen shift and start to climb to his feet but he stumbled, trying to bear my weight as well. As he started to rise a second pair of arms appeared out of nowhere and steadied us both.

I turned my head to look into the concerned face of Young. He looked at Avery's body then back to me. "Crazy Fae with a death wish," he muttered.

"Is Simon dead?" I asked, ignoring his comment for now.

He shook his head. "No, he fled while I fought off his three goons. We should get out of here though. Both of you need medical attention as soon as possible." He glanced down at my charred and bloody hand. "If you weren't a Dragon's mate, that would have been melted off."

"Not helping," I told him as he helped us towards what we prayed was a door out. Staggering through a labyrinth of stone corridors, we finally made it outside. The sun was just setting as we approached the exit. Panting and tired, we stopped to rest.

Young disappeared to look for horses, leaving Vallen and I to stand there and hold each other up. I looked up at my Dragon and stroked his cheek with my non-injured hand. "Still love me?" I asked.

He narrowed his gaze on me. "You are a difficult, headstrong, pain in my ass, but yes, I love you. I don't love you in spite of those things. I love you because of them."

Young reappeared shortly with a couple horses in tow. Vallen and Young lifted me to the back of one and while we all knew who I would have preferred to ride with, Young swung up behind me after helping his brother onto the other horse. It was decided it was better to put me in the hands of the person least injured should we encounter trouble on the ride back to civilization.

Sometime well after dark we reached the town we had been captured in and opted to stay in the stables with our actual horses rather than the inn again. I did my best to walk Young through first aid for both

Vallen and I, but quickly gave up and sent the stable boy for Millicent.

The poor maid felt terrible about what had happened. She really had believed that she was helping us, and bore the bruises from the beating Avery had given her to keep her quiet. The maid was considerably better at first aid and I made a mental note to make sure to better train Young before returning him to his knight.

The next morning, despite Millicent's arguments, the three of us headed out for home. We were injured, heartbroken at the loss of a friend, and still angry that Simon had managed to escape. The hours dragged on as I kept looking over my shoulder, expecting to see the noisy Wolf girl. Each time she wasn't there my heart ached and felt colder.

Young didn't speak except when spoken to and refused to eat almost anything. I caught him on more than one occasion staring at the nail that Heather had given him. There was a sadness in his eyes I hadn't thought I would ever see. One I had never wanted to see.

We stopped in the cave we had slept in the first night up. Vallen and I built a fire and prepared some food. Young disappeared, but somehow I knew where he was, and my heart ached even more knowing he wouldn't willingly be coming here for a long time either. When he returned his hands were covered in dirt and his cheeks were painted with spent tears.

Neither Vallen nor I said anything to him. It would just hurt more if we did. Instead we ate in silence and went to sleep without a word. Young sat with his back against the wall, staring at the spot we had slept that first night.

The ride home the next morning went faster than the ride out had gone, as the horses were walking downhill. Horses aren't fond of going downhill, especially steep paths, but we seemed to have conveyed some of our mood to them. We wanted to get as far away as possible from the mountains and the memories they held. By late afternoon we had arrived at the village in the foot hills.

The food was warm and wholesome. Exactly what we needed at this moment. As we were all weary, I pushed for us to stay the night here, rest the horses, and return home on the next day. Vallen agreed out of concern for me. Young agreed because he didn't have the spirit needed to argue, responding with a halfhearted shrug when I asked.

We purchased two rooms for the night at the inn. Vallen and I both took long hot baths and settled into bed early with a light meal. Having seen Young head directly to the bar upon our arrival, I had a good idea I knew how he would spend the night.

"He's taking the Heather's loss much harder than I expected him to," said Vallen as he stroked the hair from my face.

My head rested on his chest as we lay there silently for a moment. "You remember what it was like losing Melody, right?"

"Of course. She was my first love. I was devastated. This is different though," he argued.

"Your brother was crazy about her. He hasn't kept his eyes off of her since the first night they met in the woods," I told him.

Vallen seemed dumbfounded. "I hadn't even noticed."

"In your defense, you were sort of preoccupied with keeping me alive and all." He smiled at the memories.

"Still, my brother was in love and I didn't even know it," he said.

"How did you get over Melody?" I asked.

"I made a deal with a Mage and gave up my Dragon Fire. Then I threw myself into my work. Then I pined for Melody's reincarnation." He stopped. "Then I rescued a Fairy who was trying to have herself made into soup. I looked into her eyes and saw all the pain I had felt and carried with me for years. I thought maybe if I could give her a fresh start, I could give myself one too."

"Crazy Fairy, everyone knows Virgin Soup is so last century," I joked.

Vallen leaned forward and kissed the crown of my head. "True love is a strange thing. It heals even the most painful wounds. I will be there for my brother so he doesn't have to shoulder this pain alone."

"We both will," I assured him.

Chapter Thirty-Two

We awoke the next morning to a heavy pounding on the door. Vallen stumbled out of bed to go see what the fire was about. I snuggled into the warmth of where Vallen had been, enjoying the smoky scent he left behind. From where I lay I could make out most of the conversation.

"I know it's early Sir, but he's passed out naked on one of the tables. He has two of my serving girls so unnerved they won't even enter the building to start preparing for breakfast." The innkeeper began to relay the story of how Young had spent the night.

"I'm sorry," said Vallen. "I'll come down and try to get him to move in just a moment."

"I'm not trying to cause trouble. I heard him tell the story last night about the girl he lost. With such a fresh wound, it makes sense he tried to drink away his pain. I tried to tell him to declare his love and see if she would give him another chance." The innkeeper obviously had his own memories of unrequited love.

"He would if he could," Vallen assured him.

"My missus was headstrong and turned me down a few times too. You ought to encourage him to try again." The man really was on Young's side.

"The girl is no longer living," Vallen explained.

"Oh!" the innkeeper said a moment later. "You know what? I'll just get a blanket and cover him up. I'm sure the girls will be fine once they understand."

If the grief hadn't been so fresh I think I might have laughed about the situation. Someday, when the wound wasn't as recent, I would tell Young about the kindly innkeeper. I knew it would amuse him.

Vallen shut the door and turned back to face me. "I don't know what to do," he told me.

"What do you mean?" I prompted him.

"The brother in me wants to baby him and take care of him. Hug him and tell him it will all be all right, but I know it won't. The realist in me knows the best thing is distraction and that I should send him back to Sir Leon the day after we get back." Vallen looked torn.

"When you lost Melody, what did your parents say?" I held my breath.

"My father told me to come home. He said I should be around family to help me heal." He shook his head. "I didn't want to deal with it and so I didn't heal like I should have."

"Then I think you have your answer. I think Young needs his brother more than Lord Vallen the Knight right now." I offered my best reassuring smile.

He looked at me. "I'm really sorry I haven't asked this, but how are you coping with her loss? I know she was special to you."

I struggled to sit up, and Vallen quickly rushed over to help me. Leaning back against the headboard, I thought about it for a little while. "I guess it hasn't totally hit me yet. I feel an empty ache in my chest when I think about it, but I also keep expecting her to just reappear at any moment."

"I can understand that. She had a way of popping in and out of trouble," he commented.

"It's not just that. The last person I really cared about that I thought was dead, turned out to be alive. It sort of messes with your perception of life and death." I looked down at my still perfectly flat belly and rested my bandaged hand on it. "I think if it's a daughter, I want to name her Heather. If that's all right with you?"

Vallen beamed back at me with pride and reached out to rest his hand on my stomach. "I think that's a beautiful idea," he said. Suddenly he grew still. "I'll need to tell Uther when we return."

I winced and let out a slow breath. "Let me be the one to tell him. She was like a little sister to me so I think I may be able to relate a little easier than you can."

"Do you want me there?" he asked.

"You can be, if you would like to be," I told him with a nod.

We rested a few more hours before going down and wrestling a hung-over Young onto the back of a horse. There was no way he was going to successfully steer in his condition, so I took the reins and Vallen rode beside him to make sure he stayed mounted.

It took us all morning, but we arrived back at Maht around lunch time. With the help of the stable lad and two of the maids we got Young inside and in bed. I all but collapsed into a chair in the living room while Vallen sent word for Captain Lucius to come join us. I munched on apple slices as we waited.

Less than an hour later the captain was welcoming us home from our most recent adventure. We let him know that Simon was still on the loose but that Avery had been slain. He didn't seem surprised that I had been the one to slay her.

He sipped tea and talked about what had happened since we left a week ago. Uther had found a passion for sewing. The vendor's wife had made him help with the mending and He had done such a good job that she had arranged an apprenticeship for him with the tailor once he finished his community service. "I'm sure Heather will be happy to hear her brother is back on track."

I paused, my breath catching in my throat. "Well, you see…"

Vallen covered my hand with his. "Heather was lost on this mission," he explained.

We both watched as the captain's eyes filled with sorrow. "It's always painful to know a light has been snuffed out so young. How is Lord Young handling the loss?" he asked.

Vallen seemed shocked. "You knew of his feelings for her?"

It was the captain's turn to look surprised. "Everyone knew of his feelings for her. The only other person I've seen more smitten is you."

Vallen grumbled but let it go. Obviously, he didn't handle not knowing something very well.

"Have you told her brother yet?" Captain Lucius asked.

I shook my head. "Not yet. You're the only one we've told so far. Please keep it to yourself until we've had a chance to speak with Uther?"

The older Dwarf nodded his understanding. "She was a good girl, and she will be missed. We should give her a grave here in the city. She fought and died as one of us. It's the least we can do. Besides, maybe it will offer some peace for Lord Young and her brother."

I nodded. "I would like that too." Tears welled up in my eyes but I fought to hold them back. *Now is not the time*, I told myself.

We did our best to turn the conversation, but after that news there was no real way to save it. Captain Lucius excused himself to return to work. Vallen and I headed upstairs for some much needed rest.

The next few days tumbled by in a blur. I sat down and explained what had happened to Uther. As expected, he fell apart. He asked the tailor if he could postpone the apprenticeship. He stayed long enough to see us set up a grave marker in her memory, then left to carry the news home to their family. He vowed he would be back and that he would live his life the way she would have wanted him to.

Young spent much of his time reading at her grave. Vallen and he had a massive argument when he found Young wading in the pool in the basement. Now that I better understood the purpose of the pool and what had happened with Princess Alizeyah, I could understand why Young was splashing around and why Vallen was so upset by it.

After all the yelling and door slamming, Young decided he would return to Sir Leon at the end of the week. Vallen didn't argue with him. If I brought it up, he asked me to just let it go. They were both hurting and I didn't have a way to fix it.

On morning of the day before Young was set to leave, I asked if he would keep me company while I cleaned out Heather's chamber. My thought was that maybe he would find something he could take with him as a memento. I also thought it may be a last chance for me to try and convince him to stay longer and work things out with Vallen.

I sent Vallen off to do whatever he did when he wasn't home and met Young in the kitchen. He looked at me with pained eyes over a cup of tea. "I don't know if I can do this, Morgan," he admitted.

"I don't know if I can either, but it needs done. I thought since you are leaving tomorrow, you may find something you want to take with you to remember her by." I bit my lower lip as I watched the emotions cross his face.

"Let's just get this over with, then," he said.

We walked silently down the hall to her chamber and pushed the door open. Most of her belongings fit into a single trunk. When I first met her, all she had were the clothes on her back. I opened the trunk and began pulling out the items within.

A few tunics, a few sets of leggings, a blanket, a tea cup, and a hair brush. I knew there were a few dresses hanging in the closet, but since she never had the chance to wear them I was sure they held little value to him. Young picked up the tea cup and looked at it.

Isabelle Saint-Michael

"When we first met, she didn't have anything, and since I didn't know how long we would be traveling together, I bought her a tea cup so I wouldn't have to share mine." I smiled.

"She admitted the night we met that she didn't even like tea, but because you drank it she was determined to learn to like it," he laughed as he confided in me.

He picked up the blanket and lifted it to his face to smell it. "When she tripped over me in the woods she was in wolf form and then naked. I wrapped my blanket around her so I would stop trying to stare at her. She was so beautiful." We both teared up.

"She was," I agreed.

"You gave me that whole lecture about not leading her on, so when we went out the morning we left the cave I told her that I wasn't interested in her as more than a friend. I could see my words hurt her and it took every ounce of strength I had not to tell her I was lying and that I was crazy about her." He sniffled. "I just thought I would wait until things were settled down and then tell her how I felt." He bit back a heart-wrenching sob. "She died without knowing that I returned her feelings."

I reached out and wrapped my arms around him, finally crying my own tears of loss. We sat there for what seemed like hours, sharing memories and letting out the tears and pain we had bottled up for days. When next I looked up I noticed the sun had set and the sky was dark. "We've been in here all day," I said, wiping my eyes.

Young nodded and looked down at the blanket. "You keep the tea cup and I'll take the blanket, if that's all right with you?" I nodded.

"Young, I know it's painful to be here and the new friction between Vallen and you isn't helping, but won't you consider staying? At least a little while longer?" I had to try.

"I wish I could, Morgan, but I know what was done to bring Hudraer back, and staying here is too tempting. Heather would want me to finish my training and I can't do that if I break Draconic laws. It's better that I go, work hard, and make her proud. It will be like I'm training for both of us." He offered me a smile. "I won't be gone forever. Besides, I want to be back for when you have my niece or nephew. Vallen is going to be useless for running things here for at least the first month."

Young leaned over and hugged me once more before taking the blanket to go pack with his belongings. I looked at the tea cup in my hands and decided to add it to the china cabinet. I strolled through the manor to the dining room and was just deciding where to display the cup when I heard the door swish open behind me. "What do you think?" I asked. "Top shelf with the pink ones or middle shelf dead center?"

"Dead is always the best option" said a familiar voice.

In that moment I forgot how to breathe. I whirled around, dropping the tea cup. It shattered on the tile floor below. "What are you doing here, Simon?"

"Well that's not a very warm welcome for an old flame," he said with a sneer.

"Welcome be damned. Why are you here? Shouldn't you be fleeing for your life right now?" I asked.

"See, I thought about that. I did." He sounded borderline crazy. "But then I remembered you cut down my mate and that it would be rude of me not to return the favor."

I suddenly remembered that it was already dark and that Vallen still wasn't home. "What have you done, Simon?"

"Nothing," he said with a shrug. "Well, nothing yet," he corrected himself.

My mind started racing, trying to remember where the nearest weapon was. I feverishly thought through my exit strategies. Keep him talking, I told myself. "How did you get in here?" I asked.

He smiled. "Funny story, that one. I walked right in the gate past an archer who was too preoccupied playing with a child's bow to notice me. Then I strolled up to the Manor and knocked. One of your lovely maids was only too happy to let me in when I told her how we had been young lovers and decided to just be friends." He started walking around the dining room table.

I casually copied him, doing my best to keep it between us. "You know, my husband will be home soon, and I don't think he'll like that I had a gentleman caller here without him. Perhaps you should leave and come back tomorrow," I offered. I glanced around the dining room for anything that might save me. Not even a butter knife was in sight. Our maids were entirely too good at their jobs.

"Your husband is probably very busy dealing with the fire and the arson charges brought up against Uther. I'm sure he will be disappointed to learn that he fell off the wagon again, but once a bad egg, always a bad egg." Simon rushed around the table and I stumbled into a run, slowed by my still-healing feet.

I made it out of the dining room and into the main hall. I started speaking louder and looking for anything I could use to defend against the sword he now had drawn. "Well it's been really great seeing you SIMON, BUT YOU SHOULD BE LEAVING NOW!" I was almost screaming by the end.

"Interesting tactic, making me think you aren't here alone, but I saw the last of your maids leave for the night and I highly doubt that the stable boy can hear you from here. Not that the lad would be much help even if he could hear you." Simon started strolling towards me at a leisurely pace.

"You're right," I said. "You're too smart for me. I was trying to scare you off." My eyes finally landed on a fireplace poker nearby. I started backing up towards it, hoping he wouldn't realize what I was really doing. "That's why we were such a good match. You were the brains of the operation. I never could have pulled off a death scene like you did."

He seemed to like having his ego stroked. "It was a bit of genius. I was rather proud of it."

"So I am really sorry my mate isn't here for you to slay. He's been really busy." I reached behind me with my good hand, closing it over the cold brass handle of the poker. "I can try and set up an appointment if you like?"

"You know what else is great about maids?" he asked. I shook my head and grinned, preparing to defend myself. "They simply *love* to gossip. I just heard the wonderful news that you and Lord Vallen are expecting."

"Thank you. I'll make sure to not send you an invitation to the shower," I offered.

"I was thinking maybe rather than killing Vallen, I would just kill you and his child." Simon thrust his sword at me.

Twisting quickly and ignoring my injuries the best I could, I avoided the attack. I managed to knock away his next blow with the poker. He seemed surprised. I dodged to the right, giving myself the space of the room to maneuver in. He swung hard with the next strike and I threw all my weight behind the poker.

Lesson learned. A fireplace poker is not a sword. The iron snapped under the force. He was knocked back a step but I was now defenseless. I prepared to dive. He swung wide and I flinched, knowing I would be hit. Instead there was the sound of steel against steel. I blinked, looking up to see Simon crossing swords with Young.

Young forced me behind him and maneuvered us both while defending against Simon's attacks. He slowly forced Simon back into a corner and I watched approvingly as Young handled his sword masterfully. There was a confidence there I hadn't seen in him before. For the first time ever I acknowledged what only he already knew. He was already a knight.

With another firm blow, he knocked away Simon's sword. Simon grinned and held up his hands. "I am unarmed, Sir. Return my weapon and we can finish this like gentlemen."

I started to yell at Young but it was too late. As he crouched to pick up Simon's sword, the Elf kicked him in the knee, knocked away his sword, grabbed hold of his hair, and held a dagger to his throat. Simon looked at me with a grin. "Three for the price of one. Lord Vallen is going to know more suffering than ever. The loss of his entire family in a single night."

"Let Young go," I told him, doing my best to keep my voice soft and controlled.

"Run, Morgan!" Young commanded.

"No, I won't leave you," I said, before looking back at Simon. "Be reasonable. You can leave now without harming us and I will tell Vallen to stop looking. You can take your harem girls and go play sultan at Drakehaven, but if you kill Young or me Vallen will *never* stop hunting you."

I caught the flicker of a dark shadow behind Simon as he laughed. I stayed quiet and let him talk, hoping that Vallen was about to step in and save the day. "I would rather die tomorrow knowing I took revenge then have one hundred years of emptiness ahead of me."

I digested that information. "Are you trying to tell me you actually loved Avery?"

"From the day I first saw her. I begged her father for five long years to allow me to propose. She refused me, saying I was untitled, poor, and all-around unworthy. I didn't know that what was really wrong the whole time was that I wasn't Vallen. I devoted my life to getting everything she wanted me to have but they kept giving it to you. Title, land, wealth, and none of it meant a thing to you. I thought maybe if you fell for me you would either share or be willing to help me advance my career. All you cared about, though, was *everyone else*." He sneered again.

"What made Avery change her mind?" I asked, wondering why Vallen was taking so long to kill Simon. Maybe he wanted to face him in honorable combat?

"A year ago Vallen's long-lost love came back into his life and Avery realized she had lost him. So she switched her focus to crushing him and wanted my help. We planned the whole thing because I knew you would never just let me and half our men go." He spit on the floor. "Then I find out when you show up in Everbloom that you're with Vallen, and once again he had something that was mine."

"I was never yours. You never wanted me to begin with. You were only using me," I argued.

"You were always mine. It's why none of the other men would make a move on you." He gripped Young's hair tighter and pulled his head back, exposing more of his throat. Young struggled against his grip, his eyes begging me to run. "Now the tables have turned and I will take EVERYTHING that ever meant anything to Vallen. Starting with his brother!" Simon pressed the dagger to Young's throat, causing a bright red line of blood to form. As I lunged for the dagger, Simon stopped and jerked forward. I watched as a blade exited through his chest and was pulled free. He looked shocked and tried to turn to see his attacker. There was another sharp movement from behind him and he gurgled what could have been a scream right before his head fell from his shoulders and rolled across the floor. I stared where it stopped just feet away from me.

Simon's body crumpled to the ground and the dagger fell free, clattering on the marble floor. I looked at our savior and blinked, struggling to comprehend what I was seeing. "Do all villains talk too much?" Heather asked.

I couldn't breathe and the room started to spin. She saw the look on my face and rushed forward, urging me to sit down. "Hey there, don't go passing out because of a little bit of blood. You're Lady Morgan after all, what will people think?"

I clasped my arms around her and sobbed tears of joy as my head still spun. Heather patted my back and stroked my hair. Suddenly she was wrenched from my arms and dragged to her feet.

"Thank the sun, the stars, and the moon! You're alive!" Young gasped, and pressed his lips to hers while crushing her against his body. She leaned into the kiss, sliding her hands around his neck.

Finally Heather pulled back to look at him. "Not that I'm not thrilled to see you too, but dead bodies don't really put me in a romantic mood, so if we could discuss other things now and come back to this later...."

Young smiled so broadly he kissed her again. "Whatever you like, you're alive!"

She looked at me with confusion. "Is that really all it takes to make a Dragon happy? A set of lips and being alive?"

I burst out laughing. The more confused she looked, the harder I laughed.

"I missed something, didn't I?" she asked.

"Only your funeral," I told her.

At that moment, Vallen walked in. First he saw the dead body and his eyes filled with panic. Then he saw me and relaxed. Then he saw Heather and staggered backwards a few steps. He looked at Young with hurt in his eyes. "Tell me you didn't use the pool?" he pleaded.

Young shook his head and smiled. "She's alive."

I waited for Vallen to come collect me off the floor so we could explain things. We decided, after having Simon's body removed and the house cleaned, that the rest of the talking could wait for morning.

Chapter Thirty-Three

The next morning we all sat around dining room table and talked about what had led us to that moment in time. "I thought they dumped you off a cliff," I said to Heather.

She was busy stuffing her face but in between bites she was kind enough to explain. "They did," she nodded, swallowing more food. "I shifted into my Wolf form, which can take a greater beating. I ended up hitting a ledge about twenty feet down. I was pretty badly beaten up, but luckily nothing was broken." She stuffed more food in her mouth.

"So you just found your way off a cliff?" Vallen asked.

"Not exactly. Nothing was broken, but I sure as heck wasn't in any position to go much of anywhere. A couple scouts from an Orc tribe spotted me. At first they were thinking dinner, but when I shifted back into my Human form to convince them not to eat me their shaman took an interest in me." She reached out and poured a cup of tea. The action amused me but I said nothing.

I nodded for her to continue. "So he nursed me back to health and explained to me that his spirit animal was a Wolf and that he had always wanted to meet a Were because he felt a kinship to us." She threw her hands up. "Long story short, I made some new friends and when I was well enough to travel, I came home. When I got here I heard you arguing or whatever you were doing with Simon, so I waited for the best moment to attack, only to have it ruined by Young getting himself caught. So... I figured out a plan B, which was a sword. You know, for a house with three... I mean, four warriors living in it, it was surprisingly difficult to find a weapon."

"I know, right?!" I said, throwing up my good hand in agreed frustration.

Vallen rolled his eyes. "Yes, I know. Young and I are horrible Dragons since we keep our homes tidy and our weapons put away."

I patted the back of his hand. "Admitting you have a problem is the first step in recovery."

"Of course it is," he said sarcastically.

"So yeah, finally found a sword and used Simon as a pincushion. Now, on to the important stuff. I heard the rumor I'm going to be an auntie?" She smiled excitedly at me.

"That is the rumor," I said.

"Yeah, but is it true? And now that I'm not dead, are you still going to name it after me if it's a girl?" she wiggled her eyebrows at me.

"We'll discuss it," I told her.

"So are Dragons like Humans and need nine months? Werewolves take nine to ten months. What about Fae? I heard they're only pregnant six months." She grinned. "How long until you get fat and we have a reason to eat sweets every day?"

Vallen looked at me "Dragon pregnancies normally run between a year and fourteen months."

I took in that information then looked down at my stomach. "Don't you even think of staying in there that long. Just because your Daddy is a cranky old lizard doesn't mean you get to be."

Young blinked and looked at Heather. "What do you mean, WE get to eat sweets?"

Heather grinned. "Were women believe in solidarity with their own, so when one of us in a family gets pregnant all the women go on binge-eating diets."

"You're going to get fat if you do that," he told her.

She shrugged. "So? I'm beautiful no matter what. Is that going to be a problem for you, Dragon?"

Vallen sat across the table trying to subtly shake his head no. Young ignored him and we all prepared for the oncoming storm.

"What if I want to eat sweets in solidarity?" he asked.

Heather thought about it for a moment then reached out and patted his nice flat stomach. "I don't care, but what is your knight going to say?" she asked.

"I'll be working off the baby weight with Lady Morgan, so it won't be an issue, but I don't know about you."

Young paused and looked at Vallen. "I have something to ask you, brother?"

Vallen took a deep breath. "You know I want you to finish your training."

Young nodded. "I have a request, but I don't think you're going to like it much."

"Go ahead," Vallen cautiously prompted him.

"I want to finish my training under Lord Hudraer. I would just be in Everbloom, so it would be easier for me to come home on breaks." He held his breath.

"Lord Hudraer and the Princess are not in a position to train you. They need to redeem themselves to the nest," Vallen insisted.

"Yeah, here's the thing. I'm the second born and I will always guard the gate, but the baby you're growing right there means I'm no longer your heir. I'm free to carve out my own path and I'm going to swear fealty to Hudraer and Alizeyah. You know if you would just forgive them, and yourself, you would too. Geren has already said he will be taking an oath, and with him and Lady Jura backing the two of them…" Young shrugged.

Vallen growled at Young. "This isn't open for discussion."

Young stood his ground. "If Morgan had died at the hands of Avery, trying to save you, what would you have done?"

I felt Vallen stiffen, then turn to look at me. I searched his eyes, knowing this was the last piece he needed to let things go. His eyes softened and he took a deep breath. "I would rip apart the very bonds between heaven and hell to get her back."

"So does that mean okay?" Young pressed.

"No, it means I will go to Everbloom in the next few days and discuss Lord Hudraer taking you on as a squire. I don't want you learning any of Alizeyah's bad habits. That girl makes Morgan look like all her plans are well thought out." I considered kicking him.

"My plans *are* well thought out. Just because I don't require a decade to make a decision doesn't mean I'm reckless," I argued. All three of them turned and glared at me.

"Throwing yourself from Iron Warrior to Iron Warrior," said Young flatly.

"Taking on an entire encampment of bandits by yourself," commented Heather.

Vallen looked at me. "Two words - Virgin Soup."

"All right, all right… I get it. They all worked out, didn't they?" There was a collective sigh from the group.

Vallen looked around the table. A smile spread across his face. "It's rather nice to have a family again."

"So, do I get to go with you to meet this Princess Alizeyah and Lord Hudraer?" I asked innocently.

"No. In fact, keeping the two of you as far apart from each other as possible sounds like the best plan."

Two days later Heather and I waved goodbye as the Dragons headed off to Everbloom to discuss all those things most important to heroes: friendship, loyalty, kindness, and forgiveness.

When I started this adventure, I had been a Dragon Slayer, a virtuous hero who was too busy saving people to have time for love. In the end I was the one slayed by a grumpy old Dragon, and in place of my lonely warrior virgin stands a knight, a sister, a wife, a mother, and anything else I choose to be. Real strength comes from our hearts, not from our swords. So arm yourself with love and surround yourself with people who share your happiness.

"Are we done staring at the horizon while you do the whole inner monologue thing?" asked Heather.

I turned and glared at her. "I do not *inner monologue*."

"Right… you just think a lot. Just so you know, when you're inner monologueing, you're only one step below the villains that tell you their evil plans or backstory right before they try and kill you. If you haven't noticed from this adventure, it doesn't work out so well," she informed me.

"Hey! Be nice. I'm pregnant and cranky. I can inner monologue if I want to inner monologue," I growled.

"Ha! I knew you were doing it. I'm getting really good at reading you." She grinned, turning back towards the manor. "Now, the guys are gone for almost a week. Let's go put at least five pounds of baby fat on. I have a strange hankering for cookies."

"Keep it up and I won't share my cookies with you. Has it occurred to you maybe I don't want to get fat?" I huffed behind her.

"See, every day a little closer to a villain. First it starts with hogging the cookies and refusing to gain weight, next thing you know you'll be stealing the world's supply of ice cream," she taunted.

I stopped at the doorway. Heather turned to look at me. "What's ice cream?" I asked.

"Oh, honey. I think we're going to need to take a field trip while the boys are gone. Ice cream may be the best part of pregnancy," she explained.

"How do you know so much about pregnancy?"

She grinned. "Contrary to what you think, I'm not the youngest. I have nine younger siblings and three older sisters who all have pups of their own. I know."

I considered her words carefully. "How would one go about stealing the world's supply of ice cream?" I asked. "And can I bring my sword?"

More fun from Isabelle Saint-Michael

If you enjoyed Dragon's Guide to Slaying Virgins you can follow more of Vallen and Young's adventures at http://elvenlife.com

Also check out Isabelle's other books

About the Author

Isabelle Saint-Michael is a cupcake enthusiast, shoe addict, and world traveler. She is known for her sense of adventure and geekier hobbies. She is frequently seen haunting coffee shops and pubs in the wee hours of the morning. No matter where she goes, shenanigans and laughter are never far behind.

ISABELLE
SAINT-MICHAEL

Bunny
Be Were
AN OTHERWORLD REALMS NOVEL

Coming Fall 2015

www.ingramcontent.com/pod-product-compliance
Lightning Source LLC
Chambersburg PA
CBHW030537260626
47157CB00006B/2075